NECESSARY RETRIBUTION

MIKE MCNEFF

WHIDBEY WRITERS GROUP PRESS

Whidbey
Writers
Group Press

PRINT ISBN 978-1-944215-12-5

For further information regarding permissions, please contact
wwgpress@gmail.com

Library of Congress Control Number: 2013940459

For Dad – Maj. Gen. Edward McNeff USAF (Ret.). Fighter pilot, father, grandfather and the man who helped me fight off the ravages of polio and kept me from being crippled.

PROLOGUE

Chiu Huang, a Chinese intelligence agent, watched as James Chapple beached his small fishing boat at the campground on the north end of Lake Eaton in the Adirondacks. The Special Assistant to the Director of the Central Intelligence Agency owned a vacation home on the south end of the lake. He climbed out of the boat and walked to the parking area of the campground, which was deserted on this late fall day.

Chapple opened the passenger door to Huang's Jeep Cherokee and got in.

"Good afternoon, Chiu."

"Good afternoon, James. I trust you are well."

"I am, thank you." Chapple handed Huang an 8x10 manila envelope. "Here's the latest brief on the CIA's intelligence on your country. I think you'll find it particularly interesting that there is still a squadron of nuclear capable US Air Force F-16 jet fighters at Hualien in Taiwan."

A jolt went through Huang. "Excellent, we have suspected your military did not totally pull out of Taiwan. That is valuable information." He handed Chapple an envelope containing five thousand dollars in cash.

"Thank you. Are we making any headway on my appointment to Director of the CIA?"

"We are applying pressure on certain members of Congress and the administration. We have to proceed carefully, so it will take a little time, but we will be successful."

"I know, it's just that I will be more valuable when I get into that position. There are things that the Director of Operations is doing I'm not privy to."

Huang's face tightened. "Yes, Mr. Yates and his subordinate, Mr. Grassley are particularly dangerous. When you are Director, we expect your first act will be to dismiss those two."

"Don't worry. I can't stand them. They act like I'm not even there."

Huang looked away for a moment and then turned back to Chapple. "Our friends in Iraq want to know what the president might do if they decide to take military action in their region."

"I'm sure that would depend on what the action would be."

"Well, see if you can determine the response to different alternatives."

"I really don't think this president is as hawkish as his predecessor and probably won't do anything as long as we are not talking about Saudi Arabia, but I'll find out."

"Good. Well, until next time, James."

"Uh, well, yes. I'll see you later."

As Huang watched Chapple leave, he thought about Yates and Grassley. *Those two are indeed dangerous. They are doing things we need to find out about and stop. Especially, if Hussein invades Kuwait. Such a move could cause problems...and opportunities. Now that we have confirmation the US military is still active in Hualien, we can start working toward creating an international incident that will allow us to attack Taiwan.*

Huang started his engine and drove out of the campground.

CHAPTER ONE

C aptain John Sorels sat back in the shadows of a second story room, watching a house across the street. He never thought he would be tasked to evaluate another team on a real time mission, especially on the western outskirts of the Gaza Strip. A US Army psychiatrist from Fort Lewis, Washington, was a hostage in the house. She had come to Israel on her own time to treat Israeli and Palestinian citizens suffering from Post Traumatic Stress Disorder. Hamas rewarded her compassion with a kidnapping.

The US insisted they would find and rescue her and Sorels' Delta team was tasked with the mission...with a wrinkle. A new team, a supposed top secret direct action team, would do the mission. Sorels had been told the new team did well in training, but he was to determine if they were ready to be on their own in the real world. The brass chose him because he knew nothing about the new team. They wanted an impartial opinion.

Sorels raised his binoculars. His jaws clenched. *Final exam time, my friend. I hope it isn't final for you.*

IN THE GLOW cast from windows and a few door lights, the old man in the donkey cart moved slowly down the narrow, rock strewn, dirt street. The cart, full of old pots, pans and other odds and ends, banged and rattled the ancient song of the tinker. The old one's long beard, streaked with grey and stained from tobacco juice, swayed back and forth as the stiff wooden wheels rolled over stone and rut. A turban covering his long grey hair, sat askew on his head.

Three young men standing in the doorway of the third house from the corner looked at the old man with narrowing eyes and sneers on their faces. Their heads were wrapped in checkered wool scarves and they wore military style pants and boots like most men from Hamas. Each loosely held an AK-47 automatic rifle in his hands. The few people on the street walked on the other side from where the three men stood...out of both respect and fear.

As the old one came abreast of the three men, one of them spat an insult towards him. The old man replied with the flash of two rounds from the muzzle of a silenced HK MP5 submachine gun into the chest of the surprised terrorist. The muzzle swung left and sent two rounds into the next fighter. The third man brought his rifle up to shoot the old one, but a large black man appeared from the alley between the mud brick houses and terminated the threat with a quick burst from his silenced submachine gun and the Hamas terrorist plowed head first into the graveled dirt. Two other figures ghosted in behind the black man.

The old one sprang from the cart and threw off his robe, beard and turban and they stacked up at the door with the old one at the rear, fourth in line. Number one in the stack, the black man, tried the door handle. It moved. He signaled by raising his thumb in the air and number four tapped the shoulder of number three, who tapped the shoulder of number two, who tapped the shoulder of number one and he flung the door open. The stack moved into the building... swift, silent and ruthless.

In the first room, two men rose from wooden chairs only to be cut down mid-stride by bursts to the head from the submachine guns of numbers one and two. Blood and skull fragments splattered on the far wall. Numbers three and four moved past them and turned right down a narrow hallway. Numbers one and two followed. Number three tossed a grenade through a door to the left. It exploded with a brilliant flash and loud report as the team entered the room. An armed fighter, stunned by the flash/bang grenade, staggered towards them through the thick swirling smoke until number three put two rounds in the junction of the man's nose and eyebrows. Another terrorist struggled to his feet and pointed a pistol at the head of a blindfolded woman tied to a chair, but the two rounds fired by number four mottled the hostage's blindfold with blood and grey matter before the gunman's finger could curl around the trigger. Number four posted at the room's door while numbers one and two freed the woman.

"What's your name?" Number two asked the hostage.

"Captain Kathleen O'Connor, United States Army," came the trembling reply.

"We're getting you outta here, Captain."

"Extract, Extract, Extract!" Number four spoke into a hand held radio.

"Inbound," a voice replied.

The team hustled to the front door, two of them carrying the woman between them by lifting her under each arm. Two armed Hamas men ran towards the house, but were cut down by unseen snipers. Other Hamas fighters faded back into doorways.

A black van skidded up to the rescue team. One and two got into the back seat and pushed the woman to the floor telling her everything would be all right. Number three climbed into the back of the van and opened a back door. Number four jumped into the front passenger seat and the driver handed him a remote detonator. Twenty-one seconds had elapsed.

The driver stomped on the gas pedal and careened down the street, engine roaring and tires kicking up clouds of dust. Three cars skidded around the corner carrying gunmen firing automatic weapons at the fleeing van. Suddenly, a bullet hole appeared in the driver's windshield of the first car and it veered sharply to the left and slammed into a concrete wall sending jagged chunks flying in all directions. Number three fired at the remaining pursuers to keep them at a distance. Number four watched the cars in his large side view mirror. As the pursuers approached a hay cart, he pushed the button on the detonator. A bank of claymore mines hidden in the cart exploded into hundreds of steel balls ripping through the cars' metal side panels and occupants' bodies. The first car spun broadside and the second car smashed into its left side, both exploding in an orange flash before disappearing in a thick, roiling, cloud of black smoke.

A Range Rover pulled onto the road in front of the van and two others fell in behind. The caravan sped west for ten miles. Number two comforted the still trembling hostage. Strong arms held her as he wiped the remains of the man who tried to kill her off her face. Captain O'Connor clung to the man, sobbing. Number one, a trained combat medic, began treating her injuries. The radio crackled.

"SpearTip, this is Condor Four-Seven," the extraction aircraft called.

"SpearTip control, Go Four-Seven," the team's tactical air controller replied.

"We have two wagons two miles out from LZ One."

"Roger, Four-Seven, we're there. Winds are from the north, light and variable, temperature eighty-two degrees, barometer three zero eight six."

"Roger, SpearTip."

The van and the Range Rovers pulled off the road. Infrared goggles made Firefly Flashers visible down the middle of the road. Shadows of armed men appeared out of the darkness.

One of the men reported to number four, Colonel Robin Marlette, at the car window. "360° security set and area clear."

"SpearTip control, we have Fireflies in sight. Starting final approach."

"Roger, Four-Seven, LZ is clear."

Robin watched an infrared vision of the first US Air Force C-130 setting down on the road. It roared by the vehicles and slowed to a stop a half-mile away. Two of the Range Rovers sped after it and drove onto the lowered loading ramp. The LZ security team at that end of the area scrambled on board and the loading ramp lifted.

The turbo prop engines ran up again and the plane started its take-off run.

"SpearTip control, Condor Four-Eight on final."

Robin spotted the second C-130 making its approach.

"Roger, Four-Eight. LZ clear," the controller advised.

It touched down and rolled to a stop. The security team jumped on the running boards of the passing vehicles headed for the loading ramp. Once in the plane everyone stayed in place as the loadmaster and his crew secured the load. Robin saw the loadmaster speaking into his headset and felt the airplane shudder as the engines roared and the plane raced down the road until it lifted off into the air.

Robin leaned back in his seat and took a deep breath.

"Man, am I glad to get out of there!" the driver, Gary Perkins, said brightly.

Robin looked at Captain Sorels, who got out of the Rover in front of the van. The Captain simply nodded.

A HUMVEE WAS WAITING when the planes landed at the Israeli Hatzerim Airbase.

"How did it go?" Bill Grassley, CIA Deputy Director of Operations, fell in beside Robin as they walked to the hanger serving as the mission command center. "Delta Command has been bugging the hell out of me about the rescue of the hostage."

Robin didn't break his stride and Bill had to hurry to keep up. "We got her, Bill. She's shook up and has minor injuries, but otherwise appears okay."

"What did Captain Sorels say?"

"Not much."

"I don't know if I like that."

"There's only one way to find out."

They walked over to where the rest of the team were gathered. Robin saw number two, Burke Jameson, get out of an ambulance and watch as it left the tarmac.

"The hostage?" Robin asked number one, Emmett Franks.

"Yeah, she'll be all right. What's the score, Rob?"

"Don't know yet. We're on our way to find out."

"Do you think we're going to make it?"

"We'll make it." number three, Rocky Barnett, added. "We did a damn good hit!"

"There's a reason I picked the four men who did the assault phase of this mission. Just follow my lead," Robin cautioned.

Robin and Bill led the team to Captain Sorels who was conferring with some of his men.

"Captain, we're anxious to know what you think about our operation."

The captain looked at Robin with steady, concerned eyes. "Colonel, I have some questions, if you don't mind."

"I'll answer what I can."

Sorels scanned the faces of the team. "How much combat experience do you guys have?"

"Well, these men are Vietnam vets. Emmett, my gentle giant, served two tours as a LLRP, earning the Distinguished Service Cross, the Bronze Star and the Purple Heart. Burke here served three tours in Special Forces, earning the Distinguished Service Cross and the Silver Star." Robin put his hand on Rocky's shoulder. "Rocky was a Recon Marine for two tours and earned the Silver Star, the Bronze Star and the Purple Heart." Robin pointed to Gary. "My friend, Gary, is a highly trained and experienced pursuit driver."

"What about you?"

"I've been in combat, just can't say where. All of us have many years' experience in tactical operations and training. I can't really tell you anymore about us."

"How long did you work on this op?"

"I'm sure we got the original intel when you did."

"I gotta say, you guys put it together in damn quick fashion."

"Well, Captain, we have a lot of experience doing investigations. We know how to get the right info quickly."

"I believe it. You certainly did on this mission."

"Thanks."

Sorels took a deep breath. "You guys did this by the numbers. Your planning and briefing were thorough. Your infiltration with disguises was well done. Your execution was low drag and high-speed complete with effective high ground sniper cover." The Captain looked around at the men. "I'm going to wholeheartedly recommend your team go active. You're definitely ready."

A murmur of approval went through the team.

Robin shook Sorel's hand. "Thank you, Captain. We worked hard to get here."

Bill Grassley shook the captain's hand. "Thank you, Captain. I appreciate your assessment."

"You've got one hell of an asset with this team, sir. I hope you use them well."

Bill nodded and turned to Robin. "We need to go."

"You're the boss. Mount up, guys. We're burning daylight."

Robin watched as the men quickly moved to pack up their gear, their banter and smiles showing their spirits were high. He thought of the hell they all had been through the last two years, including the unforgiving training by the best special ops teams in the US military. *Yes, we are ready!*

BARZAN AL TIKRITI sipped tea at a table in a Damascus cafe and contemplated the changes in the world. As of today, the Americans elected a new president, a good thing in Al Tikriti's estimate. The former president was not afraid to use military power. Al Tikriti didn't think the new president was of the same mind, making it easier for Saddam to maneuver. As operations chief of the Mukhabarat, the Iraqi Intelligence Service, it was Al Tikriti's job to figure these things out. He was also Saddam Hussein's main contact with terrorist groups who targeted western interests.

Today, he was meeting Abu Nidal, a freelance terrorist, formerly from Fatah and the Palestinian Liberation Organization. The temperature was pleasant and there were outside tables, but Al Tikriti took no unnecessary chances. Damascus could be a very dangerous place.

Nidal came through the door, immediately spied Al Tikriti and came to the table.

"Good afternoon, Barzan."

"And a good day to you, Abu. Would you like some tea?"

"Yes, thank you."

Al Tikriti poured a cup.

"You have new work for me, Barzan?"

"I do. I need you to put together a team for two very important missions."

"What are the targets?"

"I have several picked, but I don't know which two I will assign to you until events unfold."

"How many men?"

"Twenty should be sufficient."

"And how much are you willing to pay?"

"Two million US dollars now, for your preparations, and ten million when the job is done."

"Two million is hardly enough to prepare for a mission. We will need weapons, transportation..."

"All of those will be supplied. You will only have to provide twenty trained men."

"When will you provide the two million dollars?"

"There is a briefcase under the table. Take it when you leave."

"As always, you are very persuasive."

"I trust your Libyan friend will be interested in helping us?"

"Of course."

"Thank you Abu. I will be in touch."

Nidal nodded, picked up the briefcase, and left the cafe.

CHAPTER TWO

The team's second in command, Ernie Jackson and Charles "Chucky" Osgood, a former informant of Robin's, walked through the large, empty warehouse with him. It had eight loading docks, most of them out of public view and a nice suite of offices on the third floor. Just outside, the port of Seattle busily unloaded the large container ships bringing the world to Seattle, and loaded ships taking Seattle to the world.

"I think this will do nicely, Ernie," Robin observed.

"Yep, all we need to do is dig out and finish a secure basement. Just a minor thing."

"It won't be that tough if we get the right company to do it. We'll also need a way to conceal the two satellite dishes and a bunch of antennas Grassley says we'll need on the roof."

"Who are we going to get to do this?"

"Grassley gave me a referral for a construction company." Robin pulled a card from the inside pocket of his sport coat and handed it to Ernie. "KBR construction. Bill says they can be trusted to do the job and keep quiet. That's the number for our contact in the company."

"Why are you giving it to me?"

"I've just designated you our contractor liaison."

"I don't know jack shit about construction!"

"It's time you learned. Besides, it's either contractor liaison or you run the regional recruiting. I can't do both."

"Okay, okay. I sure as hell don't want to do all that traveling. I'll handle the warehouse."

"I knew you would see it my way."

"We've been best friends for a long time, but sometimes I really don't like you, Rob."

"Yeah, but you always love me."

Ernie put his arm around Robin's shoulders. "I do, brother. I surely do."

"Okay guys," Chucky cut in. "I'm really happy your families are doing well and you love each other, but just what in hell am I supposed to be doing?"

Robin put his arm around Chucky's shoulders. "You're the most important man on the team."

"Yeah, right, Rob."

"You are, Chucky, because you're our front man."

"What do you mean?"

"Well, we can't apply for permits, business licenses and official things. We're officially dead. So we need you to do those things and be the face man for the company."

"That doesn't sound like fun. I thought you said I'd be helping protect the national security of the United States."

"Being the front man for the company is just part of your job. The other part is to connect with your former associates in international crime."

Chucky's face brightened. "Now that sounds better, but you're confusing me. Whose side are we on?"

"That will depend on what we're doing, but whatever it is, we'll need all the contacts we can get."

Chucky grinned from ear to ear. "Rob, this could be the start of a beautiful relationship."

THE GUARDIANS WERE GATHERED in the conference room at the warehouse. Robin could tell everyone was antsy and ready to go to work. He was finishing explaining the plan for organizing the company and the intelligence operation.

"Basically, Burke and Rocky are going to split the world in half. Burke will take Europe, Africa and Canada. Rocky will take Asia, the Middle East and South America. Ernie and I will cover the U.S. and Mexico. We already have a worldwide list of potential contacts with the CIA stamp of approval. All of them are disabled military or law enforcement, but each team will run a background, and investigate the potential contact by reputation and surveillance."

"Are these guys going to be part of our company?" Mark Warren asked.

"Yes, their primary job will be to find interesting products for us to import and markets for our American products. They'll also set up networks for product gathering and distribution."

"What about the other side of the business?" Emmett asked.

"They'll be our in-country experts and our channels to contact reliable assets during our operations. We want to be damn sure they're reliable and have the integrity we need. Once you complete your investigation, I come in and close the deal. Any questions?" No one spoke up. "All right, Burke and Rocky get moving. We're burning daylight."

CHAPTER THREE

O n a pleasant fall early afternoon in Le Crotoy, France, Robin sipped coffee at an outside table of the Les Tourelles Hotel. He looked out over the sandy estuary where the River Somme met the English Channel and breathed in the moist, salty air. The bright sun warmed the cool fall air. The man he waited for limped around the corner and eased his large frame into a chair at his usual table facing the estuary. The limp came from an AK-47 round that shattered his left femur during the French Foreign Legion's campaign in Chad. Robin thought how close he had come to having a similar wound. The limp distracted a casual observer from realizing the man was in peak physical condition. He didn't acknowledge Robin's presence, but Robin knew he'd already been spotted by alert, intelligent eyes set deep into a face so black it wouldn't need camo paint on a full moon night.

Robin rose and walked over to the other man. "Hello, I've been waiting for you."

"Rubbish, you people have been watching me for three days." The deep, mellow voice carried a British accent.

At the same time two men moved closer to them. They were intercepted in a non-threatening way by Burke Jameson and Mike Collins. The other man noticed the contact.

"Actually, we've been watching you for three weeks."

The man's eyes flashed surprise.

"Oh, it's true." Robin smiled in a friendly manner. "We're very good at what we do. We've followed you despite the recent efforts of your fellow Legionnaires, but I'm happy to see the Legion's legendary emergency number still works. May I join you?"

The Legionnaire waved Robin to a chair at his table.

"My name is Robin Marlette. I'll get to the point. I want to offer you a job."

The Legionnaire's eyebrows lifted.

"It's a legitimate job," Robin added.

"No danger?"

"It can get as dangerous as you want, I suppose."

"Why me?"

"My company only hires former military and law enforcement personnel who are disabled because of injuries incurred in the line of duty. So, as a disabled Legionnaire, you meet the first of our criteria. Our background investigation showed you were born in Algiers. You also have worked extensively in the Middle East and Africa. The company can use your expertise and connections.

"The company?"

"You're also fluent in five languages." Robin continued, leaving the question hanging in the air between them. "Most importantly, you have integrity."

"How did you find me?"

"You were recommended to us."

"By who?"

"Is that important?"

"Not really. Are you CIA?"

"No. I am the CEO of an export/import and services company."

The other man laughed. "You have been reading too much James Bond. What do you import and export?"

"Anything where we can legitimately make a buck."

The Legionnaire gave a quizzical look.

"Sorry, anything that makes a dollar, a franc, a pound...we're in business to make money."

The Legionnaire nodded. He leaned back in his chair and looked at Robin long and hard.

"Do I have to leave France?"

"We prefer you relocate to the Middle East."

"I have no desire to leave here."

Robin shrugged. "Your base salary will be two hundred and fifty thousand dollars a year plus commissions."

The Legionnaire's eyes grew wide as he leaned forward.

"That should be enough for you to visit here regularly."

"How do I get started?"

Robin reached into his coat pocket and handed the Legionnaire an envelope containing an open round trip ticket on the Concord from Paris to New York with a connection to Seattle, accompanied by ten thousand dollars. The Legionnaire reviewed the tickets and thumbed the money without expression. He looked at Robin.

"I will expect you in Seattle, Washington on the twenty-fifth of next month. That should be enough to get you there and back comfortably. Call me when you get to New York. We'll show you the company and our operations. Is that acceptable?"

"Yes." The Legionnaire allowed his voice to show he was impressed. "Will you join me in a bottle of wine?"

"Shall we include our friends?"

"By all means."

Robin signaled to Burke as the Legionnaire called the cafe

owner over to the table. "Henri, four bottles of your best Medoc and six glasses, please."

The six men drank wine and enjoyed the conversation of men who have lived lives filled with danger. Robin ordered lunch. Jonathan Marchaux, the Legionnaire, was the last of this stage of country contact recruitments.

ROBIN CAME out of the bathroom of the room at the Les Tourelles where he and Karen were staying and saw Karen looking out the window. She wore a light dress with bare shoulders and arms. The late afternoon sun shone through the dress and outlined her figure. He walked up behind her and put his arms around her waist.

"Do you know how beautiful you are?"

"I just know I love it when you tell me I'm beautiful."

"You're beautiful." Robin nuzzled her neck and his hands moved to her breasts.

"Oh my, are you getting fresh with me?"

"I have a proposal."

"What might that be?"

"Let's have dessert before dinner."

Karen turned to face him and kissed him deeply. "I think that's a wonderful idea. I can get used to this globetrotting lifestyle, Mr. Marlette."

"Hopefully, we can bring Laurie and Eddie on some trips next summer."

Karen gave Robin a concerned look. "How long do you think it will be before Bill starts giving the team missions?"

Robin took a deep breath. "It could happen anytime now. The CIA has invested a lot of training and money getting the team set-up and ready, not to mention keeping us all out of prison for going into Mexico and raiding Rodriquez's compound. They'll be wanting a return on their investment soon."

Karen held Robin tightly. "I'm scared, Rob. I know this is going to be more dangerous than police work. I'm worried the CIA will start to rely on you and the team to solve a lot of serious problems."

Robin started to say something, but Karen put her fingers on his lips.

"Don't try to bullshit me, Rob. I feel the same worry in you and I see it your eyes."

Robin deflated. "You're right. I am worried. All I can say is the team is ready. We've had the best training from the best units in the business and we have the best equipment I know of. We'll have to take it one day and one mission at a time."

Karen kissed Robin and ran her hand through his hair. "Thank you for being honest with me. Keep it that way. Trying to protect me from knowing the bad things just makes it worse."

"Okay, kiddo, I'll you give the straight scoop all of the time. Just remember this conversation."

"All right, I've said my piece. I'm ready for dessert."

ROBIN LOOKED over the people assembled in the company's conference room. Worldwide Enterprises, Inc. actually lived up to its name; fifty-two men and women from all nationalities, cultures and color. The regret of being forced to disappear from his job with the Arizona Department of Public Safety's Narcotics Special Enforcement Unit faded as he found the new challenges interesting and exciting.

"Ladies and gentlemen, may I please have your attention." It wasn't a request, but a gentle command. "As you know, we've recruited all of you to facilitate our import/export and tactical services business. We want you to also identify markets in your areas for American products." A few chuckles filtered through the group.

"Your secondary job is to be prepared to provide us with contact assets and in-country logistical support for tactical operations in which we may engage on behalf of our clients." A murmur of approval filtered through the room.

"Let's get something straight. We are a legitimate business group. The more products and markets you identify and develop, the more money you can make. If you take this aspect of our company seriously, you can become millionaires or even multi-millionaires." A loud rustle filtered through the room. "We want you to be successful because the richer you become, the more contacts you make. The more contacts you make, the more influential you become. We have some very demanding clients. They will ask us to do some difficult things. We'll need your contacts and support."

A hand shot up from the middle of the room. A detective from the Japanese National Police had received a severe beating from some Yakuza gangsters when he got too close to shutting down their black market operation. It cost him the use of his left eye and most of the hearing in his left ear.

"Shosi." Robin nodded in his direction and the short muscular man stood.

"Mr. Marlette..."

"Please call me Robin."

"Thank you, Robin," Detective Shosusha Tanyaka said with a bow. "I am concerned about what your clients may ask you to do. I will not compromise my integrity for any cause."

"And we would never ask you to. We may, however, draw a fine line between what is ethical and what is legal in any particular country. In other words, we will never ask you to violate your integrity or ethics. On the other hand, we may ask you to violate the law of a particular country, but the choice will be yours. You can choose not to help us on any particular operation or part of an operation."

"Will that mean we will be fired if we choose not to assist you?"

"I'll decide those times on a case by case basis, but I don't think it'll be a problem. If you're really standing firm on principles, I won't fire you. I will say, however, if you believe you can never violate a law of any country in your area of operation, this would be a good time to bow out of your association with our company."

"Under what circumstances would you ask us to violate a country's laws?"

"Just off the top of my head, we might ask you to violate a country's laws to rescue an innocent person, if the person is being held against their will with the tacit approval of that government."

Shosi nodded.

"I take it that might be acceptable to you?"

"Yes, that would be acceptable to me."

"Good, Shosi. Any other questions?" Robin waited for silence to settle in the room.

"Ladies and gentlemen, the services section of our company is primarily geared to those kinds of operations law enforcement officers would perform. You are here to protect the innocent and bring fugitives to justice where governments simply can't or willingly don't. You were chosen to be here today because of your proven courage and integrity. We will only do operations that further the free world's sense of justice. The emphasis is on the word 'free'. Does that answer the tough questions?" Heads nodded and Robin noticed all eyes were fixed on him. "Good. Your area directors will show you around our facilities and will brief you on the strategic plans for your areas of operation. We're happy to have you aboard."

CHAPTER FOUR

A s Robin drove towards the Clinton/Mukilteo Ferry that would take him across Possession Sound to the mainland, the new day started to filter through the pine trees lining Highway 525. Glowing white cumulus clouds dotted the rose color of the early morning sky. He never tired of the beauty of his new home.

Seattle was the company headquarters. On any given Friday, the team trained with special operations teams stationed at one of the five major military bases in the area. The CIA believed in the event of an emergency, the military could transport them anywhere in the world in a matter of hours. But, after considering Robin's arguments for the unit to be self-contained, the CIA decided to equip the team with its own assets for rapid deployment.

Robin allowed the men to live anywhere they wanted in the general Seattle area. He and Karen considered Seattle a beautiful city, but after living in Phoenix, they were determined to live in a small town. They explored many small towns in the Puget Sound area, but none seemed to be just what they wanted, until they took a trip to Whidbey Island.

They drove through deep forests, farm fields with the pleasant smell of new mown hay and towns that came from a picture post card until they reached the town of Coupeville. They drove down Main Street and then turned on a street lined with buildings built in the 1800s sitting on the shore of a body of water called Penn Cove.

Karen looked at Robin and said, "This is it."

"I like it too, Dad," Eddie chimed in from the back seat.

"How 'bout you Laurie?" A long silence filled the car. "Laurie?"

"I don't want to live in a small town. I'd rather live in Seattle."

"Well, you enjoyed Pinetop when we lived there."

"Get real, Dad. I was twelve."

Laurie's voice became loud and harsh. "What do you want from me? Cathy and Casey have started their own lives. It's just Eddie and me and he will do anything you say. So do you really think I believe you care about what I want? I wanted to do things, to be someone who did good things and now you want to stick me in a small town on a dumb island." Laurie choked back tears.

Robin slowed and parked near the Coupeville Wharf. He looked over to Karen who gave him the *It's your problem* look. Eddie wore a confused and hurt look on his face.

"It's all right, Eddie," Robin said in a quiet voice. "C'mon, Laurie. Let's take a walk." He got out and opened the door for Laurie. She stepped out, but wouldn't look at him. He put his arm around her shoulders and guided her to the pier, a redwood carpet stretching to the wharf at the end. Blue water framed the wharf with a background of deep green forest and the lighter green of pastures on the other side of Penn Cove. A bright blue sky graced by white cotton ball clouds topped the scene. Robin was struck by the beauty of it all.

"Laurie, it might do you good to look up." Laurie slowly raised her head and as her eyes went higher, her steps slowed to an eventual stop. She looked slowly to the right and then slowly back to the left, taking in the deep soothing color on nature's canvas before her. Her breath seemed to stop for an instant.

"I have never seen a more beautiful place, Dad."

"Same here, kiddo."

She looked into Robin's eyes. "I'm overreacting, aren't I?"

"No, you're not. Our family has been through hell...because of me. Last time I checked, you're part of this family. You've never said a word about the attack. Never said a word about the hell that followed. Never said a word about the move out here. You just did what we as a family needed you to do. No, sweetheart, you're not overreacting...you're just now reacting, which you have every right and reason to do. We do care about what you have to say. It's about time you said it."

"Oh, Dad!"

"What, honey?"

"You make it so hard to stay mad at you!"

"Well, that's a good thing. Laurie, we don't have to live here." They stopped at the end of the pier and Laurie leaned on the rail. Robin waited as she looked at the vista of Penn Cove before her.

"Actually, Dad, I think this might do. I'll figure something out about the rest."

As they headed back to the car, Robin stopped and looked at Laurie. "You sent your little brother into a tailspin a while ago."

"Don't worry, Dad. I'll fix it."

"I know you will. You know me, I love to point out the

obvious. That way I'm always right." Robin spotted Karen and Eddie coming out of a store across the street eating huge ice cream cones. They both were smiling until Eddie saw Laurie.

She crossed the street and walked up to Eddie. She put her arms around him. "I'm sorry, little brother. You know I didn't mean what I said."

"I thought you were serious, Sis." Eddie's eyes started to well up.

"If you think I was serious, then you have a lot to learn about girls. I love you, Eddie. Sometimes girls get crazy about little things."

"Sis, nothing that's happened lately is a little thing."

Robin, Karen and Laurie looked at Eddie with surprised expressions.

Karen spoke quietly. "I think we all need to find ourselves a quiet place to live in this town and bring some peace to our family. It has been a rough two and a half years."

"I think that's a very good idea," Robin said. Laurie looked at Eddie who seemed more relaxed now.

"We do too, Mom and Dad." Eddie grinned at his sister.

Robin knew he would treasure that moment for the rest of his life. He pulled the car into the ferry toll booth lane. He waved at the toll collector, who was always at this booth on the early weekday mornings with a bright smile, as she acknowledged his monthly pass and pointed him to the line in lane three. Robin had about fifteen minutes before the next ferry, so he decided to get a cup of coffee and a pastry. He was about to walk over to the little snack stand at the end of the ferry dock when a man at the window pulled a gun. The man's hand shook.

"Damn!" Robin quietly opened the pickup door and slipped out. He moved quickly and silently across the asphalt of the dock toward the man's back. The woman behind the counter looked terrified as she stuffed cash into a paper sack. She glanced at Robin. The robber started to turn...too late. Robin grabbed the gun hand and jerked it down pulling the right side of the gunman down off balance and slammed a fist into the back of the man's head at the medulla. The robber's legs folded and he collapsed in a heap. Robin grabbed the gun, stripped the magazine and cleared the chamber in two swift movements.

"State Patrol! Don't move!" Robin froze. He slowly raised his hands, spreading his fingers as he did. A man in plain clothes moved into view holding a semi-automatic pistol, which Robin knew to be the issued State Patrol duty weapon. Although he saw no badge, he didn't move. His eyes, however, followed the man's every move.

"I think I know what happened, but I saw what you did. You don't move unless I tell you to."

Robin nodded.

The trooper was young and wide eyed at this point.

"The guy on the ground tried to rob me!" the woman behind the counter yelled pointing to the suspect. "He saved me!" She pointed to Robin.

"Who are you?" the trooper demanded.

"Robin Marlette." He could hear sirens in the distance.

"No, not your name. What are you? Who do you work for?"

"I'm a businessman just trying to help."

"Bullshit! No businessman can do what you did!"

"I'm trained in martial arts."

"That was not martial arts! That was combat training!" Robin knew he had to change the subject.

"Officer, I don't want to tell you what to do, but I would appreciate it if you would point your weapon at the ground instead of at me."

The trooper lowered his gun, but it didn't look like his curiosity had lessened.

"I have a concealed weapons permit and I'm armed. I am carrying a Colt .45 and a folding knife. If you care to, you can remove my gun and knife and search me for other weapons. I'm on your side."

The trooper kept his distance. The sirens were getting close. Robin sighed. *Grassley isn't going to like this.* His pager started vibrating.

DETECTIVE MEL ROUSH of the Island County Sheriff's Office was a twenty-two year veteran of the department. He really didn't care why or how this Marlette guy stopped the armed robber. He had an ironclad case against the suspect with very little work. This made the detective very happy. Trooper Echoles, on the other hand, would not let his concerns drop.

"Mel, you had to see that guy in action to understand what I'm telling you. He was good...too damn good."

"Let it go, Tim. If he's some kind of operator, he isn't going to say shit to us about it. Marlette did us a favor and he is willing to testify. He's as good as gold to me." Det. Roush wrote a few more notes on his pad then walked to where Robin leaned against his pickup.

"Mr. Marlette, you're free to go now. Thank you for your quick action and thank you for your cooperation."

"No problem, Detective. Glad I could help."

"The sheriff is probably going to give you an award for what you did."

"With all due respect, Detective, I would appreciate it if you would dissuade the sheriff from any kind of an award. I'm not good at such things."

Roush had to fight to suppress a smile. *I'll bet you're not.*

"WHERE THE HELL HAVE YOU BEEN?" Burke fell in step at Robin's elbow as he walked through the door.

"I ran into a little...situation."

Burke's eyebrows rose sharply.

"I had to take down an armed robber."

"Oh shit. Grassley's going to go ballistic. He's been calling."

"About what?"

"We have our first mission. He wants you to call him on the secure line ASAP."

Robin took a deep breath. "Great! I don't even have time to practice how to tell him I'm going to be front page news in a small town paper." He walked down the stairs and swiped a magnetic code card over a square tile that dropped down revealing an ocular scanner. Robin put his eye up to the scanner allowing red lines to flash over his retina. An elevator door opened in the wall. If a person didn't know it was there, they would walk right by it.

The elevator door opened on a room crammed with electronics. There were five television monitors, four computers and a dizzying array of two way radio sets and telephones. Jamie Slater and Emmett Franks were manning the center.

"Hey, Boss. Grassley says he really needs to talk to you."

"Okay, Jamie, connect me." Robin sat down at a white telephone as Jamie pushed some buttons and dialed a number. He nodded and Robin picked up the phone.

"I hope that's you, Rob." Grassley's voice had a tinge of irritation.

"It's me."

"Where have you been?"

"Well, to get right to the point, I stopped an armed robbery." A long pause hung on the other end.

"Did you have a choice?"

"If I did, I wouldn't have taken action."

"Okay, we'll have to do damage control. Just tell me it didn't happen in Seattle."

"No. It happened at the ferry dock on the island. The Island County Sheriff's Office is doing the investigation. The detective doing the case is pretty cool. A young trooper, though, was a little too impressed with my moves."

"Okay, you can give me the details later and I'll take care of it. In the meantime, we have a mission."

"It's about time. Where are we going?"

"Bangkok, Thailand. There is a fugitive there named Anton Ivanov we need to bring in."

"What's the catch?"

"He is wanted for trafficking children for sex. The U.S., Britain and France all have warrants out for his arrest. He was arrested by the Thai government, but they're stalling on the extradition. The guy is a Russian citizen with close ties high up in the Soviet government. We got word that he's not actually in jail, but is being held, and I use that term loosely, in the penthouse of the Landmark Hotel. We're afraid the Russians are going to smuggle him out. Your job is to get him out first."

"I take it that means today or sooner."

"You are very astute."

"What do you mean by 'high up in the Soviet government'?"

"KGB."

"Wonderful! Couldn't make the first one easy, could you?"

"We don't need you guys for easy missions."

"I guess. I don't have time to figure the budget...deposit five million."

"That's pretty high!"

"Do you want him alive? I can do it a lot cheaper if you'll take him dead, which I have no problem doing to an asshole like this."

"You win. Your five million is deposited...now."

"Alive it is! We'll be airborne by 2300."

SADDAM HUSSEIN SLOUCHED BACK in his enormous chair at the head of a long conference table surrounded by his ministers and generals. Saddam's left arm stretched out on the table, his right hand rested on the butt of his pistol. Through narrowed eyes, he listened to the Deputy Prime Minister, Izzat Ibrahim report the events at the Saudi sponsored conference with Kuwait in Jeddah.

"I presented our four demands to Crown Prince Sa'ad Al-Abdallah. The first, Kuwait must abide by OPEC quotas; second, Kuwait must cede the southern part of the border including the Rumaila oilfield; third, Kuwait must write-off the war debt from the Iraq/Iran war; and fourth, Kuwait must compensate Iraq for oil market losses as a result of the oil price decline due to Kuwait's over production. The prince demanded that writing off the debt must be in return for border demarcation that settled the dispute forever. We, of course said this was negotiable. We negotiated for less than two days and ended with disagreement remaining on all issues."

Saddam surveyed each man around the table. He used this tactic of intimidation with great success his entire reign as President of Iraq. After staring into the eyes of the last man, Saddam leaned forward with a smile.

"I have decided that our great country has done enough negotiation through the accepted diplomatic channels with the government and people of Kuwait. Kuwait is not a legitimate country. Its territory belongs to Iraq and has since the Ottoman Empire. Its oil should not be enriching the people of Kuwait. It should be enriching the good people of Iraq. It is time for us to take back what is rightfully ours."

The usual and expected cheer rose from the table. Assistant Defense Minister Assad Tareq raised his hand.

"Yes, Assad." Saddam's voice had the tone of a threat.

"Excuse me Excellency, I know you have considered the response from the Americans and NATO, could you tell us your conclusions, sir."

Saddam waved his hand dismissively. "The Americans and NATO are nothing but weak whores. They will never intervene. They have no balls! We already have one hundred thousand men at the border and they do nothing!"

Another forced enthusiastic cheer rose from the group.

"If they do attempt to interfere, Barzan will have some surprises for them." Saddam nodded to Barzan. Al Tikriti smiled.

CHAPTER FIVE

T en hours of furious activity had Fatboy, the Guardians' Boeing 747-400, airborne. The CIA and the Boeing wizards performed their magic and the plane had some features that would make 007's "Q" envious. Fatboy also carried four Range Rovers and two RIBs, Rigid Inflatable Boats.

After a refueling stop in Honolulu, Robin walked up to the cockpit.

"How are things up here?"

"Just peachy, boss," Jack Moore, the team's most experienced pilot said as Robin stepped through the door.

"Good. I want the people who hold my life in their hands to be happy."

"Rob, ol' Fatboy here practically flies himself. You're just paying us exorbitant salaries to babysit him."

"Oh, I feel better now. You left a real flying job with US Customs to get paid more to babysit."

"You guys see a problem with that?"

"I've been looking for an angle like this my whole life," engineer Eric Newman replied.

"Same here," copilot Oscar Leighton added.

"I don't know why I ever agreed to bring you cowboys on board this gig."

"Because you love us, boss, that's why."

"I guess that's it. Just remember when we get one hundred miles from Bangkok, arm the defense suite on this baby. If the Russians know we are coming, it could get nasty."

Jack turned and looked at Robin. "Jesus, Rob. It's our first mission and you're already getting cynical."

"It's my job to get everyone home. People other than Grassley know we're moving on this guy. Just stay alert for threats."

"You got it, Mother Marlette," Oscar cracked.

"It's so good to hear a familiar refrain. How long do we have before landing in Bangkok?"

"The flight computer says ten hours and seven minutes."

"Thanks, Jack. See you guys later." The pilots saluted as Robin started up the stairs to the intelligence deck.

"What's the latest intel, Jamie?" Jamie turned and smiled at Robin, a broad true smile that showed the attachment and respect between the two men. The head wound Jamie received in the gun battle with the Rodriquez drug cartel permanently affected his ability to move his right hand and leg. He reported for duty expecting to be put out to pasture, but Robin had other plans. A year of training on electronic surveillance, computers and communications at CIA headquarters in Langley, Virginia, produced a first class intelligence officer. Jamie took to it all like a duck to water.

"Chien reports the Soviet ambassador went up to see Ivanov today." A former South Vietnamese Navy SEAL, Chien Nguyen-Tran, the team's area representative, lost his left foot to a land mine. When the South Vietnamese government collapsed in 1972, he escaped to Thailand, settled in Phuket and opened a tourist shop.

"How did he find that out?"

"He says his wife comes from a large Bangkok family. One of them is the assistant head housekeeper at the Landmark."

"You're kidding me!"

Jamie grinned broadly at the intelligence coup. "Scout's honor, boss."

Robin felt a lot better about pulling this mission off. "All right, the next contact you have with Chien, tell him we need a way around Thai Customs at the Bangkok airport. We can let them inspect if we have to, but the less they know about Fatboy, the better. Also tell him to rent four surveillance cars. Nothing fancy, just cars that fit in."

"Will do, Rob."

"Have you finished loading the info I need for the briefing?"

"Yep, maps, photos, mug shots and dossiers. You're all set."

After the team assembled, Robin continued the briefing done on the first leg of the trip. Everyone stared at the small computer screen at their seat in the briefing room as he covered the geography of Bangkok and the surrounding area in more detail. A large red dot pinpointed their target...the Landmark Hotel.

Robin tapped the screen and it zoomed in on a set of schematic drawings showing the interior of the Landmark from the service basement to the penthouse. "As you can see, we have a straight shot with the service elevator from the service basement to the penthouse because it gets special treatment." Robin touched the screen again. "These are the pictures and intel on Ivanov and the Russian ambassador. The code name for Ivanov is Stinky. The code name for the ambassador is Uncle."

"We launch as soon as we get clear of customs. Our man on the ground is Chien Nguyen and he'll have transport waiting for us. Weapons will be silenced pistols and they should only be used if your life is in danger. Each two man team will carry four Rattlesnake knock-out syringes. Remember, we want this guy alive.

Plan A is to use Chien's contact to get us up to the penthouse. We'll knock Stinky out, put him in a laundry cart, go down the service elevator, then we'll make a beeline for the airport. A Range Rover will meet us just outside the airport and we will transfer Stinky into the Rover and it will go directly to Fatboy. The rest of us will drop off the rental cars, but Chien will handle the payment details.

Plan B will activate if we have to deal with any outside interference...namely the KGB or the GRU, the Russian military intelligence unit. If they are in the area we will have to neutralize them before we move the target out. That's why I want you to carry the extra syringes. We'll still have to get up to the penthouse, but we won't move until we have taken care of the Russian agents. The rest will go as we briefed before. Any questions or comments?"

Later, Robin looked up from his desk as Ernie Jackson came into his cabin.

"Sorry to bother you, Rob, but we need to talk."

"What's up, brother?"

"We are less than two hours from Bangkok. We got a message from Grassley. The KGB is going to make a move to get Stinky today."

"Are they on the ground?"

"They don't know."

Robin thought for a minute. "Any word from Chien?"

"We had contact an hour ago. Everything is still go with him, including getting us past customs...it'll just cost us."

"Chien said Stinky is still at the Landmark?"

"Check."

"Okay, on the next contact, I'll need to talk to him. Plans will stay the same. We will just have to play it by ear."

Thirty minutes later, Chien called again.

"Chien, this is Robin."

"Robin! How are you?"

"Doing good my friend. Can you put together a surveillance team ASAP?"

"I don't know. I can start calling relatives. Why?"

"I am not sure we're going to get there before the Russians. If they grab Stinky before we get there, we're going to need to know where they are."

"I'll start calling relatives. My cousin says he is still at the Landmark."

"That's good. Get a surveillance team up and keep me updated every half-hour. Turn your radio on and put it on Tac 8 scrambled. I'll contact you when we are on the ground."

CHAPTER SIX

Ground control directed Jack to park the aircraft in a remote part of the Bangkok Airport. Robin exited the plane by the internal stairway and was wrapped with sticky, warm air. A short, wiry man in a very officious uniform stood next to a car waiting for him, with an expectant smile on his face.

"Good afternoon, sir. I'm Robin Marlette."

"I am Captain Alak Shenawatra, Supervising Airport Customs Officer."

Robin bowed slightly and handed the officer an expanding file containing the plane's documentation, passports of the entire team and a plain brown envelope. The officer went to his car and motioned for Robin to follow. He retrieved a set of rubber stamps and proceeded to stamp the visa in each passport. Pulling out another form, he stamped it too. He put the passports and the form back into the folding file and removed the brown envelope. He thumbed the currency and looked at Robin with a smile.

"Welcome to Thailand. Your vehicles are waiting for you in front of the cargo terminal to your right."

"Thank you, Captain. You're very kind."

The Captain drove away as Robin called on his portable. "Okay, let's rock!" As the team came down the ramp, Robin smiled as he read the form the Captain had put in the file. It was their exit clearance.

THE TEAM WAS STILL fifteen minutes out from the Landmark when Chien called on the radio.

"The Uncle went up to the penthouse."

"Shit!" Robin cursed as he mentally clicked through options, none of which made him happy.

"Pick it up, guys."

"Not easy in this traffic, boss, but I remember a side street on the map about five hundred meters ahead that could cut a few minutes."

"Do it!"

Driving fast proved difficult in the teeming city of Bangkok. The team went through alternating districts of wealth and poverty. The fading day slowly wrapped the city in a warm and humid evening. The pungent aroma of Asia; a mixture of spices, flowers, food, exhaust, smoke, garbage and sewage permeated the air. In some districts, just as many people walked in the streets as were on the sides. Vehicles of every description careened down the streets with horns blaring, mindless of any traffic laws. Driving was a game of chicken as well as a method of transportation.

When the team was five minutes away, Chien radioed.

"SpearTip, a black sedan pulled up to the service entrance to the hotel and two white men went in. There's a driver with the vehicle. They reek KGB."

Robin's heart pounded and his mind churned. "All units,

same set up. SpearTip Two, you follow us to the service entrance. We'll go to the service door. You hang back until we have the target in custody, then you come and bag him. We'll get back to our car and boogie. SpearTip Three and Four, you follow Two to the airport and cover them. All units understand?"

"Two, good."

"Three, Roger."

"Four, also."

"Chien, we are thirty seconds out. Release any surveillance units you have and engage the driver in a conversation."

"Roger."

Burke drove the car slowly past the alley at the rear of the hotel.

"Stop here." Robin signaled Rick Santos and Emmett in Unit Two to stop. He and Burke exited their car and sneaked a peek around the corner. Chien and the driver were yelling at each other.

"Burke, go to the driver's door and mess with him." Burke moved to the left as Robin walked quickly to the passenger side of the car. He stopped by the rear quarter panel.

Burke walked up to Chien. "Hey, is this guy giving you trouble?"

The Russian cursed and started to get out of the car, but Burke and Chien pushed back on the door.

Robin jerked opened the rear passenger door, slipped in and reached over the front seat jamming a rattlesnake syringe into the driver's left shoulder. The man yelped as Burke pulled the driver's head out and smashed his face with a knee strike. Robin motioned Chien to leave, but Chien bent down to help Burke with the driver.

As Robin came around the rear of the car, the service door opened. Stinky stepped out. Two KGB agents carrying luggage were behind him. Robin grabbed Stinky and spun, flinging the fugitive to Burke and Chien and then threw his body against the door, slamming it in the face of the first KGB agent. Robin heard a thump and a loud curse when he did so.

Chien pushed Stinky to the ground.

Burke dragged the driver over to the wall.

Emmett and Rick came screeching up to the service door. Emmett jumped out, grabbed Stinky, threw him into their car and jumped back in. Rick gunned the engine and they rocketed out of the alley.

"Look out!" Chien yelled. Robin heard an engine and looked back to see Burke maneuvering the KGB car towards the service door. He jumped out of the way and Burke banged into the door blocking it.

"Let's go!" Robin yelled as he threw a salute to Chien limping to his car. Robin and Burke sprinted to their car. Seconds later they were in Bangkok traffic both wide eyed and breathing heavily as adrenalin coursed through their bodies, which were dripping with perspiration. Robin began to laugh. Burke soon laughed too.

"What a clusterfuck!" Robin yelled above the roar of the engine.

"No shit! It all went down so fast, I'm not really sure what happened!"

"What happened is we got Stinky and no one got killed! That's all that matters." Robin keyed his radio.

"SpearTip to Fatboy."

"Fatboy, go."

"We're inbound. Send out SpearTip Five and get ready for departure."

"We're already on it."

Ninety minutes later, Robin appeared on the flight deck.

They were already taxiing toward the runway.

"Are we cleared for take-off, Jack?"

"Not yet. We are number three in line."

"I'll feel a lot better when we're airborne."

Jack taxied the aircraft to a position behind a Luftansa 727. Minutes ticked by. He suddenly cocked his head and pressed his headset to his right ear.

"Rob, they want us to come back to the cargo terminal."

"Hold your position."

"What do I tell them?"

"Tell them unless it is an emergency, we already have our exit clearance."

"Worldwide 305 Heavy, Bangkok Center, we already have our exit clearance. Unless it's an emergency, we'll hold our position. We do have a schedule to meet." By now they were next to take off. They lined up on the runway. There were four aircraft behind them.

"They're telling us to standby, Rob."

Robin's jaws were grinding. "Come on...Come on...Jack..." Robin was about to tell Jack to take off.

"Roger and thank you, 305 Heavy." Jack and Oscar pushed the throttles forward and the big jet started down the runway. It gathered speed and began to tremble. After what seemed forever, Jack eased back on the wheel and the airplane rose into the night sky. Robin breathed a sigh of relief.

"Wonder why they let us go?" Jack mused.

"I imagine the good Captain shared some of his largesse." Robin felt relieved he paid the amount Chien suggested. "Activate the defense suite, Oscar."

"Done, Mother Marlette."

Robin put his hands on the shoulders of the pilots. "Now you know why I demanded you guys be our fly boys."

"There's no way we would've let you guys have all this fun without us, Rob," Oscar replied.

"Get us home."

"Roger that."

Robin walked back to the team quarters and worked his way to the holding cells. Emmett and Burke were there carefully repacking Emmett's paramedic bag. Robin looked in the cell window. His stomach turned at the thought of what this man did.

"How's Stinky?"

"He's still out, but he'll be fine."

"I'm going up to see Jamie. Let me know when Ivanov is conscious."

"Will do."

Robin walked up to the intelligence deck. "How is it going, Jamie?"

"Good, Rob. I'm ready to contact Grassley if you are."

Robin put on a headset and plugged it in. "Let 'er rip."

"Bill Grassley."

"It's Rob. We have the package and are headed home."

"Good job. The Soviets are beside themselves. They suspect the CIA did it, but they're not sure because the FBI and DEA in the Bangkok embassy are just as confused as the Soviets."

"I may have injured one the KGB agents."

"We haven't picked up anything like that. Do you think you hurt him badly?"

"Naw, I probably just broke his nose."

"Don't worry about it. I have something else for you to worry about."

"Nothing about home is it?"

"No, I have another mission for you...a very urgent mission."

"We can't go home first?"

"No, because you're not far from the trouble."

Robin took a deep breath. "Okay, what's the mission?"

"A group of about thirty men from the Moro Islamic Liberation Front kidnapped seventeen international aid workers on the Philippine island of Mindanao. The Philippine Army attempted a rescue that resulted in the death of thirteen of the hostages. The Army has pulled back to regroup. They're a little shaken. The commander was relieved and they're waiting for the new one to get on the scene."

"What does this have to do with us? Why can't our guys go in and get them?"

"I think you know the Filipinos are exerting their independence from us. Our guys are there, but they are being prevented from participating. We need you guys to rescue the remaining hostages, but make it look like the Filipinos did it."

"Jesus, Bill, we're good, but we're not magicians!"

"One of the hostages is the daughter of a multi-billionaire named George Lanthrop, who is a very important supporter and advisor to the President. Lanthrop is asking the President to do something. You guys are our 'something'."

Robin rubbed his forehead. If he took this mission, it would require a High Altitude Low Opening (HALO) jump. His men were already tired and a HALO jump was a dangerous proposition in the best of situations. He knew, however, that Grassley and Yates were simply calling in their markers...and the team was only three hours away from Mindanao. "Okay, Bill, where are they?"

"I've sent a satellite image to you. It will show the current location of the hostages and a river delta you can drop into about three miles away."

"You know this will require a HALO jump tonight."

"I know it's asking a lot, but you're our quickest option and our best chance for success."

"Are your people sure we are only dealing with the thirty tangos?"

"No, they're sure you'll probably be dealing with a lot more. We believe the thirty tangos were probably just the assault group. They've probably hooked up with the main force by now."

"That's just wonderful!" Robin stared at the wall trying to bring his rising blood pressure down. "Give me about an hour to get a plan worked up. I'll get back to you."

"Okay, Rob. Please let me know as soon as you can."

Robin took off his headset.

"You look pissed off, boss."

"I am, Jamie. Pull up the satellite image Grassley just sent. Get the coordinates, send them to Jack and check the weather and winds up to thirty thousand feet in the area."

"You got it."

Robin walked down to the flight deck. "Jack, set a course for Mindanao to the coordinates Jamie just sent you."

Jack turned and frowned.

"We may have a new mission. I'll let you know more when I do."

Jack saluted and Robin went into the team quarters.

The men were in high spirits. Robin knew they were happy about a successful mission. He also knew part of their happiness was the thought of going home.

"All right, everyone...listen up!" The group quieted and all eyes turned toward him. "We just had our first mission and it was a success." The men let out a cheer Robin felt sure reverberated from the nose to tail of Fatboy. "That's the good news." A disquieting silence blanketed the room.

"What's the bad news?" Burke asked.

"We just received a new mission."

Robin saw half the men were disappointed, but the other half showed excitement.

"American citizens are being held hostage in Mindanao by a group known as the Moro Islamic Liberation Front. The Philippine Army screwed up a rescue attempt which resulted in thirteen hostages getting killed. The army guys are apparently pretty messed up over this incident and the kidnappers fled into the jungle with the remaining four hostages. The CIA thinks they have the kidnappers and the hostages located. They want us to HALO in tonight and rescue these people. We need to get a plan worked up. Burke, you and Rocky get with Jamie and start the plan. The rest of you guys start getting your gear ready. Make sure you triple check your HALO gear and start pre-breathing oxygen in ninety minutes. Ernie, you are C&C again. Emmett, you have Ivanov duty. Gary, you need to be working on an extraction plan..."

"Wait a minute, big guy," Ernie interjected.

"What?"

"I was C&C last time. It's your turn to be C&C and I'll lead this mission."

Robin considered his friend for a moment. "I can buy that normally, but not this time. This is our first combat HALO jump. I've got to lead it." Both men eyed each other through a long charged pause.

The other men quietly created distance between themselves and their team leaders.

Ernie walked next to Robin and spoke in a low voice.

"You can't protect me, Rob. If either of us gets hurt or killed, it will be the same for our families. It's not fair to me as the second in command here. Either you trust me to do the job or you don't."

Robin looked down at the floor. He searched his mind trying to figure out an excuse or a plausible retort, but none came to mind.

"You know I trust you with my life, Ernie and maybe I am

trying to protect you. On the other hand, this is our first combat HALO jump and I need to lead it....you know I need to lead it. After this, we'll alternate."

Ernie slowly nodded his head. "Okay, Rob, I'll go with you this time, but I lead the next mission...no matter what it is."

Robin put his hand on his friend's shoulder. "10-4, you stubborn ol' coot."

CHAPTER SEVEN

Burke and Rocky came up with the best plan under the circumstances, their Vietnam combat experience once again proving invaluable to the team. Robin called Grassley and told him they accepted the mission. Grassley was relieved, but not surprised. He didn't even argue when Robin set the price at twenty million dollars. Still, Robin's nerves were taut. They had no real team preparation time. It went against every principle of their training... except one...*improvise, adapt and overcome*.

An hour and a half later, the men were assembled at the rear of the aircraft with fifteen minutes until the jump. Each man's equipment was inspected by the man next to him and then Burke and Rocky did final checks. Burke finished inspecting Robin, the last man to be checked.

"Everybody ready to go?"

"Roger," Burke replied.

"All right, gentlemen, listen up. We want to maintain radio silence as long as we can. I don't think they can monitor our Tac frequencies, but since the element of surprise is essential to this mission, we won't chance it. Keep the guide lights on Burke and Rocky in sight the minute the door opens. Their GPS receivers should get us to Ingin River delta drop zone. When the chute opens, activate your firefly and go to your infrared goggles. If you run into any problems during the jump, you can break radio silence to let us know. Make sure you tell us who you are and don't cut yourself off. Key the mic for at least one second before you tell us your emergency. Remember, the closest town is Sindangan, about five miles to the northeast as the crow flies, but a helluva lot longer on foot. The Philippine Army guys are still there.

This is our first combat HALO and I don't mind telling you my asshole is a little tight, but we have the best training and the best equipment. We should be fine. Any questions or comments?"

Mark Warren spoke up. "I hope someone brought some extra toilet paper because I'm probably going to need it when we get down."

"Shit, Mark, you're so young, you'll probably bounce even if your chute doesn't open," Doug Ariel joked.

"Five minutes to jump," Ernie's voice came over the intercom. Emmett, the designated jumpmaster, signaled for everyone to form up. The men stood abreast to each other in two loosely formed lines facing the compartment cargo door. Each man activated a chemlite attached to the top rear of his partner's helmet. Emmett signaled for the men to go on oxygen. He pushed a button and a wall rose up from the bottom of the compartment and sealed off the chamber. Emmett raised his hand.

"Starting decompression."

The rear cargo door slowly opened and the men stared into the darkness. The stars winked bright in the sky and a half moon softened the harshness of the black void. The frigid air at thirty thousand feet punched their bodies and some men wrapped their arms around themselves hoping to retain some extra body heat. The big jet's nose pointed at an extreme angle of attack with the engines screaming. The pilots slowed the plane down to jump speed.

"Standby the door!" Every eye fixed on the jump light. After an eternal thirty seconds, it turned green.

"GO, GO, GO!" Emmett yelled with an urgent voice.

In an instant, the entire group of men dove into the night. Robin, the last man out, saluted Emmett and followed his men into the darkness, the shepherd of this flock. He momentarily fought for control as he arched his back and spread out his hands and feet as he achieved controlled free fall. He kept his eyes on the blue light on Burke's helmet, while doing a mental head count. The number of chemlites equaled the number of men who jumped and no chemlite appeared to be spinning...a very good sign. Their training and discipline brought the team to a level of operational competence beyond everyone's expectations... except Robin's. Now, if every man's equipment worked as advertised, this could be fun.

The team rocketed towards the earth, thrilling Robin to his very core. This was as close to flying like a bird a man could get. He checked his altimeter...passing through 20,000 feet. He smiled behind his oxygen mask. His body surged with the pleasure of doing an extraordinary thing well and this inevitably led to thoughts of Karen. He wished she could experience what he felt.

KAREN MARLETTE'S eyes fluttered open. She had been trying to fall asleep when she felt her husband's presence. She sat up in bed. Her heart felt happy even though Robin wasn't home. He was thinking of her...she knew it. She lay back down and closed her eyes. Somehow, sleep finally overtook her.

AT SIX THOUSAND five hundred feet, Robin's chute opened. The ram-air parachute allowed Robin to fly it like a hang glider. He had set his chute to open five hundred feet higher than the other men so he could spot anyone in trouble. He activated his firefly, unhooked his infrared goggles and flipped them down. A few seconds later, other fireflies began flashing. Robin soon counted eight floating in the night. All were moving through the air smoothly in a predetermined landing pattern.

When he reached fifteen hundred feet, Robin prepared for landing, picking an area where no fireflies were flashing. He released his equipment bag so it hung from him on a line twenty feet below and flipped up his goggles. The Ingin River glistened in the moonlight and he headed for the edge of it. Robin made one full turn and pulled on the control handles to flare out slowing almost to a hover. His bag thumped on the ground and he landed standing, pulled the handles and collapsed the chute. Popping his harness open, he shucked it onto the ground and moved quickly to his bag. Robin retrieved his pack and looked around as he shouldered it. He hit the bottom of the magazine in his silenced Colt Commando assault carbine and pulled and released the bolt handle to load a round in the chamber, hitting the bolt assist for good measure. The team gathered around him as he circled the chemlite from his helmet above his head. Everyone was accounted for. Rick complained of a sore ankle, but said he'd be all right. Mark was soaked from a water landing, but confirmed his weapons ready. The team hid their chutes, jump gear and equipment bags in the brush under a thick stand of trees.

"Okay, were movin' out. Rocky, you're point. Set a quick pace."

"Roger, boss."

The team started up the river staying close to the embankment using the concealment of the foliage growing there. Robin walked in the middle of the team and he appreciated it was night because the air was warm and humid. He knew daybreak would bring soaring temperatures.

The river was one hundred yards wide flowing with a good current and the sound of the water along with the sandy bank masked the sound of the team's movements. After going for about a mile, Rocky turned left and the men started climbing through mountain jungle consisting of canopy and long needled pine. They moved along primitive paths for two hours, everyone acutely alert. Rocky stopped and the men all dropped to one knee forming a defensive perimeter.

"We are about a half mile away now, Rob."

"Take Marv and do a recon. You got forty-five minutes. We'll get off the trail and move in the jungle on the left side.

"We're gone." Rocky moved out tapping Marv on the arm. Marv fell in behind Rocky and the men melted into the jungle. Burke saluted them as they went by. Robin motioned to Burke.

"We can slow down now. Start moving us forward off the trail to the left." Burke saluted and went forward to the point position, knelt and silently listened for a full minute. He then waved the men to follow. The team moved toward their objective one careful step after the other. They stopped often and listened carefully. After about forty minutes, Burke signaled to stop and after a few tense seconds, Rocky and Marv appeared out of the night.

"We got good info and a plan, boss," Rocky reported.

Robin indicated for the men to gather. In quiet whispers, Rocky and Marv explained what they saw and how they planned to do the rescue. Three hostages were around one of the several campfires in the area. They could hear a woman moaning in an old shack who was probably the fourth hostage and she sounded in bad shape. Time to move.

CHAPTER EIGHT

The team walked in single file until Rocky indicated they were at the camp. Immediately Rocky led six men to the right. Robin and Burke moved to the left. Mike Collins started setting up claymore mines along the trail.

Robin and Burke crept silently, merging with the shadows in the jungle until they were at the back of the shack Rocky had described... putting it between them and most of the terrorists. Still, there were three men at the back. Loud snoring confirmed two were asleep, but one stood awake and fully on guard. He turned towards the shack when the woman cried out or moaned in between her sobbing.

Robin signaled Burke to take the alert man and he would take care of the sleepers. Both drew their knives.

The woman cried out again and a laugh followed a man speaking broken English and describing sexual acts too brutal for Robin to contemplate.

The guard let his weapon hang on its sling and rubbed his crotch...his last sexual act. Burke dropped the man's lifeless body as Robin efficiently inserted his knife into the medulla of both his targets, twisting the blade to put them in permanent sleep.

As they moved to the rear door, Robin found it hard to control the seething anger burning inside him. The woman yelped and a man laughed at her pain causing Robin to want to smash the man's face into the rough logs of the shack. He pushed these thoughts back and breathed deeply, focusing on the mission as he and Burke drew Glock 9mm pistols loaded with subsonic ammunition and attached silencers.

Burke had the same cold, resolved look Robin now felt.

He pressed his mic button to send a static hash and signal the team to move in. He and Burke entered the shack through the partially opened door.

In candlelight, Robin's sights found a head directly in front. He squeezed the trigger in a double tap, then swung to the left and sighted on the head of a man standing with his pants down. Robin fired another double tap. Then scanning the room he saw Burke shoot a man naked from the waist down with an erection. A fourth man lay on the dirt floor, his pants around his ankles.

A nude woman was tied down over a rough-hewn wooden bench, badly beaten and bleeding from the mouth, vagina and anus. The horror of what these men had been doing turned Robin's stomach. He bent down and gently put his hand on the woman's forehead. Her eyes fluttered and she whispered something in Russian.

"We're getting you out of here." Robin whispered in his text book Russian.

"Americans?"

Robin held his finger to his lips.

The woman nodded with a sob of relief.

Burke handed Robin a blanket.

Robin lifted the woman's body as gently as he could to the

sitting position and wrapped her. He picked her up and she shuddered, but put her arms around his neck.

Two men came around the corner of the shack as Robin and Burke were leaving through the door they came in. Chunks of both men's heads went flying as Burke took both of them out with successive shots. The two men moved through the jungle as quickly as they could without causing the woman too much pain.

A shot rang out, then another. Automatic weapons began to chatter and bullets started flying everywhere. Men shouted and a woman screamed. Ahead, Robin saw Mike Collins waving them toward the trail. Robin knew the claymores were within the next fifty feet.

"Burke, stay and help with the holding action!"

"Roger!"

ROCKY HAD LED Doug and Mark, his hostage rescue team, around the edge of the camp. He told Marv to set up the cover team. Rocky scanned the immediate area from overgrowth about twenty yards from where the hostages were located.

By the light of two campfires, Rocky saw two hostages were asleep on the ground and one sat on a log with her head in her hands. There were at least four terrorists in the immediate area of the hostages. Two were awake and talking to each other and the other two slept on the ground nearby. Rocky tapped Mark's shoulder and pointed to the hostages.

Mark nodded.

Rocky tapped Doug's arm, pointed to the sleeping men and ran his finger across his throat.

Doug nodded.

Rocky pointed to himself and then pointed to the two

terrorists who were awake. Doug and Mark acknowledged and the men then focused their attention to the camp. A few seconds later, Robin's static hash broke in their ear pieces. They moved forward...dark, dangerous shadows gliding through the night.

Rocky held his silenced Glock at eye level, the tritium night sights lined up on the awake terrorist farthest from him. At fifteen yards, Rocky fired two rounds and the man fell over. He swung his pistol to the right, his shots made the other man's head snap back as he dropped to the ground.

Doug took care of the sleeping men and Rocky motioned for him to help Mark with the hostages while he covered them. Rocky holstered the Glock and unslung his Commando assault carbine.

JESSICA LANTHROP HAD no emotional reserves left. She believed she was going to die all because she wanted to prove she wasn't a mindless, spoiled rich girl. She looked up at the stars. Well, at least she did prove that before she died. Jessica almost screamed when she saw three shadowy figures moving toward her from the dark jungle, but the closest man to her put his finger to his lips. She realized they were there for her and her friends. She jumped when one of the men shot two of her captors who were talking to each other and then again when the third man shot two who were sleeping.

"Americans," the closest man whispered. "We're getting you out of here. Wake your friends."

She bent down and shook Alana. Betsy raised her head and started getting up. A man yelled and a shot rang out. Then more shots. Fear churned through Jessica's gut and she screamed as her rescuer grabbed her and pulled her to the trees.

MARV'S TEAM was set to cover the extraction. He saw Rocky take out the guards. Marv repeatedly scanned the area in front of him and could see there were a lot more than thirty terrorists.

A head popped up.

Marv put his night sights on it and fired one round. The head disappeared. Other men rose only to be cut down by Marv's team. The number of awakening terrorists grew rapidly and soon there were more shooting terrorists than the covering team could handle. Fortunately, the terrorists were undisciplined and fired wildly in the night.

Rocky's voice came over Marv's headset. "We're moving out, Marv."

"Just in time. We're right behind ya."

ROBIN BARELY NOTICED it started raining as he moved as quickly as he could down the trail carrying an extra one hundred and ten pounds. He wanted to create distance so he could give the woman first aid until Willy Young could get to them with his paramedic kit. Heavy gunfire reverberated in the jungle until he heard an explosion and then three more. Robin smiled. *Mike's handiwork.*

He went for another half mile before he began to feel an all too familiar pain in the middle of his back. He stopped and gently propped the woman against a tree. He suddenly gasped and arched as an invisible fist twisted the muscles in the middle of his back. The spasm passed and he bent over to help release the tension. When he straightened, the woman looked at him with questioning eyes.

"Just an old wound."

She nodded in understanding.

Robin pulled off his pack, retrieved his trauma kit and started cleaning the wounds on her face.

"Please do not move." A deep male voice with a Russian accent spoke from the jungle. "We would rather not kill you." Robin slowly raised his hands.

Men in Russian Spetsnaz jungle fatigues armed with AK-47s moved in around them. Two of them lifted the woman onto a stretcher.

"She's badly injured and needs immediate medical attention," Robin said quietly.

A man in civilian hiking clothes stepped forward. "She will get it." He looked closely at Robin. "You took Ivanov!"

Robin just looked at the man.

He laughed heartily. "Good riddance, although if you ever meet my KGB comrade, be prepared for a boxing match!" The man laughed again, but then his face turned to stone. "What happened to the men who did this?"

"We sent them to hell."

The Russian's face brightened. "I hope you will let me buy you a drink someday."

"I'd be delighted," Robin said with a smile.

The woman said something to the men holding the stretcher. They brought her closer to Robin. She raised her hand and put it on his cheek. "Thank you, my angel. I will never forget."

"You're welcome. Take care." She gave a weak smile as the sound of a helicopter in the distance had the Russians hustling down the trail.

Robin heard people coming down the trail, so he stepped into the jungle until he saw Rocky, then the rest of the team and the other three hostages.

Rocky looked at Robin and then around the ground.

Burke walked up.

"What the hell is going on, Rob?"

"The Russians have come and gone."

"What?!"

"The woman in the shack was Russian and I suspect one of their agents. Probably a very important agent. Spetsnaz and the GRU came and got her."

"Holy shit! I'm glad we didn't have a fight over her!" The sound of the helicopter faded in the distance.

"Me, too. Everyone okay?"

"Yeah, just some minor injuries, but we gotta get these ladies out of here."

"Okay, Rocky move us out."

The rain kept on coming as the team worked their way back to the river. The men made a raft out of logs and bamboo so they could float the women and save them the walk. Robin contacted Ernie by satellite radio.

"SpearTip, you have to watch out!" Robin could hear the excitement in Ernie's voice. "There are hostiles in the area!"

"Yeah, we know, Fatboy. We just had tea."

"What?!"

"It's okay, they just wanted one of theirs."

"It's not that simple."

"Roger, we'll sort it out later. Just get the Filipinos to the delta ASAP.

"Roger, I'll get them rolling."

The team finished the raft and taught the three women how to control it with long bamboo poles. The group moved down the river and the men had to hustle to keep up with the raft in the rain swollen river. After thirty minutes the night gave way to light grey overcast with the coming dawn and the sound of helicopter blades blended with the rush of the river.

"Okay, ladies, your ride outta here is coming. Remember, we were never here. The Russians came and got the other woman, whatever she called herself and you escaped. Don't contradict anything you see in the press. It's essential to our survival you follow that script."

"Thank you, everyone." Jessica said. "You're truly wonderful." She reached out and touched Mark's shoulder and he put his hand on hers.

"Sometimes," Robin replied. "Now, on your way."

The women started polling as the team faded into the jungle and Robin saw Jessica looking back at Mark.

The team moved two miles down the coast to the Talinga River delta. Marv found a cave one hundred yards from the beach and everything dropped; packs, recovered chutes and tired bodies.

"SpearTip to Fatboy."

"Go SpearTip."

"What's our estimated extraction time?"

"We're in Davao City, so it will be forty-eight to seventy-two, SpearTip."

"Roger," Robin replied with a tired voice.

He looked at his men around him, their faces ghostly and showing disappointment in the glow of chemlites.

"Well gentlemen, you heard the news. Looks like this will be home for a couple of days. Before any of you turn in, I just want you to know how proud I am of all of you. We pulled off a very difficult mission with less than ideal prep time. The important thing is four terrified women are going home and none of us got hurt. It doesn't get much better..."

"Okay, boss," Burke interjected. "Enough with the speeches. Can we just go to sleep now?"

Robin laughed. "Yeah, go to sleep. I got first watch."

CHAPTER NINE

The rain continued coming down two days later when Gary Perkins showed up in a fishing boat. It took three runs in a small life boat to get all the men and equipment on board. They were all glad to get out of the cave.

Robin looked out on the transom of the boat. The monsoon weather had the boat riding waves like a roller coaster and half the team were bent over the rail even though rations ran out the day before.

"Well, I guess we're separating the men from the boys!" Rocky flashed a sardonic grin.

"Be gentle, Rock. Most of those guys over there were born and raised in the Arizona desert."

"I know, Rob. I'm just feeling a little superior right now. We pulled off two great capers with none of us getting more than scratches and bruises."

Robin looked up at the sky as rain incessantly splashed on his face. "We were damn lucky. I wouldn't want to HALO in a storm like this."

"In my experience, success in operations like these

depends on luck more than we care to admit. I suppose that's why we always say God is on our side."

Robin looked at his teammate. "I'm glad to have your experience on this team, Rock. There are very few team leaders who can depend on every man. I can."

"I wouldn't have missed this gig for the world. We're doing important work and making good money to boot."

"It is pretty damn good right now." Robin looked at the rail huggers. "Well, for some of us." Both men laughed.

"Rob!" Gary Perkins slid down the ladder from the bridge. "We have radar contact with two high speed boats coming towards us on the starboard bow. They've been shadowing us for at least four hours before we picked you up."

"Do we know who they are?"

"The skipper isn't sure, but he thinks they may be Indonesian pirates."

"Rocky, get everybody on deck ready to fight and please ask Burke to bring up my rifle and tactical vest."

"That's a big roger, boss."

Robin climbed up to the bridge and entered the wheelhouse.

A grizzled mariner who had manned a landing craft during the invasion of the Philippines in 1944 at the age of seventeen, Gary found Johnny "Whisky" Walker after doing a little investigating on the Davao docks. Walker's landing craft sunk and he ended up fighting with the infantry. He fell in love with a Filipino girl and never left.

"Hey, Skipper," Robin nodded to Walker. "You ever deal with Indonesian pirates before?"

"That I have, Colonel." Robin cocked his head. "Gary told me your rank. The boy thought he had to impress me I think, but I figured you for an officer right off."

"Is that good or bad?"

Whisky looked to the transom where the team prepared for trouble.

"Judging by the way those men look up to you, I'd say it's a good thing."

Robin looked at his men for a thoughtful moment. "Tell me more about these pirates."

"They took one boat from me, when I was young. Kids were little, didn't think I could chance a fight. They tried again last year. Me and my boys fought 'em and beat 'em. I figure we killed four of 'em. If those boats are pirates, they're coming after me. It ain't your fight."

"Bad guys on the prowl are always our fight."

"Well in that case, there is a forty mike-mike grenade launcher in the forward hold just under the doors on the bow. Might come in handy."

"How'd you manage to get permission to carry that on your boat?"

"Who said I had permission?"

Robin laughed. "I'll put a man on it. You maneuver, we'll do the shooting. I suggest you head right for them, to present a smaller target."

"We'd better get on it. The scope shows two circling and two more coming up on our starboard beam."

Burke brought Robin his rifle and vest. "Burke, there's a forty millimeter grenade launcher under the doors on the bow. Get it manned with a radio!" He turned back to Walker. "Skipper, does your radar give us accurate range?" Robin asked as he buckled his vest.

"Aye." Robin stepped up to the windshield. Mark Warren, who had an uncanny ability with the grenade launcher, stood behind the weapon. Burke looked up at him and Robin held up four fingers and their radios were ready on Tac 4. Robin searched his mind for the spec sheet on the M19 40mm grenade launcher until it surfaced. It had an effective range of about sixteen hundred yards and a maximum range of twenty-two hundred yards. He couldn't lock on a target so he would have to estimate between sweeps of the needle on the screen. He peered into the scope.

The Skipper made the turn into the pirates, putting two of the targets at two thousand yards off the port bow.

Robin picked up his radio. "Target...013 degrees...1900 yards... fire two!"

Mark sent two rounds out.

Robin saw two water spouts, but no explosions.

One pirate boat kept charging forward, but the other slowed way down and started to turn. The two starboard targets were now off the bow within maximum range.

Robin quickly re-worked the calculations for the remaining port target.

"Target...016 degrees...1600 yards...fire four!" Robin immediately re-focused on the two boats on the starboard bow. "Target...089 degrees...1900 yards...fire two!"

The advancing pirate boat on the port side exploded in a fireball as his partner raced away apparently not wanting to end up the same way.

The men cheered.

Robin turned to check starboard. Water spouts erupted just missing the pirates. Large green tracers whipped over and around the fishing boat followed by the sound of a heavy machine gun ripping across the water.

"Target...dead ahead...1200 yards...fire four!" Water spouts shot up again and one of the boats took a hit, but no fireball bloomed. The boat, however, turned away. More tracers came at the fishing boat and men hit the deck as rounds smashed into the lower cabin spewing shrapnel in all directions. Robin looked back at the transom and saw Doug Ariel and Willy Young lying on the deck. Robin grabbed his rifle and went on the bridge deck. "Fire at will!" The whole team opened fire.

A rocket propelled grenade (RPG) swooshed over the transom along with the tracers from the machine gun. The 40mm grenade launcher thumped rhythmically. The sheer amount of metal hurtling at the pirate boat began to take effect, even at five hundred yards. A man fell off the boat as pieces of it flew in the air. At three hundred yards, the boat began to disintegrate. A grenade made a direct hit and the boat disappeared with a loud bang in a huge black cloud.

Robin jumped down to the transom. Both Doug and Willy Young had been peppered by shrapnel. Doug had a large ugly wound in his left shoulder. Willy had taken hits on the upper part of his back. Robin could see a large piece of metal embedded in Doug's shoulder. Burke had opened Willy Young's medical kit and he handed Robin a syringe of morphine. Robin pushed it into Doug's thigh. Willy rose off the deck and crawled over to Doug.

"I'll take it from here, Rob."

Robin started to object until he saw Willy's hands move confidently into the bag and retrieve scalpels and a large forceps to remove the metal.

He looked at Robin. "We should get him below."

Doug shook his head. "No! I'll just get seasick again. Just do what you got to do here."

"Give me another morphine, Willy." Willy handed Robin another syringe.

"Don't knock me out, Rob. I hate..."

"If I knock you out, you dumb shit, you won't be seasick."

Doug thought for a minute. "Okay, stick me."

Three hours later, the rain finally let up. Robin stood on the bridge deck sucking in deep breaths of ocean air. If he didn't know better, he'd have thought he was seasick, but he knew almost losing a man ate at his gut. The metal in Doug's shoulder was a chunk of a shattered 12.7mm machine gun bullet. A direct hit with such a large round would've killed him. Burke treated Willy's wounds and they were not serious.

Robin looked up and marveled at the lush blanket of stars. They seemed to be mysterious, but reassuring companions on his journey through life. He and Karen spent hours on camping trips teaching the kids about the constellations. Robin's heart filled and he longed for Karen's arms around him. A kaleidoscope of recent memories cascaded through him. He focused on one overriding thought. His love for Karen grew every day. She was his constant companion, even seven thousand miles away.

CHAPTER TEN

R obin stood in the wheelhouse as the boat gently kissed the dock in front of a large compound on the northwest coast of Mawes Island across from Davao City. Several young men from a group of thirty people stepped forward to grab mooring lines.

"That's quite a crowd, Whisky."

"Don't worry, they're all family. No loose tongues. This is our home."

"You've got one hell of a big family!"

"Yes, sir. And one hell of a good family."

Robin made his way through the crowd coming up the gang plank then walked up the wharf to where Ernie and Jamie waited by a Land Rover.

"Here's the money you wanted." Ernie handed Robin a plain brown envelope. "You sure you want to give him that much?"

"You see all those people?"

"Yeah."

"They're all family."

Ernie's face lit up. "Gotcha, boss. A ready-made army, no less."

"Amen, brother."

Robin walked back to the boat swarming with "family" unloading equipment and checking machinery. Walker and a man of about forty were looking over the damage from the bullets. Robin took him aside and handed him the envelope.

"Skipper, your fee is in there, plus a sizeable retainer I hope you'll accept in case we need you...or your family battalion here...in the future."

Whisky looked in the envelope and gave a low whistle. "You certainly are persuasive, Robin."

"It's my job."

"Hold on boys," Walker said as Burke and Willy were coming down the gang plank carrying Doug on a stretcher. He motioned to his family and a beautiful dark haired woman stepped forward. "Rob, this is my eldest daughter, Dr. Maria Walker. I thought you might want her to look at your man."

"I've already made arrangements..."

Maria's eyes flashed with annoyance. "I'm a board certified neurosurgeon. I know what I'm doing."

Robin nodded and Maria walked over to the stretcher. She asked Doug some questions then knelt, removed the bandage and took a long look at the wound. She spoke with Willy for a minute and then carefully replaced the bandage and touched Doug's cheek. Robin didn't like the look on her face when she returned.

"It's a good thing you called ahead, Papa. I have an ambulance waiting to transport him."

Robin hesitated. "Doctor, we can't..."

"We need to get him to my hospital immediately. It may have already been too long, but at least I can prevent further nerve damage. I have an idea of what you are worried about and I guarantee his identity and presence will be confidential."

Robin took a deep breath. "All right." He knelt by the stretcher. "You know we have to get Ivanov back to the states, Doug. You'll be on your own for a while. Any objections?"

"No, boss." Doug's gaze locked on Maria.

Robin looked from Doug to Maria and back. He smiled. "I guess not. Burke, Willy, take Doug to that ambulance."

"He'll be well taken care of," Maria said smiling down at Doug.

Robin thought Doug was going to float off the stretcher. "I'm sure, Doctor."

As Maria led the way to the ambulance, Whisky whispered to Robin. "I trust that man of yours is a good man."

"He is, Whisky."

"Is he married?"

"No, why do you ask?"

"I haven't seen my daughter look at a man like that for many years. She was married once. The no good son-of-a-bitch stole her blind and left her with a broken heart."

"Doug's pretty much in the same boat, on that score. There seems to be a connection there, but who knows? They just met."

"Just makin' sure."

"As a father of two daughters, I completely understand."

THREE HOURS LATER, the team winged for Hawaii. Robin sat with Jamie, waiting for a connection with Bill Grassley. "Pick up the headset, Rob. He'll be coming on."

Robin put the headset on just in time to hear, "Bill Grassley."

"Hi, Bill. We're headed back."

"Rob, it's good to hear your voice. How is everybody?"

"We had to leave Doug in Davao City, he'll have to undergo surgery to minimize nerve damage to his shoulder. Willy got some minor wounds to his back. Everyone else is fine."

"Do I need to do anything about Doug?"

"He's in good hands."

"Good work on these missions, Rob. You guys are proving your worth in spades."

"We do our best."

"What can you tell me about the Russian woman you rescued."

"She was in bad shape, beaten mercilessly and repeatedly raped before we got to her."

"What you don't know is she's one of the KGB's top assassins. She's taken out several western operatives. The Brits and the French are a little peeved we had her and didn't terminate her."

"When we saw her, she was a victim. We don't kill injured hostages even if they are assassins. But I won't let that affect future decisions if we meet again."

Robin thought it best to change the subject. "On another note, get a hold of Chris Fleming and tell him to get his butt up to Seattle."

"Why?"

"I want to turn Ivanov over to him. We can do it quietly and smoothly with Chris and avoid any complications."

"That's a great idea. I'll get on it."

"I'll call again when we're a couple of hours out of Seattle."

"Okay, that'll be fine."

Robin took off the headset and leaned back in his chair. "So Jamie, how've you been?"

"Worried about you guys."

Robin nodded. "There probably were some things to worry about."

"That doesn't sound like you."

"So far, our worst casualty has been you. The events over the last two years have taught me the difference between luck and skill. In a combat operation, we need both to survive. We increase our odds by having top skills, but we need at least a little bit of luck to get back alive. We've had a good run of luck, but I just don't know how long it will last before we lose someone."

"You guys are one of the best trained teams in the world."

"You mean 'us guys'. Training is one of our edges. The other is you."

"Me? What do you mean?"

"You're our intelligence analyst. I will not commit our team to action without your intelligence estimate the mission has a probability of success."

Jamie's face took on a very serious look. "I don't like the idea the team's success is based on my decision."

"It isn't. It's always based on my decisions. I know the nature of intelligence. It can be unreliable. But I know you're absolutely reliable. You give me the best intelligence and I make the decisions."

"I appreciate your confidence in me."

"You've earned my confidence, Jamie." Robin stood up. "Now, I've got to check on Ivanov."

"Damn, I missed you guys!" Emmett promptly gave Robin a bear hug the minute he came through the holding area door. "Promise me you won't leave me behind next time."

"I didn't want to leave you behind this time."

"What's the deal with Doug?"

"He's in good hands. He needed surgery and I think the doctor is also going to work on other wounds."

"What other wounds?"

"The doctor is a lady and they seemed to click."

Emmett's face broke out in a grin. "A little lovin' would do that boy a world of good."

"How's Ivanov doing?"

"Okay. He gave me some problems in the beginning, but I straightened him out. He's been asking me about American prisons and I think he wants to work a deal to do all of his time in our country. He ain't too keen about going to Britain or France."

"He apparently isn't too dumb."

"Not on that score."

"I'll talk to you later, I want to get a debrief done before we land."

"Roger, boss."

Robin walked up to the team area conference room where the men were assembled. He looked over the team and smiled. Ernie had opened the bar and the men were relaxing with their favorite adult beverage.

"Listen up, gentlemen. I want to do a final debrief while things are fresh in our minds. I know we debriefed our main missions while we waited for pick up, I just wanted to make sure there weren't any final thoughts.

Rick Santos raised his hand. "I just want to say from the time we formed up to jump out of the plane until the time we got back, I was scared shitless." Knowing chuckles floated around the team. "I also want to say working with this team is the highlight of my life. We are the best damn team in the world. Tell Grassley to bring it on."

The team cheered and they rose up and pounded Rick's back. Rocky gave Rick a bear hug. Robin smiled with satisfaction as he looked on. Yes, we are the best damn team in the world.

COLONEL GENERAL IVAN PICUSHKIN, Commander of the Soviet Union Nuclear Arsenal, took a long drag from his cigarette in the rear seat of his official car parked in a wooded area on the south end of Lake Ladoga near St. Petersburg. Viktor Danshov sat across from the general. Danshov ran the narcotics and fencing business for the Russian Mafia. Bao Ma Teo, an intelligence agent for the Ministry of State Security for the Peoples Republic of China, sat next to the general.

Danshov leaned forward in his seat. "General, Mr. Teo is my contact for the people who wish to purchase your merchandise. I think you will be pleased with his offer."

General Picushkin turned to Teo. "I am listening."

"My contacts would like to purchase five devices. They are prepared to pay ten million US Dollars apiece"

Picushkin's cigarette stopped on the way to his lips. "How can I be sure your clients have that kind of money. They are not from any government."

They do have support from several of our allies."

"I understand they are Muslim Jihadists."

"That is correct."

"Will any of these devices be used in this country?"

"Aside from the Chechnya question, they do not want to make the Soviet Union an enemy. One of the clients, is Saddam Hussein, so you can be sure he certainly doesn't want that to happen."

The general sat quiet for a moment. "The price will be twenty-five million for each device. I will deliver them in Pakistan as you previously asked as long as Pakistani Intelligence (ISI), is still willing to provide protection."

"That presents two problems. The first is you want too much for the devices. The second is, one of the devices needs to be delivered to North Korea."

"Well, then Comrade Teo, I'm sure you can find other sources for your needs."

The back of the car fell quiet for a few moments until Teo spoke. "I guess there is an occasional time when the concept of supply and demand applies. We will agree to your price, but one of the devices must be delivered to North Korea."

"No, I will not deliver anything to North Korea. I will make delivery of that device in Vladivostok since that is the closest port to North Korea and it must be before the other devices are delivered in Pakistan."

Teo slowly nodded his head. "Very well, I will make the arrangements. Your demands make for difficulties, but you are doing a good thing, General. I fear your government will soon be a paper tiger and will no longer be part of the movement to destroy America."

"Thank you. I cannot sit idly by and watch us give up. I am taking a serious risk to do this, so I must do what I can to make it worth my while."

"Well, then I must leave you. I have much to do." Teo went to his car and drove away.

"You almost brought tears to my eyes, with your patriotic talk, Ivan," Danshov said with a sardonic grin.

"Screw you, Viktor. Let that monkey think it is patriotic. I just want my money before everything goes to hell."

Danshov laughed. "We are of the same mind."

CHAPTER ELEVEN

From his room at the Silver Cloud Hotel, Special Agent Chris Fleming watched the late afternoon sun create a golden shimmer on the water. His many years as an FBI agent had conditioned him not to question strange assignments, especially when the assignment originated from high up in the CIA. He had been told to get to Mukilteo, Washington, go to the Silver Cloud Hotel and wait for further instructions. So, he watched Possession Sound and waited.

At exactly five pm his phone rang. "Chris Fleming."

"Hey you ol' fart, are you hungry?" That voice sounds familiar.

"I am."

"Well, get your raggedy ass up to Arnie's just up the hill from you. You're already a drink behind."

"I'm on my way." He walked up to Arnie's, his memory searching for that voice. He made his way through the crowd at the entrance, but stopped in mid stride on the way to the hostess. Robin Marlette stood next to the podium, with a grin on his face.

"Rob!" Chris rushed forward and gave his old friend a warm handshake. "Damn, it's good to see you!"

"Good to see you too, Chris. C'mon, there's a bunch of hooligans waiting for us." Robin led Chris down the stairs to a banquet room and when they walked through the door, the Guardians mobbed Chris and subjected him to bear hugs and thumps on his back.

Chris looked around at the twelve friends who dared to cross into Mexico and take on the most dangerous drug cartel to rescue Robin's daughter, Cathy. A tear or two welled up in his eyes. "For a bunch of guys shot to shit a couple of years ago, you all look pretty damn good! Where's Doug?"

"Doug is taking some time off for medical treatment," Robin said.

"Is he going to be all right?"

"When his treatment is done I suspect he'll be healed in more ways than one."

"That's good to hear."

"C'mon, have a seat, order a drink and catch up."

"What do you know about us?" Robin asked as he and Chris enjoyed Arnie's great seafood an hour later.

"Nothing. After the raid on Rodriquez's compound you guys and Bill Grassley disappeared and all information stopped as if you didn't exist anymore. The last time I saw you all was at Davis-Monthan when they brought you back from Mexico and you all looked like hell. I honestly thought some of you were dead."

"We weren't too far away from it, especially Jamie and Marv."

"So what are you guys up to?"

"We're in the import/export business."

Chris cocked his head sideways.

"We have reps all over the world and we're always looking for good people."

Chris looked around at the team. "Rob, you're so full of bullshit. All of you guys had the tactical operator look back when you all were SWAT cops, but you guys really have the look now. So, are you going to level with me?"

Robin handed Chris his business card. "Come see me when you retire. I guarantee it will be worth your while. I'll even pay for your travel."

"I can't believe you're not going to tell me now!"

"I am telling you, Chris. You know more about us than any other person not involved in our company. The rest will come naturally."

Chris took in a deep breath. "I plan on retiring within the next year. I'll come up the next day. Or better yet, you're all invited to my retirement party. We'll come back here together!"

"We'll be there in spirit."

Chris laughed and shook his head. "Okay, Rob. Have it your way."

"That's the way I like it. Now sit back, relax and enjoy yourself. It's damn good to see you."

THE NEXT MORNING, Chris rose at six-thirty. When he got back to his room last night, there was a message on the phone telling him to report to the Special Agent in Charge at the Seattle FBI office at nine in the morning. He did a three mile run and then prepared for the day. After checking out, he headed to his rental car. As he approached the car, he saw a figure in the front passenger seat. He dropped his bag and put his hand on his gun under his sports coat. Coming up behind the person, Chris looked in and saw a man who was shackled, gagged and blindfolded with a typed message pinned to his chest.

The agent opened the car door and removed the gag and blindfold. He then pulled the paper off the man.

"I demand to be taken to the Russian Consulate immediately!"

"I'm Special Agent Chris Fleming of the FBI. Who are you?"

No reply.

Chris looked at the paper and read the name Anton Ivanov, the man's date of birth and reference to several arrest warrants from the United States, Britain and France for Trafficking of Children for Sex and other related crimes. A photo matched the man in his car.

"Mr. Ivanov, I presume." Again, the man didn't answer. "Well Mr. Ivanov, we're going to the FBI office in Seattle and get this figured out. In the meantime, you're under arrest for the warrants listed on this sheet of paper, which include Trafficking of Children for Sex. You have the right to remain silent. Anything you say can and will be used against you in a court of law. You have the right to an attorney prior to and during questioning and if you cannot afford an attorney one will be appointed to represent you free of charge. Do you understand these rights as I have explained them to you?"

"I want to speak with an attorney."

"That's fine. Sit back, relax and enjoy the ride." Chris closed the door and retrieved his bag. As he walked to the driver's door he grinned broadly. *That damn Marlette is always a step ahead of everyone else. Strictly speaking, I don't know how Ivanov got here...strictly speaking...like in court.* Chris smiled all the way to Seattle.

CHAPTER TWELVE

R obin turned into his driveway and parked. The colonial style house overlooked the Strait of Juan de Fuca and in this mid-morning, sparkles of sunlight danced on the water under a deep blue sky dressed with wisps of cloud.

He turned his attention to the beautiful woman standing in the front door. She started toward him as he walked to her and they met in a loving embrace and kiss. Robin could feel Karen wore nothing under her sundress. Passion urged them together and Robin dropped his bag and lifted Karen into his arms. "Are the kids home?"

Karen smiled. "They're in school."

Robin carried her to their bedroom, laid her on the bed and kissed her deeply. "I've missed you so much. I think about you all of the time."

"I know. I can feel you. Robin, I love you with all of my heart."

"I know. I love you with all of mine."

"I know."

Robin kissed his wife again and they made love,

treasuring each other. When they were spent, Robin rolled them over onto their sides and held his wife close. *God I love this woman!* He continued to embrace her without a word.

Karen gently pushed him back with a happy smile. "Welcome back!"

"I like this kind of homecoming." They both laughed.

Robin put his hand on her cheek and looked into her beautiful green eyes. His heart felt so full, he thought it might burst. He kissed her gently and pulled her closer to him.

The sun set low in the September sky as they sat on their deck enjoying a glass of wine and filling each other in on events the past two weeks, when they heard a car pull into the driveway.

"Laurie and Eddie are home."

Robin rose from his chair just as the front door flew open and Eddie came running into the house.

"Dad!"

"Out here, Eddie."

Eddie ran out onto the deck and wrapped his arms around his father, squeezing tightly.

"Damn, son, you're getting strong!"

"I'm working out because I'm on the JV football team."

"So mom told me. Good going. What position are you playing?"

"I play end and quarterback."

"Wow! That's pretty darn good for just starting out."

Eddie grinned and Laurie came out onto the deck and hugged her father and kissed him on the cheek. "Hi, Dad."

"Hi, honey, how are you?"

"I'm doing good."

"What does that mean?"

"I like the school and the kids are very friendly...and I love my car." Laurie smiled brightly. "Thank you for getting it for me."

"You're welcome. What else?"

"I've started writing more and have joined a writer's group in Seattle. I'm also volunteering at the Veterans Hospital there."

"Well it sounds like you're not wasting any time. You going to let me read some of what you're writing?"

"Sometime...maybe."

Robin laughed. "Okay, Laurie, but don't make it too long."

Eddie spoke up. "There's a guy who's sweet on Laurie."

Laurie's face turned the color of the wine in Robin's glass. "Eddie, stop!"

"It's okay, Sis, I like him."

"You going to tell us about him?"

"Oh, Dad!"

"C'mon, you have to tell us something about him."

"I'll tell you about him!" Eddie offered. "He's a senior, an honor student and a half-back on the football team. He wants to be a fighter pilot and he's helping me get better at football."

Laurie's eyes slid over to Eddie with a dark glare.

Eddie just grinned back

"Does he have a name?" Robin asked.

"His name is Dan Hansen," Laurie sighed with exasperation.

"He sounds like a good guy."

"I think he is."

Robin put his arm around his daughter's shoulders. "I'm glad you're doing well here, honey."

ROBIN WALKED up to the receptionist at the Island County Sheriff's Office.

"Hi, I'm Robin Marlette and I have a nine o'clock meeting with the Sheriff."

"Oh, yes, Mr. Marlette. He's expecting you. Come with me." The receptionist let the Sheriff know his nine o'clock was here and led Robin to the end of a short hall.

The Sheriff was a tall, blond muscular man who looked vaguely familiar, but Robin didn't say anything.

"Come in, Mr. Marlette."

"Please call me Robin." He shook the sheriff's hand. "It's nice to finally meet you."

The sheriff smiled. "Call me Pat. We've met before."

Robin took a deep breath. "I was afraid of that."

"I used to be a team leader on the Seattle SWAT team. I attended a conference in Phoenix where you gave a presentation on the tactical aspects of taking down air smugglers and I talked to you afterward. Don't worry, I have a good idea of what's going on. As you know us SWAT guys have occasion to come in contact with some lesser known federal agencies, so it wasn't hard to figure out what's going on when I saw your name in Mel's case report. I haven't mentioned this to anyone and I won't. I'm just glad the rumors of your death are premature."

"Actually, the rumors came close to being true for several of my team, but we all survived, although some of us not in the same condition as before."

"Well, I appreciate what you did for us the other day and whatever you're doing now, I just want you to know if there's anything we can do to help out, let us know."

"I appreciate the offer and if there is anything my team can do, just let me know."

"I will. You don't have to worry about going to court on the armed robbery. Mel tells me the suspect is going to take a plea."

"That's a relief. Mel struck me as good detective. Has is priorities straight."

"He's my best."

"The young trooper did a good job too, really. I think he figured the bad guy was out for the count and I was his only threat. He'll grow into a fine officer."

"I guess you haven't heard about Trooper Echoles."

"No, I haven't."

"He was arresting a suspect on a felony warrant. The suspect started to resist and they struggled in between their cars. A drunk slammed into Echoles' patrol car pinning Echoles and the felony suspect. The suspect was killed and Tim is in critical condition at Harborview."

"Damn, the same thing happened to some of our guys in Arizona. One of them died. What are Tim's chances?"

"They think he'll survive, but the doctors are saying he'll never walk again, which might kill him in the end."

"What do you mean?"

"Tim lived to be a trooper. He has a master's degree in economics and a doctorate in business administration, but he loved being a trooper and that's all he wanted to do. Now, that's over."

"Sheriff, please keep me informed of Trooper Echoles' condition and if his family needs anything, I want to know about that also."

"The State Patrol is doing a good job of taking care of them, but if I hear anything, I'll let you know. They have set up a fund for the family with Whidbey Island Bank."

"Thanks for the information. I've got to get going, it's been great talking to you."

"Same here, Robin."

"I'll be seeing you, Pat."

Robin left the Sheriff's Office and walked over to Whidbey

Island Bank where he transferred ten thousand dollars to the Echoles fund as an anonymous donation.

TWO HOURS LATER, Robin walked into his warehouse office suite. Ann Newman, who now handled all of the business phones and clerical work followed him into his office. Ann was the sister of Fatboy's navigator/pilot, Eric and the wife of a lawyer that the team put in prison for life. Ann divorced her husband and refused money the government offered her as a settlement concerning the seizures of all of her husband's assets because it was "dirty money." When the team became operational, Robin hired her.

"I'm sure glad you're back here." She plopped a stack of folders a foot high on his desk. "You need to make some decisions on the shipment and purchase contracts or Worldwide, Inc. will be out of business before you can say Worldwide, Inc. We're backed up with the ones you need to make decisions on. We also need to decide what shipments we are going to pick up in our plane or have shipped by common carrier."

Robin stared at the stack. "Transfer the phones to the com center and bring the rest of the stuff in. We'll work our way through them until we're finished."

It took twelve hours to plow through half of the contracts and after a two hour drive home it was three in the morning when Robin finally crawled into bed.

Karen spooned her body along his and wrapped her arm around his waist. "Do you really think you can run this company and command missions all by yourself?"

"I honestly don't know." Robin relaxed in Karen's warm embrace. "I didn't think the business end would get this busy so quickly. Our in country reps are working their tails off.

They're finding great products at good prices, finding good markets for US products and products other reps are finding in other countries. The logistics are a nightmare and keeping up with import/export laws and taxes is almost worse than SEAL training."

"Can't any of the other guys help?"

"They are. Ernie's managing the facilities; Burke's managing the loading docks and the other guys are managing the country reps. These two back to back missions really screwed up the business end of things."

"You need to hire more people."

"Ann said the same thing."

"We women always know best." He could hear the smile in her voice.

"Is there any way I can answer that without getting into trouble."

"Just agree."

Robin chuckled and laced his fingers through Karen's. "I think I'll go to sleep now."

But Robin didn't sleep. Ann and Karen were right. He had to find some good people to manage the day to day business of the company. The reps were relying on the home office to process orders and shipments in a timely manner. He just didn't know where to start looking for the kind of talent who could deal with the other side of the business and keep it secret.

CHAPTER THIRTEEN

Barzan Al Tikriti listened intently to President Hussein's words. That is what one did if he expected to survive a meeting with his Excellency.

"We must show the Americans this war they have fostered upon us will cost them dearly."

"Mr. President, I will immediately issue strike orders. I already have a list of targets and plans for attack as you ordered when you decided to take back our land. We should be able to strike within thirty days."

"Very good, Barzan. I'm sure you have enlisted the assistance of our Palestinian, Korean and Libyan friends."

"Yes, sir, and the Russians and the Chinese have offered logistical support."

"Good…and Barzan…"

"Yes, Excellency?" Al Tikriti looked into Hussein's dark narrowing eyes.

"Do not fail me."

MARK WARREN HELD Jessica Lanthrop closer as they danced, elated he took the chance and called the number she had given him in Mindanao. He took her for a quiet dinner and now they were in a night club in downtown Seattle. Jessica took her head off his shoulder and smiled at him.

"You're not nearly as intimidating as the night you rescued me."

"I'm sorry about that. I didn't mean to scare you, I was just ready to fight for your life. It takes a certain mindset and I'm sure it showed on my face."

She put her head back on his shoulder. "I feel safe with you."

Mark's heart pounded. Jessica's perfume was intoxicating and her body pressed against his stirred intense desire in him he never felt before. The band finished the slow song and launched into a rock 'n' roll number.

Jessica took Mark's hand and led him out of the club. "I need to smell the ocean."

"I'll get a cab."

"No, Mark. I want to walk and don't tell me it might be dangerous. I think I'm with a man who can handle anything...and I felt your gun."

"Okay, we'll walk."

As the couple strolled down towards the Seattle waterfront, Jessica took Mark's hand. "How come you don't have a girlfriend?"

"I haven't met anyone who interested me enough...until tonight."

Jessica smiled at Mark. "You must be demanding!"

"No, I don't think so. It's just I know when I fall in love, I'll devote myself to that person. So, she needs to steal my heart."

"And no one has?"

Mark did not answer for a moment. He stopped and took Jessica into his arms. "Not until tonight." He kissed her softly.

"Do you live far from here?"

"My condo is just two blocks away."

"Will you take me there and make love to me?"

Mark became a little embarrassed and looked down. "Jessica, I never...I'm a virgin."

Jessica flung her arms around his neck and crushed her open mouth against his, her tongue swirling and darting into his. Then she put her lips next to his ear. "So am I, Mark. Let's explore love together."

ROBIN WALKED into Tim Echoles hospital room.

"Remember me?" Robin approached the hospital bed and shook the state trooper's hand. Sheriff Pat Stewart told Robin Trooper Echoles' recovery wasn't progressing as it should. He seemed to be almost fighting his physical therapist's attempts to facilitate his healing.

Tim nodded his head.

"What's the matter? Can't you talk?"

"I can talk. I remember you."

"I just talked to your wife. She's really worried about you. In fact, everyone's worried about you."

Tim turned his head away.

"Look at me!" Robin snapped.

Tim's head jerked back. "Who in the hell do you think you are?"

"I'm exactly who you think I am and I'm the guy who is going to offer you a job."

Tim's mouth twisted with confusion and annoyance.

"Mind if I sit down?" Robin asked in a more gentle tone.

Tim nodded to the only chair in the room and Robin sat down.

"I head up a covert direct action team. Our cover is an export/import business in Seattle. It's a legitimate business and it's growing too fast for me to keep up and still conduct missions. I need someone to come in and become the chief operating officer. Our success as a covert team is directly dependent on the success of the business side of the company."

"So you want me to be a pencil pusher and sit on my ass while you guys do the important stuff."

"You're not listening to me. I just said the success of the covert operations are directly dependent on the success of the company. We have operatives all over the world whose income is tied to the business. Did you hear about the arrest of Anton Ivanov?"

"Yes."

"That was us. Our operative in Thailand was essential to the mission. He's a disabled Vietnamese Navy Seal. Did you hear about the rescue of the hostages in Mindanao?"

"Yes."

"That was us."

"But the news said the Filipino Army rescued them."

"We rescued them and made it look like they did."

"Why did you do that?"

"Because the CIA said to." Robin leaned forward. "Tim, I know how much you loved being a trooper. I also know you have the education and ability to help me out. You can certainly find a position, where you can put your education and ability to work, even with your disability. But you won't find a position where you are directly contributing to solving serious problems in the world."

Robin could almost hear the gears turning in Tim's head, so Robin played his final card. "As you progress and get a handle on the daily operation of the business, we can get you working with our intelligence analyst." Tim's eyes lit up. Bullseye! The hook was set. "Currently, we rotate operators into the intel center to help out, but it would be good to get a more constant person in there, especially when we deploy. Our analyst is also developing software for different needs we have and could use help in that area."

"Suppose I agree to come on board. What would my salary be?"

"How about five hundred thousand dollars a year plus bonuses?"

Tim's eyes just about popped across the room. "You're making it damn tough to say no!"

Robin walked over and put his hand on Tim's shoulder. "You've been dealt a terrible blow, Tim, but you have a lot to live for. You're a good man and you're married to a good woman. I need your help, but I think we can help you, too. What do you say?"

Tim put his hand on Robin's. "Thank you...I don't remember your name."

"Robin Marlette."

"Thank you, Mr. Marlette. I'll think about your offer."

"Fair enough, but please call me Robin. I'll get back to you in about a week." He shook Tim's hand and started for the door.

"Wait!"

Robin stopped and looked over his shoulder.

"I don't know who I'm trying to fool. Of course, I'll accept your offer."

"Whew, had me worried there for a second. Shall I call your wife in?"

"Yes, thanks."

ROBIN WALKED out to the hallway where Sheriff Stewart patiently waited.

"Mission accomplished, Pat."

Then Pat let out a long breath. "I'm glad he accepted. You've probably saved his life."

"Hell, I think he saved mine!"

Pat put his hand on Robin's shoulder. "Remember, Rob, if you guys need anything, just let me know."

"The only thing I'd ask is for your boys to check on Karen and the kids when I'm gone."

"You got it. Just have Karen call me when you leave."

"I appreciate it."

"Let's head home. We can grab a bite at Ivar's before we take the ferry."

The two men had just walked into Ivar's when Robin's pager went off. He looked at the screen and saw the emergency code. "Pat, I've got to get to Paine Field. Can you drop me off?"

"Sure, Rob. Let's go."

CHAPTER FOURTEEN

J ack Moore was perusing the latest updates to the 747's Pilot's Manual with his feet up on the desk when Robin walked into the office next to the company's large hangar at Paine Field. "Hey, Rob," Jack stood and followed Robin to the back of the office. "What's going on?"

"I'm about to find out." Robin picked up the secure phone and was immediately connected to the communication center.

"Worldwide Enterprises, Jamie speaking."

"It's Rob. What's up?"

"Grassley's on the line."

"Okay, patch him through."

"Rob?"

"Hi, Bill. What do you have for us?"

"NSA has intercepted communications between Iraq and several known terrorists indicating Hussein is trying to organize attacks against U.S. interests all over the world. One intercept indicates an attack will originate from North Korea. We need you to terminate their plan."

"Have you sent the intel to Jamie?"

"I have…Rob, this situation necessitates your team take out the terrorists in North Korea."

Robin did not immediately respond to the comment as knots started forming in his neck and shoulders. "And I thought the last mission was difficult."

"I know this is a bad situation. If you guys are caught, the North Koreans won't be merciful, but we need you guys to do this. If we sent spec ops in, we would risk war…nuclear war. With you guys, well, you know the score."

"Yeah, we don't exist."

"That's what I mean. You'll also have to send part of your team to Hualien, Taiwan. We have indication there is a Palestinian recon team there already."

"Why do these guys want to hit Taiwan? We pulled out in 1979."

"Not quite. We have two squadrons of nuclear capable F-16s hidden in a mountainside at Hualien Air Force Base and the Chinese suspect this. We think they're using Hussein's boys and the North Koreans to play their own game, which is to smoke us out and create a reason to attack Taiwan."

"I know they're itchin' to do that."

"Yes they are. This would give them a screen to appease the international community, if they did attack. It would also spread our forces out much too thin and leave us vulnerable in several areas."

"Is this the only threat in the area?"

"It's all we know about, but that could change."

"Robin took in a deep breath. "We'll look at the intel and get back to you…and Bill…"

"Yes?"

"This is going to be extremely expensive."

JAMIE STOOD in front of the assembled Guardians. He had just finished giving a briefing on the situation. Several low whistles greeted the photos on the screen against the wall in the briefing room.

Ernie Jackson stepped in front of the group. "As you can see gentlemen, we've been handed an operation that can have enormous consequences if we fail. I'll lead the mission and Rob will be command and control along with Jamie and Mark."

"Why me?" Mark blurted.

Robin stepped forward. "We've decided at least one operator needs to be with command and control to handle incidental problems, like Emmett did last time. We set up a rotation starting with the youngest man...I believe that's you, Mark."

Mark's displeasure was evident, but he remained silent.

Ernie continued, "Burke and Rocky, you'll work with me on the plan. Gary, start working on infil and exfil assets-either boats or helicopters. Jamie, start working on North Korean radar and patrol coverage for the Chongjin area. Any questions? Okay, let's get with it."

Robin walked over to Mark. "Mark, get with Jamie and get up to speed on all the intelligence and our sources. I also want a strategic situation report for the region, including political and economic updates."

"Okay." Mark started after Jamie, but stopped and turned to Robin. "Sorry, Rob. I didn't mean to get pissed, I just don't like missing the action."

"Don't count yourself out of the action yet. According to Grassley, this shindig is just starting and they really don't know the full scope of the situation."

"Yes, sir."

Robin got on the phone and called Paine Field.

"Worldwide Air Services, this is Jack."

"Hi Jack, how are you doing?"

"That depends on why you're calling."

"Get the plane ready to head to the Far East...either South Korea or Japan."

"Roger, the crew is already here."

"We'll give you the details when we get there."

"Okay, see you then."

Robin dialed Grassley next.

"Bill Grassley."

"Bill, it's Robin."

"Yes, Rob."

"I don't want to piss off the South Koreans, so do you have a contact that can get us into a military base so we don't have to go through customs?"

"As a matter of fact I've been working on that. You can land Fatboy at Osan Air Force Base. I'll send you the information and frequencies.

"Our South Korean rep will handle our transportation from Osan."

"That won't be necessary, Rob. The Air Force people are spec ops. They know the score and they'll get the team to Sokcho by C-130. That'll be the closest jump off point for the operation."

"You do good work, Bill," Robin hung up the phone. *But I'm still going to charge you an arm and a leg...and a head!*

SEVEN HOURS LATER, the Guardians were in the air. They had worked out the basic plan and now the details were being put in place. Emmett and Rick were going to split off in Hawaii and go to Taiwan. They were to locate and identify the Palestinian recon team and neutralize them.

NSA updates indicated the North Koreans had agreed to

provide the weapons, explosives, RIBs and other equipment for the attack and load them onto a Libyan freighter. The rest of the team studied maps, satellite imagery and intelligence to finalize the plan, but a missing piece of critical information made this task difficult. US intelligence had yet to identify the target freighter with several of them in the harbor and ships coming and going.

Against this backdrop, Ernie met with Robin, Jamie and Mark in the upper deck intelligence center. "The plan calls for the team to launch from Sokcho in a fast, medium sized boat or helicopter to take us to a point about twenty five miles off shore from Chongjin. A two man recon team will immediately go in to try to identify the target freighter. When the recon team calls in 'feet dry', the assault team will follow."

"What if the recon team can't find the freighter?" Robin asked. "Shouldn't the assault team at least sit off shore until we confirm the freighter is there?"

"I'm thinking the trip from the boat to the harbor will take enough time for the recon team to make that determination."

Robin pulled the satellite photos over. "There are two harbors and they're separated by a river. I really don't see how they can do a recon of both in the hour it's going to take you to get there. If you go in before they're finished, you're jeopardizing six men instead of two."

"It won't take an hour because the recon team will split up and do both harbors at the same time."

"Are you sending four men to do the recon?"

"Rob, I know how you feel about solo recons, but in this case we need to do it."

Robin remained silent for a long moment. "This isn't the movies. None of us are Rambos. For as long as I've been a tactical team leader, I've nixed the solo recon because two minds are better than one and four eyes are better than two. Either live with a possible long recon or send four men in."

"I'll talk to them and see what they say."

"Who's your recon team?"

"Rocky and Marv."

"Understand, I don't want to tell you what to do, Ernie, but I've lived by this rule for almost eight years and it has never failed us."

"I do understand, Rob. We'll take a look at it."

Robin nodded to Jamie and Mark. "Do you guys have anything to say?"

Mark spoke up. "I'd consider taking some food, like several cases of MREs or some other food rations. My research into the strategic intelligence for the region indicates a widespread famine has engulfed North Korea. Thousands are dying of starvation and there are indications of civil unrest in the country. The international community offered food aid to North Korea, but those idiots rejected it. Something like food could be more powerful than a gun."

"That's not a bad idea, Mark," Ernie replied. "I'll go get this plan finished."

Robin stood up, "Okay, let's get back to work." He went over to the secure phone and called Shosi Tanyaka in Japan.

"Shosi here."

"Hi Shosi, it's Robin."

"How are you?"

"Doing well and yourself?"

"I am well also."

"Good to hear it. Are you secure to talk?

"Yes, I am clear."

"We have a mission in progress and we're looking for a fast, large helicopter with a range of at least five to six hundred nautical miles. Know where we can get one?"

"I don't know what its actual range is, but a friend of mine flies a CH 53 for a shipbuilding company. He owes me a favor or two."

"CH 53 would be perfect. Can you put him on standby for a charter flight?"

"He flies a lot to China and Russia delivering parts. I don't know what his schedule is, but I'll talk to him."

"That'll be great. We may need it as a backup exfil method. You can get back to me on the Fatboy secure phone."

"I'll call as soon as I hear anything."

Robin put the phone down and looked up at Jamie and Mark. "Well guys, what do you think?"

"Going into North Korea when we don't have the target identified seems very risky to me, Rob." Jamie's frown reinforced the seriousness of his concern.

"North Korea is a dangerous place to be...period. Ernie knows that and he'll take the best precautions, short of scrubbing the mission. The chance of us being successful doesn't seem very good right now, though. My main goal is to do the best we can and get everybody back in one piece."

"Given the situation," Mark said, "I'm kinda glad to be in the command and control group for this one."

Robin laughed. "See, Mark, things tend to work out. Keep monitoring the intelligence stream and hope the CIA or NSA comes up with something that'll make things a little easier."

CHAPTER FIFTEEN

F atboy refueled in Honolulu where Emmett and Rick split off and headed for Taiwan. Robin gave them a new handheld satellite phone supplied by the CIA. He also told them Doug would be joining them in Taiwan, which was welcome news.

The team used the flight to Incheon, South Korea to review and refine the plan. The CIA sent four possible freighter configurations for the team's consideration. They were trying to narrow down the odds, but they were a long way off from attracting the interest of a Vegas gambler.

After finalizing the plan, Ernie met with Robin alone.

"I think it's the best we can do with the intel we have, Rob. Rocky and Marv agree we need to do solo recons of the harbors, with Mike as back up. He'll stay with the boat so he can go to whoever may need help.

Robin let out a long breath. "I just don't like having them alone in such hostile territory, but I'll go along with your call this time. Hell, the wisdom of the entire operation itself is questionable."

"Why do you think Grassley is sending us?"

"Plausible Deniability. The geopolitical ramifications are enormous. I'm betting the CIA wants to be able to deny any US involvement if we get caught on one hand and say they tried everything to prevent the worse-case scenario on the other hand, if asked by the White House."

"Well, if we don't find that ship, we are going to do a good recon of the harbors. If they used it once, they'll use it again and we'll have the information."

"Just remember, a good recon means no contact with the enemy."

"Ten-four on that score." Both men smiled at Ernie's use of police radio code.

DOUG WALKED through the international terminal at Taipei Chiang Kai-shek Airport. As he approached the terminal doors he recognized Cái Song, the company rep in Taiwan, walking towards him.

"Hey Cái, how ya doin'?"

"I am fine, Doug. How is your shoulder?"

"Aw, it's okay. Still aches a little, but I've got a great doctor. It will be good as new soon."

Cái nodded with a smile. "I have commandeered a plane to take us to Hualien. I have a friend who has a yacht there and he's given us use of it under one condition."

"What's that?"

"He wants to come along."

"I don't know if Robin would like that."

"Well, he retired as the commanding general of the Taiwan Marine Corps."

Doug laughed. "Hell, I don't think even Robin would argue with a general!"

They exited the terminal where Cái showed Doug to a car

idling at the curb. Without a word, the driver drove to the private aviation terminal. Once Doug got situated in a seat on a Lear Jet, Cái handed him a shoulder holster rig with a Sig Sauer P220 .45 automatic pistol and two extra magazines.

"The General has any other weapons we may need."

Doug started checking out the pistol when he noticed Cái rubbing the back of his neck while he gazed vacantly out the door.

"What's bugging you, Cái?"

Cái let out a long breath. "The general felt it necessary to inform our government about the threatened attack," Cái said. Then he added quickly, "They promised not to interfere and offered all the assistance we need."

"Damn! We gotta tell Ernie about this right away." Doug could see his statement caused Cái even more concern. "Don't worry, Cái, you're not in trouble. Whatever happens, we'll deal with it." Relief spread across Cái's face. Still Doug worried about the secrecy of the mission being compromised.

Cái moved to the plane's door. "I'm going back to the main airport to pick-up Emmett and Rick. The bar is well stocked and there's food in the refrigerator."

"You're a good man, Cái!"

CHAPTER SIXTEEN

F atboy landed close to 0900 hours and was directed to a tarmac in front of two large hangars. Jack guided the big bird onto the tarmac and turned Fatboy around. The plane was too big to fit in the hangars. Kwan Thay, the company rep for South Korea, and two US Air Force pilots came on board.

"Robin, this is Major Jesse Arnold and Captain Art Wiseman from Air Force Special Operations."

"Nice to meet you." Each man had a firm grip as Robin shook their hands. He liked a pilot with a steady hand.

"Same here, Colonel," the major replied.

"You can skip the rank, Major. Robin will do just fine."

"The guy with CIA told us your rank, so I thought I'd cover my ass. You never know."

"Can we start loading the equipment onto your aircraft?"

"You bet and we can take off as soon as it's done."

"I like it," Robin said as he led them through to the cargo hold.

Two hours later, the Chongjin team was loaded on an Air Force C-130 headed for the air base at Sokcho. Robin, Jamie and Mark set up the systems needed to monitor both the Taiwan and the Chongjin teams in Fatboy's communication center.

"Do we have any updated intel, Jamie?" Robin said as he checked the new handheld satellite phones. They were much better than the commercial version because they could access military communication satellites, which gave almost full worldwide coverage twenty-four hours a day. Given how spread out the team was, they could certainly come in handy.

"Everything is still the same. Emmett and Rick hooked up with Doug and Kwan. Ernie and his team should be landing at Sokcho in ten minutes."

"Well, let's round up something to eat while we can. I expect things are going to get hot soon."

"You're a great leader, Rob!" Mark cracked.

"I just can't deny you growing boys your daily bread."

DESPITE HIS YEARS of experience as police SWAT team leader and the two years of intense special ops training, the pit of Ernie's stomach churned as the C-130 touched down in Sokcho. He wanted to command a mission, he just didn't think it would be on such a vague target.

As the plane came to a stop Ernie's mind completed yet another review of the plan. He wondered if Robin felt the same way when he led the men. Ernie's fists tightened with resolve. "Let's move out!"

The men grabbed their gear and hustled down the ramp to two Chevrolet Suburbans with dark tinted windows waiting on the tarmac. Kwan gave instructions to a location in Sokcho Harbor and the drivers moved out. Fifteen minutes later, they arrived at a low blue building on the northeastern edge of the harbor. The team piled out of the

SUVs and were directed to a low slung motor boat moored at the stern.

"What kind of boat is this?" Ernie asked Kwan.

"It's an old fifty foot wooden power boat I rebuilt. I put in twin five hundred horsepower diesels and extra fuel tanks. She'll cruise at thirty knots with a range of eight hundred nautical miles."

"Wow, you did all that yourself?"

"No, several of my friends contributed time and money to the project. We wanted a boat that could get us out to good fishing water and get us back quickly. I thought she'd come in handy because she's wood. Not easily spotted on radar."

Ernie put his arm around Kwan's shoulders. "Did I ever tell you that you're a good man?"

Kwan grinned from ear to ear.

"Load up guys," Ernie barked. "Let's get this boat underway. We're burnin' daylight!"

WASTING no time after they landed, Cái took Emmett and Rick to meet up with Doug and the Lear Jet got them to Hualien in twenty minutes. A private car picked them up and Cái took them to a large home on the beach north of the city off Road 193. It was a beautiful two story house with large verandas all around. As the men got out of the car, a distinguished looking older man came out of the front door to greet them. He warmly greeted Cái who introduced the man to the team.

"Gentlemen, please meet General David Leung."

Emmett stepped forward, saluted then offered his hand. The General broke into a broad grin and shook Emmett's hand.

"Glad to meet you, General."

"Please call me David. I'm long retired from being a general."

"I'm Emmett Franks, sir and this is Rick Santos and Doug Ariel."

David shook each man's hand. "Please, come inside and have some refreshment before we get down to business."

The team grabbed their gear and followed David into his home.

A beautiful woman dressed in a red, silk, mandarin gown floated into the living room followed by a man pushing a cart with drinks.

"Gentlemen, this is my wife, Ching Lan."

"Welcome to our home, gentlemen. Please sit down."

Emmett said, "Good afternoon, ma'am," as the other men respectfully nodded to her.

Ching Lan extended a well-manicured hand toward an intricately carved side board laid out with an eye popping array of dim sum. "After you have refreshments, I'll show you to your rooms."

"Ma'am, I believe Cái has a hotel set up for us," Emmet said as he was handed a glass of something that smelled like an exquisite combination of honey and mint.

"He did, but we told him to cancel those reservations. You men are here to protect our country and we will make sure you are well taken care of. It is not a point for discussion." Ching Lan smiled graciously, but her eyes held a determined look.

Having been married for almost twenty years, Emmett replied with the only acceptable answer of, "Yes, ma'am."

A pleasant hour of discussion passed before the men got down to business.

"Whatever you need, please let me know and it will be taken care of," David said after Ching Lan left the room.

"We're going to need cars," Emmett began, "and we'd like

to rent them from a company that will rotate them daily for us."

"You will have cars," David said without a second's hesitation. "They will be delivered here early each morning."

Emmett nodded and sat back in his chair.

"Before you leave to check out the situation, I will supply you with appropriate weapons."

"Thank you, sir," Emmett said as he set his drink down. "Quite frankly, we'd like to get started. Our intel is still pretty sketchy on this whole situation. The sooner we get an eye on these guys the better I'll feel."

"Do you know where they are?"

"We've been told they are staying in a two story house across the road from the northeast corner of the air base."

"Hmm, I hadn't heard that."

"Our main goal right now is to bug their location and hopefully find out more about their plan."

"Yes, I agree you should get started immediately. I'll arrange everything while you get settled."

Emmett didn't spot a signal, but Ching Lan reappeared and showed the team to their rooms. Emmett took the middle room of the three to have easy access to both his team members. Huge sliding glass doors opened onto a veranda with an expansive view out over the Pacific Ocean.

"This beats the heck out of even a five star hotel," Rick said as he gazed out over the water.

"Yeah, sure does," Emmett said. "But we're not on a vacation here. Get changed and let's get moving."

They met David back in the living room and he took them into a basement. Walking over to a steel door, David punched a code on a key pad. The door clicked and then the sound of metal moving within the door signaled it was unlocked. David turned the handle and opened the door.

"Take any weapons you need," he said as he ushered them into a large room lined with weapons.

"Ammunition is in that steel chest against the far wall," he said before disappearing back up the stairs.

All three Guardians chose silenced HK MP5 submachine guns. Rick also chose a MacMillan sniper rifle in NATO 7.62 with a GEN III night weapons scope, a set up on which he trained extensively. They loaded magazines, packed cases and walked back up the stairs to find cars waiting for them.

Cái walked up to Emmett. "If you want, I can drive for you and we have two marines from our intelligence division who can drive for Rick and Doug. They know the area well and will not interfere with your operations."

"Okay, bring them over here." When the men assembled, Emmett laid out a quick plan. "You and I will go to the area where we think the house is. We'll try to verify they are there. The other cars hang around the area. If it is the house, we'll set up surveillance and wait for an opportunity to plant some bugs. Cái before we go, can you do a quick frequency check and make sure we won't be on a frequency that'll interfere with a station here?"

Emmett handed Cái a frequency list and he went in the house. By the time the men loaded their gear into the cars Cái returned.

"Four of your frequencies are clear."

Emmett looked at the sheet. "We'll use Tac 3. I'll be Echo unit, Rick you'll be Romeo unit and Doug you'll be Delta unit. The men nodded. "Okay, let's rock and roll."

CHAPTER SEVENTEEN

Relief flooded through Ernie to see the sun edging lower and lower in the blue Pacific sky. Even though they were well outside the twelve nautical mile limit the North Koreans considered their territory, they also claimed a two hundred nautical mile "exclusive economic zone." The zone primarily protected their fishing industry, but the North Koreans weren't known for being predictable when it came to stopping any kind of boat.

From the cabin of Kwan's boat, Ernie searched the horizon towards North Korea through binoculars. They were two hours into the eight hour trip and had crossed the DMZ an hour ago. The possibility of a patrol boat or aircraft spotting them increased with every revolution of the props.

The boat cruised effortlessly at thirty knots and it handled well, even in the developing swell. Nodding to Kwan, Ernie walked out on the back deck and found Rocky and Burke doing final checks on weapons and explosives.

"Nothing like a little evening cruise to relax a person."

Burke rolled his eyes, chuckled and shook his head. "Take

a deep breath and chill out a little, boss. You have to realize the worst thing that can happen to us is we get killed."

"Now those are comforting words. You really know how to ease someone's nerves."

"If you think about it, Ernie, Burke's right," Rocky said as he jacked a round into the chamber of his silenced MP5 . We all are gonna die someday. It's just a matter of when and where. So relax, there's really nothing to lose."

"Thanks, I feel better already. Everything okay with the things that go bang?"

"Yeah, we're good," Rocky replied. "I just hope we get to blow something up."

"Amen," Burke said as he slapped Rocky's raised hand.

Right," Ernie muttered and then silently added *and we all get back in one piece.*

ROBIN AND MARK were going over maps and satellite imagery for North Korea and Taiwan. The satellite pictures showed a lot of ship traffic in the East Sea, the Sea of Japan and the Eastern China Sea. There were several ships in both harbors at Chongjin, but comparison of photos on different days showed ships replaced with others. Finding the target ship, if it even existed, seemed about as easy as picking out a particular wave in a choppy sea.

Jamie put down his headset and walked over to the map table. "I just got an intel update."

"What's the score?" Robin said as he put aside the satellite picture of the western harbor at Chongjin and picked up the one from the eastern side.

"Still no positive location on the target, but the chatter NSA is picking up still indicates a threat against an American base."

"That's not very helpful."

Jamie kept twisting a pen in his hands until Robin looked up.

"Spit it out, Jamie."

"I requested the suspect transmissions and reviewed them myself."

"Go ahead."

"I know those guys are the experts, but I see something there NSA isn't looking at. It seems to me the chatter is talking about two targets and one of them is a big one."

"That would be the base in Taiwan."

"No, Rob. Bigger than that. One that requires a large attack."

Robin leaned forward in his chair giving Jamie a serious look. "Is there any info about a large contingent of men anywhere?"

"No, but what if it doesn't mean a troop movement, but a large scale weapon?"

Jamie now had Robin's full attention. "Who has that kind of weapon?"

"Saddam Hussein, according to some reports."

"Are we talking about a chemical weapon? Because I thought the intel indicated he didn't have any nukes?"

"That could be it."

Robin rubbed his chin as he mulled over Jamie's news. "Okay, I'm going to call Grassley and tell him to pipe all raw intel on this mission to you."

"They won't do that, Rob. We're not cleared."

Robin gave Jamie a hard look. "Get ready to receive the info."

"Yes, sir."

"Mark, help Jamie. We need to sort this out."

"Roger."

Robin walked over to the secure phone and dialed.

"Bill Grassley."

"It's Robin."

"What do you need?"

Robin related Jamie's information to Grassley.

"You know, Rob, those NSA guys know what they're doing."

"So does Jamie. What I'd like you to do is relay Jamie's info to them. If they look at the intel and agree, then I want all raw intel on this mission sent to Jamie, real time."

Grassley remained silent for a while. "Okay, Rob, I'll get back to you."

CHAPTER EIGHTEEN

Cái and Emmett parked a block away from a white house two tenths of a mile from the northern Nineteen end of the Hualien Air Force Base runway.

"Do you think we have the right house? It's been two hours," Cái noted.

"It's the closest thing around here matching the intel," Emmett replied as he scanned the area. "We're going to have to go with it for a while."

"Echo, this is Romeo," Rick's voice crackled through Emmett's radio.

"Go ahead, Romeo."

"Got a green Subaru station wagon carrying two Middle Eastern subjects heading your direction."

"Roger, watch out for counter-surveillance."

"Will do."

A few seconds later the vehicle came down the street from the north and turned into the driveway. Two men entered the house.

"Okay, the suspect vehicle just pulled into the target house," Emmett advised.

"All units hold your positions. We have a possible counter-surveillance car in the area and headed towards you, Echo...a blue sedan."

"Roger, Romeo."

Emmett watched as the second vehicle turned into the driveway. The driver looked around and then entered the house.

"It's definitely a suspect vehicle, also. Everyone sit tight for a few."

Five minutes went by and then two men came out of the house, exchanged some words and then started walking in opposite directions on the street.

"Damn," Emmett whispered.

"Shall we move?" Cái asked.

"Too late now. Just sit tight and hope he doesn't come this far. Echo to all units, they now have counter-surveillance on foot. If you're not in line of sight with the house, pull back."

Emmett flattened his seat back and ducked down as far as he could. If the suspect saw him, it would probably blow the surveillance, as a large black man was not a common sight in this area.

Cái watched as the man kept coming in their direction. "He is still coming and he is looking all around, even the bushes. He is definitely counter-surveillance. Still coming...still coming...still coming. Emmett, we may be in trouble. He's getting close!" Cái's voice seemed an octave higher.

"Just stay calm, Cái." Emmett's statement belied his pounding heart.

"But he's getting...hold it!" Cái's voice dropped to a whisper. "He stopped and pulled a small radio out of his pocket. He's turning around and starting back...fast."

Emmett slowly raised his head and peeked over the dash just as the other suspect came back.

"Echo to all units. Move closer to the house, but get a new position."

"Roger," Rick answered.

"Roger also." Doug confirmed.

Emmett watched the suspects go into the house. "Okay, Cái, let's move back a ways."

Cái pulled the car onto the road and made a u-turn and moved to a dirt road a tenth of a mile from their previous location. Darkness began to brush the day away as Emmett surveyed the orchards around him and the target house.

"I'm going to check out the house on foot."

"Be careful, Emmett."

Emmett grinned. "I was born careful. Just listen to the radio."

Cái nodded in the gathering gloom. Emmett quietly got out of the car and retrieved a backpack from the rear seat. He put it on and hurried across the road into the orchard. Reaching the edge of the trees nearest the house, he stopped. Pulling a night scope from his pack, he checked out the area for cameras or wires, but didn't see any. The blinds were closed around the house, so he approached the nearest window. He looked past old blinds fraying at the edges, but couldn't see or hear anything. He moved to the next window and as he got to it, he could hear voices.

Through the edge of the blind he saw the man from the sedan. He'd changed from street clothes to black fatigues and his face was smeared with camouflage paint. A pistol sat on the table he leaned against as he pointed to various spots on a paper he'd spread on the table. Unfortunately, Emmett didn't recognize the dialogue being spoken, but he knew the signs of a briefing when he saw one. They were preparing for an operation.

Going back to the orchard, Emmett moved to a position from where he could see the front of the house. He found a place with concealment and a good view. Ten minutes later, two men came out of the house and got into the Subaru. One had a backpack. Both were dressed in black and wore camo paint. Both were armed.

"Echo to all units, two suspects are about to leave the house in the Subaru, dressed in black and cammied up. Both are carrying AKs. Standby for direction of travel."

"Romeo, roger."

"Delta, ditto."

"Okay, they're headed east."

"We're ready for them," Doug replied.

Emmett wondered what the third man was up to, but didn't have to wonder long. The other car's lights came on and it pulled out and headed east also.

"Counter-surveillance just headed east, too." Emmett didn't see him come out and figured another door led to the parking area.

"Roger, we'll watch for him," Doug affirmed.

"Cái, go to our previous position and wait."

"Roger."

As the second car disappeared down the road, Emmett approached the house. He walked past the eastern wall of the building and saw the door the third man must have come from. Sweeping the eastside with the night vision he didn't see any security equipment, but did see the power box. Emmett went to it, located the main switch and turned it off. He looked at the door handle and saw it didn't have a security type lock. *For tangos, these guys aren't very security conscious.* Pulling out his lock pick set, he chose a pick and quickly popped the latch.

Emmett entered the house with his silenced 9mm pistol drawn. He moved to a front room and saw nothing out of the ordinary. Two straight backed chairs. A paisley covered sofa, a beat up coffee table with an ash tray full of Turkish cigarettes. He crept to the room where he looked through the window and found the easel set up with a detailed topographical map of the area around the air base. There were satellite photos with the legend in Cyrillic, showing they originated from the USSR. Emmett looked in the closet and found three AK-47 automatic rifles, a case of 7.62×39 Chinese rifle ammunition, a rocket propelled grenade launcher, ten rocket propelled grenades, twenty soviet style hand grenades and a case of 9mm pistol ammunition.

As he backed away from the closet, he looked up and his heart slammed into this throat. A video camera stared at him. Praying his move to cut the power disabled the video system, Emmett started tracing the wires and found the recorder in the bottom drawer of the dresser in the room. There were several other cable wires coming in to a video splitter in the back of the recorder. Relief swept through him when he saw the power light on the recorder remained off.

He had turned his radio down when he entered the house, but now he could hear someone calling him. He turned the radio up and answered.

"This is Echo, go ahead."

"Suspect three is headed back in your direction."

Shit! I haven't even started planting the bugs! "Roger. Emmett to Cái."

"Cái, go ahead, Emmett."

"Can you arrange a power outage for the area?"

"When?"

"Now!"

Cái did not respond immediately and Emmett grimaced as he imagined Cái cussing up a storm. Cái finally said, "I'll try."

Emmett got to work looking for good spots to plant the

bugs. He definitely needed to plant at least two in the briefing room. Over the radio he heard Rick report suspect three was only three miles from the house. His mind worked furiously weighing the risks for several spots, but he managed to get two planted in that room.

"Suspect one mile out."

Emmett planted one in the living room and one near the kitchen table and started for the side door.

"Suspect is coming up on the driveway."

Emmett saw headlights shining on the entrance to the driveway. Suddenly, all the lights in the neighborhood went out. The car stopped. Emmett locked the door and stood at the back of the door, holstering the pistol and drawing his knife. He saw the driver get out and come toward him. The key fumbled for a minute and then made it into the slot and the door opened towards Emmett. He prepared himself for a knife kill, his heart pounding so hard he thought the tango would hear it. He heard the terrorist hit the light switches with no luck.

The tango moved into the house with a flashlight.

Emmett ducked through the door and quickly opened the fuse box and flipped the main switch. Closing the fuse box, he heard the tango call out. Emmett sprinted to the orchard. As he made it to the tree line, the tango's flashlight swept the yard surrounding the house.

Emmett stopped running, but moved deeper into the orchard. Looking back, he saw a flashlight still sweeping the back yard of the house and the edge of the orchard. He made his way back to Cái's location and keyed his radio. "Cái, I'm coming in."

"Roger."

Emmett dropped his pack in the back and got into the front passenger seat. Cái immediately did a u-turn and headed south.

"Where you going? I still have to hook the receiver to the phone line."

"The police and the power company will be all over this place soon."

"Wow, when you and the general do a cover job, you do it up good!"

"There's no cover job and the general doesn't know anything about this."

"How'd you kill the power?"

"Climbed a tree, broke off a large branch and threw it on the line. We could never get the power killed that fast any other way. Even the general does not have those kind of connections." Emmett sat stunned for a moment. Then he started laughing.

"Goddamn, Cái, I'm going to tell Rob to pull you out of the rep business and turn you into a full time operator! That was quick thinking…and gutsy. You're the man!" Emmett held up his hand and Cái slapped it with a grin.

"Did you get the bugs planted all right?"

"They're planted, but it was a close thing getting out of there. What's going on with the other two suspects?"

"They are on the mountain behind the base. Rick says they're taking video with night vision."

Emmett spoke into his radio. "Echo to Romeo."

"Go ahead, Echo."

"Break off the surveillance and head back to the command post."

"Roger. Delta, you copy?"

"Roger," Doug answered.

"We'll finish the job tomorrow," Emmett said to Cái. "I don't want to spook these guys anymore tonight."

CHAPTER NINETEEN

Rocky, Marv and Mike got into one of the two RIBs the team had brought for the mission. They seemed to melt into the night because of their black tactical uniforms and camo paint on their faces. Ernie leaned over the gunwale of Kwan's boat.

"You guys watch yourselves. We'll see you in an hour."

Mike saluted and started the engine, its noise dampened with a series of modifications developed by the SEALs. Soon the RIB and its three man crew faded into the night.

The rest of the team began final preparations for their infiltration. Ernie pored over the map and satellite pictures one more time, even though every detail was burned into his mind. The enormity of this mission laid heavily on him.

ROBIN PICKED up the secure phone. "Hi Bill."

"The NSA guys...and some of ours, have egg on their face and are very impressed with Jamie's analysis of the intel. The raw feed should be starting in a few minutes."

"I appreciate it. FYI, the Chongjin recon team is moving in right now and the Taiwan team is on their tangos."

"Sounds good, Rob. Keep me posted."

"Always." Robin hung up the phone and turned to Jamie. "You'll be getting the raw feed anytime now."

"You're amazing, Rob. I didn't think they'd do it."

"They did it because you're amazing."

"Can I be amazing too?" Mark chirped.

"In due time, Mark. In due time."

THE RIB silently kissed the shore just outside the north harbor of Chongjin. Marv climbed out, pushed the boat back out to sea and then moved to a clump of bushes and knelt down. His night vision goggles were already on so he shouldered his pack and flipped the safety off on his suppressed MP5. He did a 360° scan for threats and not detecting any, he ghosted toward the harbor in the blackness, his heart thumping against his ballistic vest.

Moving to the corner of the first building on the south side of the harbor, Marv scanned the vessels moored around it. He didn't see any cargo vessels matching those described in the intel. Knowing intel is rarely on the mark, he decided to look for vessels with a Libyan flag. He made a slow visual search for movement around the buildings and ships, but saw none. He moved out, staying in the shadows, but close enough to the ships to see any flags. He completed the search on all three sides of the harbor and didn't find anything. He headed back to his exfil point.

ROCKY STOOD stalk still in the shadow of a building.

Across from him a group of North Korean soldiers surrounded four women, but the soldiers didn't seem to be threatening to the women. They just seemed to be discussing them. The group, however, blocked the rest of his survey of the southern harbor. Rocky turned to try to scout an alternative route and collided with a soldier coming around the corner.

"Shit," Rocky hissed as he raised his weapon.

The soldier raised his hands with a terrified look. "Don't shoot! I am not your enemy!" He said in surprisingly good English.

Rocky put his hand over the soldier's mouth. "If you're not my enemy, be quiet."

The soldier nodded his head and Rocky slowly removed his hand. "You don't understand," the soldier whispered. "No soldier here is your enemy. We hate our government. Our people are starving and they do nothing. You are American, correct?"

"Yes, I'm an American."

"You are here because of the Arabs?"

A jolt went through Rocky. "Yes, I'm looking for them."

"You must talk to my colonel. We have information and we need your help." Rocky hesitated. "Please, come with me. The lives of those women you see over there depend on it."

Rocky keyed his mic. "Rock to Mike, I've made contact. Code four."

"Roger," Mike replied.

"Okay, let's go, but keep in the shadows."

"Yes, I understand. I am a soldier too."

Rocky smiled and nodded to the group across the way. When they got to the door, the soldier held up his hand for Rocky to wait and then entered the building. Rocky heard some excited talk and fingered his trigger nervously. The soldier came back with a tall, slim man showing grey hair on his sideburns. He walked with a ramrod back and as he came closer to Rocky, he saw a worried face.

"This is my colonel."

Rocky snapped attention and saluted the colonel.

The older man held out his hand and Rocky took it in a friendly shake. The man then spoke to the soldier.

The soldier nodded and translated. "My colonel wishes me to introduce us. I am Lieutenant Chong and he is Colonel Sinchu, of the 1st Battalion, 6th Army Corps. He wishes to know your name and rank."

"I'm Lieutenant Barnett."

The lieutenant translated and the colonel nodded and said something in reply.

"The colonel asks what is your unit?"

"Please tell the colonel I apologize, but I can't divulge that information."

The lieutenant translated and the colonel thought for a minute then started speaking and the lieutenant translated as he spoke. "There were two cargo ships in our harbor here, each carrying teams of Arabs planning attacks on Americans. One ship went to Hualien, Taiwan and left four days ago. The other set sail for Vladivostok and then on to attack the port of Sasebo in Japan. That ship left yesterday. I can give you a description of the ships. I tell you this as a sign of good faith and ask your help in return."

"Tell the colonel I'm very grateful for the information and I offer whatever help I can. I would like to know how he got his information."

"The Arabs were braggarts. They actually told me of their plans because I'm the only one who speaks English."

Rocky's headset crackled. "Ernie to Rock, we're in place."

"Standby, Ernie...my major is here now. What can we do to help you?"

"The women in the warehouse openly protested against

the government in the public square. We have been ordered to execute them. We need you to take them with you. We can't hide them from the secret police here. If you take them, we can simply dig graves and say we buried them."

Rocky did some quick mental calculations on the load capacity of the two RIBs they had. "Okay, let me go get my major and we'll get things worked out."

"Do you have any medicine?"

"We have a medic. Why?"

"One of our sergeants is very sick. Could your medic look at him?"

"I'll check." He turned and trotted to the meet point. Five minutes later he found the rest of the team. Mike had already picked up Marv.

"What the hell's going on?" Ernie asked.

"It's kind of complicated, but we don't have to worry about the army here. They're our friends."

"Are you nuts?! We're in North Korea!"

"Look, Ernie, these people are starving and the government is doing nothing about it. They hate the government. They gave me the scoop on the tangos. I need you and Willy to come with me."

Ernie took a deep breath. "Get your gear, Willy. The rest of you set up a perimeter and wait for us."

"And don't shoot any soldiers," Rocky added.

The three men went back to the warehouse and met the colonel and the lieutenant. During the walk back, Rocky filled Ernie in on the colonel's request.

"This is my major, sir," Rocky said to the colonel.

The colonel held out his hand to Ernie and they shook hands.

"And this is Sergeant Young, our medic. He'll take a look at your sick soldier."

"Would you please come with me, sergeant?" the

lieutenant asked.

"Lead the way."

"Before you go, Lieutenant, tell the colonel we'll get the women loaded on our boats. They can only take the essentials. We'll be near capacity."

"It is all right, Major. They have nothing, but what they are wearing. Where will you be taking them?"

"South Korea."

"I'll tell them."

The colonel, lieutenant and Willy went into the warehouse. Moments later the colonel brought the four women out. Their eyes were wide and frightened. Ernie took the hand of the closest one in his hands and bowed to her.

"Don't be afraid. We will protect you." He spoke in a soft, calm voice.

The woman managed a smile and nodded to Ernie.

"I hope she doesn't think you just proposed to her, boss," Rocky cracked.

Ernie chuckled. "Let's get them to the boats."

WILLY KNELT beside a soldier with a very pale face covered in perspiration. The soldier's breathing was quick and shallow. "How long has he been like this?"

"Four days," the lieutenant answered. "That's when he was injured."

Willy lifted the man's shirt and started removing the bandage on his left side. The soldier flinched and gritted his teeth. Willy stopped and pulled a morphine auto injector out of his bag and punched it into the man's thigh.

"Tell him the pain will stop in a few minutes."

The lieutenant translated.

Willy slowly removed the bandage as the soldier bravely

took the pain. Willy began cleaning the infected wound as gently as he could. The man tensed with pain at first, but then started to relax as the morphine took hold. Willy began to clean more aggressively and debriding the wound. He applied antibiotic ointment then gently covered the injury. A tetanus shot and a shot with a large dose of the strongest antibiotic in his kit completed the treatment.

"Lieutenant, I'm giving you these morphine auto injectors. All you have to do is remove this cover, insert the needle in his buttocks or thigh and push this button. Don't do it more than four times a day and only do it if he's in severe pain. This is morphine and it's extremely addictive." Willy then handed the lieutenant the rest of his antibiotic syringes and a bottle of antibiotic pills. "Give him a shot of antibiotics in the morning and another tomorrow night. Then start him on these pills...four a day until they're gone. Keep the wound clean, but don't bandage it for three days."

The lieutenant handed the medical supplies to another man and gave him the instructions. The man nodded he understood.

"Does that man have any questions for me?"

The lieutenant asked the man the question and he said something back. "This man is one of our battalion medics. He says thank you for treating their sergeant. He wishes he had the same training and supplies you do."

Willy looked at the man and smiled. "You're welcome."

To Willy's surprise the man hugged him. Willy hugged him back, picked up his bag and looked at the soldiers around him. Their condition tore at his heart. They were malnourished and most of them did not look well. "When did the injured man last eat?"

"All of us have been sharing what we have, but he had only a little to eat this morning."

Willy reached into his bag and pulled out two MRE

rations. "Here is some food for him. He needs nutrition if he is going to get better."

"Yes, Sergeant."

"Okay, Lieutenant, let's get me back to the boats."

ERNIE SAW Willy and the lieutenant coming out of the warehouse. The colonel had given him drawings of the ships the terrorists were using. Ernie identified them as the Norwegian Tween Deck/RO/RO Geared cargo ships listed in the intel. Ernie considered the intelligence bonanza the colonel and his men could provide on an ongoing basis about North Korea and Chongjin shipping traffic. He decided to take a big risk.

"Lieutenant, I want to give the colonel this satellite phone. It will enable us to communicate with your unit on a regular basis. You just have to be careful about when and where to transmit as I'm sure the air waves are monitored here, but you don't have to worry about receiving messages."

The lieutenant translated and the colonel seemed to be interested, but troubled about the phone. After a minute of thought he spoke to the lieutenant, who became very upset and started arguing, but the colonel cut him off with a curt order. The lieutenant stood rigid with tears running down his cheeks. The colonel's face softened and he put his hands on the lieutenant's shoulders. Ernie thought he was witnessing a conversation between a father and his son.

The lieutenant turned to Ernie. "Major, my colonel says the only way this will work is if you take me with you. The colonel and I have a code, which only we know." The lieutenant's voice broke and the colonel put his arm around his shoulders and spoke looking at Ernie as the lieutenant translated.

"Lieutenant Chong is a very capable officer. He has risked a very bright career to do the right thing for his men and people we serve here in Chongjin." The colonel choked back tears. "Years ago, my wife died in childbirth because I did not have sufficient rank to get the special care she needed. I lost her and my newborn son. Lieutenant Chong is the son I never had. Please take him with you. Then the phone will work well."

Ernie turned to Rocky. "What about the capacity of the boats?"

"It will be touchy, but I think we can make it."

Willy spoke up. "Ernie, we need to get these people food and medicine."

"That would be damn near impossible, Willy!"

"Boss, you don't understand. These people are starving to death. The guy I just treated will definitely die if he doesn't get food and all of these people are sick. If they get hit with the flu they are all dead!"

Ernie's gut churned. *And I insisted on leading ops.* "Lieutenant, please tell the colonel to expect us back tomorrow night. If we don't make it, it will be the next night. In the meantime, we have a couple of cases of MREs we'll leave with you. We'll need one of your men to come get them from our boats."

The lieutenant translated.

"Okay, let's get out of here. C'mon, Lieutenant, the colonel's right. You're more valuable with us."

The lieutenant and the colonel had a last father and son embrace and then Rocky led the way to the boats. When the women saw the lieutenant climbing aboard, they all started whispering and smiling. The lieutenant reassured them everything would be all right. After unloading the MREs, the RIBs headed back to Kwan's boat, with Ernie wondering if he had made the right decisions.

CHAPTER TWENTY

Upon receiving the colonel's information from Ernie by satellite phone, Robin started issuing orders.

"Get us to Sasebo ASAP, Jack."

"Roger."

"Jamie, get a hold of Shosi and tell him to line up the chopper he and I talked about. Alert the Taiwan team to the description of their target ship. Tell them we'll have it located soon."

"Okay, Rob."

"Mark, get us geared up for a maritime op including scuttle charges according to the plan Ernie worked up."

"Will do."

Rob picked up the secure phone and called Grassley. He relayed Colonel Sinchu's information and asked Grassley to locate the vessels by satellite ASAP. Then he pulled up satellite photos of Vladivostok and the Sea of Japan and started studying them. The pit of his stomach twisted. *We started with iffy intelligence that caused us to split our team and now Mark and I have to infiltrate into Vladivostok and sink a ship full of tangos.* He leaned back in his chair. *It's damn near too crazy to even contemplate doing this! I should just call Bill and tell him to sink the damn ship with an air strike. Why should I risk killing a young kid like Mark for this? Not to mention my own self.* Robin reached for the secure phone, but the nagging thought of a nuclear war stuck in his mind. *Dammit! I guess we can work up a plan and see how it shakes out. If it's too risky, I'll tell Bill we're off.* He hung up the phone.

By the time Fatboy landed in Sasebo, Robin and Mark had a plan that reasonably satisfied them under the circumstances. That didn't mean they weren't apprehensive about the operation. Shosi met them at the Sasebo airport, after flying there in the CH53 he had procured.

Upon their arrival at Sasebo, it became clear why the port was targeted. It played a vital logistics role in Operation Desert Shield/Storm by serving as a supply point for ordinance and fuel for ships and Marines operating in the Persian Gulf theater. A successful attack would have major adverse effects on the war.

Robin and Mark spent an hour going over the plan with Shosi and Kuro Nakamuro, the helicopter pilot and his co-pilot Ryuu Yoshio. Kuro was a retired Japanese National Police commander and Japanese Naval Reserve captain. He flew helicopters for the Navy. Ryuu retired as a major in the Japanese Air Force. When they retired, the Mitsubishi Shipbuilding Company hired them as company pilots ferrying parts and repair crews to China and Russia.

Kuro did express some concern when he looked at the satellite photos and saw the target ship docked less than three hundred yards from the helipad where he usually landed. Robin assured him he would set the charges to go off long after Kuro flew back to Japan. Although he accepted this promise, he still seemed a little nervous, so Shosi agreed to go with them on the trip.

"What's security like at this part of the port, Kuro?" Robin asked.

Kuro laughed. "There is no security. Things are falling apart in Russia. Government workers are not getting paid most of the time, so they have simply stopped working. The only security I think you need to worry about is any private security the ship owners hire, but I have not seen much of that either."

"Well that makes things easier, I suppose. Let's get going."

NSA had located both target ships by satellite and fed regular updates to Robin and Emmett. As the men waited for the helicopter to be fueled and preflighted, Robin watched the sky turning dark . The coming night didn't bother him for the night was an ally… it was the gathering storm on the horizon. For the first time, Mark had a lack of enthusiasm about a mission. His face showed the same tension Robin felt.

Robin turned to Mark. "Nervous?"

"No. I'm terrified."

"Me too."

"Let me get this straight. The success of this mission depends on us remaining undetected going into the Vladivostok cargo docks, getting onto the ship, setting the charges in the hold, disabling the communications on the bridge, getting off the ship before the charges go off and successfully rendezvousing with the helicopter in the open sea…at night and now apparently in a storm. We're going on what seems to me to be a very iffy mission because our government doesn't have the balls to piss the Russians off. Right?"

"Simply put, but essentially the case."

"It kinda pisses me off, boss."

"The problem is we are supposedly in détente with the Soviets. So our government doesn't want to be the ones who publicly jeopardizes the negotiations."

"That's crazy! The Russkies are the ones supporting these terrorists and in cahoots with Saddam Hussein!"

"As they always have. The problem is two nuclear armed nations trying to keep each other at bay...by the throat. So the negotiations go on while the shooting war is mostly covert."

"Why aren't Delta or SEALs doing this mission? Why little ol' us?"

"It is a big deal for a ship under a national flag to be assaulted by another country. Even though pirates do it all the time without much repercussion, if another country does it, it's an act of war. In this case, probably nuclear war. If U.S. military assets get caught in such an assault, the government would have to admit the U.S. did it and try to negotiate their release. That would put tensions right to the edge. That's why Delta or the SEALs can't do this mission, even though I'm sure if they know about it they're mightily pissed off they're not." He turned to Mark. "You know the score with us."

"Yeah, if we get caught, we're just fucked. What did they do about situations like this before we came along?"

"Oh, I doubt we are the only team like this out there. We just pulled the short straw on this one."

Having explained this to Mark suddenly made Robin feel a little better about the situation.

"Yeah, but Rob, if the ship does an attack with a Russian or North Korean flag, it's the same thing. Things will explode anyway."

"I'm sure that flag will disappear just before the attack. They're flying them so they won't be molested enroute to their target."

"Hell, if you put it that way, looks like you and I are about to save the world!"

Robin looked at Mark who grinned ear to ear and patted him on shoulder. "It's good to have my old Mark back."

"I'm always with you, Rob. Just sometimes it helps to talk it through."

"I know, it just helped me."

SHOSI SIGNALED they were ready and Robin and Mark picked up their gear and headed for the chopper. The pilot took the gear, which included an RIB, and started distributing it in the helicopter to maintain the balance of the aircraft. With the equipment secured, the pilot got in and began his start checklist. Minutes later, they were in the air and headed out to Toyama where they would refuel...and then on to the Union of Soviet Socialist Republics.

CHAPTER TWENTY-ONE

At first light the Taiwan team continued the surveillance. Taiwanese Marine Intelligence sent an agent into the area in a telephone company service truck. He attached the bug receiver to a phone line at the box servicing the target house and put a tap on the telephone. The intercepts were fed to David's house to a recorder and relayed by satellite to NSA by burst transmission. They translated the intercepts and sent the information back to the team.

The intercepts indicated the tangos weren't spooked the night before. They were acting normally and by the end of the first tape, they were in contact with someone who updated them on the location and estimated time of arrival of the ship, now less than twenty-four hours away. Emmett's brain worked overtime.

Emmett received an urgent message from Robin saying he now commanded the strategic and tactical aspects of the Taiwan operation. He wanted to do a good job commanding his first operation. He had a thousand questions he wanted ask Robin, but he realized he needed to settle down and figure things out for himself. He decided to split the team up. He would take Rick and Kwan with him and leave Doug to handle the tango recon team with the help of the Taiwanese Marines. He reasoned since the tango recon team were operating on Taiwanese soil, they were fair game for the Marines.

The tangos didn't move much as the surveillance day wore on, but they had a steady stream of communications traffic. Early in the afternoon, David radioed Emmett and told him they should terminate the physical surveillance and meet back at his house. When they returned to the house, David told Emmett the intercepts indicated the recon team would meet the rest of the assault team on the beach just off Road 9 by the Taroko Bridge tonight. That meant the team taking down the ship needed to leave and get set up at Yonaguni Island to intercept the freighter.

Emmett addressed the team. "Okay, listen up. We are going to split up. Rick and Cái, you're going with me and David to take down the ship. Doug, I need you to take care of the tango recon team with the help of the Marines..."

"Whoa there, bud, you're not taking down that ship without me!"

"Doug, I need someone on the tango recon team."

"The Marines don't need my help, but you're going to need my help with that ship."

Emmett started to argue, but David spoke up. "Emmett, I don't mean to interfere, but Doug may be right. By the time you board the ship, I suspect the entire crew and the assault team will be awake and on edge. It could be a difficult endeavor."

Emmett rubbed his forehead. "Doug, I'm also worried about your shoulder and the fact you haven't trained for over two months."

"My shoulder is fine and I've been training Whisky's sons and nephews on tactical movements and such. We went on the range two or three times a week this last month and I've been running. I'm good to go."

"Okay, we'll leave the tango recon team to the Marines. Cái, since you'll be our boat man, who will be our contact with the Marines?"

The Marine who had been driving Rick, Lieutenant Martin Cho, raised his hand. "I'll be commanding that aspect of the operation, Emmett."

"Sounds good, Marty. Keep the radio you've been using so we can coordinate your take down with ours. As soon as we hit the ship, we'll let you know and you can take down the recon team."

"Will do."

"Well, David, I guess it's time to load up your boat and head to Yonaguni Island."

EVEN THOUGH EXHAUSTED, Ernie and Gary spent hours rounding up MREs, rice, other food staples and medicine to take back to Col. Sinchu's battalion. He turned the women over to U.S. military intelligence agents, but didn't tell them about Lt. Chong. During the trip back, he and Lt. Chong convinced the women not to mention Chong to the intelligence guys. To give the women incentive to do so, Ernie promised to give them money to help them in the relocation. He gave each of them $5,000 when they got to Sokcho and promised to send them more later. The women were extremely thankful and happy...so far so good.

Ernie surprised himself by deciding to try to keep Chong as part of the team. During the trip back to Sokcho, Chong fit easily into the group and Rocky and Burke started calling

Chong "Gunner" because his given first name was Gun-woo. The next part of his future plans for Gunner needed Robin's approval and Bill Grassley's help. After setting this all up, he went to the hotel where the team rented rooms, called his wife, and collapsed into bed for a few hours' sleep.

CHAPTER TWENTY-TWO

Kuro flew the helicopter at a low altitude even though they already had clearance to enter Vladivostok airspace. Night had wrapped itself around them as they approached the coast of the Vladivostok Peninsula at 1722 hours. A sprinkle of lights appeared ahead of them, growing more intense to the right where Vladivostok sat along the bay.

Winds buffeted the chopper the entire trip and Mark and Shosi, weren't looking too good.

Robin talked to Kuro over the intercom. "Kuro, are you going to make it back to Toyama all right in this weather?"

"Yes, we will make it back just fine. It takes very heavy weather to stop us from flying."

"How 'bout picking us up?"

"Same thing. Get ready to push the RIB out. There is a patch of brush near the clearing you can reach by following the road I showed you on the satellite photos."

Robin moved back to the cargo area and began untying the lines securing the RIB. Mark started helping.

"Hold on to those two lines, Mark and we'll lower the boat into the bushes Kuro hovers over." Mark nodded.

"Thirty seconds to go, Robin," Kuro announced.

Robin pulled the door latch and pushed the door open. A blast of cold, wet air hit him. The chopper went into a hover and Robin could make out the bushes through his night vision goggles.

"Okay, drop it."

Robin signaled Mark and they pushed the RIB out and let it dangle for a moment and then lowered it into the bushes, letting the lines go.

"We're good, Kuro. Take off." The big chopper moved forward at a slow speed to the landing pad just over the next hill. Robin and Mark went to a large tarp at the back of the helicopter and got underneath it with their gear. Just before securing the tarp, Robin signaled Shosi they were good to land.

KURO MANEUVERED the helicopter for landing while Ryuu lowered the landing gear. The pad lay in between a row of trees bordering an empty field on the left and an open storage area on the right with the harbor directly in front of them. He saw a truck waiting for him at the entrance to the pad area and also noticed the target ship further to the left. He set the big chopper gently down and began shutdown and the turbines started to wind down from a roar to a whine.

The truck moved closer and two men got out. Kuro recognized Sergey Bostroff, his customer in this area. Sergey waved and Kuro waved back. He let Ryuu continue the shutdown while he went to the back to greet Sergey. He slid open the door and greeted the Russian in English, the mutual language the men spoke. "Good evening, Sergey, how are you?"

"I am well, Kuro. I am glad you decided to come early. I have a customer who immediately needs one of the electronic parts you brought because they are leaving tonight."

"I'm happy we can accommodate your demanding customers."

"Ha, I only sell to them because I need the money. They are damn Arabs and none too friendly looking. Are you staying with us tonight?"

"Unfortunately, we have to get back."

"But surely you can stay for one cup of vodka."

"Of course, Sergey. I cannot leave without toasting our friendship."

"Ah, good. Let's load the truck and get over to my shop. We'll drink first and do business later."

The men unloaded several boxes of parts and got them into the truck. When they were finished, Sergey wanted them all to crowd into the cab, but Kuro told them he needed to check something in the helicopter and he would walk over to the shop. The truck left and he went to the helicopter and undid the tarp hiding Robin and Mark.

"Robin, did you hear about the Arabs?"

"Yes, we did. We're going to have to move fast."

"Look, I can keep Sergey busy for at least an hour, maybe a little bit more, but that is the best I can do."

"That'll be good enough."

"Now is a good time for you to move."

"We're outta here."

Robin and Mark put on their gear, which included each man carrying two twenty pound haversacks of C4 explosives. They were dressed in black BDUs over wetsuits and wore watch caps which blended with their blackened faces. Robin appreciated the wetsuits which prevented the cold, wet air seeping to his bones.

They jumped off the helicopter and moved to the trees to the left. The trees were against a clay wall surrounding the empty field. The men climbed over the wall and started slowly moving along it to the northwest corner of the lot, directly across and only forty yards away from the target ship. The area didn't have much light.

The two men would move twenty yards and then stop and clear their surroundings of any threats. It took them fifteen minutes to reach the corner. Robin peeked over the top of the wall and saw a small building in a stand of trees and bushes to the right and still only forty yards from the ship. He also saw the open rear cargo door to the ship.

"We're going over the wall and to the right to a small building surrounded by trees and bushes," Robin whispered to Mark. "You go first and I'll cover."

Mark nodded and rose up and looked to the right and went over the wall. Robin kept his weapon ready for any threats from the target ship. He saw Mark disappear into the trees. Then he went over the wall and moved next to Mark.

"We'll watch for about fifteen minutes to see what's going on before we move in."

Mark nodded again and the men surveilled the area for any movement. Within five minutes, a car drove up to the ship and a man got out and sat on the trunk of the car. Another man came out of the rear cargo door. He carried a large briefcase. He stepped on to the dock and walked over to the car.

Robin and Mark were only fifty feet from the men and could see what they were doing. Robin could make out distinct features, but no color with night vision goggles. The men talked to each other for a moment. They didn't act like they knew each other. The man from the ship handed the other man the briefcase and he opened it. Robin could see him taking out bundles of currency.

"If I didn't know better, I'd say we got a dope deal going down," he whispered.

"That's what it looks like."

The man from the car took the briefcase off of the trunk of the car and opened the trunk. The other man reached in and took out a backpack, but this one looked different. It looked like a cylinder about three feet by two feet and had some weight to it going by the way the man handled it. The shape of the backpack rang a bell in Robin's mind, but he couldn't grasp the thought. Whatever it was, the guy from the ship paid a lot of money for it.

The two men shook hands and parted company. Out of habit, Robin noted the license number of the car as it backed up closer to them. Then it drove away. The other man shouldered the backpack and disappeared into the cargo door.

Robin took the satellite radio and checked to see if he had a connection. He did and he sent a message to Jamie describing the backpack. Five more minutes went by without movement.

"Okay, Mark, let's rock." The two moved out of the trees and over to the ship. Robin got to the left side of the open door and looked in the lower hold. Seeing no one, Robin jumped onto the deck and dropped to a kneeling position. He swept the deck with the night vision and saw no threats. He waved to Mark who jumped onto the deck. They moved to the center seam of the hull and Robin put his C4 charges on the port seam. He pulled wires out of both haversacks and connected them together. He took a digital timer out of one of them, connected the wires to the timer and set the time for three hours.

Robin smiled to himself as he looked up and saw Mark

diligently covering the area for any threats. He's learned well. Robin tapped Mark's shoulder and motioned to the starboard seam and the men moved over. Robin started to get the wires out of Mark's haversacks when he heard a sound toward the rear of the ship. He looked over and Mark had his weapon trained on something. Robin moved his head slightly and could see feet on the top of the stairs where they met the tween deck. He heard shouting and talking and recognized Sergey's voice. Robin saw him coming to the cargo door. At the same time, the helicopter started up drowning out the conversation. A man came down the stairway to the bottom hold. The two men met at the corner of the hold, but they were out of sight.

Robin's heart pounded as he raised his silenced MP5 and bent on one knee next to Mark and covered to the front of the ship. The men could barely see each other's face in the gloom. The helicopter took off and as it faded into the night Robin could hear talking again. It stopped and he heard someone going up the stairway. Mark signaled all clear. Robin let his MP5 hang in his sling and resumed setting the other charges. He set them for two hours and fifty minutes. He then tapped Mark on the shoulder and signaled for them to move out.

"What about the ship's communications?" Mark whispered.

"It's too dangerous to try to get up to the antennas while the ship is docked. We'd be seen for sure. Besides, we won't be anywhere near it when the charges go off."

Mark nodded and they went to the cargo door and checked out the area. They couldn't hear any noise on the tween deck, so Robin signaled for them to move out. They leaped onto the dock and made straight for the corner of the wall around the empty lot and jumped over. They waited for a couple of minutes and hearing nothing they headed back along the wall to an opening at the southeast corner. They used a dirt road Kuro said would take them to the other side of the peninsula and they could find the RIB from there. Robin looked at Mark who grinned. Robin felt good too. They may just get out of this alive.

They were fifteen minutes away from the ship when Robin's satellite phone vibrated.

"Mark, stop. We're getting a message." The men moved to some bushes and Robin cupped his hand around the screen, hit the unscramble button and read the message.

ALERT ALERT ALERT
PACK IS NUCLEAR WEAPON. MUST RECOVER.
ACKNOWLEDGE.

HIS HEART POUNDED into his throat and for a moment he remained still. Then he leaned over to Mark and showed him the screen. The same fear Robin felt appeared on Mark's face. Robin looked at the screen again, hoping he misread it, but the words seared into his brain. He slowly pressed three buttons, hit the scramble button and then the send button.

ACK

HE TURNED THE PHONE OFF. He looked at Mark and simply said, "Let's go." They started back to the ship with Robin setting a double time pace. They worked their way back to the small building surrounded by the trees. Scanning the area, they saw no one, but heard the ship's engine running. Robin tapped Mark's shoulder and moved in a fast walk to the left side of the cargo door with his weapon ready. The hold was clear and he dropped onto the deck moving to the darkest corner he could find in the front, with Mark following. The cargo door started closing. The two men huddled next to each other and waited in the dank gloom.

CHAPTER TWENTY-THREE

D avid kept the boat at a low speed as he guided it in an area twenty-five miles west of Yonaguni Island. Emmett stood next to him, fidgeting and scanning the night sea with low light binoculars. Other men searched the night from different parts of the boat.

The last position from NSA put the target ship approximately two miles northwest of their location. Emmett thought they should've spotted it by now. He looked over at David, who seemed a lot calmer than Emmett felt. He reached for his satellite phone and David gently put his hand on top of Emmett's.

"Give us a few more minutes, Emmett. The ship is close, I can feel it."

"Now you're beginning to sound like our boss. He says shit like that."

"You mean Robin?"

"Yep."

"I must meet him."

"Oh, I'm sure you will."

They motored on in silence until Doug's voice called out, "Navigation lights, ten o'clock!"

Emmett raised his binoculars and caught a flash. He settled the binoculars down and then clearly saw the lights. He took his eyes off the binoculars and could still see the lights now.

"Do you see them, David?"

"Yes, I have them."

"We'll get ready to launch the RIB."

David held out his hand. Emmett wrapped his huge hands around David's in a warm handshake.

"Good luck, Emmett. I'd tell you to be careful, but if you were careful, you wouldn't be here, would you?"

"I'm careful in my own way." Emmett saluted David and walked out of the cabin.

David began maneuvering the boat to bring it behind the tango ship, but keeping a decent distance between them. Gradually, he completed the turn and started pacing the ship. Cái came into the cabin.

"We're ready to launch, General."

"Good. The ship is doing ten knots, Cái. At that speed and this sea, there shouldn't be any trouble catching and boarding her."

"Yes, sir."

David smiled. "I wish I could board her with our friends."

"I do too, sir, but I am sure they will take care of business."

"I'm sure they will, too."

Cái saluted and left to join the team.

AS THEY CLOSED distance on the freighter, Emmett glassed

the rear deck for any movement. Suddenly the glow of a cigarette appeared near the stern.

"Rick?"

"I see him." Rick lay prone over the left side of the RIB with his sniper rifle.

Emmett tried to keep an eye on the stern of the ship and Rick at the same time, but decided to just watch the ship. They came closer and Emmett began to fidget. Several seconds went by and he wanted to scream for Rick to shoot when he heard the muffled shot leave Rick's silenced rifle and the cigarette floated to the sea.

"He's down," Rick quietly observed.

Emmett saw no one else and waved Cái forward, pointing to the right side of the stern. Emmett readied a boarding ladder. He could see the small deck above the rear cargo door and prepared the hook attached to the rope ladder.

Cái made a good approach and Emmett got the boarding ladder hook on the railing around the small deck in two tries. He grabbed the ladder with his hand and got his foot on the first rung. He climbed to the hook, made sure it held securely and waved Rick up. He could see Doug covering the stern with his silenced MP5.

THE EVER AGILE Rick caught the boarding ladder and got his foot onto the bottom rung on the first try. He thought he did pretty good considering he was carrying forty pounds of C4 explosives, as were the other two men. Emmett waved him up and then helped Rick over the rail. He went to the back of the small deck and using a handhold, pulled himself up onto the area in between the superstructure and the starboard exhaust stack. From there he inched his way over an inclined piece of support and dropped down onto the second deck of the superstructure. He cleared right and saw the body of the man he shot. He pulled the body against the base of the exhaust stack. He then cleared a corner to the left and saw a ladder leading up to the top deck and climbed it. Reaching the top, he saw his objectives...the communication antennas for the ship. He set to work disabling them.

EMMETT SAW Rick go onto the upper deck, turned and waved Doug up, who slung his MP5 back and grabbed the boarding ladder with his right hand. He stepped onto the ladder and grabbed further up with his left. Emmett had moved down to help Doug and in light of the full moon saw him wince, but he made it to the small deck. Emmett pulled him closer.

"You good? I saw you wince."

"I'm good to go. Let's rock!"

The two men climbed onto the second deck of the superstructure, cleared the outside, set up security and waited for Rick to come down from the top deck, which he did a few minutes later. The ship's bridge sat just forward and up from them and Emmett pointed to it. The other men nodded.

Emmett quietly climbed the steps to the door of the bridge and peeked through the window. He saw two men talking to each other, but not touching the helm or throttle. That meant the ship steered on auto pilot and a good thing to Emmett. Doug came up behind and Emmett signaled for Doug to follow him in and Rick to maintain outside security. Both men nodded.

Doug crouched and moved to the door handle. Emmett pointed to himself indicating he would go straight in and pointed to Doug indicating he should buttonhook to the right. Doug nodded. Emmett raised his weapon and nodded. Doug pushed the handle down and pulled the door open. In one second both men moved into the bridge. The man on the left instantly reached for a pistol on the chart table. Emmett put a two round burst into his head, which pitched the man forward onto the chart table in a crimson shower and he crumpled to the deck. The other man stood stock still with his hands raised. Doug grabbed the man and pushed him face down to the floor and put his knee behind his neck. Emmett put plastic handcuffs on his hands and feet. linking them together and put duct tape on his mouth.

Emmett and Doug came out of the bridge and Rick led the way to a ladder down to the weather deck. All three had their weapons ready and continually scanned the area around them. Once on the weather deck they found the door to the inside stairwell to the tween deck and Rick very slowly led the way down. Suddenly, he stopped and raised his hand in a fist, indicating to the others to stop. He bent down and peered under a ledge. He eased back up, pointed to his eyes and then showed seven fingers, indicating he saw seven enemy.

Emmett pointed to his eyes and then to his weapon.

Rick nodded indicating he did see weapons.

Emmett signaled that the team would go down the stairs fan out and take out all seven enemy. The other men understood, in a fan, left side takes out targets starting on the left, the center takes out targets in the middle and the right side takes out targets starting on the right. He held up three fingers and the others nodded. They readied themselves to go down the stairs.

Rick held up three fingers and pulled one in...then another...then the third.

Emmett saw Doug move to the left and followed Rick as he stopped in the center. Emmett saw seven men dressed in camouflage around two RIBs. They had the center cargo door halfway open. The man furthest to the left saw them coming and yelled as he reached for a weapon and Doug fired a burst into the man's torso spinning him around. Emmett focused on the man furthest on the right. He had a quizzical look on his face that disappeared as his head exploded from Emmett's 9mm rounds hitting it. Emmett swung his weapon to the left and targeted a man diving behind the closest RIB. Emmett fired a five round burst that tore through the boat and smashed into the terrorist's torso. Swinging his weapon further left he looked for more targets, but all seven men were down.

The team quickly checked the bodies, making sure they were dead. They put the bodies in the RIB's along with all the tangos' weapons. They pushed everything overboard after puncturing the air cells of the boats with their knives and. Emmett waved the men back to the stairwell and led the team down to the main cargo hold in the bottom of the ship. He peeked under the ledge there, but saw no one and led the team all the way down. They quickly fanned out, with Emmett going to the starboard seam in the middle of the ship, Doug to the port seam.

RICK WENT to the engine room as Emmett and Doug started setting their charges, but Rick froze at the door. A man wearing dirty green coveralls stood inside. The man turned, saw Rick and reached for an AK47 leaning against a bulkhead. Rick had slung his MP5 and held the haversacks full of C4. The man grabbed the rifle by the barrel with his left hand and pulled it up and grabbed the trigger area with his right hand. At the same time, Rick dropped the haversacks and drew his pistol. Rick fired first hitting the man in the chest. The man started falling backward and his dying reflex pulled the trigger of his rifle firing a four round burst with the first round hitting the bulkhead to the left of Rick's leg, spraying it with shrapnel. The second round hit Rick's upper left leg, smashing into the thigh muscle and exited at an angle. The third round hit him in the right side of his stomach just under his vest, coming out the back of his right side, leaving a large hole. The last round hit the bulkhead just to the right of Rick's head, slamming shrapnel into the right side.

EMMETT HAD JUST SET his charges for ten minutes and saw Doug finished his when he heard the shots. He looked to the engine room to see Rick crashing to the ground. Both Emmett and Doug ran to Rick. Emmett bent down over Rick.

"Rick! Talk to me!"

Rick tried to mouth words, but nothing came out.

"Doug, cover while I check him out!"

"We gotta go, Emmett! The charges are set! Let's get him outta here and work on him on the boat!"

"Standby, dammit!"

Emmett worked feverishly to stop all the bleeding he could and he gave Rick morphine. "Okay, let's go!"

Doug set Rick's charge and threw it into the engine room. Emmett picked Rick up in his huge arms and cradled him like a baby. Doug led the way back to the stairs, MP5 at the ready. He stopped at the top and saw a man coming quickly down the stairs with a panicked look on his face and pointing an AK 47. Doug put his sights on the man's head and fired a burst. The man fell back and then started slipping down the stairs at Doug. Doug kicked him off the stairs so he wouldn't hit Emmett and Rick.

He cleared the tween deck and motioned Emmett up.

Doug led the way up the stairway to the weather deck. He stopped at the door and cleared the area.

Doug scrambled up the ladder to the second deck of the super-structure and took a rope out of his pack. He held on to both ends and dropped the loop to Emmett who put it under Rick's arms. Doug pulled Rick up while Emmett helped by holding Rick enough to halve his weight on the rope. They got Rick to the deck and moved to the exhaust stack and over the incline. Then Emmett climbed down to the platform at the top of the rope ladder. He aimed his flashlight toward the rear of the ship and flashed three times. Immediately, Cái arrived at the stern with the RIB. Doug lowered Rick to Emmett and then climbed down to the platform. Emmett started down the ladder when an explosion rocked the boat...then another.

Doug steadied himself and lowered Rick to Emmett and then together, they worked him down the ladder. The ship had slowed considerably and settled lower in the water. Emmett let Rick hang for a moment and stepped into the RIB. Then he grabbed Rick's feet and pulled him into the boat as gently as he could. Emmett waved for Doug to come down. Men were shouting on the boat now.

Doug looked up at the superstructure. "Emmett! Get away from the ship! The engine room is going to blow!"

"Get your ass down here, now!"

Doug saluted Emmett and climbed back up the ladder and moved to the second deck. He cleared the area and went to the bridge. He looked through the window and saw a man screaming into a microphone. He had a pistol in the other hand. The man threw the microphone at the bridge console just as Doug entered the bridge. The man turned and Doug fired a burst into the man's chest and then his head. He fell backwards onto the bridge console and then hit the deck with a dull thud.

The crewman they had hogtied still lay there with terrified

eyes. Doug cut the plastic cuffs, waved to the man and ran out the door. Another explosion rocked the ship. He looked around and saw no one so he scrambled over the incline and climbed down to the platform at the top of the rope ladder. To his surprise, the crewman from the bridge followed him and when he landed on the platform, he raised his hands in a gesture to show he meant no harm and then indicated he wanted to come with Doug.

The water splashed around the small deck and Doug grabbed the man, flashed his light three times out to sea and jumped into the water holding the terrified seaman. Moments later the man started shouting. Doug looked back and realized the crewman couldn't swim. He swam to the man and grabbed him. Turning him around, Doug put his left arm under the man's armpits and began a lifeguard carry away from the ship. Doug truly worried he couldn't swim fast enough away from the ship before it sank and took him down with its suction.

He swam as hard as he could until he heard an outboard engine. He reached into the vest and pulled out a chemlite, lit it and held it up. His arms and legs ached and he didn't know how long he could hold the other man up. The outboard came closer and it bumped into him.

"Emmett! I'm here!"

The engine went into idle and Cái's face appeared over the side of the boat. "Emmett's back on the General's boat, working on Rick. Get in!"

"Here, help this idiot get on board." Cái flashed a surprised look and then reached over and pulled in the crewman. Doug then climbed on board and flopped down on the deck, his left shoulder throbbing. Cái jumped to the helm and gunned the engine, pulling the RIB in a tight turn away from the ship and back to David's boat. Doug sat up and watched as the ship broke up and sank into the sea. The man looked at him, put his hands together and bowed to Doug. He nodded back.

As they approached David's boat, a helicopter flew away. Cái brought the RIB up to the stern and Doug scrambled onto the swim platform and secured the line. Cái took the crewman's arm and led him off the RIB. Doug and David pulled the RIB onto the boat then David went to the helm and headed the boat back to Hualien.

"Is Rick on that chopper?"

"Yes."

"How is he doing?"

"Not good. Emmett had to restart his heart twice here. It's a good thing he is a medic or Rick would be dead."

Doug dropped into the seat next to David, his mind and stomach churning at the same time. A plan formed in his mind. "Where is the chopper taking Rick and Emmett?"

"To the Navy hospital in Taipei."

"You still have one of our sat phones?"

"Yes, it's over there," David said pointing to a waterproof bag.

CHAPTER TWENTY-FOUR

R obin and Mark watched from their dark corner as two men talked at the door to the engine room. The men had come down a few minutes after Robin and Mark settled into their hiding space. Since then, one stayed there while the other kept going up the steps and coming back a few minutes later.

The ship had been underway for almost an hour and it rolled and pitched in the storm. Robin figured they had a good hour, maybe even an hour and a half to take care of business and get off the ship before the charges blew. The ship wasn't large, so he figured it wouldn't take too long to find the nuke. Of course, they had to get by the tangos and the crew to find it...minor problem.

The two men at the engine room headed for the stairs, still talking to each other. Robin could just hear enough to understand they had some kind of problem with the engine.

Mark looked at Robin. "What's the plan, boss?"

"I was about to ask you the same thing."

"You're not bolstering my confidence, Rob."

Robin smiled at Mark. "We have Ernie's plan, we're just

going to have to adapt it to a two man team instead of a six man team."

Mark had a silent thinking moment. "Well, once on board the ship, his plan called for disabling the ship's communications."

"Right, but he counted on getting on the ship from the outside. We have to get to those antennas from the inside or blow the radios in the bridge with our grenades. Either way, my guess is we're going to have to fight to get there."

"That's what I figure, too."

"This time we can't ignore the communications because it could bring ships and planes out to the area when we are trying to get away."

Mark nodded.

"Okay, so when we get to the weather deck, I want you to go up and take care of the communications. It'll be your call on how you do it. I'll start looking for the nuke. When we come across anyone, we try to take them out quietly. I know this isn't exactly how we're wired, but we take no prisoners. We see someone, they're history. Any other way and we won't get off here alive."

"Given what these fuckers are up to, I'm good to go."

Robin put his hand on his friend's shoulder. "You're amazing, Mark."

Mark grinned.

Robin cuffed him on the chin. "Let's get ready."

Mark put his hand on Robin's arm. "I have a confession to make."

"What?"

"I broke a major team rule and called Jessica Lanthrop awhile back." Mark waited for Robin's reaction.

"So, how did it turn out?"

"We're engaged. If I don't..."

"Stow it, Mark. We're both going to make it. Congratulations. Let's get this done and get home."

The two men checked their weapons and magazines. As they were finishing their preparation, one man came back to the engine room. When Robin saw Mark was ready, he nodded to him and Mark nodded back. They started moving to the engine room and into the dim light.

Robin went to the starboard charge and looked at the timer. He was shocked to see they only had fifty more minutes. Time had gone by faster than he'd estimated and he cursed himself for not paying more attention to his watch.

"We only have fifty minutes," he whispered to Mark.

Mark's face showed concern, but not panic. He had a hardened look of resolve and Robin thought he'd aged five years.

As they moved closer to the engine room, the man came out, saw them and ran for the stairs. Robin fired a burst and the dull thump, thump of the silenced weapon knocked the man against the bulkhead and he collapsed to the deck. Robin went over and confirmed he was dead. They dragged the body back to the dark front of the hold. The two men moved up the stairs with Robin in the lead. As they got near the tween deck, Robin could hear several voices. He took a quick peek at the top of the stairs and saw five men around RIBs near the side cargo door, with weapons all over the area.

He whispered to Mark. "Five tangos, many weapons near the side cargo door. The tangos are standing together. We'll take positions on either side of the stairwell and shoot from there. I'll take right, you got left."

Mark nodded.

They moved to the stairwell with Robin standing on the right side and Mark going prone on the left. Bringing his MP5 to bear on the tango on the right, Robin figured he had to move fast and only needed to see his targets drop. The rolling of the ship caused him to take more time than he wanted, but he got a good sight picture, squeezed the trigger and the tango dropped with a two round burst to the upper chest. He heard Mark's weapon fire as he put another two round burst into the next tango he saw standing to the left, and that man dropped from Robin's vision. He moved the sights further left and shot a man running for the cargo door. The bullets ripped into the man's back. He slammed into the door and dropped to the deck. Sweeping further left showed Mark had dropped the other two. Robin cleared around him and saw nothing.

"Clear!" he said in a hoarse whisper.

"Clear!" Mark replied.

They moved forward and checked the bodies. The first man Robin shot was still alive, so he put a round in his head.

"These assholes never knew what hit them," Mark whispered.

"Let's hope we can keep it that way. These RIBs are our ticket out of here. When you disable the antennas, get down here and protect these babies. Let's move."

The two man team moved up the last flight of stairs to the door leading out to the weather deck. When they stepped out, the wind howled and sheets of rain pelted them. They moved to the ladder going to the second deck of the superstructure. The walkway to the crew quarters ran to the left of the ladder.

Robin stopped and whispered to Mark. "Good luck, partner. If you get compromised, break radio silence. Otherwise, I'll see you on the tween deck."

"Good luck to you, too, Rob."

Robin saluted and headed down the walkway.

MARK CLIMBED the ladder and peeked over the top. He saw

two men working on something by the ladder he needed to climb to get to the antennas. They were in foul weather gear and their backs were turned to him. He slowly put the muzzle of his weapon over the edge of the deck and rested it there so it moved with the roll of the ship and his intended targets. He pushed the selector switch to semi-auto and took careful aim on the head of the man on the left. He fired and the man dropped. He moved the sights to the right and the other man turned with a surprised look filling Mark's sights. The man died with that look and a bullet hole in his forehead.

Keeping low, Mark stepped onto the deck and ghosted to the ladder to the communications antenna. He climbed the ladder, at times holding tight in the roll, which got worse the higher he went. He reached the upper deck and knelt on one knee while he surveyed the area. The ship had a pronounced roll at this level and he held on tight. He saw a communications satellite dish to his left. He decided to save it for last in case it was video the crew may be watching. He saw several antennas to his right, which looked easy to disable, but immediately in front of him stood a high mast with a long range antenna on it. The base of the antenna was a good twelve feet up the mast. Mark swallowed his pounding heart. *This could be worse than a HALO jump!*

He raised off his knee and shuffled on the slippery deck over to the base of the mast to a metal ladder surrounded by circular braces running up it like a tube. Mark reached up and grabbed the bottom brace, pulling himself to the bottom rung. The horizontal rain stung his face and he climbed back down and knelt again, taking off his pack. He opened it, fished out his goggles and put them on. He unhooked a pack shoulder strap and looped it around a handhold. He started back up the ladder.

Each rung was slippery and the roll of the ship made balance difficult, but he made it to the base of the antenna. He pulled out a wire cutter from his vest, wiped his goggles and started cutting wires. He prayed the crew wouldn't transmit or he would get a good jolt. He finally cut through all the wires, put the cutters back in his vest, went down the ladder and retrieved his pack.

Now Mark knew he had to move fast. Time was running out. He quickly crawled to the smaller antennas and disabled them. Then he crawled to the back of the deck and removed the transponder from the satellite dish. He started for the ladder to the second deck when gunfire erupted just below him.

WHEN ROBIN LEFT MARK, he started down the walkway and stopped at the first porthole on the starboard side. He did a quick peek and saw four men sitting on bunk beds. He looked again and they seemed to be just discussing something. He ducked and went to the second porthole which looked into the same room from a different angle. He didn't see the nuke pack in either view.

He moved to a causeway and could see it had four doors, two on either side. He figured they were entrances to cabins like the one in which he just looked. He moved back out to the second deck and to the next porthole on the starboard side and looked in, but it was dark. He went back to the causeway and as he passed the door of the rear port cabin, he saw two men arguing. He went around the corner and peeked in the porthole and saw the same man from the dock holding the nuke pack in front of him. Another man yelled at him. Robin went back to the door and tried the latch...it moved. He stepped back with the muzzle of his weapon at eye level and opened the door.

The tango with the nuke yelled when he saw Robin, who

immediately put a burst into the other man knocking him forward into the tango holding the nuke and then he fell to the deck. The man with the nuke hit his back against a bunk bed, but kept standing using the nuke as protection. He made a move for a pistol on a small table. Robin couldn't shoot because of the nuke, so he rushed forward and slammed into the man knocking him down and sending the pistol flying. Robin grabbed the nuke pack and pulled, but the man just came with it. Robin took a step backward to pull harder and stumbled over the body of the first man he shot and fell on his butt. He quickly rolled to a crouching position as the man rushed for the door swinging a metal bar. The bar hit Robin on the left side of his neck just under his jaw and against his larynx. He grabbed the hand with the bar, but he choked and struggled for breath. With all his might, he slammed the man's right arm against the metal end of the bunk bed frame and heard it snap. The man screamed and dropped the nuke. Robin smashed his fist into the middle of the man's face. The man fell backwards and crashed into the small table and hit the deck in a flurry of shattered wood and splinters. He rolled over and struggled to his feet.

Robin bent down to pick up the nuke, but he dropped to his knees trying to breathe. The man charged Robin again ready to strike him with one of the legs from the table. He swung, but Robin blocked the blow with his left hand and drawing his knife with his right, he rammed it into the man's gut, cutting edge up. The man gasped as Robin used both hands to pull the knife up cutting from the gut to the sternum. Their eyes met and Robin tilted the point of the blade and shoved it into the man's heart. The terrorist's eyes went dull and his body shuddered to limp.

Robin collapsed with the man's body. He forced himself to calm down and breathing became easier. He coughed and spit blood. He staggered up with the pack and slowly opened the door. A man stood at the opposite corner on the port walkway with an AK47. He looked right at Robin and fired a burst, but Robin ducked behind the steel door as bullets smashed into it. He fired a burst through the crack and then took one of his frag grenades and tossed it out to the walkway. It went off with a loud bang and then Robin heard screaming. He put a fresh magazine in his submachine gun and leading with this weapon, checked the area. A head poked out of the cabin where the four men were. Robin fired a burst at the head and it ducked, leaving the door cracked. He ran to the door and tossed another grenade into the room and slammed the door. He ran to the stairwell to the tween deck, almost slipping on the wet weather deck in the wind as the second grenade went off. There he found Mark lying at the top of the stairs.

UPON HEARING the gunfire below him, Mark was torn. He wanted to go to Robin, but he knew he had to protect at least one of the RIBs they saw on the tween deck. He ran to the ladder and slid down to the second deck of the superstructure, seeing a man come out of the bridge as he did so. Mark hit the bottom of the ladder in a crouching position and fired at the man. At the same time he saw the muzzle flash of a pistol in the man's hand and felt a searing burn on the top of his right shoulder. The man fell back against the rail at the door of the bridge and crumpled down against the door. Mark then heard a loud bang on the port side of the ship.

He ran for the ladder to the weather deck balancing against the roll of the ship and wind. He heard a yell behind him and a shot. A heavy blow hit his right buttock spinning him around and off of the second deck onto the weather deck twelve feet below. He landed on his left foot and heard a snap as he slammed onto the deck sending a sharp shot of searing pain from this ankle to his hip that felt like someone stuck a red hot fireplace poker up his leg. For a moment his whole body knotted in pain. Another loud bang reverberated throughout the ship. Then he rolled over on his back in time to see a head come over second deck rail and he fired a four round burst. The head disappeared in a red mist carried away by the wind, but the body folded over the rail and then slipped down.

Mark crawled to the door leading to the stairwell to the tween deck, pulled himself up to the latch and opened the door. The wind caught the door and flew it open and he crawled inside to the top of the stairs. The intense pain again made his body taught and lightheaded, causing him to vomit. He heard footsteps and turned to see Robin coming through the doorway.

WHEN HE SAW Mark lying there in a pool of blood and vomit, Robin's heart stopped as Mark gave him a weak smile. "Boy, am I glad to see you."

Robin noticed Mark's left foot canted out in an odd angle. "I hate to do this to you, but we gotta move and it's probably gonna hurt like hell."

"I know. Let's go"

Mark raised his arm and Robin pulled him up and got under his armpit. "Here we go, partner." At that moment an explosion shot through the holds, jarring the men and hurting their eardrums.

"Shit, now the boat's sinking!"

Mark yelled in pain as Robin got them down the stairwell over to the RIBs, struggling under the weight of Mark and the nuke pack. There a shout sounded from the top of the stairs.

"Cover the stairs, Mark!" Robin picked up a tarp and laid it in the bottom of the largest RIB, a twenty-two foot boat. Mark fired a burst at the top of the stairs. Robin put the nuke pack and his MP5 in the RIB and pulled Mark up and helped him into the boat. Drawing his pistol, Robin ran to the side cargo door controls and hit the lever to open the door.

Water immediately flooded in the tween deck and at the same time another explosion painfully ripped through the hold. Bullets slammed in the bulkhead just over Robin's head and he turned and fired at a man on the stairs, but missed as he fought the surging water. The man pointed his gun at Robin again, but the ship lurched and the man fell down the stairs.

"Get in the boat, Rob!"

Robin struggled to get to the boat in the rising water. Then he saw Mark at the controls of the boat and the engine started. Mark steered the boat over to Robin and he crawled in.

"I got it, Mark. Get down."

The real danger to them became clear to Robin as he looked up. The door was not going up as fast as the water was rising. He did a full circle, dancing around the other RIB which floated aimlessly, trying not to panic and looking for a way out. The thought of drowning flushed him with terror. Then Robin realized he could get the bow of the boat under the door. He maneuvered the boat and pushed the throttle forward getting the bow under the door, stopping at the helm pedestal.

"Mark, take the wheel!" Mark struggled up and took the wheel, half kneeling, half sitting and cursing at the searing fire in his body. Robin got underneath the door and with all the strength in his legs and back, he pushed against the door, trying to lower the boat enough to get the door over the helm pedestal. At the same time Mark slowly increased the throttle and the edge of the door dug into Robin's back, causing him to grunt with pain.

With a grind the door rose to the lip at the base of the small windshield. Then the door stopped and Robin pictured the generators flooding. Adrenalin surged through him and he pushed again straining with every ounce of strength in his body.

"Full throttle, full throttle!" Robin yelled. He heard the engine roar. The boat momentarily stuck and then with the crack of the windshield breaking off, it shot onto a tumultuous sea.

CHAPTER TWENTY-FIVE

L aurie Marlette walked into the family room and saw her mother out on the deck, looking towards the west and the open Pacific. Karen turned and walked to the edge of the deck and Laurie could see her mother wringing her hands. She seemed to be looking for something...or someone. Laurie opened the door and walked out onto the deck and put her arm over Karen's shoulders.

"Mom, are you all right?"

Karen didn't answer right away, but continued to look out to sea. Then almost absent mindedly said, "Your father's in trouble."

Laurie turned her mother so they were face to face and saw tears welling in Karen's eyes. "What do you mean?"

"Your father is scared, worried and hurt."

All her life, Laurie had heard her parents talk about being connected even when they were apart. They would say they could sense each other's feelings. Laurie didn't know if she believed it or not, but more than once, she witnessed one say something about the other which later turned out to be true. Now her mother scared her. "Do you know where Dad is?"

"Oh, yes."

"Where?"

"Honey, you know I can't tell you."

Laurie sighed with exasperation. "I know what's going on. I know we can't talk about what dad and the team do and I never have. What makes you think I would say anything?"

Karen looked at her daughter and put her hand on Laurie's cheek. "I'm scaring you aren't I? I'm sorry, honey. Your dad is somewhere around Japan or Russia. Jamie told me he and Mark had to split off from the team to take care of a problem."

"What problem?"

"Jamie didn't tell me, but I know your dad is really worried about someone and I suspect it's Mark."

"Mom, do you know how weird you sound?"

Karen smiled at her daughter. "Laurie, I hope someday you meet someone you can connect with like your father and I do."

Laurie hugged her mother. "You're going to make yourself sick worrying about him."

"I'm a little worried, but I know your father and he'll figure out how to get Mark and himself home safe...and God help anyone in his way."

"WHAT THE HELL do you mean they're MIA?!!" Ernie almost screamed into the phone to Jamie. Burke jumped to his feet and glared at Ernie. The others were glued to Ernie's words.

"I mean exactly that. NSA has confirmed the ship sunk about fifteen nautical miles off the coast of Russia, but we've had no word from either Rob or Mark. The storm makes it impossible for NSA to see enough to find people or even a small boat in the water."

"So that's all we know? That's as good as they can do?"

"I'm sorry, Ernie, I'm just as worried as you."

Ernie let out a long breath. "Okay, Jamie, I'm the one who should apologize. I know it's not your fault. Just keep me posted on the situation. What about the Taiwan team?"

"More bad news. Mission accomplished, but Rick is badly wounded. He's at the Taiwan Navy Hospital and Emmett is there watching over him."

"Jesus, things are going to shit!"

"I got a call from Doug. He's alerted Maria and she's willing to go to Taiwan and make sure Rick gets the best treatment. He wants us to pick her up."

"Do it. Tell Shosi to monitor things from Japan. Make a stop at Osan and pick up Burke and Rocky on the way down to Mindanao."

"If you say so. You sure you want us to leave here?"

"Yes, I'm sure. How are you going to help Rob and Mark, land in the water? Just get moving."

Ernie ended the call. "Burke, Rocky, come with me." Ernie led the two men out of the boat and onto the dock, where they could talk in private. "You guys remember Rob's instructions to us about getting a captured team member out?"

Burke's eyes narrowed. "I do, but what makes you think Rob and Mark are prisoners."

"I don't know they're prisoners, but just think about it. The ship sank fifteen miles from Russia. If they got off it, there's only one place they can go..."

"Russia," the other men chimed.

"So, we'll get you back to Osan and then you guys get on Fatboy and start doing what you need to do to get us some Russian bargaining chips."

"We're talking serious shit, Ernie," Rocky said with a concerned face.

"Just get it set up. I'll make the final decisions."

Burke's mouth bent in a whimsical smile. "You know, Ernie, you're starting to sound like Rob."

BILL GRASSLEY LEANED over the NSA deputy director's shoulder and studied the screen before them.

"The sky's clearing, so we'll try an infrared shot," the deputy director advised.

Bill watched as the magnification increased. The technician, a man named Stevenson, gingerly fingered the controls, making the movement of the satellite imagery seem silky smooth as he moved it toward Vladivostok. "There, sir! Got something moving on a steady bearing towards the outer entrance to Vladivostok."

Bill looked more closely. "That might be them. There's no other small craft in the area."

"And that's a really small craft. Like a life boat or RIB," the deputy director added.

"Well, that means the nuke is either at the bottom of the sea or they're about to repatriate it to the Soviets."

"Why would they do that?"

"If I know Rob...and I do, he might need that nuke as a bargaining chip. Whatever he's doing, he has a good reason."

They continued to watch for a half-hour as the image moved into the harbor. It slowed down and then turned and headed for a flashing light just in from the beach.

"I wonder why he's headed for the light?" the technician asked.

"Can you change from infrared and get the color of that light?"

"Just a moment, sir."

A few seconds later the screen changed. "It's a blue light."

"Well, I'll be damned," Bill said under his breath.

"What's he doing?" the deputy director asked.

"He's going to contact a cop!"

Bill's satellite phone rang. "Grassley."

"Bill, it's Jamie. We just got a flash message from Rob."

"What's it say?"

"Mission accomplished. Mark WIA. Expect to be prisoners soon."

"Thanks, Jamie."

"Yes, sir."

"Well gentlemen, that's the case. Robin is going to trade a nuke for his team member's life."

"I'd say he's making a good trade," the technician blurted. "Sorry, sir...just my opinion."

"For what it's worth, Mr. Stevenson, we agree with you and we better tell the Chief of Naval Operations that he can pull his sub out of there. It won't be needed now."

CHAPTER TWENTY-SIX

The boat shot out onto the sea, throwing Robin backwards. He hit the side of the boat and bounced into the water, grabbing onto a rope lining the outside of the RIB. The boat bucked like a wild stallion in the waves and the rope cut into his hand. He pulled himself up so his left arm got over the side and then he felt Mark grab him and pull. Robin surged with a kick and flopped into the boat.

The rain lessened and a full moon radiated through cloud breaks, but the wind was howling, agitating the sea. Robin crawled to the pedestal taking control of the boat, guiding it over and down the five to seven foot waves at an angle. They came at him as looming, dark, undulating masses with pale, luminous tops. The bucking became less pronounced, but the boat still made a wild ride. He gave thanks they were in an almost enclosed sea, which limited the wave action. He remembered from the mission work up that the currents ran counter clockwise. With the winds coming out of the east, he could only go one way...back to Russia.

Robin saw Mark lying in the fetal position in the bottom of the boat.

"Mark, get under the tarp!" he yelled.

Mark raised his head, but seemed unresponsive.

"Goddammit, Mark, get your ass under the tarp before I kick it from one end of Asia to the other!"

Mark raised himself higher and fumbled with the tarp. Robin leaned to help him, but almost lost control of the boat.

"C'mon, Mark, move it! You've got to fight shock!"

Mark started moving more deliberately, managing to get the tarp unfolded and lay down on it. He got the other side almost over him, but the wind fought him.

Robin leaned over enough to grab the edge of the tarp and pull it over Mark, who pulled it tighter around himself like a cocoon. It was all he could do for Mark at this point. He concentrated on getting to Vladivostok as fast as he could. He fought the waves and the wind for a good hour. His body was shaking and he knew hypothermia was imminent. He saw lights and gradually could make out Ostrov Russiky. Soon he guided the boat between Russkij Island and Skryplev Island and entered Vladivostok Bay where the surrounding land masses calmed the winds and wave action.

Robin took a minute to check on Mark. Barely conscious, the young man was in the early stages of hypothermia and Robin knew he had to get help quickly. He pushed the throttle forward and decided to head for the headquarters of the Russian Pacific Fleet, although he only knew its approximate location. He moved through the bay and then headed up the main harbor.

Suddenly, Robin picked up a flashing blue light in his right peripheral vision. *That may be a cop! If it is, based on what we were told about government workers not getting paid and not showing up for work, this guy's got to be dedicated to still be doing graveyard shift. At least I may be able to talk to him before the shit hits the fan. What the hell, it's the best shot we got. Here we go.*

Robin put the boat in idle for a moment and sent a message to Jamie. Then he dumped the satellite phone and all of Mark's weapons into the water. He put the boat in gear and glided to the shore just below the light. He jumped out and pulled the boat onto the beach. He checked on Mark.

Mark looked at him and Robin saw he didn't look good.

"Hang in there, partner, I'll be back in a minute with some help."

Mark nodded.

Robin headed up a small hill and just before the top, he stopped and surveyed the area. The short climb warmed his body a little. He saw a police car and an officer bent over his hood writing. Another car rested on its side just in front of the police car. Robin didn't see anyone else. He silently came within five feet behind the officer. Although Robin had learned Russian during his training, his fluency needed work, unlike his Arabic. He spoke carefully.

"Greetings, comrade."

The officer spun around and blanched at the sight of Robin's MP5 pointed at his head. Robin saw a man with an intelligent face wearing a clean, pressed uniform with his leather and brass shined. Good! A professional.

"I don't want to hurt you, officer. I need to talk to you and I need you to listen. When I'm through, I'll give you my weapons." Robin thought he said it right.

"Would it be better if we spoke English? Your Russian is not very good," the officer replied.

"That would be a great help."

"I understood you to say you do not want to hurt to me, but you should repeat the rest."

"I just need you to listen to me and then I'll surrender and give you my weapons." *And brother, you have no idea what kind of weapon I have.*

"I'm listening."

"My name is Robin. First of all I want you to know that until three years ago I was a police officer for fifteen years. I tell you this in hopes you'll consider me a brother officer and know I'm not lying to you."

"Go on."

"A few hours ago, my partner and I recovered a Russian tactical nuclear device stolen from your country."

The officer's eyes grew wide. "How did you know this?"

"That's not important right now. What is important is I have the device in a boat just below us...don't panic, it's not armed to detonate. I want to give the device back to your country in exchange for medical treatment for my partner, who is also in the boat, badly wounded."

"I'm sorry, I cannot help you. This is far too large a problem for me to handle."

"No it isn't. I can give you a contact in the GRU who can help us solve this problem, but we can only give the device to him. If we do this, you'll probably become a Hero of the Soviet Union."

"Ha, the Soviet Union is finished. The country is bankrupt."

"Look we have to do something. My partner needs immediate medical attention and the device needs to be in your custody. Are you going to help me or not?"

The officer thought for a moment. "I will help you."

The two men looked each other in the eye for a few seconds, then Robin unslung his MP5 and handed it to the officer. "Who am I surrendering to?"

"Sergeant Lev Rogov of the Militsia, at your service."

"Good to meet you, Lev." Robin handed over his Colt .45. "Let's go get my partner and the device."

The two men walked down to the boat. Robin lifted the tarp.

"Mark, I have help. We have to get you up."

Mark looked at Rob with a vacant stare and in a shaky, hoarse whisper said, "I'm s-s-oo c-c-cold."

"We'll use the tarp as a stretcher. Careful with his left leg, it's a mess."

The two men lifted the tarp as gently as they could, but Mark grunted with pain. They struggled up the hill trying to be gentle as Mark growled and grunted, but Robin could tell Mark tried not to show how badly he was hurt. They finally got to the car and they could see Mark wouldn't be able to lie down in the small back seat.

"Lev, we need to put him in a sitting position with his legs facing out. Then you go to the other side and pull him over while I hold his leg. That way he'll have the left leg on the seat."

Mark spoke up. "I-I-I can h-help, Rob. J-just give me a m-m-minute to get r-ready." Robin watched as Mark closed his eyes and focused on absorbing the pain about to come. His heart went out to Mark.

"Okay, I'm r-ready."

They got Mark to a standing position and then gently lowered him onto the seat. Robin steadied the left leg in the tarp. Lev went to the other door, reached in and started pulling Mark in as Mark pushed with his right leg. Robin could see the pain on Mark's face, but he didn't utter a sound. After a short time of careful effort they had Mark settled in the car.

"God, the heat feels good," Mark said in response to the heater blowing warm air at him.

"Lev, I'll go down and get the device." Robin could see hesitation on Lev's face. "If I do something wrong, you can shoot me. You have my guns."

Lev nodded and Robin went down and retrieved the nuke pack. When he got back to the car, Lev put the device in his trunk. They got in the car and started driving.

"I'm going to take you to City Hospital #2. It is the medical school hospital and my wife is the head nurse at night. The doctors and nurses there are less Communist Party oriented than Hospital #1." They drove for about fifteen minutes and then arrived at a large building. Robin told Lev about meeting the GRU agent in Mindanao. He noticed they had turned on a street called Russkaya and the number on the building was 57.

"Wait here." Lev got out of the car and hurried up the steps. Five minutes went by and Robin started to get nervous. He contemplated stealing the police car and getting away, but one look at Mark nixed the idea. Then Lev came out of the hospital with an attractive, but clearly concerned nurse and two orderlies with a gurney.

"This is my wife, Rada. She is going to help us, but we must do exactly as she says."

"We will." Robin turned to Rada. "Thank you for helping us."

She shot him an icy look and then said in English. "My husband is doing a stupid thing. It's a good thing I love him."

"You sound like my wife."

Rada smiled briefly. They put Mark on the gurney and wheeled him into the hospital. Lev didn't come with them.

"Where's Lev?" Robin asked.

"He will return."

Based on the signs, Robin saw they were bypassing the emergency room. They got into an elevator and went to the fourth floor and into a private room. The orderlies left, but Robin noticed one of them seemed a little pissed off.

A doctor came in and talked to Rada in a concerned tone.

Robin picked up that he was worried the two men would try to escape and harm hospital personnel.

"Excuse me, doctor, we're waiting to turn ourselves in to the GRU. We're here because my partner needs medical attention. We won't try to escape."

"You speak our language! Why are you waiting for the GRU? They are not known to be kind and gentle."

"I've met some of them and I think we can work with them towards a solution of this situation. You have my word we won't try to escape."

The doctor looked at Robin for a moment and then walked over to Mark and asked in English, "Are you in much pain?"

"It hurts like hell, doc."

"Rada, get his clothes off."

The doctor went over to a sink, washed his hands and went back to Mark. Robin helped Rada take off Mark's clothes and while doing so he palmed Mark's folding knife and slipped it under his pillow. Mark noticed Robin do this.

"Where is this blood from?" The doctor rolled Mark over on his right side. "You've been shot!"

"Yes, sir. Helluva place to get shot."

"No actually, if you have to get shot somewhere, the buttocks are not necessarily a bad place. The worse result is you won't be able to sit comfortably for awhile." The doctor then started examining Mark's leg, which took about fifteen minutes of him touching and asking Mark questions. "We are going to have to take x-rays of this leg. I am sure surgery will be required. Excuse me, while I make some arrangements."

Thirty minutes had gone by since the doctor left. Robin heard a commotion outside the room and then three men burst in, their faces mean with the desire to cause trouble.

"You must leave this room...now!" Rada ordered.

One of the men pushed her aside, calling her a whore.

This didn't set well with Robin. She ran out the door. The larger of the men gave an order to the other two.

"Take him outside," referring to Robin.

Robin saw Mark reaching underneath his pillow. As the two men approached him, he could smell a strong odor of booze coming from them. He saw the larger man reaching to grab Mark's broken leg. One of the men tried to grab Robin. He caught the man's arm and pulled him close, kicking the man in the groin and hitting his Adam's apple with his closed fist. The man crashed to the ground holding both his groin and throat. The other man leaned in mid swing with his right hand. Robin used a circular motion to trap the on-coming arm in a hold. Grabbing the man's hand, Robin dropped to his knee taking the man's inverted hand with him. This act dislocated the man's shoulder, causing him to scream. Robin jumped back to his feet and in rapid succession punched the man in the throat and kicked him in the groin. That man also fell to the ground incapacitated.

Robin whirled around to look at Mark and with great satisfaction saw Mark had pulled the larger man close to him and put the folding knife to the man's throat. Knowing Mark did not understand Russian, but for the larger man's benefit, Robin growled, "Kill him."

"Please don't kill me, please! I'm sorry!" the man cried.

"Why shouldn't we kill you? You came to torture my friend. I think he has the right to kill you."

At that point the man urinated in his pants.

The door flew open and Lev, Rada and the doctor rushed into the room."

"Stop! Put the knife down!" Lev ordered.

Mark lowered the knife, but didn't drop it.

"Boris, you idiot. You don't come to work for a month and then you show up here drunk?! What kind of fool are you?"

"Up yours, Lev. You're protecting American spies."

"No, Boris. I'm holding them for the GRU, who will be here from Moscow in four hours, which is just about how long you have to live, I think."

Boris turned white and began to shake uncontrollably. "Lev, y-y-you must tell them we made a mistake. W-we didn't know!"

"Get out of here and take these miserable excuses of human beings with you! To think you are police officers! Go home and keep your mouths shut or I will tell the GRU what idiots you are."

Boris gathered his two cohorts and staggered out of the room. Lev stared at Robin with anger in his eyes.

"You retained weapons. You told me I could trust you."

"I did tell you that and you can still trust me. We didn't use the knife on you and we wouldn't. I just didn't know who else I could trust here."

"What other weapons do you have?"

Robin hesitated for a moment and then unbuckled his pants and reached to his inner thigh to a waterproof pocket on the wetsuit. He pulled out a .22 Magnum Derringer and handed it to Lev. He looked at it for a minute, turning it over and around. Then, to Robin's surprise, he gave it back.

"Please keep it hidden."

"I will."

The doctor walked over to Mark and held out his hand. Mark gave him the knife and the doctor handed it to Robin.

"Your friend is going in for surgery. He won't need this."

Rada and another nurse wheeled Mark out of the room and Robin and Lev followed.

"You know, the GRU almost hung up on me until I mentioned Mindanao. Whatever you did, must have impressed them."

"It was an interesting situation. I wish I could tell you more, Lev, but you'll have to ask them."

"I understand."

They arrived at the surgery area and Rada motioned for Robin and Lev to stop. She came back in two minutes carrying a bag. "You are filthy and you smell. Come with me."

"But my part..."

"You promised to do exactly as I told you. Please do so. Lev will watch over your friend."

Robin followed Rada to a room down the hall from the surgery area. She put the bag on a bed and turned to Robin and started inspecting the left side of his neck.

"You have been injured on your neck. What happened?"

"A guy hit me with a piece of metal."

She walked behind him. "You have blood across your back. Please take your clothes off."

Robin took off his vest and shirt and unzipped his wetsuit, but just peeled it down to his waist.

"Take everything off."

"I don't have anything on underneath my wetsuit."

"I am a nurse. You have nothing I have not seen before. You have obviously been in a fight and we need to inventory your injuries."

Robin took a deep breath and pulled off his wetsuit. Rada began inspecting his body with warm and gentle hands. She seemed to know just how far to go in touching his wounds. She also touched his old wounds. She came around and faced Robin.

"Open your mouth." Robin opened his mouth and Rada shined a light into his throat. "You have been bleeding in your throat. It has stopped, but I do not know how much blood you swallowed."

"I don't think I bled too much. I could feel it."

"Come."

Robin followed her to the bathroom.

"You must take a shower. I will clean the wounds on your back. You can clean everything else."

Robin turned on the shower, got the water at the right temperature and stepped in. He got his back wet and turned it to Rada who stood just outside the door. She began gently cleaning his back. As gentle as she tried to be, it still hurt, but it also felt good...good enough for Robin to start to get an erection. He put his hands over himself.

"My husband has put our family at risk of imprisonment or execution because of you and your friend."

"Why? He recovered a stolen nuclear weapon!"

"The GRU will only see he knows about a stolen nuclear weapon. The Soviet Union does not like its failings known to the proletariat. They will send us to the Gulag or execute us."

Robin turned to face Rada. "I won't let them take you anywhere."

"You are insane! You have no control over them!"

"They owe me. My team saved one of their agents and I have other bargaining chips. I won't let them harm you or your family."

Rada looked into Robin's eyes. "I hope so." She then looked at his genitals and a smirk formed on her lips. "Perhaps you should turn around."

Robin looked down feeling himself blush and quickly turned around.

Rada finished cleaning his back.

"There, you can finish your shower. There is a robe just outside the door to the left." She closed the door.

Robin lost himself in the warm water and exhaustion began to set in. He shook himself out of it and turned off the shower. Toweling off, he put the robe on and walked out of the bathroom.

Rada waited with a cart full of bandages and dressing. "Lay face down on the bed, please."

Robin did as asked and Rada began putting an ointment on his back and then bandages. She finished and told Robin to sit up. "You have other minor injuries, but they do not require bandages. Here, put on these clothes. They are probably too small around your chest and shoulders as well as too large around your waist, but it is the best we can do."

"Thank you, Rada. I appreciate it."

"You have fought many battles. Do you get tired of being in danger?"

"I really haven't fought too many battles, just a couple of tough ones."

Rada shrugged her shoulders. "Follow me."

They walked back to the surgery waiting area where Lev waited and Rada went into the operating room. She came back out a minute later.

"The surgery will take a few more hours. The leg and ankle are badly damaged and the doctor is working hard to save their full function, but he's making no promises."

"Tell him his efforts are very much appreciated."

"You should go back to the room where I bandaged you and get some rest."

"If you don't mind, I'll wait here."

Rada shrugged and walked out of the surgery area. Robin sat down and put his head back. "You have one smart wife, Lev."

Lev chuckled. "She is not one to trifle with when at work. She is much different at home."

"You're a lucky man." The sentence faded as Robin slipped off to sleep.

CHAPTER TWENTY-SEVEN

E mmett paced up and down in front of the surgery suite at the Taiwan Navy Hospital, with a heavy heart. Rick was in a bad way. His wounds caused immediate massive bleeding and shock, putting him on the edge of death. Emmett couldn't figure out why Rick stayed in the doorway. He knew it was the fatal funnel.

"Emmett!" He turned to see Doug coming toward him. They hugged each other. "How is he?"

"I don't know. He's been in surgery for six hours. Hey, why the hell didn't you get in the boat?!"

"I just couldn't leave the guy we left hog tied on the bridge without cutting him loose. I just had to make sure he had a chance."

"Well, you'll never know if he made it."

"Yeah, I do. He followed me out to the platform. I ended up taking him on our RIB to the boat. The Marines got him now."

Emmett looked at Doug and put his arm around his friend's shoulders. "We've come a long way from a cop's way of thinking, haven't we?"

"I don't know. I still believe I think like a cop…still making fine distinctions in a split second.

"Yeah, you're probably right about that. Some things never change. Have you received any word about Robin and Mark?"

"The last I heard they were MIA."

"What??!!"

"Jamie said they sunk the ship, but no one has heard from them for about six hours."

"Can you call Jamie and get an update?"

"I'll get my sat phone and do it right away. I just wanted to let you know Maria is on her way to supervise Rick's treatment."

"Man, that could piss off these doctors."

"Not if Maria tells them she's his doctor. They have to respect the doctor/patient relationship."

"I hope so. Please find out about Robin and Mark."

"I'm on it."

Now Emmett truly fretted with worry. *One friend seriously hurt and two missing. Is any of this worth losing men who are closer to me than brothers? Why do we get the shit missions and always at the last minute with no real planning time. We've just been asking for trouble. What the hell are we going to do if we've lost Robin?!*

Emmett continued to pace with these thoughts whirling through his head, twisting his gut. His name echoed in his brain until a strong hand gripped his shoulder.

"You okay, Emmett?" Doug asked.

"I'm sorry, man. I'm just worried about everything."

"Well you can ease up about Rob and Mark. They're alive. Rob sent a message to Jamie saying Mark was wounded and they were about to be prisoners in Russia."

"What else did he say?"

"That's it. Jamie said Robin most likely dumped the sat phone into the sea."

"How are we going to get them out of Russia if they're prisoners?"

"Jamie said Ernie is on it."

"What does that mean?"

"I don't know. Jamie says Ernie is acting a lot like Robin."

"Hmmm, that can't be a bad thing at a time like this."

"No, brother, it surely can't."

ERNIE'S TEAM loaded Kwan's boat with all the food and medicine they could safely pack into it. Kwan told Ernie they should leave earlier than the last run because the loaded boat would travel much slower. The team now consisted of Ernie, Kwan, Willy, Marv, Mike and Gunner. Ernie decided to send Gary with Burke and Rocky, since Gary's job was to extract team members out of danger areas. Gary jumped at the chance to help get Robin and Mark out of Russia.

Ernie knew going back to North Korea with a light team was risky business and his decision to move ahead with the mission even surprised himself. Robin's admonition to focus on the mission kept repeating in Ernie's mind along with Robin's other favorite saying of "improvise, adapt and overcome." *Well, Rob, I'm doing my best.*

The boat's engines roared to life and after they were warmed up to Kwan's satisfaction, he steered her out of the Sokcho harbor and pointed the bow towards North Korean waters.

ROBIN JOLTED awake at Lev shaking his shoulder. "What's up?"

"The surgery is over."

Robin's eyes slowly focused and he saw Rada and the doctor standing in front of him.

"How's Mark?"

"I am happy to say I believe the surgery was successful. I have repaired the damage, although your friend's ankle is now about twenty-five percent metal. He should fully recover, but it will be a long and painful process."

Robin stood up and shook the doctor's hand. "Thank you, doctor. We'll repay you for your service."

The doctor cocked his head with a quizzical look. "I'm not sure you're going to live long enough to accomplish much more in your life."

"Oh, I think I'll survive just fine, Doc."

"I hope so for your sake...and theirs," the doctor said nodding to Lev and Rada.

"Robin, the GRU will be here in a half-hour," Lev warned.

"Okay, I'm ready."

"I am not sure I am."

"Just tell them the truth, Lev. I'll handle the rest."

"When will I be able to talk to Mark, Doc?"

"He will be in recovery for at least two hours. I will let you know."

"Thank you."

"Come, Robin we need to go to the Navy Headquarters."

"You tell the GRU I'm not leaving this hospital without Mark." Robin saw Lev turn pale. "Never mind, Lev. I'll go with you."

Lev let out a sigh and looked to the heavens.

FATBOY TOUCHED down at Chiang Kai-shek International Airport and taxied to the cargo area at the northeast end of the field. The middle ramp came down and Maria Walker climbed down into Doug's arms.

"Oh, Doug, I'm so happy to see you!"

"Not as much as I am to see you!"

They kissed and then Maria stepped back at arm's length with a stern look. "How is your shoulder?"

"It hurts, but it'll be okay. You can check it out later. Right now Rick really needs you."

They got into a Jeep Cherokee Doug had rented and headed for the Navy Hospital.

Shortly after they left, Fatboy took off again...headed for France.

ROBIN AND LEV were seated in a conference room in the head-quarters of the Russian Pacific Fleet. The Navy boys weren't very enthusiastic about letting them in until Lev mentioned the GRU. Things changed quickly and they were ushered into the conference room. Shortly after they were there, the GRU officer who Robin met in Mindanao came into the room and sat across from the two men. He didn't smile.

"So we meet again and this time you have some preposterous story you have recovered a tactical nuclear device stolen from our country."

"It's only preposterous if you want to play ostrich and hide your head in the sand and I don't think you're that kind of man." Robin detected a slight smile on the man's face.

"Where is the device?"

"Aren't we going to introduce ourselves first?"

"Fine, who are you?"

Robin stood up and reached across the table. "I'm Robin Marlette, nice to meet you..."

The GRU officer stood up and took Robin's hand. "I am Colonel Alex Prokenzi. He still didn't smile.

"This is Sergeant Lev Rogov of the Militsia, a true Hero of the Soviet Union."

"We will be the judge of that. Now, show me this supposed device."

Robin turned to Lev and shrugged his shoulders. Lev stood up. "Come with me, comrade. I did not think it wise to let anyone know about the device until you arrived."

"That is good thinking, Sergeant. Lead the way. You stay here, Mr. Marlette."

"Can I get a cup of coffee, Alex?"

Alex looked at Robin and then burst out laughing. "You are an interesting man. Would tea be satisfactory?"

"Sure, without sugar, please."

Alex laughed again. "Without sugar, of course."

Alex and Lev walked out and Robin took a deep breath. *Damn, it took a while to get that boy to smile. This could be harder to work through than I figured. I may have to start pitching hard ball sooner than I thought.*

A few minutes later, a young girl in uniform came in with a cup of tea. Robin thanked her in Russian and she smiled and quickly walked out. Robin sipped his tea and waited. The tea tasted strong and bitter, but hot and it felt good going down, except for the sting along the injured side of his larynx. Forty-five minutes later, Alex came in with the nuke pack, but without Lev.

"Where's Lev?"

"That is not your concern."

"Yes it is. Get him in here."

"Where do you think you are? I could kill you right now

and none of your people would know. You would just disappear."

Robin's fingers gripped the derringer in his pants pocket. "I know exactly where I am...and so do my people."

Alex shot Robin a concerned look.

"The CIA knows about this stolen nuclear weapon?"

"You mean the preposterous one?"

"You are angering me!"

"Well, start acting like the professional I met in Mindanao and maybe we can stop playing games."

Alex's back went stiff for a moment and then he leaned back in his chair.

"Let's recap where we're at," Robin began. "My partner and I recover a nuclear device stolen from your arsenal. We bring it here to return it. I contact Sergeant Rogov, I surrender to him and tell him to call you. Based on our contact in Mindanao, I figured you were a professional and reliable. Are you going to prove me wrong?"

"This problem is going to be resolved at a much higher level than me. I'm just investigating the matter."

"We'll have to change that."

Alex laughed, but it was a cynical laugh. "You really don't understand what dire straits you are in. We do not negotiate solutions to problems. We eliminate problems and you, my friend, are a serious problem."

"Actually, Alex, you don't know what you're dealing with."

Alex snorted. "You are CIA. We know what you are and we know just how far you will go before you cave in. I am not impressed."

Robin leaned forward. "I'm not CIA. I'm not bound by their policies or the political bullshit that cuts their balls off."

"Then who do you work for?"

"The highest bidder, as long as we like the mission."

"Who is 'we'?"

"My team."

"You are a mercenary?"

"Of sorts."

Alex drummed his fingers on the table and looked at Robin for a good minute. "I have the feeling you are not telling me everything."

"Of course not. I need to keep my bargaining chips close right now."

"How do I know you have anything worthwhile?"

"You don't, but if I have nothing worthwhile, I know you'll just kill me. So it is in my best interest to not be bullshitting you."

"I have been ordered to bring you to Moscow."

"Fine, we'll go as soon as the doctor says my partner can travel along with Sergeant Rogov and his family."

"You are mad! You are not giving me orders!" Alex shouted.

"Alex, I strongly suggest you not be in a hurry. You are going to find out very soon just how far reaching my organization operates and the extent of our willingness to take care of business. I wouldn't create problems, if I were you. I am not going to try to escape, because I don't have to. I believe we're only going to have to wait a couple of days. Then we can go to Moscow and resolve this situation where I can give you and your superiors some very important information."

Again Alex stared at Robin and drummed his fingers on the table. Then he stood up, said, "Wait here," and walked out of the room.

Robin remained still. His insides turned flips because he knew he came very close to dying during his conversation with Alex. He realized he had been gripping the derringer so tight his hand hurt. He didn't dare show a change of face because he figured the room was bugged as well as monitored with video. He kept his face frozen as he mentally went over the conversation with Alex and worried unless Ernie pushed the envelope, Alex would soon know Robin's words were pure bullshit. His mind raced to search for alternative avenues of escape, but the pickings were slim...and Slim just left town.

Alex walked back into the room. "The doctor says your friend should be able to be safely transported in two days. My superiors are willing to wait for two days until we go to Moscow. I will take you back to the hospital. If you try to escape, I will kill your friend."

Robin looked into the cold stare in Alex's eyes. "I'm not going to try to escape, but before we go to the hospital, I believe you owe me a drink."

For a moment, Alex's face showed anger and confusion. Then he burst out laughing. "You are truly a different kind of American. I have never met one like you."

"Yeah, I know, everybody says that, but remember you offered to buy me a drink in Mindanao."

"Of course, I remember. Come, we will go to the hospital, but stop along the way and as you say, wet our whistles."

"Hey Alex, you catch on fast. You've been watching John Wayne."

"Have you watched John Wayne?"

"Of course...I consider his movies to be training films."

Alex laughed again. "It upsets me that I am starting to like you."

"Why? I'm a likeable guy."

"Because in all likelihood, I am going to have to kill you."

"Oh, Alex, stop being a drama queen."

Alex burst out laughing again. "Come, I am thirsty."

"Now you're talking, buddy."

The two men walked out of the room and down the hall.

Just before the lobby, Alex went into another room and came out with Lev. Lev's face had turned white and he barely looked at Robin. They got to the steps going down to the parking lot and Alex said, "Wait here."

Lev looked straight ahead and seemed determined not to acknowledge Robin's presence.

"Relax, Lev. We're going drinking."

Lev's head snapped to Robin. "You are insane! They are going to kill us both!"

"Not if you be calm and play the game. We're going drinking and becoming good buddies with Alex. Just follow along."

"I will not. I do not drink alcohol."

"That explains a lot, but today you're going to drink alcohol and you're going to drink it like your life depends on it...because it does, along with Rada's and your kids'. Just order beer and drink it slowly. You'll be fine...and Lev, smile for chrissakes."

Alex pulled up in a Mercedes sedan and Robin got into the front and Lev climbed into the back seat.

"Now Alex, I hope you're taking us to someplace where they have good food and good vodka. I don't need rot gut booze."

"I am not a wealthy man."

"Don't worry, it's on me. I'll pay you back when my people pick us up."

Alex turned and looked at Robin and then laughed again. "Truly, I have never met an American like you."

"See, isn't life grand? We learn something new every day, but who ever said I was an American?"

Alex looked at Robin and put the car in gear. He drove for ten minutes and then pulled up and parked in front of a high rise building. Robin could see what looked like a restaurant at the top. The doorman started to say something to Alex, who flashed his credentials. The doorman backed off and waved them into the building. They took an elevator to the twenty-fifth floor and the doors opened to a posh restaurant and bar. Alex again displayed his credentials and also handed currency to the maitre'd, who appeared perplexed by the odd combination the three men presented. Alex in a suit, Lev in uniform and Robin dressed in mismatched clothes. They were seated at a table with an expansive view of Vladivostok Bay.

"Good choice, Alex. I like the view of this magnificent bay."

"What do you want to eat, Robin?"

"Why don't you introduce me to Russian cuisine. I'll trust your judgment. What about you, Lev?"

"I do not know. I have never eaten in a place like this."

"He'll trust your judgment too, Alex."

Alex laughed the same deep hearty laugh Robin heard on Mindanao and he started to feel a little better about the chances of survival. He hoped a reverse Stockholm Syndrome was taking effect, but he knew Alex was experienced, well trained and hardly a pushover.

"Alex, I think you and I should toast our reunion with some good vodka."

Alex ordered a bottle of vodka called Putinka and three shot glasses. The waiter quickly brought the order and Alex put a glass in front of each of them. Robin noticed Lev didn't object and right then he knew it would be challenging to keep Alex relaxed and Lev from passing out this evening. Robin participated in drinking contests in his younger years, but none where his life depended on his performance.

Alex poured each glass until they brimmed with the clear liquid. "This fine product of Russia is actually an elixir that wards off old age and promotes good health."

"I have no doubt," Robin replied.

Alex raised his glass, as did Robin. Robin prompted Lev to raise his. "To Mother Russia!" Alex's voice boomed.

"To Mother Russia!" the other two men responded.

Robin watched as Alex enjoyed his vodka and didn't down the shot in one gulp. He sipped and enjoyed the taste and warmth of the drink. *The drinking gods are with me tonight.*

Still the drink disappeared soon enough. "Again, my friends... again!" Alex urged as he reached to pour another round.

Robin downed the rest of his drink and Alex filled the glass. He hovered the bottle over Lev's glass, which remained almost full.

"Sergeant, you are not drinking!"

"I believe, Alex, the good sergeant is making sure one of us can drive after dinner. Besides, it just means more for you and me."

Alex pondered this for a moment and then nodded his head. He raised his glass.

"Allow me," Robin offered.

Alex again nodded.

"To the heroes of the Great Patriotic War!"

"To the heroes of the Great Patriotic War!" the other men responded.

The waiter appeared with meat and potato pies, a loaf of dark bread, plates of herring, fresh vegetables and pickles. The men began to eat, with Alex making sure their glasses remained full. Robin found he was ravenous and enjoyed the food. The herring were seasoned and baked so the fish were flaky and very tasty. But Robin's favorite, by far, was the meat and potato pie and he ate several. He also kept up with Alex on the vodka and could tell Alex felt Robin was relaxed and off guard.

"So Robin, here we are enjoying good drink and good food and yet I know nothing about you."

"That's not true. You know I do contract work."

"Yes, but who are your clients?"

"Now, Alex, you know it would be very unprofessional for me to disclose my client list."

"Ha! Client list! I bet the Soviet Union would never be on your list."

"On the contrary, we would consider any offer you have."

"But you would just turn us down."

"It would depend on the mission and what you're willing to pay."

"Are you serious?"

"Very serious."

"Hmm, I would like to test just how serious you are, assuming my superiors let you live."

"And just why wouldn't they? What have I done to hurt your country?"

"A ship is missing."

"I don't know about a missing Russian ship."

"I did not say it was a Russian ship. The ship was from North Korea."

"Why do you care about a North Korean ship?"

Alex's eyes narrowed and shot a dangerous look at Robin. "I know that ship did not have a Russian nuclear device on it."

So that's it! They think we stole the device and are trying to figure out what the hell we're trying to do with it...and that's why I'm still alive. Jeez, how do I play this? They're probably tearing that thing apart to make sure it doesn't go off!

Robin took a deep breath. "You know, Alex, I'm getting the feeling you and your superiors think we stole the device."

"I do not have any reason to believe otherwise."

Robin leaned forward and spoke in a low but forceful voice. "Okay, let's get some things straight here. My organization does not kill innocent people. We would never detonate a nuclear device...anywhere. We would never deliver a nuclear device to anyone other than a nuclear country who is part of the nuclear treaties.

"Your country, on the other hand, assisted the idiots on that ship to attack Sasebo, Japan where they would have killed innocent people. What you didn't know is they did in fact have the stolen Russian nuclear device on board and they planned to detonate it during the attack, killing hundreds of thousands of innocent people. What you also don't know is one of your countrymen sold it to them for a very large amount of cash money."

"You are lying."

"You know damn good and well I'm not lying. And here's a news flash for you. I witnessed the transaction and I know who the traitor is. Please pour me another drink."

Alex sat stone still staring at Robin. Robin reached over and took the bottle and poured himself a drink. He looked over at Lev and saw his deathly pale face.

"Lev, drink up."

Lev took his glass in his shaking hand and drank it empty, swallowing the vodka down with a tortured gulp. Robin refilled his glass. Then he filled Alex's.

"Speak up, Alex. Your silence is ruining a fine dinner."

"Tell me who it is...who sold the device?"

"I plan to tell you, so you can kill him, because if you don't, we will. But I'm not telling you until we're released, so we have some negotiating to do."

Without taking his eyes off of Robin, Alex sipped his vodka. Robin returned Alex's look in between bites of meat and potato pie. It was an act, of course, and Robin's patience neared its limit.

"I can't guarantee you will be released or even allowed to live."

Robin leaned back in his chair and let out a long breath.

"Okay, Alex, we've played this game long enough. You already know I'm not connected with any government because you've contacted the usual suspects and they don't know us. You've already told them you're going to execute us and they said they don't care...and I'm still alive.

"You're not going to kill me because you want to know more about me and my organization and you want to know who my clients are. So, you thought you'd try the smart method and use honey instead of vinegar. I, on the other hand, want to stay alive and so I've been counting on the reverse Stockholm Syndrome. But you and I are professionals and both of us are only going to be partially successful at our little game."

Alex finally laughed again and shook his head. "Perhaps you're right."

"I'm always right and the reason we're playing this silly ass game is because on your side you're not the boss. You have people you don't respect telling you what to do. I, on the other hand, have to play the game knowing other people are telling you what to do."

"Who is your boss?"

"I'm the boss. Nobody tells me what to do. At some point, we are just going to have to trust each other. I have no desire to hurt you in anyway and I don't think you want to hurt me. You certainly could have killed me anytime, if you really wanted to."

"We can trust each other, but you must not put faith in my ability to influence my superiors. They do not like being told what to do. I cannot guarantee anything."

"That piece of honesty goes a long way with me, Alex. We'll work through it. I'm not without bargaining chips that'll influence your superiors."

"I hope your organization will not do anything stupid."

"I guarantee you won't think it's stupid."

SERGEANT LEV ROGOV edged closer to panic. He was astounded and alarmed at the conversation between the two secret agents seated at the table...and he was drunk. When the American started arguing with the GRU man, Lev thought he would meet his death in this fancy restaurant right along with the insane Robin. So, Lev started drinking the vodka, keeping up with the other two men. He smirked at the thought he was drunk and he would not live to endure the wrath of his wife...because the GRU man was surely going to kill him.

Then he thought of his children and how his dedication and desire to be the best officer in Vladivostok now threatened their lives. This is the Soviet Union, the place where whole families disappear every day. The day for his family to disappear was at hand. Lev now knew he failed as a husband, father and officer. Tears were about to come when he realized the other two men were laughing. He fought to focus on their conversation.

"YES, I believe your candidate for hero of the Soviet Union is thoroughly drunk!" More laughter.

"Lev, my friend, are you all right?" Robin asked.

Lev tried to speak clearly, but he couldn't make his tongue work correctly. "Noooo, I am nooot ookay. I d-d-doo not w-w-ant tooo die and I d-do not want my flaamblee to die."

"Ease up, Lev. No one is going to kill you or your family."

"I-I thsshink youuu arrre insshaane!" Lev tried to hold a belch back, but gave up. The other two men roared with laughter.

"Well, Alex, I think we should go to the hospital."

"Yes, our friend needs a bed."

"Come on, Lev, up we go." Lev tried to work with Robin to stand up, but ended up just leaning on him. Alex paid the bill and the men went down the elevator. A valet brought the car for them and as they were getting in Lev turned to Robin and tried to talk. Robin understood the word drive in the jumbled sentence.

"No, Lev you don't have to drive. You've done your duty for now."

Fifteen minutes later they arrived at the hospital and Alex took Lev to a room. Robin went to the nursing station near the surgery area.

"Excuse me, is my friend still here?"

Rada's voice came from behind him. "Your friend is in a private room. Where is Lev?"

"He's here."

Rada came closer to Robin. "Is he as drunk as you?"

"No. He's more drunk...but we're all alive." Robin could see the import of those words was not lost on Rada.

"Come with me."

Robin followed Rada to a private room and saw Mark in bed with his eyes closed. As Robin came closer, Mark opened his eyes.

"I'm glad someone's having fun."

"You have no idea. How ya doin', bud?"

"Apparently, I'll live."

"Actually, the doctor says you'll fully recover."

"I know, he told me. He also said it would be a long and painful journey."

"Yes, he did say that would be part of the deal."

"Are we going to get out of here, Rob?"

"We're taking it one hour at a time, but it's looking promising."

"The doctor says we'll be going to Moscow in two days."

"That's the plan, so you better rest up."

"Yeah, I'm pretty sleepy right now."

"Night, night, brother. I'll check on you later."

Mark's answer was a snore.

Robin turned to Rada, who looked tired and older since Robin had first seen her.

"Rada, we're going to get out of here...all of us."

"How can you be so sure?"

"I really can't go into much detail, but our organization isn't sitting around doing nothing. They'll be working on getting bargaining chips to get us out."

"Yes, but that will be for you, not us."

Robin put his hands on Rada's shoulders. "I'm the leader of this organization and I'm telling you, we are not leaving without you and your family."

"But what if we don't want to leave our home, our family and our friends?"

"That I can't fix. In order for you and your family to be safe, you need to come with us. After some time passes, we can work on getting you back with your family and friends."

"Why do you care about us? We are nothing to you."

"I got you into this mess. You're good people. I can't let anything happen to you." A moment of silence passed between them. "Rada, you're exhausted. Go get your husband and go home and get some rest. Don't be angry with Lev, he did what I asked and later I'll explain to both of you why."

Rada turned away and started for the door then turned back around. "I don't know if I should hit you or kiss you."

"I'm like that."

She came closer, kissed him on the cheek and left.

CHAPTER TWENTY-EIGHT

E rnie paced the deck of Kwan's boat. The team had been in contact with Colonel Sinchu, but now they couldn't raise him on the satellite phone. As the night wore on, he knew he had to act.

"Marv, you and Willy do a recon and see what the hell's going on with the colonel. Mike you run the boat. Once you're feet dry, give yourselves thirty minutes to see what you can find out. If you can't make contact, get back and we'll scratch the mission for tonight."

"Sir, I would like to go also," Gunner said as he came forward.

"This is a recon job, Gunner. These guys have a lot of specialized training."

"I am a soldier, Major. I may not be as well trained as Marv and Willy, but I know enough not to get in their way. I also know all the places the colonel might be."

"That could be helpful, Ernie," Marv noted.

"All right, Gunner get moving. You guys take care of him."

"Oh, I think the ol' Gunner here can take care of himself just fine," Willy added.

The men climbed into the RIB and with a salute disappeared into the night.

MARIA CAME out of Rick's room with a concerned look on her face.

Emmett walked up to her. "You look worried, Maria. What's up?"

"Rick is in critical condition. He owes his life to you. The doctors here have done a good job to stop all the bleeding and minimize the damage to his kidney, but they can't do more until he gains strength."

"I was afraid the bullet in his side hit the kidney."

"It did, but only on the lower end. It should still function properly."

"Then you're worried about his leg."

"Yes, it's badly damaged. The bullet glanced off the bone breaking it and the circulation has been affected. The longer we wait the more damage will occur."

Doug spoke up. "Rick's a tough ol' bird and in damn good shape. He should be coming around in short order."

Maria looked at her fiancé and put her arm around him. "I know you want him to be okay and I'll watch him closely. We'll do the best we can."

"He's always been an agile, quick athlete. I don't think he could stand being crippled." Pain laced Doug's voice.

Emmett's deep voice came low and soothing. "Rick will fight, Doug, and with Maria here, he's in good hands. I think his chances are good." Emmett's gut felt otherwise.

MIKE HELD the throttle low until the RIB bumped the shore and Marv and Gunner jumped out and pulled it up. Willy slung his medical pack on and the three men saluted Mike and moved silently through the shadows, stopping frequently to listen. After two hundred yards they could hear yelling interspersed with screams coming from a warehouse next to the one where Willy treated the soldier.

They crept closer and as they came to the opening, Willy saw a man standing with a gun pointed at the head of Colonel Sinchu as they stood in front of an assembled formation of soldiers. Another man raised a wooden club and hit the side of the soldier Willy had treated two nights before. The soldier screamed. The man yelled at the soldier.

"What's he saying, Gunner?"

"He's demanding to know where they got the bandages and medicine."

"Who are they?"

"Secret police."

The soldier moaned in pain, but said nothing. The secret police agent raised the club again. Willy nudged Marv and he nodded. The two men glided into the room. The agent with the club had his arm at full height when Willy squeezed the trigger of his silenced MP5 sending two rounds into the left side of the man's head, taking off the right side and sending the man in a turning dive onto the concrete floor. An instant later, the agent holding a gun to the colonel's head took two rounds from Marv's gun at the junction of the nose and eyebrows as he turned to look at Marv. The two rounds exited the back of his head spraying blood and brains on the colonel. The lifeless body crumpled to the ground.

Colonel Sinchu and the assembled soldiers stood motionless as Gunner rushed to his mentor. Willy handed Gunner a package of moist towelettes and Gunner began to clean the colonel's face and speaking to him in Korean.

"Gunner, tell the colonel we need to get these two assholes to the RIB and get this mess cleaned up," Marv ordered.

Gunner spoke to the colonel and he nodded and then gave some orders. Soldiers rushed forward and picked up the bodies and Marv motioned for them to follow him and they headed for the boat. Other soldiers produced pails and mops and started cleaning the remaining blood, brains and skull fragments.

"Willy, I'm going to take the bodies back to our boat and dump 'em. Then I'll bring back a load of food."

"Rog."

Willy started treating the injured soldier by first giving him an injection of morphine. The clubbing did serious damage to the wound and ribs. Willy worked feverishly to stop the flow of blood. The soldier reached up and grasped his forearm. Willy looked at him and the soldier said something with eyes that spoke respect and warmth. Then life faded from those eyes. Willy immediately started chest compressions, but soon realized it was no use. The soldier had lost too much blood. Willy reached over and closed the soldier's eyes.

"Did you hear what he said, Gunner?"

"Yes. He said thank you for being such a good man and caring about us...the soldiers."

"He died a brave soldier. He took the beating and didn't say a word." Willy looked at the colonel. "I'm sorry I couldn't save him, sir."

Gunner translated to the colonel. The colonel replied, "You did all you could. There is nothing to be sorry for."

Willy stood up. "Gunner, we have to make sure the secret police can't be traced to this place. How did they get here?"

Again he translated to the colonel. "The colonel says their car is around the corner."

"We need to move it somewhere else, at least several miles away. Can you manage that?"

"I'll see it is done."

"All right, in the meantime bring me any sick soldiers, so I can try to treat them."

ROBIN BOLTED up from the chair. Then he recognized Mark's room and realized he had fallen asleep. He stood up and moved his shoulders to try and ease the pain from the damage done by the cargo door. He also wanted to get rid of the pain from his hangover. He walked over and checked on Mark and was satisfied he rested comfortably. Robin made his way to the sink and filled a glass with water and drank it down. Then another. He sat back in the chair and let his head fall back against it, quickly falling back into an uneasy sleep.

ONCE MIKE and Marv got two miles from shore, Mike opened up the throttle and sped to the boat where Ernie waited. He came up along side of the larger boat.

"What's going on? " Ernie asked.

"These two idiots." Marv pointed to the bodies.

"Shit, what happened?"

"These guys are secret police. They were torturing the injured soldier and had a gun to the colonel's head. Willy and I decided to refer them to a higher jurisdiction. We need to sink these bodies."

"I have an extra anchor with chain. That ought to sink them," Kwan offered.

"Bring it here, please."

Kwan retrieved the extra anchor and helped Marv and

Mike wrap the bodies in the chain. They fastened several parts of the chain together with wire. Once done, they eased the bodies into the sea. Mike then brought the RIB up on the rear of the boat. The men loaded both RIBs with food and medicine and then they headed back to Chongjin.

Each RIB made four trips in the darkness. The process went quickly with the soldiers helping with the unloading. Ernie looked at his watch.

"Marv, head back to Mike's RIB with Gunner and get back to the boat. I'll go get Willy. We'll get back by the other RIB."

"Okay, boss."

Ernie headed for the warehouse, stopping one hundred feet from it. The hair on the back of his head tingled and his gut got that "little voice" feeling. He slipped into the shadows and moved slowly toward a window. He got as close as he dared and staying in the shadows, maneuvered to get a look. Finally he saw the colonel and two men near him, but Ernie sensed there were more. They were dressed in civilian clothes and judging from the bodies Marv brought back, these guys were most likely secret police also. He moved back and forth looking for Willy, but didn't see him.

The colonel looked calm, so Ernie didn't want to make a move, but he worried about the sunrise. He heard a movement to his left and stepped deeper into the shadows. The person moved quietly. A figure came into view...it was Willy.

Ernie whispered quietly, "Willy, over here."

Willy froze and then grinned and came over to Ernie. "Boy, am I glad to see you. We gotta get outta here."

"Roger that. Let's move."

The men glided through the shadows ready for anything, their heads on a swivel.

When they got to the beach, Ernie abruptly stopped. "Shit, where's the boat?"

"Don't tell me the boat's gone, Ernie. I don't need that."

"Well it's not where I left it." Ernie thought for a minute. "Let's head over to the pier."

They moved to the pier stopping and listening, wary of an ambush or a trap. They got to the building closest to the pier.

"Wait here, Willy. I'm going to check under the pier. If the boat is there I'll signal you."

Willy nodded.

Ernie stepped out and as he did, Mike came out from under the pier and waved them over.

"Come on, Willy!" They sprinted to the pier. "What are you doing under the pier? You were supposed to go back with Marv and Gunner, Mike."

"I sent them on so I could watch this boat. It's a good thing I did because two soldiers came and told me to hide from the secret police. If I hadn't been here, you might have lost your ride home. We'll push the boat out and paddle until we get about a mile off shore. Then we'll turn on the motor."

"Sounds like a plan."

They pushed the boat out and started paddling. A faint pink glow peeked over the horizon.

KWAN AND GUNNER WERE NERVOUS.

"Do you think we should go in and look for them, Marv?" Kwan asked.

Marv looked at the growing sunrise. "Hell, no. If they were in trouble they'd call us. Just sit tight. They'll be here." He scanned the horizon with binoculars and then looked with his naked eye. He thought he saw something and raised the binoculars again. "There they are! Get this boat fired up. We gotta get outta here as soon as we recover them."

Soon Mike brought the RIB up on the rear of the boat.

Ernie jumped out. "Head us out 090° Kwan and step on it!"

"Yes, sir!"

"Everybody keep a sharp lookout. The secret police were back at the warehouse."

Gunner whirled around and looked at Ernie.

"Don't worry, Gunner. It looked like the colonel had it handled."

Willy put his hand on Gunner's shoulders. "They were looking for the two we whacked. We got rid of all the evidence, so I'm sure the colonel laid a good story on 'em. It'll be all right. He'll probably call us when he's clear."

"Okay, everyone, stash the tactical gear and change clothes. Cover those RIBs. It's time to become fishermen."

CHAPTER TWENTY-NINE

Rick opened his eyes because he heard Emmett and Doug talking about him.

"Are you assholes talking about me?" He croaked.

Emmett's face came into view. "Hey, Buddy, it's good to hear your voice."

"How close did I come to dying?"

"Too damn close. Maria's here. She needs to talk to you."

"Hello, Rick. Do you remember me?"

"I never forget a beautiful woman. You going to tell me the score?"

"Yes, I am. You've had a rough time. You almost bled to death. The doctors who worked on you when you came here saved your life, along with Emmett."

Rick smiled at Emmett. "Thanks, brother."

Emmett nodded.

"What's the bad news, Maria?"

"Your leg is badly damaged and no work has been done on it except to stop the bleeding and prevent infection because you're very weak. But the longer we wait, the chances of you having a full recovery are reduced."

Rick looked back and forth between Maria and Emmett. "If it's all the same to you, let's get on with it. I can handle it."

"I'll start making arrangements. You rest now."

"Good idea." Rick faded back to sleep.

ROBIN STOOD BACK in the corner of the room as the doctor and nurses examined and worked on Mark's leg. The doctor had a pleased look on his face.

"Everything looks good. There's very little bleeding and I don't see any sign of infection. Your youth and your excellent physical condition are working to your advantage."

"Thank you for a great job, doctor."

"I'm glad I was here when you came in."

Rada walked into the room and looked at Mark's leg. "Excellent work, doctor."

"Thank you, Rada."

Rada turned and looked at Robin. "And I hope you're feeling as bad as my husband."

"Your wish has come true."

"Come with me."

Robin followed Rada to another treatment room.

"Take off your shirt."

Robin did as ordered and turned his back to Rada. She carefully took off the bandages across his back. He felt her putting on a cream.

"Oh, that feels better."

"I'm sorry, I should have told one of the nurses to do this sooner."

"It's okay. How does it look?"

"It is healing." She finished putting the cream on and redid the bandages. "You can put on your shirt."

Robin got his shirt back on and turned to face Rada.

"Open your mouth. Your throat is looking better, also."

"It feels better."

"The GRU man says we are leaving tomorrow morning for Moscow." Rada started to shake and tears rolled down her cheeks. "I am terribly frightened."

Robin took her hand. "Rada, all you have to do is remain calm and tell them the truth. Neither you or Lev have done anything wrong."

"They do not care about such things as right or wrong. They do not tolerate anything that threatens their authority, such as people like us knowing they allowed a nuclear weapon to be stolen from them."

"You're going to have to put some trust in me. If you do as I ask, I know I can get us all out of here."

"I hope so, I truly hope so." She squeezed his hand. "I'll take you back to the other room."

When they got back to the room, Alex was there.

"Ah, I see you haven't escaped."

"I gave you my word."

"Yes, you did. I came by to tell you we will be leaving in the morning. I will pick up you and your friends here at nine o'clock."

"We'll be ready."

BURKE LAUGHED. "Those three Russian boys think they've died and gone to heaven."

Rocky smiled. "Well, it's not every day young guys get invited to a villa on the Riviera by beautiful women. I'd like to know how Jamie found out these guys were in Paris."

"I wonder how Chucky knew these broads...and the owners of this villa."

"I'm not asking about any of it. By the way, you do make an excellent butler."

"And you're a great gardener. Just wondering how Gary talked us into letting him be the bartender."

"Yeah, we definitely got suckered on that one."

"Oh well, payback's going to be a bitch. Do you think Jamie has sent the message yet?"

"Yeah, Ernie authorized it. The Russians are probably scrambling to verify their little darlings aren't where they're supposed to be."

"Considering they're sons of members of the Council of Ministers, I'd say scrambling doesn't come close to describing what they're doing."

Both men laughed. "Well, I better get back to butlering."

"Okay, brother. Catch you later."

IT TOOK a while for Lucy Santos to stop sobbing. "Emmett, I want to come over there to be with Rick."

"I figured that. I've talked to Wanda and she will take care of the kids. Have Ann book you on a flight to Honolulu. We'll pick you up there."

"Thank you so much, Emmett. You and Wanda are wonderful friends."

"We're all in this together, Lucy. I'll see you when you get here."

ERNIE WAVED as the North Korean patrol plane circled overhead. The other men waved also. The plane made one more pass, waggled its wings and turned back to North Korea.

"What do ya think, boss?" Marv asked.

"I think we'd better get into South Korean waters ASAP. What's our position, Kwan?"

"We're about forty-five minutes away from the border."

"Open her up. Let's get out of here."

Ernie picked up his satellite phone and dialed Jamie.

"Hi Ernie."

"What's the status of everyone?"

"We haven't heard from Robin or Mark or the Russians. I'm sure it won't be long though."

"How are our hostages?"

"Gary says the real problem may be getting them willing to go back!"

Ernie laughed. "How's Rick?"

"Maria has him back under the knife. I don't know how that's going. Emmett arranged for Lucy to get to Taiwan."

"Good. We should be getting back to Sokcho soon. We'll get to Osan as soon as we can and wait for you guys to pick us up. Let me know when there's any word from the Russians."

"I'll keep you posted."

"Thanks, Jamie." Ernie ended the phone call and looked out over the sea. He felt a great weight on him. The uncertainty of how the Russians would react to the demand worried him. If they didn't play ball and negotiate for the release of those young men, the team would be forced to play like the Russians did in Lebanon, when two of their diplomats were kidnapped by Muslim extremists. The Russians kidnapped family members of the extremists and started sending body parts of their relatives to them. If the Russians balked, the team...Burke and Rocky...would have to do the same thing or Robin and Mark would be dead. It sickened Ernie to think about it, but he knew they were in a different world now. He didn't know what he'd do if the team lost Robin and Mark. He did know, in spite of his fears, he had to project confidence and determination to the men. He put his game face on and turned to the men on the boat. "With Colonel Sinchu calling and saying all is well, we're making progress on all fronts gentlemen. We'll get back and finish this mission and go home."

Marv, Mike and Willy grinned and gave a thumbs up.

CHAPTER THIRTY

Early in the afternoon the next day, Robin and the rest were escorted into a two story grey building in Moscow. The flight from Vladivostok was uneventful except one thing. The crew called Alex forward to the cockpit and when he returned his face turned to stone and he gave Robin a hard look...a hard look laced with the kind of fear that comes with the unknown.

Robin figured the demand had been made. His thoughts rested on Ernie. If Robin was right, Ernie faced tough and ugly decisions and Robin thought how being captured might just be easier than making those decisions. The rest of the flight was very quiet.

As they entered the building, three serious looking men and Alex immediately grabbed Robin and took him away from the group. They went down a drab hall, shoved Robin into a room and jammed him down in a chair at a long table. Two officious looking men sat across from him. The men who brought him in spread out around the room. Alex stood to Robin's left and slightly behind him. Robin clearly understood he would leave this room in only one of two ways...dead or alive.

The shorter of the men across the table started to speak, but Robin saw he read from something. The man mouthed words about the Soviet Union as Robin scanned the room looking for weapons and avenues of escape, then his eyes met the eyes of the other larger man sitting across from him. Robin saw intelligence, interest and a hint of mirth. The short man said words that caught Robin's attention.

"Your organization has committed a monstrous criminal act by kidnapping Russian citizens. They have demanded your release and have threatened to start sending body parts to us if we do not comply. We have never experienced such vile, insane behavior!" The man's voice rose at the end of the sentence.

"Are we going to sit here and play games or are we going to take care of business? You people did the same thing in Lebanon. We learned from you. Only you never gave a warning, you just started sending body parts. At least we warned you, but if you don't comply the body parts will start coming, I assure you."

Nobody replied and two pairs of eyes simply stared at Robin. He kept his face still and fervently hoped his eyes were not revealing the rising fear inside him. He could hear the clock ticking. The shorter man nodded to Alex and suddenly, Robin's head was jarred by a hard blow and he flew out of the chair onto the floor. Instinct and reflex took over and Robin rolled to his feet and sprang over the table. He grabbed the larger, quiet man by the neck and dragged him into a corner of the room holding the derringer against the man's throat.

He now faced four armed men surely bent on killing him. The one who had spoken appeared to be shaken. Strangely enough, the man he held at gunpoint appeared calm.

"Put the gun down, Robin!" Alex ordered.

"Sorry, Alex. I want everyone out of this room...NOW!"

"What are you going to do?"

"I'm going to have a little chat with this gentleman, who I think is the boss here." Robin couldn't be sure, but he thought the man he held actually chuckled.

"We can simply walk out of here and execute everyone you want to be safe."

"No you won't..."

Suddenly the man Robin held spoke in Russian. "All of you leave this room now. Do nothing until you hear further from me. Do not interrupt us."

The others looked at each other for a confused moment and then Alex ushered them out of the room and with a parting glance, closed the door. Robin patted the man down and then let him go. The man went back to his chair and motioned for Robin to sit. "Do you speak Russian?"

"I understand it better than I speak it."

"Ah, let's speak English, but you will have to forgive my grammar."

"I'll bet you're being modest."

"You are a direct young man and also astute. I am General Yosef Yamurov, Commander of Soviet Military Intelligence. You are correct. We have used your tactic in past, but your organization has crossed the line. We are concerned for these hostages. They are the sons of very important people in our government."

"I assure you they will not be harmed if we negotiate a timely exchange."

"What guarantee do I have for their safety?"

"If you negotiate in good faith and any hostage is harmed, I will not be part of the exchange."

"You are either very honorable or very stupid...or both."

"Actually, I have men in my command I can trust with my life and who I can trust to do the right thing."

"You would be the first commander I have met who could say that with such confidence."

"Well, now you have."

General Yamurov remained silent for a moment, but his face was animated as he thought through the situation. Then he reached for the telephone on the table, pulled a piece of paper out of his shirt pocket and handed it to Robin. "Is that a good number?"

"If they told you to call it, it's good."

Yamurov put the phone on speaker and dialed the number.

"Yes?"

Robin recognized Jamie's voice.

"This is General Yosef Yamurov, Commander of Soviet Military Intelligence, the GRU. To whom am I speaking?"

"I'm Jamie."

Yamurov looked at Robin and he nodded. "Jamie, I have Robin here, would you like to talk to him?"

"Yes, I would."

"Hello, Jamie."

"Hello, Robin. Are you well?"

"I'm well. How quickly can you connect this call to the tactical commander?"

"Thirty seconds."

"Please do so."

"Yes, sir."

Robin and Yamurov briefly waited and then Ernie's voice came over the phone. "This is Ernest Jackson, Tactical Commander. I believe I'm talking to General Yamurov?"

Robin made a gesture to Yamurov, asking him if he understood and the general nodded. "Yes, this is General

Yamurov. I must immediately enquire about the well-being of the hostages. Are they safe and well?"

"They are General and their every need is being met."

"May I speak to one of them?"

"Well, General we could do that, but it would cause more harm than good."

"I don't understand." Some irritation crept into the general's voice.

"Sir, the young men don't know they're hostages. They're actually enjoying themselves immensely and as long as we move this situation along they will continue to do so. Of course, if you choose not to cooperate, their status will change for the worse."

The general leaned back in his chair and looked at the phone for a moment...then he burst out laughing. "Tell me Ernest, would their mothers approve of their conduct?"

"Not in the least, General."

The general laughed even harder. Still smiling, he leaned toward the phone. "Ernest, I think it is the best interest for us to make an exchange. Do you have a location in mind?"

"We would prefer the Zurich airport, Sir."

"Ah, excellent choice. The most neutral place in the world. Do you have a date and time?"

"Is tomorrow evening at 2000 hours Zurich time convenient for you?"

"Yes, that will be fine."

"You'll be directed to a clear holding ramp north of the terminals and east of the runway. We can park side by side and make the exchange."

"Excellent. We will see you then."

"Yes, sir. Good afternoon." The connection ended.

"I suppose, Robin, the call cannot be traced."

"Of course it can. It'll just be a dead end. I wouldn't waste time and manpower tracking it down."

The general smiled. "You play along a fine line, but you play it well. I can see why you are so confident of your organization. You are most definitely not CIA, although I suspect they are a client, as you say. Alex tells me you would accept us as clients under the proper circumstances."

"Yes, sir, we would."

The general looked at his watch. "I have several appointments I must attend to, but I hope you will accept my invitation to dine with me this evening. I would enjoy lively and interesting conversation."

"I would be delighted. May I check on my party now, General?"

"Yes, of course. I will have Alex escort you so you will not be bothered and he will bring you to dinner."

Robin rubbed the side of his head. "Alex is a good man, with a hell of a punch."

"Judging from the look on his face, I don't think he enjoyed hitting you."

"Oh, I didn't take it personally."

The general smiled. "I hope not. Alex is one of our best officers... and he is my nephew."

Robin chuckled. "I thought I recognized a similarity. I hope he's not too upset over my grabbing you at gunpoint."

"If he is, I'll take care of it." The general rose and opened the door. "Alex!" he called out.

A moment later, Alex entered the room appearing tense. He looked at his uncle and then at Robin.

"Alex, we have resolved this situation. Your analysis of Robin was accurate. We are dealing with honorable people. Please take Robin to his party and make arrangements for them to stay at the Leningradskaya Hotel. Then take him to get some decent clothes at my tailor, after which I want you to bring him to dinner."

Alex did nothing for a moment and then simply said, "Yes, sir."

The general saluted Robin and left the room. He and Alex just looked at each other for a moment and then Robin said, "Are we going to be pissed at each other or are we going to call it even."

A slight smile came across Alex's lips. "I suppose we call it even."

Robin held out his hand. "Good."

Alex shook Robin's hand. "I'm not sure I would want to fight you anyway. I have never seen a man move like you did going over the table."

"My friend, the body can do amazing things when the mind is terrified."

Both laughed. "Come, let's go reassure your friends."

When Robin entered the room where the others were being held, the apprehension was palpable. He noticed Rada checking on Mark's bandages and felt thankful for her presence. All eyes turned to Robin.

"Hello everyone. General Yamurov, the head of the GRU, has agreed to release us. We will be in Switzerland tomorrow evening."

Relief flooded the room and Lev pulled his children to his chest and held them.

"What are we being exchanged for?" Rada asked.

Robin ignored the question. "Are you folks hungry?"

"Yes!" Lev's son, Ilya, chirped.

"Well good, Ilya. You are all going to the Leningradskaya Hotel. I'll be there later this evening. You can eat there. If I don't see you tonight, be ready to travel by nine in the morning." Robin turned to Lev. "Lev please make sure Mark is put in a room with two beds and tell the front desk I'll be coming in later."

Alex appeared at the door with a tough looking female in a military uniform. "Are you ready?"

"Yes."

"Good. This is Lieutenant Sonin and she will escort everyone to the hotel."

"I assume they can order meals there."

"Yes, of course."

"If the food they order exceeds any allowances, I'll send you the money. In fact, please see they are put in the best rooms. We'll pay for everything."

"That will not be necessary. They will be comfortable."

"Thank you, Alex." Robin nodded to the Lieutenant. "Thank you, Lieutenant."

CHAPTER THIRTY-ONE

General Yamurov and Robin sat in large wing backed chairs in front of a picture window looking out over Moscow. They smoked Cuban cigars with a glass of one hundred year old fine champagne cognac. Robin wanted to ask the name of the cognac, but didn't want to seem impolite. He just enjoyed the marvelous drinking experience.

The dinner was delicious wild caught Russian salmon seasoned with ginger and dill. Their conversation was indeed lively and interesting. The general loved good books and his extensive library provided great starting points for conversation.

The discussion did touch upon contentious issues between the United States and the Soviet Union, but it soon faded when both men agreed the Soviet Union was about to drastically change. Neither man professed to know the future. As the evening progressed, they were on a first name basis.

Robin dragged smoke from his cigar and exhaled. Then he sipped his cognac. "You know Yosef, I really don't know why America and Russia aren't partners in this world. Even if the governments are at odds, the people have more in common than differences."

"There is some truth to that observation. While I serve the Soviet Union, I am not particularly in favor of communism. I think it creates more poverty than it cures. It certainly does not eliminate the upper class. Very few Russians can enjoy the dinner we just did."

"I study war. Not because I like it, I think it is a stupid endeavor. I study it because it brings out the best and the worst in the human race. Your country's stand against Germany in World War II was heroic in every way. So much so, that I am proud of your country, even though I'm not a Russian. On the other hand, I don't understand why you have to control the other countries that make up the Soviet Union."

"Actually, there is a very logical reason. Our borders are vulnerable, especially along our borders with Europe. Throughout history, we have been repeatedly attacked from the European Plain. We are also vulnerable to attack by China from the Mongolian Plateau, although to a lesser extent because of the harsh wilderness of Siberia. So, we extend our borders with satellite countries by forming the Soviet Union to protect Moscow and the Republic of Russia."

"I've never considered that before. I now have a better understanding of your nation's motivations."

Yosef smiled. "And what nationality are you? I believe you are American, but you have never said."

"Out of necessity, I've become a citizen of the world."

Yosef shifted in his chair and looked directly at Robin. "Do you know why you are still alive?"

"Not really, I've just played the hand I was dealt the last couple of days."

"The Council of Ministers want you dead. You have angered them and you worry them. You have brought home the reality that no one is really safe in this world. I have been stalling the ministers because you remind me of myself in my years as a young agent and I think you can be useful in the future."

"Apparently, I haven't given them the same impression."

"No, and I assure you if any of those boys are hurt in anyway, you will not survive the following twenty-four hours. That is the only certainty of your situation. It's not personal, you understand."

"I do."

A man came into the room and whispered something into the general's ear. He swallowed the last of his cognac and stood up. "It is time for me to retire for the evening."

Robin stood and Yosef took him by the elbow and led him to a door.

"This is the door to my study. There is somebody in there who would like a word with you. I will see you in the morning. Have a good evening, Robin."

"Good evening, Yosef." Robin opened the door and stepped into the room. A woman who stood at the window turned to face him. He recognized her as the KGB agent he rescued from the terrorists in Mindanao. She stepped closer to him and in the low light, her face seemed the color of porcelain accentuated by her black hair which lightly curled around her dark eyes, small nose and lips appearing like oblong rubies in the low light. She was indeed beautiful...and dangerous, Robin reminded himself.

She came closer and touched his face as she did the morning he rescued her. "My angel, it is good to see you again."

"It's good to see you're healing."

"I am, but I still have much healing to do."

Robin simply nodded. He looked into her eyes and saw a jumble of pain, fear, love and hardness he found unsettling. "I hope you're being given the time to become well. After what you went through, you need a lot of rest and time to sort through your feelings." Robin felt like he talked just for the sake of it. He really didn't know what to say. "What's your name?"

The woman hesitated for a moment. "Svetlana, but I am called Lana."

"I'm Robin, Lana."

"I know." She put her arms around his neck and whispered into his ear. "Be very careful, Robin. Powerful men do not want you to leave this country alive. If they do let you leave, the KGB will still be looking for you." She pulled her head back keeping her arms around him. Robin started to say something when she put her finger on his lips. Then she rose on the balls of her feet and put her lips on his. She trembled and her tongue touched his lightly and briefly.

Robin felt her fear and anxiety. She moved her head back and looked at him with those confused eyes. He pulled her to him, gently holding her trembling body. The embrace wasn't one of passion, but an embrace of healing. He felt her clinging to him and tasted the tears running down her cheek. Lana let her arms drop and ended the embrace. She touched his face again and left the room.

Robin took a deep breath. *That was one of the strangest experiences of my life.* His thoughts were interrupted by Alex, who entered the room.

"It's time to go to the hotel, Robin."

"Okay, Alex." Robin looked at the door Lana went through. "Is she going to be all right?"

"Do not be concerned for her."

"I already am."

"Robin, some day she may come to kill you."

"I don't think she'd kill me."

"You don't understand. She has no choice. She will do as she is told."

"Why?"

"Please, Robin, we must go."

Robin looked back at the door and then at Alex. He walked out of the room without saying another word.

CHAPTER THIRTY-TWO

Things moved fast the next morning. Alex came to the room Robin shared with Mark. He insisted the group leave immediately, but Rada hadn't finished changing Mark's bandages, so Robin and Alex had a few tense minutes. They finally made their way to the van waiting for them at the front of the hotel. The van had an escort of two black Volga sedans in front and a limousine and third Volga in the rear. Robin then understood Alex's urgency. Not everyone was willing to let his group leave. They were in the middle of a conflict in the Russian government.

The convoy sped through the streets of Moscow with the Volga sedans displaying flashing blue lights and screaming sirens. They weaved through heavy traffic as vehicles careened out the way, causing some accidents. This further raised Robin's concern. It pegged when Alex, seated in the front passenger seat, turned and handed Robin his Colt .45 and extra magazines.

"Is it that bad, Alex?"

"It could get very bad. Our government is in a crisis and you are part of it."

"Glasnost versus hard line communism?"

Alex nodded.

Robin checked to make sure a round was in the chamber and inspected the magazines. He put the extra magazines in his pocket and slid the gun into his waistband. He looked at Lev and Rada whose eyes were now large and fearful. "We're taking this one step at a time. We do as Alex says and we don't panic."

Robin could see a military airfield up ahead. He looked back and saw more blue lights behind the convoy. Up ahead, he saw vehicles gathering around the gate to the airfield. "Are they on our side, Alex?"

"We are about to find out."

As Robin looked ahead, he saw gunfire erupt between the cars and people at the gate. He heard Alex say something to the driver and the van shot forward with a burst of speed. The lead Volga also increased speed and as it neared the gate, the people scattered. Only a few rounds were fired as the convoy crashed through the wooden bar across the road. The Volga smashed into two cars blocking the entrance, sending them spinning in opposite directions, but the Volga veered sharply to the left on a deflated front tire and rolled. The rest of the convoy raced to the tarmac.

Robin could see a medium sized jet passenger aircraft on the tarmac with a platoon of soldiers around it. One of them waved the convoy forward and the van skidded to a stop next to the stairs leading to the door of the plane.

"Get in the plane now!" Alex ordered.

Robin jumped out of the van and helped Rada and the children get out. "Get in the plane, Rada!" Then he and Lev opened the back doors and lifted Mark's stretcher and headed for the stairs. Robin could see vehicles surrounding the plane. "Come on, Lev. We gotta move fast." The two men went up the stairs as quickly as they could.

Alex followed them into the plane. "Robin, get everyone into the rear compartment."

Robin and Lev carried Mark and Rada followed with the children. Alex came in and handed Robin his MP5 and tactical vest. He then hurried out of the plane. Robin stepped over and handed Mark his pistol and the extra magazines for it.

"Rob, if they get this far, a .45 isn't going to do much good."

"It's a bargaining chip." Robin looked at everyone. "Stay calm. General Yamurov must have a plan. We'll just have to see how this all plays out."

He went to the forward compartment, closing the door behind him, taking a position where he could see out of the aircraft. A man exited the limousine and walked over to a group of men being held at bay by the soldiers. After a brief discussion, one of the opposing group headed to the limousine with the first man. The opposing representative got into the limo while the first man stood outside.

Fifteen minutes went by and the opposing representative left the limo and went over to his group. General Yamurov got out of the limo and came into the plane. "Robin, please put the weapon away. You already possess the most powerful weapon you could have in this situation."

Robin put the rifle down and took off the vest. "What's my weapon?"

"The identity of the person who stole the nuclear device. You do have it, don't you?"

"Yes."

Yamurov nodded with satisfaction as Alex led three men into the aircraft. Their faces were stern and heavy with concern. All of them were dressed in tailored suits and wore expensive watches and jewelry. They sat across from Yamurov and Robin with a table separating them.

"Robin, will you please tell these comrades what you came to Vladivostok to do and what you saw." Yamurov put his hand on Robin's arm. "The whole story please. Alex will translate."

Robin related the operation Mark and he conducted including seeing the transfer of the nuclear device. At the mention of the nuclear device, the eyes of two of the men grew in size. The other man's eyes narrowed. Robin told them he and Mark came to Vladivostok by boat and the RIB should still be where they stashed it. While he did talk about the sinking of the ship, he skipped much detail about the assault. He concluded by saying he came back to Vladivostok to return the device and seek medical attention for Mark.

One of the men asked a question and Robin understood he asked about the identity of the man who sold the device.

Yamurov turned to Robin. "I know this is sooner than you planned to identify the thief, but I am sure you understand the urgency."

Robin reached into his shirt and handed the general an envelope, who opened it and grunted with acknowledgment. He handed the envelope to the man sitting in the middle of the three. His face had a stony and grim look. The man's demeanor raised alarms in Robin.

"Comrade Chairman, the license plate identifies the car as the one belonging to General Ivan Picushkin. The physical description matches that of Ivan. In addition, we have received word General Picushkin and two of his officers went on vacation three weeks ago and are now one week overdue. We had this information for two days, but we did not yet know Robin's information. It would seem we have a serious problem."

The sound of a helicopter landing close to the plane interrupted the conversation. Alex looked out the door and then announced the Soviet Premier had landed. Everybody rose to their feet, including Robin, as the premier entered the plane.

The chairman curtly told Yamurov Robin had to leave.

"Robin, will you please join your friends."

"Of course, Yosef." Robin went to the rear compartment. When he walked in, all eyes were on him.

"What is happening?" Lev asked.

"The top officials of the Soviet Union are in the next compartment, including the premier."

Lev's mouth dropped open and his eyes almost came out of their sockets. "The premier is here?!"

"Yes Lev, it's an interesting situation in there. Just stay calm."

"What's the interesting part, boss?" Mark asked.

"Well partner, it appears the GRU hadn't told anybody about the nuclear device until now."

"You're kidding!"

"No I'm not. All I can say is the three members of the Committee of Ministers here sure as hell didn't know."

The door to the cabin opened and Alex motioned for Robin to come with him. Robin walked into the middle cabin and saw two of the three ministers there. Alex led Robin to the next cabin forward. He opened the door and waved Robin in, closing the door behind him.

Only three men were in the cabin, Yosef, the Soviet Premier and the Chairman of the Council of Ministers. The premier pointed to a chair. "Please sit."

"Thank you, Mr. Premier." Robin knew the premier spoke excellent English.

"Yosef tells me you speak passable Russian, but you are more comfortable speaking English."

"Yosef is a kind man. I've been told several times in the last few days my Russian is terrible by other less kind men. I understand your language very well, but I need to practice my own Russian much more."

"Well, this is no time for practice, so we'll speak English. Yosef told me of you a few days ago and of how you returned the nuclear bomb stolen from us. I would like to thank you for doing so."

"You're welcome, sir."

"I hope your friend found our medical facilities sufficient."

"We both found them to be excellent."

"Good, but now we have the problem of you, your friend and some Russian citizens, who apparently fear their own government more than they fear you, and three sons of our ministers here who are in the hands of your organization...so to speak."

"With all due respect, sir, all we have to do to solve that problem is get to Zurich and make the exchange."

The Premier studied Robin for a long moment. "Were you sent here to conduct operations against our country?"

"No, sir and I have no desire to do so."

"Have you been here before?"

"No, sir."

The premier became quiet again and Robin understood the man was testing his veracity.

"I am told you do not do work for the CIA."

"I never said I didn't do work for the CIA. I said I am not with the CIA."

A slight smile came across the premier's face.

"I am also told you would do work for us."

"As with any other client, if we like the mission, we'll do it."

"If we agree to this exchange, I have a mission for you."

"What would that be?"

"Help us find General Picushkin."

"We'd accept the mission."

"What would the fee be?"

"Given what the man has done, we wouldn't charge a fee."

The premier gave a surprised look. "You would do it for nothing?"

"No charge to your government."

The premier sat back, folded his hands across his stomach and nodded his head in thought. "Thank you, Robin. Now if you'll excuse us, we have some final discussion to conclude."

"Thank you for your time, sir. It's been an honor."

The premier nodded and Robin went back to the rear compartment.

"Where were you?" Lev asked.

"I had a conversation with the premier. We'll soon know what is going to happen."

Lev just looked at Robin like he was an alien from space.

Rada put her arms around her children and bowed her head.

Mark smiled.

Sounds of activity around the aircraft became evident. Alex opened the cabin door once again. "We are moving you to the forward cabin. It is best the family goes first and then we can carry Mark." Alex looked at everyone. "We are going to Zurich."

CHAPTER THIRTY-THREE

Lucy Santos sat in a chair with her head on her husband's bed as she dozed. Doug walked over and put a blanket over her shoulders. She was exhausted from the trip, but refused to go to a hotel and get some rest. He leaned against a wall and sipped coffee.

Emmett went with the team to cover the exchange of the Russians for Robin and Mark, leaving Doug and Maria to take care of Rick and Lucy. Cái and David visited often and were all over the hospital making sure Maria had everything she needed and Rick had the best nurses.

Doug worried about Rick. Maria said the repairs went well, but Rick's weakened condition did cause concern. She added that Rick's top physical condition was key to the success of the surgery. A weaker man would've died.

Rick stirred and Doug put his coffee down and stepped to the head of the bed. Rick's mouth moved, but his eyes were still closed. Doug saw them moving like they wanted to open. Then they did open and Rick tried to blink his surroundings into focus. Doug reached over and gently nudged Lucy. She lifted her head and looked at Doug. He nodded toward Rick and Lucy rose up so Rick could see her.

Rick blinked a few more times and looked at Lucy. "Well hello there, beautiful." Rick's voice was a barely audible hoarse whisper, but it was music to Doug's ears and he could tell it had the same effect on Lucy.

Lucy put her hand on Rick's forehead. "Hello there, you Latin lover. How are you feeling?"

"Like shit, but awfully glad to see you."

Doug pushed the nurse call button. Rick didn't look good at all and a second later, he vomited. Lucy immediately tried to clean up the mess as two nurses hurried into the room and took over. Doug pulled Lucy back as the nurses worked. Five minutes later, Maria came in.

Lucy trembled and cried as she watched the medical team work. Doug tried to put himself in between Lucy and the scene on the bed, but Lucy wouldn't submit and insisted on watching. Doug had to be satisfied with just holding her back.

Maria and the nurses cleaned Rick up and got him settled. They administered drugs to minimize nausea and pain.

Maria walked up to Lucy and hugged her. "Hi, I'm Maria and I'm the team doctor. This big lug next to you is my fiancé."

"I know, Doug has told me all about you and everything you've done for Rick. I'm so grateful."

"Don't worry too much about Rick. Right now things look worse than they really are. His body has taken horrific punishment, but he is a very strong man, physically and mentally. He will be fine in time."

Lucy choked back a sob. "Thank you, so much."

"I'm just glad I could be here to do what I can."

"Lucy..." Rick's voice croaked.

Lucy hurried to Rick. "I'm here, Babe."

Rick took her hand in his. "Glad you are, honey. I'm going to be okay. We'll just take it one day at a time."

Lucy leaned over and kissed Rick on the forehead. "You rest. I'll be here."

"Who has the kids?"

"Wanda is watching them for now and both grandparents are on their way. They'll be fine."

Rick nodded and then slipped off to sleep.

"Doug, I think you better get Lucy to the hotel so she can get some sleep. I'll stay with Rick until you get back."

"Yeah, she's going to crash soon." Doug walked over and gently took Lucy by the arm. "C'mon, Lucy. You need to get some sleep. Maria is going to stay with Rick until I get back. When you get some rest and some food, I'll bring you back."

"I can't leave Rick and I couldn't sleep anyway."

"Lucy, how do you think Rick's going to feel if you get sick or collapse from exhaustion? He's going to be out at least for a day or two. You need to take care of yourself, so you can take care of him."

Lucy looked at her husband and then bowed her head. "You're right. I at least can rest a little bit."

"And get a good meal. Let's go."

ERNIE STOOD at the bottom of Fatboy's lower door at the Paris airport. Emmett, Willy and Marv came down the stairs. Eric Newman stood at the top of the stairway.

"We'll send the ladies and Chucky back over, Eric. We'll see you in London in a little bit."

"Roger, boss."

The four men walked over to the door of the corporate jet the team rented to run the hostage scam. The door opened and Chucky and the ladies came down the ramp.

"Thanks, Chucky. You and your friends did a great job."

"Enjoyed every minute of it. Just get Robin back."

"We will. See ya in London." They shook hands and Ernie climbed the stairs into the business jet. He saw the three young men surrounded by Guardians. They were all joking except for one, who sat in the middle of the three. He looked at Ernie with a concerned face.

"How is everyone doing?"

The concerned young man looked around. "I get the feeling we are not going skiing in Switzerland."

Gary, who had the most interaction with the three while they were at the villa, walked over and stood in front of the three men. "Ernie, let me introduce you to our friends. This is Yuri," Gary said pointing to a heavy set young man sitting to the left. "The young man sitting in the middle is Stephan and the gentleman on the right is Georgy. Gentlemen, this is Ernie."

"Good to meet you all. We are in fact going to Switzerland, but the skiing will be up to you and your fathers."

That statement captured the attention of all the young men. "Our fathers have talked to you?" The concerned one asked.

"Yes, they asked us to find you, make sure you're all right and bring you to them in Zurich and that's what we're doing. So, sit back, have a drink and relax. We'll be there in about an hour." The jet's engines started and soon they were taxiing.

Gary smiled at the men. "You guys have had a good time, right?" The three nodded their heads. "There's nothing to be nervous about. In an hour you'll be with your fathers."

The jet roared, raced down the runway and lifted into the air.

AFTER THEY WERE MOVED to the forward cabin, Robin heard men and the definite sound of equipment coming onboard. He also heard muffled discussions and a few orders being given. Then things quieted and the jet took off. Robin understood enough to know a contingent of Spetsnaz boarded the plane. For the next two and a half hours, he tried to swallow the lump growing in his throat. *If anything goes wrong, this will be a blood bath and a disastrous international incident. I hope to God everyone stays cool and calm. About the only good thing about all this is everybody involved are pros...except those young men.* Robin took a deep breath. *Shit! They could be the wild card in all of this. I hope the guys are keeping them happy.*

Robin looked over at Lev and his family. He felt a pang of regret he got the honest policeman involved in all of this. He knew he owed it to Lev to get his family safely out of this mess. Then he looked at Mark. *The kid has been a good troop through all of this. I gotta get him home.* Robin rested his head against the back of the seat as he felt the jet tremble through slight turbulence as it descended into Zurich.

CHAPTER THIRTY-FOUR

E rnie walked around the perimeter of the business jet surveying the situation. As requested by Bill Grassley, the two aircraft were instructed to taxi to a remote parking area on the northeast end of the Zurich airport. Ernie could see several Swiss Army armored personnel carriers strategically placed around the area, their cannons and machine guns pointed at the two aircraft. Grassley relayed the Swiss Army's edict they expected a peaceful exchange and they would not tolerate any violence. Ernie wholeheartedly agreed. He hoped the Russians did too.

He headed back to the stairway to the door of the aircraft. He looked at Emmett stationed at the front of the aircraft and then at Willy at the rear. Their weapons were hidden underneath their jackets. Ernie also noticed the Russians had deployed their own sentries around their aircraft. He climbed up the stairs and walked over to the three young Russians. "Are you ready to go home, gentlemen?"

Yuri and Georgy both nodded in agreement, but Stephan remained still. Ernie walked past them, picked up his satellite phone and walked to the rear of the aircraft. He waved Burke to come back to him.

"Keep an eye on Stephan. His attitude could bring us trouble we don't need."

"Yeah, I noticed. I'll watch him." Burke went back up front.

Ernie punched in the number for Fatboy.

"Jamie here."

"Hey Jamie, it's Ernie. Connect me to Yamurov."

"Roger. Standby."

After a brief delay, Yamurov answered, "Good evening, Ernest. I hope you are well."

"I am, General, and I hope the same for you."

"Thank you. I trust our young friends are still well."

"They're fine, General. Yuri and Georgy are in good spirits. Stephan seems a little put out with us, but I'm sure he'll get over it."

"Ah, Stephan can be a hot head and he so loves western culture. He is probably not too happy to have his good time cut short."

"Shall we start the exchange before our Swiss friends get nervous?"

"Yes. I suggest you and I meet at the exchange point to make sure all goes well."

"I think that's a good plan. I'll start out now."

"It will be a pleasure to meet you in person."

Ernie ended the call and walked forward tossing the phone to Gary. "We'll use the radios now."

"We're ready."

Ernie went down the stairs and saw a distinguished looking man about sixty years old coming towards him. They met on a walkway in between the two aircraft and shook hands.

"General Yamurov, it's an honor."

"It is very good to meet you Ernest. Do you have a military rank I should address you by?"

"I prefer being called Ernie."

Yamurov chuckled. "You belong to a very peculiar organization."

"I prefer to believe I belong to a very special organization."

Yamurov studied Ernie for a moment. "Yes, I can see why Robin has such confidence in you and your men."

This statement made Ernie fill with pride for a moment.

"Shall we start the exchange, General?"

"Yes, let's start by you sending Yuri in exchange for the Russian family your Robin has seemed to have adopted."

"All right." Ernie keyed his portable. "Gary, bring out Yuri."

"Roger." Gary appeared at the door with Yuri at the same time Rada started down the stairs of the Russian plane with her children in hand and Lev behind her. They approached Yosef and he gave Lev a piercing look.

"Are you sure you want to do this, comrade?"

"To be honest, Comrade General, I really don't know what to do. I just think it is better for us to go with Robin now and take time to sort everything out."

Yosef's gaze softened and he sighed. "Yes, it is probably better for you and your family now. Godspeed to you."

"Thank you, Comrade General."

The family went past Ernie, Gary and Yuri. Yosef waved Yuri forward. "Yuri! Go to your father."

Yuri walked quickly to the stairs and scampered into the plane.

"Georgy for Mark?" Ernie asked.

"Yes, that will be good."

Gary brought Georgy out as two Spetsnaz soldiers carried Mark out. Marv and Rocky walked up to the Spetsnaz men, saluted them and took hold of the stretcher. The two Spetsnaz men stepped back. Rocky thanked them in Russian for being careful with Mark. Gary handed Goergy over to them and the soldiers saluted and took Georgy into the plane. Marv and Rocky carried Mark into their plane.

Yosef smiled at Ernie, but a commotion inside the business jet erased it. Stephan could be heard yelling and screaming. Burke and Rocky appeared in the door with Stephan in arm locks. He still yelled and tried to kick both men.

The Spetsnaz sentries produced weapons and started to move forward. Emmett and Willy went to prone positions, weapons ready, but still not visible.

"Stop you idiots!" Yosef yelled to the Spetsnaz men. "Put those weapons away!" The Spetsnaz soldiers hesitated. "Do as I say before you get us all killed!"

Stephan's father, the Chairman of the Council of Ministers appeared at the door. "No! Get my son! Don't listen to him!"

"Andrey, look around us! The Swiss Army is coming! Do you want us all to die!"

The Chairman suddenly realized the totality of the situation as did the Spetsnaz soldiers. They immediately put their weapons away.

Yosef yelled to the Russian plane, "Alex, get out here and get Stephan." Then he turned to the Spetsnaz sentries. "You two help control him. He is the problem."

Alex sprinted down the stairs as Burke and Rocky brought the struggling young man to the exchange point. Alex grabbed him and the Spetsnaz men put him in arm locks again. Stephan kicked one of the Spetsnaz men and paid for it. The Spetsnaz soldier smashed his fist against Stephan's head, and the young man went limp. He was dragged not too nicely into the plane.

"Okay, Yosef, please bring Robin out."

"In a moment, Ernie. You have my word I will send him

out, but I need a moment with him to finalize an agreement we have." With that, Yosef spun on his heels and went into his plane.

ROBIN HEARD the commotion and started for the middle cabin when Yosef came into the forward cabin and sat down, wiping his forehead with a handkerchief.

"I'm afraid one of the young men acted badly out there and created quite a scene. Our Spetsnaz also reacted quite unprofessionally. Your people however, performed flawlessly. I am convinced more than ever I want you as an ally and not an enemy."

"Okay, so what are we doing?"

Yosef handed Robin a large thick envelope. "We have completed an inventory of our strategic and tactical special weapons. All of our strategic weapons are in place. However, we are missing at least three tactical nuclear weapons and maybe one biological weapon. Unfortunately we don't know exactly."

"How come you don't have an accurate count?"

"Picushkin controlled all the records. They are not in good order."

"And you think Picushkin is the culprit."

"He and his two security officers are the logical suspects, but I think we need to keep an open mind on this. The envelope contains all the information we have on the situation. Are you still willing to help us?"

"Of course."

"And we still have your promise of confidentiality?"

"Absolutely."

Yosef rose from his seat and held out his hand. Robin stood and took the offered hand. Then Yosef put his hands on

Robin's shoulders and kissed him on each cheek. "I wish you were a Russian, my friend."

"That's a very nice compliment, Yosef."

"And one more thing, Robin. The chairman wants you dead and I don't think he is going to change his mind. Always be careful."

"I'll be careful."

"Let's finish the exchange."

The two men walked into the middle compartment where Robin was greeted with a mixture of looks ranging from admiration to pure hatred. He did not miss the looks were also directed at Yosef. They went down the stairs and Robin could see the relief on Ernie's face.

"Here is your commander, Ernie. Thank you for your professionalism. I hope we can meet sometime under friendlier circumstances."

"Thank you, General. I hope we can, too. Goodbye."

"Goodbye."

Robin looked at Yosef and saluted him. Yosef nodded and they parted.

As they walked up the stairs, Ernie put his hand on Robin's shoulder. "I guess we're in the big leagues now."

"Let's get going and I'll fill you in on just how big the league is."

"First why don't you tell me what the hell we're going to do with the Russian family you brought to us."

"Oh, yeah, I better talk to them."

"That'd be a good idea. They're about to jump out of their skins. Also, Rob, Rick is in serious condition in Taipei. He's going to make it, but it was touch and go there for a while."

"You can tell me more in a minute. Is he in good hands?"

"Oh yeah! Maria flew in to take care of him. She is now our team doctor by her decree."

"Good."

Robin entered the aircraft and walked over to Lev and his family as Ernie ordered the pilots to take off. Robin sat down across the aisle.

"How are we doing?"

"We are scared," Rada said.

"You don't need to be. First of all, you won't have to worry about money. I'll see you're taken care of. Second of all you can be American citizens in a matter of weeks, if you choose to do so. Third..."

Lev interrupted Robin. "We can be American citizens?"

"Yes."

"Can we still stay Russian citizens?"

"If I can maintain contact with General Yamurov, I'm sure that can be arranged."

Rada's back stiffened. "We are not beggars and we do not need to be treated like children and supported by you. We can earn our living!"

"Rada...," Lev began in an imploring voice.

Robin put up his hand and smiled. "It's okay, Lev." He looked at Rada. "I never expected to support you. In fact, Rada, you already have a job if you want it."

"What would that be?"

"In the last two days, several members of our team have been injured. Besides Mark, one other member was seriously hurt. We need a medical team to tend to our needs and the needs of our families. We already have a doctor, I'm offering you the job of team nurse."

Rada sat speechless for a good thirty seconds and Robin had to stifle a chuckle.

"What would my salary be?"

"What do you think it should be?"

"I believe the salary should be the same as my salary at the hospital, three thousand, six hundred rubles a month."

"Let's see, that would be roughly about eighteen hundred

US dollars a month. How about we pay you ten thousand dollars a month to start. That would be the equivalent of approximately twenty thousand rubles a month."

Rada's eyes, along with Lev's, grew wide and Rada went speechless again.

"Things are different in America. You both have good skills and good work ethics. You can be successful in America, especially since you speak English so well and since your children speak English, they will have little problem adjusting to American schools. Why don't you relax and talk over what you want to do. I have to tend to other business, then we can talk about this some more."

Robin walked back to where Mark lay on a fold out bed as Willy worked on his bandages. "How we doing, partner?"

"I was hurtin' there for awhile, boss, but Willy fixed me up."

"The wounds look good, Rob. Those Russian doctors did a helluva job." Willy glanced past Robin and he turned around to see Rada coming down the aisle.

"If you don't mind, I would like to check on my patient."

Robin nodded to Willy, who stood up. "My medic bag is there, ma'am. You can use whatever you need."

"Rada this is Willy, one of our team medics."

"Nice to meet you, Willy. I've just been hired as the team nurse. I can take care of Mark now."

"That's fine with me, Rada. I'm sure ol' Puppy Dog here likes your touch better than mine."

Rada rolled her eyes and as she bent down to take Mark's temperature Robin heard her say, "Men!" He smiled at Willy and walked up front to talk to Ernie. Robin sat next to him and Ernie hung up a call on the satellite phone and handed it to Robin.

"I'm sure you want to talk to your wife."

"Yes, I do. After that you can brief me."

"Just kick back and relax. It's a long story."

"Where are we going now?"

"RAF Mildenhall. Fatboy is there."

Robin nodded and punched in the number for his home phone.

CHAPTER THIRTY-FIVE

As Fatboy winged its way to the United States, Robin briefed Jamie on the mission to find Picushkin and the missing weapons.

"Get the Russian info out to all of our reps right away and tell them it's top priority. Then I want you to give me an intelligence assessment of who wants these kinds of weapons, who can pay for them and who has the will to use them."

"Can I use my contacts at the Agency?"

"Not yet. I'll let you know. Here is the number you can call to keep current on what the Russians have come up with. In the meantime, try my home again. Karen didn't answer last time."

"You got it, boss."

Robin put the headset on as the phone rang...and then he heard Karen's voice.

"Hello."

His throat caught for a moment. "Hello, beautiful."

"Oh, Rob, thank God it's you! I've been so worried..." Karen broke down and started crying.

"It's all right, honey. I'm okay. I'm on my way home."

"I'm sorry, Rob. Ever since Jamie told me the Russians had you I've been frightened."

"We had some rough spots, but all in all, the Russians treated us just fine."

Karen laughed through her tears. "I'll bet they just didn't know how to deal with you."

Rob chuckled also. "I did have them guessing for awhile. I'll tell you all about it when I get home."

"I love you, Rob. I can't wait to hold you in my arms."

"I'll be looking forward to that myself. I love you."

"How long before you get here?"

"I'll keep you posted. We picked up some personnel on the way and we will have to deal with some immigration issues, but we shouldn't be too long."

"Oh, Rob, I'm so excited. Please just get home."

"I'm on my way, honey. I love you."

"I love you."

"I'll call later."

"Okay, bye."

"Bye, Babe."

Rob turned to Jamie. "Try to get me Bill Grassley."

"Don't have to try. He's waiting on the other line. I'll switch you over."

Robin heard a click and then a connection. "Hello, Bill."

"So you got yourself out of the Russians' grasp."

"Yeah, but it was iffy there for awhile."

"I'll bet. What's next?"

"You need to meet us. We need a secure place to land somewhere near you."

"Okay, plan to land at Langley Air Force Base in Virginia. I'll get back to Jamie with the clearance codes. Do you need anything special?"

"We need some fast track immigration processing."

"You don't make things simple do you?"

"After this mission, call it payback."

"Hmm, I guess that's fair."

"I'll see you when we get down."

"Okay, talk to you then."

Rob took off the headset and went to the flight deck to see Jack, Oscar and Eric.

"Well, look what the cat drug in," Oscar drawled.

"I hear you three have been sittin' on your asses the whole time I was gone."

"That's true, but we've been sitting on our asses flying at five hundred knots over half the world trying to keep this baby in the air with minimum maintenance until we get back to home base."

"Yeah, Ernie kept on saying, 'Fly here, fly there, fly everywhere.' He sounded a lot like you," Jack chimed in.

Robin looked at Eric. "You got something to say, too?"

"Nope, I love my job. I can't help it if you saddled me with these two ne'er do wells."

"Well, I'm glad to see nothing has changed on the flight deck. Grassley wants us to land at Langley Air Force Base in Virginia. He'll be calling Jamie with the clearance codes."

"Okee dokee, boss, I'll dial it in," Eric replied.

"I'll talk to you guys later."

Robin went to the team quarters and found Ernie talking with Gunner in the conference room. Gunner came to attention when Robin entered the room.

"At ease there, Lieutenant. I'm Rob." Rob held out his hand.

"Yes, I know, Colonel. I am very pleased to meet you." He shook Robin's hand.

"Please call me, Rob, Gunner. The rank is used only when necessary with people outside of the team. Please sit down. Ernie told me all about you and the great help you were to him and the team. You have a couple of choices here. You can go to work for the CIA, and become a covert agent in North Korea. I'm sure the CIA would love to have you in that capacity. You can join the US Army and become an American soldier, which will be a path to citizenship. Lastly, you can join us. We would put you through about two years of tough training, before you would become operational, except for occasional trips to Chongjin. You'll have time to think it over before you decide."

"I do not want time to think it over. I want to join you. I want to be like Rocky and Burke."

"Well, that's a damn good goal to shoot for. If it's what you want, we'll get started on it as soon as we get back."

"Thank you, sir."

"Call me, Rob, Gunner."

"Yes, sir...I mean, Rob."

"Don't worry, you'll get used to it. Welcome aboard." They shook hands and Robin went back into the team area and found the team in the workout room.

"Hey, boss, getting the details worked out?" Emmett asked.

"Slowly, but surely. What's the latest on Rick?"

"We should be able to bring him here in another week. Maria says he's coming along as well as can be expected. Having Lucy there is doing him wonders."

"That's good news." Robin turned to Burke and Rocky. "Gunner says he wants to be like you two, God help him. You need to prepare him for Ranger School. That's where we'll start him."

"We'll take care of it, Rob," Burke replied. He looked at Rocky, who shrugged. "No time like the present, Rock. Let's get him in here."

"When are you going to give us more details on this new gig?" Mike asked.

"After we get home and get some rest. Right now it's up

to our intel network to develop some leads. You guys need to keep your reps motivated to find these people. We have to get those weapons back."

"Will do, boss," Mike replied.

Ernie came into the room. "Rob, Emmett and I need to brief you on the Taiwan op. We have some loose ends there."

"Okay, let's go back to the conference room."

The men went to the conference room and Emmett briefed Robin on what happened in Taiwan.

"Why did Rick stand in the door? That goes against all our training. He knows it's the fatal funnel."

"I haven't had a chance to ask him."

"Has anyone told us what the prisoners from the terrorist recon team are saying to the Taiwanese Marines?"

"All we know is they are talking."

"Well, that's a good thing. We need to follow up and get the intel also."

Emmett shifted in his seat. "There's one more thing, Rob."

"I get the feeling this isn't good."

"Well, it could be."

"Okay, Emmett, out with it."

"We're sorta hiding one of the tangos."

Robin mulled over this statement for a moment. "Okay, I know you have a good reason. Let's hear it."

"Well, it seems Doug saved this tango's life and now he feels he owes Doug the world. He's willing to go back to the Middle East and work undercover for us. We've kept him under wraps."

Robin's mind automatically started working out the details. "Do you think this guy is capable of pulling off an undercover op?"

"I think he's trainable."

"All right, I'll need his identifying information and where we have him. I assume he's in Taiwan with Doug."

"Yep."

"Then we'll take him with us when we pick up Doug and Rick."

Ernie looked at Emmett. "See, I told ya."

"Told him what?"

"That you'd approve of what Emmett did with the tango."

"Look you guys, I approve of everything both of you did. I learned a few things while I was with the Russians. One of them is I have the honor of commanding the best team in the world...and I'm not the only one who thinks so. In Russia, I did things and made promises based on my faith in you guys and the team. You didn't let me down."

"Thanks, Rob. That means a lot to both of us," Ernie responded.

"What you guys did means a lot to me." Rob stood up. "Now gentlemen, if you'll excuse me, I need some sleep before I deal with Bill Grassley."

Robin made his way to his berth when Rada intercepted him holding bandages and ointment. "I need to check your back."

"I appreciate that. It's been hurting for awhile."

"Please, take off your shirt."

Robin started taking off his shirt as he walked into his berth. Rada followed him. "I can get a chair and put it out the door, Rada."

"My husband knows full well what a nurse does. We have been happily married for twelve years and we trust each other. Just sit down and be quiet."

"Yes, ma'am, just trying to be polite."

"I suppose I should thank you for getting us out of Russia."

"I'm not sure if I'm overreacting or not, but based on what Alex and Yosef told me, it seemed to be the best thing to do right now."

"It probably is. It's just frightening to know we have to start over in a new country. We have lived in Vladivostok our whole lives."

"We'll help you make the transition. I don't think it will be as hard as you fear."

"There, I am finished. The wound is healing nicely."

Robin stood up. "Thank you."

Rada gathered the rest of the bandages and ointment. "You look tired, please get some rest."

"That's exactly what I'm going to do."Rada kissed Robin on the cheek.

"Thank you. I was wrong about you. You are not crazy and you are a good man."

"I just kinda grow on people."

Rada smiled and then left. Robin closed his door and shed his clothes. He crawled his exhausted and sore body into bed and fell instantly asleep.

CHAPTER THIRTY-SIX

Fatboy landed at Langley AFB six hours later. Robin felt much better after four hours sleep. He stood at the top of the stairs for the bottom hatch waiting for Bill Grassley.

Fifteen minutes later Bill came up the stairs, without his usual smile. Another man carrying a large briefcase followed him.

"Hello, Rob."

"Howdy, Bill. Good to see you."

"Really?"

"Yeah, really."

"Rob, this is Ralph Goodson. He's with the intelligence unit of the Immigration and Naturalization Service."

"Glad to meet you, Ralph."

"Nice to meet you, Rob. I understand you have foreign nationals we need to admit into the country."

"Yes, sir. They all assisted in the protection of the national security of this country. Their actions required them to leave the country they were in for their own safety."

"So, do we need an application for political asylum?"

"Well, actually I was thinking more of a permanent resident status with application for citizenship."

Ralph's eyebrows raised and he looked a Bill. Bill hesitated for a moment and then nodded his head.

Ralph turned to Robin. "Okay, where are these applicants?"

"Ernie will take you to them."

Ernie waved Ralph forward and the two went to the conference room.

"Come on, Bill, we'll go to the com center."

Robin and Bill walked up the stairs to the center where Jamie and Emmett were working.

"Gentlemen, why don't you take a break for awhile."

"Roger, boss. Hi, Bill."

"Hello, Emmett. Jamie, hope you're doing well."

"Doing just fine, Bill. Good to see you." Emmett and Jamie went down the stairs.

Robin and Bill sat down at the round table in the room. Robin poured them both a cup of coffee.

"Rob, I'm sorry to hear about Rick and Mark. How are they doing?"

"Mark should fully recover after a while. We don't know the full story on Rick yet."

"I hope he'll be okay."

"He's a tough guy. He should be all right."

Bill looked down at his coffee for a silent moment. Then he looked at Robin. "Tell me about Russia."

"I probably put too much faith in them being thankful we recovered the nuke."

"So how did you get out of there?"

"We had three young men who were sons of members of the Council of Ministers. We told the Russians we would start sending body parts to them if they didn't release us."

Bill looked back down at his coffee and Robin could see

Bill's jaws were clenched. "That's totally against US policy. We don't condone or do such things."

"Good for you. It's not against our policy, especially when dealing with the Russians. As you know, they understand that kind of action."

"You can't go around kidnapping sons of high ranking government officials!"

"I don't think you want to get into a moral argument about this, Bill. After all, in our first mission, we kidnapped a man for you."

"That's different. He's a criminal."

"He wasn't convicted of anything and in the custody of a foreign government that's supposed to be a US ally. Like I said, it's not a good idea for you to make a moral argument."

"You work for the CIA..."

"No we don't. Unless you're prepared to put us on the payroll with full benefits and the guarantee to negotiate our release in case we're captured, we don't work for you. You set the rules, you're the one who put us on contract. When I was floating in the Sea of Japan with Mark in bad shape, was the cavalry coming? Was there a helicopter or a submarine coming for us?"

Bill decided not to tell Rob about the submarine, mainly because it was there to sink the freighter if necessary, not to rescue Rob and Mark. "You know the deal."

"Your damn right I know the deal. It's you who seems to have forgotten the fine print. I did what I did in Russia to survive, get Mark medical treatment and get us home. You're the one who said we would be on our own if we got caught."

"I know you agreed to work for the Russians."

"I didn't agree to work for the Russians. I agreed to a contract for a mission. It's the same basis as we have with you."

"How can you say that? What if we want to send you into Russia for an operation?"

"It's the same thing. If it's acceptable, we'll do it."

"And what if they want to send you on mission into the United States?"

"If it's acceptable, we'll do it."

"Jesus, Rob, you know we have a new president, but what you probably don't know is the director died last night. They've appointed James Chapple as the acting CIA Director and he'll probably get the appointment. He's a political hack and with you pulling this crap, I don't know if I can protect you guys under these circumstances."

"You told me you knew we had a deal with the Russians. That means you know what the deal is, because you have a mole. You know exactly what's going on."

Bill suddenly became nervous. "You're jumping to conclusions."

"Bullshit. You have a mole and you know the mission we agreed to is more than compatible with the national interest of the United States."

"Rob..."

"Don't insult me by telling me not to talk about this. You know damn good and well this conversation won't leave this room."

Bill sat back in his chair and took a deep breath. "Okay, we know you're looking for General Picushkin and the Russians are missing either nuclear or biological weapons or both."

"All right, good enough. I need you to get your people looking for Picushkin and get them talking to Jamie. Between the Russians, our people and yours we should find him pretty quickly."

"I'll get it going, but you need to understand the president is very upset about the way you handled the Russians. He's questioning the viability of the team."

"I love it. You send us to do your dirty work, but you don't want us to get too dirty. Please tell the president, if he doesn't like us, don't use us, if he has another team as quick and effective as we are. We'd love to be home with our families."

"What makes you think there aren't other teams?"

"I don't know if there are other teams. I don't care. It boils down to the simple fact that if you need us, you know we're here. If you don't need us, that's okay too."

Bill rose from his chair. "I didn't mean to piss you off, Rob."

"Well, you did. We have two badly wounded men, prevented a nuclear attack on Sasebo, prevented the Chinese from having a reason to attack Taiwan and established a reliable intel source in North Korea and all I hear is the new president is upset. Well, that makes two of us."

"I think we should leave it at that for awhile."

"Fine with me. I've said my piece."

"Shall we go see how the immigration process is going?"

"Not yet. We have some loose ends to tie up."

"Like what?"

"I need to get Gunner, the North Korean Lieutenant, into Ranger School and I may need to get Lev in as well if he decides to join us."

Bill didn't immediately reply.

"What's the matter, Bill?"

"I'm not sure I can do that, at this point."

Robin started rubbing his head. "Are you going to make me play games like the Russians did?"

"What do you mean?"

"Never mind."

Robin rose from his seat and headed for the door.

"Okay, Rob, I'm sorry. I should be playing the games with

the politicians, not with you. I'll get them into Ranger School. Same class as Carlos."

"Same class as Carlos?"

"Yeah, we've done all we can with him. He wants to work for you, so I'll see they're all in together."

Robin let out a long breath and turned his head back and forth in a futile effort to loosen his neck muscles. He thought of Carlos, a Cuban agent who flipped and went into Mexico with the team. Carlos had been doing counterespionage work with Chris Fleming ever since. It would be good to see him again.

"What else do you need?"

"We have a Palestinian under wraps in Taiwan. He's agreed to work undercover for us. I want to bring him to you and get him trained to be a covert agent."

"Damn, why didn't you tell me that before?"

"Because I want him to be a successful covert agent and not a dead one. I only wanted to tell you about him in person."

"Good point. Get him to me. I'll take care of it."

"Thanks."

Bill held out his hand to Robin. Robin clasped it warmly.

"I'm sorry for the outburst, Bill. The president's concern just rubs me the wrong way."

"It's all right, Rob. I know you've been through hell."

"C'mon, let's go to the conference room and see how things are going."

"One more thing, Rob."

"Yeah?"

"There is no other team like you guys. Nobody, not even the military, can deploy as fast as you guys can and there is no other non-military team that can take care of business like you guys. I made that clear to the president."

Robin put his hand on Bill's shoulder. "Thanks, Bill. I

know you mean well and I know some day politics may come crashing down on the team, but I'm going to call 'em like I see 'em. It's the only way to get the job done."

Bill laughed. "It's good to see you haven't changed. Let's go to the conference room."

Rob led the way to the conference room. They saw a lot of paperwork being filled out and discussed with Ralph, whose fingers flew on the keyboard of an IBM Selectric Typewriter creating permanent resident cards. "I should be done in a couple of minutes. They have more paperwork to fill out, but Ernie is going to forward it to me."

"You're my kind of guy, Ralph," Robin complimented.

"I don't hear that very often, thanks!"

Five minutes later, Ralph packed up. "Okay folks, you're now permanent residents. I don't know what these two gentlemen have in store for you, but I wish all of you luck."

Lev came forward and shook Ralph's hand as did Gunner. Then Bill and Ralph left.

Robin walked to the flight deck. "Get us home, Jack."

"Amen, boss."

CHAPTER THIRTY-SEVEN

obin and Ernie pulled into the driveway to the Marlette house. People poured out and Karen flew into Robin's arms as he walked up the driveway. Laurie and Eddie were right behind and it turned into a group hug with the dog trying to get in the act. Ernie held his wife, Sally and daughter Judy. Robin looked up and saw Cathy and Andy coming toward him. The others moved so both men could get a hug in. Then Karen hooked her arm in Robin's as they headed for the front door.

"We have some surprises for you."

"No kidding! Cathy and Andy are a surprise."

Karen just smiled at him. They entered the house as Casey came walking into the living room.

"Well, if it isn't the third year West Pointer! Hello, son."

"Hey, Dad. It's good to see you. Hi Uncle Ernie." Casey shook Ernie's hand.

"Same here." Robin and Casey embraced. "How are things going at the Academy?"

"The third year is more about learning and less about

hassle. It's much more enjoyable and I'm doing well in my classes."

"As usual. How's the military training going?"

"Good stuff. I stay in the top five percent in performance."

"Not number one?"

"Come on, Dad. I get first in a lot of the stuff, but there are a lot of smart, physically capable people there. It's tough competition."

"I know, Casey. I'm proud of your accomplishments. You should get one of the first picks of assignment when you graduate."

"That's what I'm shooting for."

"Still looking at the Rangers?"

"Yep, and working my way into Special Forces and then Delta."

Robin put his hand on Casey's shoulder. "I have no doubt you'll get there."

"Let's all sit down, shall we?" Karen gently ordered.

Everyone found chairs or the floor. Robin noticed Andy paying close attention to Cathy. He also noticed a certain glow on Cathy's face and a knowing smile on Karen's. He figured out the second surprise, but didn't say anything. He glanced at Karen again and she gave him the act surprised look.

Andy stood up. "Can I have everyone's attention please." Everyone quieted down and Andy surveyed the room, barely able to contain a wide grin forming at his mouth. "Cathy and I have an announcement to make."

Cathy took Andy's hand.

"We're going to add to this wonderful family. We're going to have...twins! A boy and a girl!"

"Hooray!" Eddie yelled. "I'm going to be an uncle!" Laughter and congratulations flooded the room as everyone took turns hugging the expectant couple.

Karen, Sally, Laurie and Judy headed for the kitchen and soon produced trays of food and put them on the dining room table. The group gravitated to the food and passed the afternoon and evening celebrating being together and new additions to the family on the way.

ROBIN AND KAREN lay in their bed. Karen gently rubbed ointment on Robin's back. "Does it feel okay, honey. Am I hurting you?"

"It feels wonderful."

"The wound is healing well."

"That's a good thing."

Karen put a new dressing on the wound. Robin rolled over and saw concern on Karen's face.

"What's bothering you, babe?"

"The team keeps getting seriously hurt. First Doug, and now Rick and Mark...not to mention you."

"This mission stretched our skills and capabilities to the limit. We had to take risks I normally wouldn't have, but we didn't have a choice. The bad guys were up to some serious shit."

"And it's not over."

"No, it isn't."

Karen reached out and touched Robin's face. "I would start to whine about the danger and you not being home, but I guess I can't complain when you stop the detonation of a nuclear bomb."

"Okay, you don't whine and I will."

"What are you going to whine about?"

"Missing you."

Karen sighed. "I know you miss me. I can feel you."

"You're not even touching me."

"No, silly, I can feel you. I can feel your heart, your soul and emotions when you are stressed or very happy."

Robin looked into those deep emerald eyes and felt his spirit merge with Karen's. He knew it wasn't supposed to be scientifically possible and he didn't believe in myths, but he felt this. "I can feel you. I'm not sure it's the same intensity as you feel, but I do feel it. Your face always comes to me during those times you describe. When I'm stressed you calm me and make me more determined. When I'm happy or exhilarated, I see your face and I know I'm sharing with you."

Karen smiled and reached for Robin and he pulled her to him and held her close.

"Promise me you'll always come back to me."

"That's a promise I made a long time ago. You're the love of my life and I can't live without you. One of these days this will all be over and we can live on this island in peace and happiness and let this screwed up world pass us by."

Karen put her lips on Robin's and opened her mouth invitingly. They merged with tenderness and love.

ROBIN AND KAREN walked into the lobby of the Silver Cloud Inn in Mukilteo just as Lev, Rada and their children came down the elevator.

"Hello, folks. Hope you had a restful evening."

"The hotel is very nice, Robin. Thank you for letting us stay here," Lev said.

"No problem. Lev, Rada, this is my wife, Karen."

Karen shook hands with them. "Thank you for saving my husband."

Rada laughed. "He doesn't need much help. Your husband is a very resourceful and determined man."

"Believe me, I know." Both women laughed again.

"I'm glad you're not laughing, Lev," Robin observed.

"I'm remaining neutral, like Switzerland." Everyone laughed at Lev's comment.

"Karen this is Ilya and I'm sorry, young lady, but we've never been formally introduced." The young girl smiled shyly and looked at her shoes. "This is Sasha," Rada offered.

Karen held out her hand to Sasha who tentatively took it. "You're a very pretty young lady, Sasha. How old are you?"

Sasha looked at Karen with admiring eyes. "I'm nine years old."

"My, and you speak English so well. We have a son about Ilya's age and a daughter who's older. They'll help you get settled in school."

Robin looked at his watch. "Let's get your luggage in the truck and head for the island."

During the ferry ride and the drive back to the Coupeville area, the Rogov family looked around in awe, except for Sasha. She had taken a definite liking to Karen and asked all kinds of questions about Whidbey Island, the United States and told Karen about Vladivostok.

Robin drove down beautiful country lanes along the west side of the island. Lev and Rada commented on the beauty of the sea and forest together. Robin occasionally came back onto the highway, but then turned off onto more county back roads. Eventually, he pulled into the driveway of a nice home on a high bank overlooking the Strait of Juan De Fuca.

"You have a very beautiful home, Robin," Lev observed.

"We do actually, but this is your home for now."

Lev's eyes grew wide and Robin heard Rada gasp behind him.

"Our company has rented this home until you find the house you want. It's fully furnished, you'll just need to go grocery shopping. I've got an appointment to tend to for a while, but Karen is going to help you get settled. I'll see you in an hour or so."

Karen was already out of the car with Sasha following her and Ilya not far behind.

"Robin, this is all overwhelming."

"I know, Lev. Just take it one day at a time and everything will fall into place." He turned and looked at Rada and saw tears streaming down her face. "I hope those are happy tears."

"Some are, but I remember how I treated you in the beginning. I am very sorry."

Robin laughed. "I deserved it back then. Come on, let's see your new house."

When Lev and Rada entered the home, Rada cried more and held Lev tight. Robin could see Lev fighting back tears of this own. It made Robin feel better about all that had happened to the family.

Ilya and Sasha came running into the living room and grabbed their parents. "Momma," Sasha cried, "come, come see our wonderful new home! It's the best home in the whole world!"

Karen came into the room. "Everything looks good, Rob."

"Great. I'm going to leave now. See you all in a little bit."

Robin left and drove to Oak Harbor to visit Tim Echoles. Tim had been released from Harborview and now recovered at home. Alice let Robin in.

"Hi Alice. I was pleasantly surprised to get your message about Tim being home. I thought it would be weeks."

"That was before you came. He's really perked up since then."

"That's wonderful. Where is the rascal?"

Alice led Robin into the family room where Tim sat in a hospital bed. The back of the bed was fully cranked up into the upright position and Tim exercised with a spring tensioned muscle builder.

"Robin, you're back!"

"Yes, sir I am. How are you doing?"

"I'm getting stronger by the day. The doctor says if I keep this up, I'll be able to go to work in about two weeks."

"What about working from home?"

"What do you mean?"

"We can get you set up here with an IBM computer and it will be hooked to our office and we can bring what paperwork you need to look at every day and take it back. I wouldn't expect you to do it all day, just as you feel good enough. That way you can ease into the position."

"That would be great. I'm really going nuts without enough to do."

"Okay, I'll get it set up." Robin looked around. "Do you have a nursing service looking after you here?"

"Yeah, we have one."

"Is it good?"

"Well, they change them all of the time and it's a pain to retell things, but it's all right."

"I'm going to bring a nurse in to meet you. She is now our company nurse. If you like her, she can take over."

"Wow, you have a company nurse?"

"Yes, she's Russian and she's very good. We picked her up in Russia this trip."

"Holy smoke, a Russian nurse. You guys really are international!"

"We are international. You're part of the team now."

Tim grinned. "Thanks, Rob. That means a lot to me."

"Well, make no mistake; your job is going to be a tough one. We had a rough go this time. Two of our guys got seriously hurt. Rada, the nurse and our team doctor will also be looking after them. I'm going to figure a way to get the other two on the island."

"We have a team doctor, too?"

"Yep. She's in Taiwan now, taking care of our other wounded man."

"Man, Russia, Taiwan...you guys were busy."

"Yes we were. I've got to run, but I'll check back on you in a day or two."

"Okay, Robin. I appreciate all you're doing."

"You can pay me back by getting up to speed and start running the business end of this company."

"I will."

"Good, I'll see you two later."

Robin drove to his own home, got the secure phone and called Doug on his satellite phone.

"Doug here."

"Hey, Doug, how are you?"

"Going nuts waiting around."

"What's the word on Rick?"

"His strength is building back up, but he's still pretty weak. Maria thinks he should be able to fly back in about five days."

"Okay, I want you to get back here. Do you think Maria can handle things alone?"

"No problem because she won't be alone. Cái and his former general are helping."

"Good. Get on a plane and get back here ASAP. We need to move on the current problem."

"Roger. I'll be back in a jiffy. The Taiwanese Marines are treating us like royalty and told me when we're ready to go, they'll fly us back."

"Whatever works. Just get back. Tell Rick I said to get off his ass and get healed up."

Doug laughed. "He'll appreciate your usual soft heart."

"Yeah, tell him I'm worried about him and do what the doctor says. I need him to be able to get back to one hundred percent."

"I will, boss. I suppose you know about Kahlid."

"Who?"

"My Palestinian friend."

"Oh, yeah. Bring him with you."

"Roger, that."

"See ya when you get here."

"Bye."

Robin next dialed Jamie.

"Com center, Jamie."

"Hey, Jamie."

"Hi Rob. I thought you'd be calling."

"Any news?"

"Nothing concrete, but NSA did pick up some signals intelligence (SIGINT) about quote 'important cargo' end quote, out of the Middle East. The source is a cell phone belonging to a known tango in Pakistan."

"Do we have anyone working on it?"

"Yeah, Jonathan is on it and has some of his Legionnaire buddies and some friends retired from the British Special Air Service (SAS) helping him out. They have a lot of contacts and hopefully they can flush something."

"Remind me to hire more Legionnaires."

"You got my vote!"

"Who's coming to relieve you?"

"Mike will be here in about an hour."

"Okay, you need to spend some time home. Take two days off. I'll handle the schedule."

"Rob, it's okay. Nancy understands. In fact, she's here helping me out."

"You guys need some time together."

"We all do, but this situation is too dangerous for any of

us to be taking too much time off. Besides, I'm the only one with the deep contacts in the intel world."

Robin thought for a moment. "Okay, but when this is over you two are gone for awhile."

"We'll talk."

"Doesn't anyone follow orders around here?"

"Yes, but what's good for the goose is good for the gander. I don't see you taking any time off."

"Okay, we'll work it out when this is over. I'm going to tell Doug to head over and hook up with Jonathan. Let Jonathan know, will you?"

"Will do, boss."

"Bye."

Robin dialed Doug again.

"Yeah, Rob."

"Change of plan. Call Jonathan and make arrangements to meet him. He may need some help there."

"You got it. You know, I'll have to take Kahlid."

"Why?"

"I can't leave him here, Rob. He's not exactly welcome in Taiwan."

"Ask the Marines to fly him to Virginia. I can have Bill Grassley arrange to pick up Kahlid since they'll be training him."

"I'll ask David, but he's used up a lot of stock for us all ready."

"See what you can do and let me know."

"Roger."

Robin next called the Fort Lewis Hospital and asked for Mark's room. A female voice answered.

"Mark Warren's room."

"Nurse, this is Colonel Marlette. Can I talk to Sergeant Warren or Sergeant Young?"

"Hi Robin. This is Jessica Lanthrop."

"Well, I see Mark is being well taken care of, Jessica."

"I'm here for moral support. Willy is here doing the actual work."

"I'm sure you being there makes Mark want to get well real soon, Jessica. Can I talk to Willy?"

"Just a minute."

"Hey, boss."

"How are things, Willy?"

"He's stable. As soon as you get a place ready, we can move him."

"Good. I should have a place in a couple of days."

"We'll be ready, Rob."

"Thanks, Willy."

Robin looked at his watch and wondered what was taking Karen so long. He went to the refrigerator and pulled out a plate full of steaks and started preparing them for grilling. The front door opened and Eddie, Laurie, Cathy and Andy came in followed by Casey.

"Hey, Dad. What's up?" Eddie asked.

"We're going to have our new Russian friends over for dinner. How 'bout helping set the table for ten people."

"Okay."

"We'll all help," Cathy offered.

"That would be wonderful, my oldest child. Can I have Andy for a little bit?"

"Of course, Dad," Cathy said kissing Robin on the cheek.

The others got busy and left Robin and Andy to themselves.

"Cathy says you've been working on some interesting projects."

"I hoped we could talk a little. My dad told me some things about the operations in terms of equipment that would make things easier, so I've been doing research and experiments to see what I can come up with and I think I've got some ideas."

"Like what?"

"Well this new cell phone technology is really interesting. I think it's going to be revolutionary."

"It is interesting, but the damn phones are like bricks. We may as well stick with the sat phones which aren't much better, but they do have worldwide coverage."

"I wasn't suggesting you change to cell service. I think you need to stay on satellite, but look at this."

Andy handed Robin an electronic device a little longer and wider than a cigarette package and just about as thick. On one side, Robin saw a moveable stick. He wiggled it and moved it into an upright position.

"I take it this is the antenna."

"Yes, sir."

"Are you sure it will pick up a satellite signal? Looks pretty small to me."

"It has the same components your current phones have. I've just miniaturized them."

"Is this one programmed?"

"Yeah, dad had Jamie program it. Push that button to turn it on."

Robin turned the phone on and the screen lit up. "What kind of light is that? That's not the usual back lit liquid crystal you always see nowadays."

"That's what is called Light Emitting Diode, or LED. It uses much less power than other types of light...almost ninety percent less."

"Wow, that will save battery time."

"That's why I used it."

Robin dialed the com center and Mike answered the phone.

"Hello?"

"That's not a very professional way to answer the phone."

"Oh, I'm sorry, Rob. I didn't recognize the phone number."

"I'm just kidding you, Mike. I'm using a new smaller version of the sat phone built by Andy."

"Really? The signal is very clear. More clear than our current sat phones and the delay isn't as noticeable."

"It sure seems like it. I think we gotta winner here. I'll talk to you later."

"Okay, boss."

Robin handed the phone back to Andy. "How much does it cost to build one of these?"

"Well, that's the problem. It's takes about twenty five thousand dollars. The guts of this thing are very expensive. Plus, I want to add a few features."

"Like what?"

"A digital camera and a digital sound connection for a tactical earpiece. You noticed there's less delay in your transmission."

"Yes."

"Well, working with L.E.D.s I became interested in light and found a way to use it to accelerate the speed of the transmission through space."

"From this phone?"

"Oh, no, there's not enough power in the phone to do that. It all takes place in the satellite."

"Andy, you're turning into a genius!"

"No, not really, Dad. I'm lucky enough to be exposed to all kinds of very smart people and inventions through the CIA. My expertise is in miniaturization, but it lends itself to a lot of other areas. Almost all of the inventions we talked about, I helped invent or helped in their further development, so the other folks are helpful when it comes to giving me a break on the patent licensing."

Karen and the Rogovs came through the front door.

"Andy, I'll start a new account and put two million dollars in it. Build us enough phones for the team. Keep me apprised of your other projects that apply to us and we'll fund them."

Andy's face lit up. "Really?"

"Really."

"That's great! Thanks, Dad."

No, thank you, Andy. We can use any edge we can get."

Karen came up and kissed Robin. "The Rogovs are very happy with their new home."

"I'm relieved."

"Relax and get cooking. We're all famished."

"I'm working on it. Can you try to get everyone introduced?"

"Looks like it's already in progress."

The family had surrounded the Rogovs. Robin noticed Eddie and Ilya talking to each other and Sasha's eyes locked on Eddie. Andy and Cathy were talking to Lev and Rada.

"Looks like it. How 'bout another kiss?"

Karen gave Robin a quick kiss on the lips, but as she pulled away, Robin pulled her close and wrapped his arms around her, holding her tight.

"Are you all right, Rob?" She whispered.

"No." He gently pushed her back and looked into her eyes. She squeezed his hands and went back to their guests.

Later in the evening Robin and Karen lay in their bed talking. The conversation had been about the family and the Rogovs, but Karen changed the subject.

"Are you going to tell me what's bothering you?"

Robin took a deep breath. "I'm very worried. We have to find those weapons and when we do, it will be tough to get to them. If we don't...well, that's just too horrible to contemplate. We can't fail."

"But you're not in this one alone, right?"

"That's true."

"Maybe the CIA or the Russians will find them first and you won't have to get involved."

Robin looked into Karen's lovely eyes. The lamp light was just bright enough to cast their color as a deep jade.

"I'm sorry...I just hoped."

"The problem with both the CIA and Russians is although they can get us the intelligence, they can't move fast enough tactically to get to the weapons. Everybody and his brother will want part of the action and that'll slow them down."

"And you don't have that problem?"

"I simply won't accept it. If we locate the weapons I know they'll tell us to wait for them."

"And you'll refuse."

"No, I just won't respond."

Karen put her head on Robin's chest. "Please come back to me. I couldn't go on without you."

Robin pulled her on top of him and kissed her deeply.

"I will always come back to you. You're the love of my life."

Robin's pager started beeping. "Goddammit, what now?" He got up and picked up his phone and dialed the com center. He walked out into the family room so he wouldn't bother Karen.

"Hi Rob. Sorry to bother you but General Yamurov just called," Jamie said.

"What's he want?"

"He says the KGB took down some Russian Mafia suspects in Chechnya. One of them says they brokered deals for eight tactical nukes for Picushkin. One of their contacts is a Chinese intelligence agent with connections to Al Qaeda and other jihadist groups. Another is a Pakistani ISI agent."

"I'm listening."

"The Mafia guy says at least four nukes are headed for Pakistan."

Robin cursed to himself. He wanted more time with his family. "Okay, call out Jack and the air crew. Then call out everyone else. I want to be airborne ASAP. Call Jonathan and Doug and get them on the ground in Pakistan. Jonathan may be able to get some real time intelligence on the situation."

"I'm on it."

"How much sleep have you had lately?"

"I'm good, Rob."

"Where's Nancy?"

Jamie didn't answer for a moment. "She's here."

"Take her somewhere for a couple of hours. We'll wait for you."

The phone was briefly muffled. "Thanks, Rob."

"See you later."

Robin went back to the bedroom. Karen had changed into a sweat suit and was packing his bag.

"I'll do that, babe. You go back to bed."

"Why? So I can listen to you bang around while you try to do it in the dark?"

Robin stood beside Karen as she put his socks in the bag. Suddenly, she turned and wrapped her arms around him and Robin felt like she tried to merge their bodies and pull him into her soul.

"It's all right. We'll get the job done and get home." Robin's throat caught.

"Sometimes you are so full of bullshit, Robin Marlette. I've loved you for almost twenty-five years. I know when you're scared…and you're scared now."

He looked into her eyes and his heart felt better…stronger. "You just keep on loving me and I will get home."

She smiled. "Then I don't have to worry." She held him tight again.

CHAPTER THIRTY-EIGHT

Jonathan Marchaux eased into a booth in the small Islamabad tea house. Two men sat across from him. One was an older Anglo with a hard look about him. The other was a young Pakistani who seemed about ready to jump out of his skin.

The Anglo grinned. "It's about time you showed up you black bastard. I thought you were going to be a typical Legionnaire and wait for the Special Air Service to take care of things."

"Blakely, the SAS couldn't fight their way out of a paper bag without Legion back up, especially one who has been retired so long. Sorry, you know how traveling is around here."

The men shook hands. "I do. This bloke is Ahmed. He plays in the cricket league I coach. He has some good scoop that may be connected to our problem."

Jonathan shifted to Arabic. "I promise I will tell no one you talked to me and I can reward you for your information, if it proves to be accurate. What can you tell me?"

The boy looked around the café and then leaned towards

Jonathan. "My brother, Bacla is a member of Al Qaeda. Do you know of them?"

"Yes, the head of Al Qaeda is Osama Bin Laden."

"Yes, yes, he is an evil man. He wants Bacla to martyr himself."

"What is Bacla to do?"

"He says he will be given a mission to attack either America or India. He doesn't know which one, but it's supposed to be the greatest mission anyone has ever seen."

"When is he going to do this?"

"He has a meeting in two days in Peshawar. He will be told then."

"Where is your brother now?"

"He is here in my mother's home, but you must not talk to him!"

"Don't worry, we won't, but we have to follow him so we can stop the people trying to get him to do this. Can you show us your mother's house?"

The young man looked around the café again. "Yes, but we must be very careful and you must promise me you won't hurt my brother."

"I promise I won't hurt your brother. Does anyone else live with your mother?"

"No."

"Then you just need to show us the house."

"All right, I will show you."

"Is it far?"

"No, only two streets over."

"Lead the way."

The young man walked out of the café and Jonathan and Blakely followed him.

"How can you promise his brother won't get hurt?"

"I said I wouldn't hurt him. That's the best I can do."

"You're a real bastard, Jonathan."

"I don't think you have much room to talk, Colin."

Blakely shrugged. "It's a nasty business and I thought I got out of it."

"Me, too, but I can't stand by and let this insanity happen."

"You're right about that, Mate."

The two men kept a short distance behind Ahmed. Colin wore a Shalwar Kameez, so with his long grey beard and deep tan a person had to be close to spot him as an Anglo. Jonathan wore the modern dress of the Sheedi, the black Pakistani tribe. The two were able to melt in the foot traffic.

After two blocks, Ahmed gave them a quick glance and walked into a small one story stone house.

"Well, there's our surveillance target."

"Yes, Doug will be landing at the airport in about two hours. The team is also on the way. We need to find a surveillance point."

"Well, there is a rental sign on that place over there. You go get Doug. I'll check on renting the house."

"All right. Let me know what you find out."

FATBOY HAD TAKEN off after a refueling stop at Anderson Air Force Base in Guam before Robin was able to make contact with Jonathan again. Ten seconds into the conversation, Robin could tell by Jonathan's voice he was more than concerned about the situation.

"One of my SAS sources recruited a young Pak whose brother is a member Al Qaeda. The brother was told he has been selected for the greatest mission anyone has ever seen and it will be either in America or India. He will be told more in two days in Peshawar."

Robin was well aware of Pakistan's two faced relationship

with the US and the Paks support for terrorists. It made sense Picushkin went there because the Paks wouldn't snitch Picushkin off to the Russians either. "Do we know who he is supposed to meet?"

"No, and I think we are only going to find out by following the brother of our source. We need to move carefully. If ISI gets word we are on the ground here, our safety will be seriously compromised."

"I understand. Northern Pakistan is an area tough for us to operate in."

"Yes, we need to be very careful."

Robin's mind sped through options for infiltration into the area. "I'll get back to you as soon as I can. I have to figure out how we can get in there without attracting too much attention, but we need enough assets on the ground to make sure we don't lose the suspects during the trip from Islamabad to Peshawar."

"I'll be waiting for your call."

"Thanks, Jonathan."

"Shall I alert the cavalry?" Jamie asked.

"No, the first thing the CIA will do is call the Pakistani President and make our job impossible. It will be shades of Vietnam where we kept the South Vietnamese military informed of our ops and got compromised numerous times. I'm not letting that happen to us."

Robin pulled maps of Northern Pakistan and the Peshawar area and began planning the insertion of the team. He asked Jamie to have Ernie, Rocky and Burke come up to the com deck to help with the planning. As he looked at the map, the difficulty of the operation became even more apparent.

At this point Robin considered Pakistan enemy territory, requiring any insertion be covert by necessity. His choices were limited by the geography. Fatboy could land in New

Delhi, India and the team could proceed. The Russians and Indians were on good terms, so Yosef might be able to provide contacts for logistical assistance. The Indian government, however, would still be in control and that meant one more thing Robin couldn't control.

The other choices all had more devilish problems. Iran was out of the question because of their hatred for all things American, as was Iraq. Afghanistan had no facilities for Fatboy to land near its border with Pakistan and the Russians were losing their grip on that country making the situation there unstable. Saudi Arabia was pro American, but they would alert the CIA as soon as Fatboy landed. As the planning team came into the cabin, Robin examined the CIA map of the area around Peshawar.

"What's our status, Rob?" Ernie asked.

"As usual we've got a shit sandwich to deal with. I'm trying to find a place we can land Fatboy and get to Peshawar without the Paks knowing we're coming."

Ernie leaned over the map with Robin. Burke and Rocky went around the other side of the table and starting looking also.

Robin moved his finger on the map to a spot in Kyrgyztan, just above the Pakistan border. "This might be the place...Osh, Kyrgyztan. There's a Russian Air Force Base there. According to the CIA info the runway is over eight thousand feet."

"That won't be a problem for landing Fatboy, even at that altitude," Burke observed.

"I don't think so either, but we'll still have to get the flyboys' opinion, not to mention the Russians' permission to land."

"I suppose that's the easy part," Burke interjected.

"You suppose correctly. To get in covertly we're going to have to go in at night and have disguises ready. At some point during the infil, we're going to need to split up in two or three man teams and come into the target area from different directions."

Burke leaned over. "Where's our target area?"

"We don't know yet. We're waiting for an update from Jonathan or Colin."

"That means we may have to stage in enemy territory. That worries me," Ernie said.

"Me too, that's why I said we needed to be ready to wear disguises."

"I have to call Yosef again. You guys start working on details."

Robin walked over to the communication console and nodded to Jamie who initiated the call.

"Hello, Yosef."

"Do you ever sleep, my friend?"

"I don't think either of us is going to get much sleep any time soon."

Yosef grunted. "I suppose you are right."

"We have a good lead in Islamabad which appears to be taking us to Peshawar. I have some requests."

"What are they?"

"First, I need permission to land at Osh, Kyrgyztan."

"That can be arranged."

"Second, I want your guarantee our plane won't be searched."

There was a pause. "That will be more difficult, but I can arrange it."

"Good. Next we need air transportation to the Peshawar area. Do you have any AN-12s or similar aircraft in Osh."

"It is likely, but if not I will get what you need."

"And last, at least for now, I need Alex to join us on this op to maintain coordination."

"He is already in the air on another mission, but I will divert him to Osh. He has his Spetsnaz team with him."

"They could be a useful augmentation to my team. I'll keep you posted."

"Thank you, Robin."

Robin hung up the phone and looked at the planning team working on the map table. He turned to Jamie.

"What's your assessment?"

"I think Jonathan and Colin are on the right track and I think the team is about to engage in its most dangerous mission."

The knot in Robin's stomach got tighter.

CHAPTER THIRTY-NINE

Karen collapsed in the overstuffed chair in the family room. Rada sat across from her.

"I don't know how Robin does all of this. Just getting the place and setting it up for Mark and Rick is enough to wear me out for two days. Thank God Lev is taking the night shift."

"My husband is a good man." Rada moved her neck and shoulders trying to loosen them. "I'm in knots and I can't seem to relax."

"Well, you've been going non-stop for days, Rada. I'd fix you a drink, but Robin said you don't imbibe."

"Maybe, I will change my mind. What do you have?"

"I personally like scotch, especially since my husband buys me the best."

"Well, give me just a little to see if I like it."

"It sounds like a wonderful idea to me."

Karen made them both scotch on the rocks. The scotch was a single malt aged in sherry casks. "Just sip it, Rada."

Rada took a sip and made a scrunched face that slowly faded. "Oh my, it feels warm going down."

"Isn't it a nice feeling?"

Rada took another sip. "Goodness, that is relaxing, but I must be careful. I have to drive the children home tonight."

"Nonsense, they're fine here and you can stay in the guest room. Casey has already gone back to West Point."

Rada sighed and leaned back on the couch. "Karen, Lev is thinking about joining Robin's team. I am worried about the things they do. I am not sure Lev is the same type of person as Robin. Can I trouble you for some advice?"

Karen looked out the windows and focused on the last glow of the sun as it dipped below the horizon. Blazing rays of orange and gold spread out over the blue water, causing diamonds of light to dance on the waves. A tear fell from her eye. She turned back to Rada. "I don't know if I'm the one to counsel anyone about how to deal with men like our husbands. I'm certainly not any good at getting my husband to pick a more mundane line of work, but you should know the team doesn't have a choice. They have to do what they do or go to prison."

Rada bolted upright. "They are criminals?"

Karen let out a hearty laugh. "Not only are they criminals, but they are international criminals." Karen saw the horrified look on Rada's face. "I'm joking, Rada. Robin and the team went into Mexico without legal authority to rescue Cathy, who was kidnapped by a drug cartel. My husband, being the man he is, made sure the cartel leader paid dearly for his crime. The rest of the team made sure the whole cartel paid dearly...it doesn't exist anymore. When they came back, they were given a choice, work for the CIA, or go to prison."

Rada leaned back on the couch. "I do not want Lev doing such things."

"I don't want Robin doing such things...all of the wives don't want their husbands doing such things, but on this last mission Robin and Mark stopped a terrorist team from detonating a nuclear device in Japan. God only knows how many lives they saved and they may have prevented nuclear war. How do I tell my husband not to do that?!"

Rada sat back up. "Lev is not like them."

Karen took in a deep breath and let it out slowly. "You're kidding yourself, Rada. Lev is a cop, right?"

"Yes, but it's not like here. He didn't have a gun."

"Did he get into fights?"

"Well, yes...it's part of the work...I mean with drunk people..."

Karen held up her hand. "Did he win the fights?"

Rada's lips started to quiver. "Yes."

Karen went over to Rada and put her arm around Rada's shoulders. Rada buried her head in Karen's chest and cried.

"Rada, we are our own worst enemies. We love men of principle, loyalty... and action. We want them to be safe, but it means trying to change them and that, my dear, rarely works out."

Rada sat upright and wiped her eyes. "Ever since Lev met Robin, it seems like he has been torn and on edge, but when Robin told him he could train to be on the team, he calmed down and has a resolve I have never seen in him before. I sense he now has the purpose in life he has always wanted."

"Don't make the mistake of believing that purpose in life means he doesn't love you or the children just as much as he always has. It's just some men are drawn to the job of protecting others who can't protect themselves. We happen to be married to two of them."

"So I should not say anything to him?"

"Oh no, Rada. Tell him exactly what you think and feel. Just don't make him feel guilty if he chooses to join the team. The only other thing you should consider is Lev will either join a police department or join the team, right?"

"That's what he said."

"Well, here's something else for you to consider. The team is the best trained and equipped team of its kind. The men are all dedicated to each other and can rely on each other in the toughest of situations. You don't find that everywhere. It's one of the things that keeps me going when they're gone."

Rada looked down at her hands folded in her lap. "I am frightened."

"Oh, Rada, I can't even begin to know what you're going through right now. You've been ripped from your home, taken to a foreign country and thrust into a very unfamiliar environment. No wonder you're frightened. I'd be terrified!"

Rada looked at Karen and smiled. Then she started laughing. Then both women started laughing together.

"I do not think I would be able to get through this without you, Karen. Thank you for being so wonderful."

"We need to get all the wives together so you can meet them, but tomorrow is going to be another busy day. We should start thinking about getting some sleep."

CHAPTER FORTY

A lex greeted Robin with a giant bear hug. "Welcome to Osh, my friend!"

Spetsnaz soldiers guarded the perimeter of the ramp where Fatboy and an AN-12 were parked tail to tail. The team and more Spetsnaz soldiers unloaded equipment from Fatboy and into the AN-12. Two more AN-12s were close by.

"It's good to see you again, Alex. Have you been briefed on our information?"

"No, Yosef told me you would brief me when we met."

"We need to brief everyone and get an infiltration plan built up. Do you have two men who can work with my planners?"

"Of course."

"Good. After we get the equipment loaded, we'll start planning and hold a briefing. In the meantime, I'll get an update from our people in Islamabad." Robin looked around. "Are these Spetsnaz men the same ones who were in Zurich?"

Alex laughed. "Are you a little worried?"

"Wouldn't you be?"

Alex laughed again. "Yes, I would be. Some of these men were in Zurich. Only part of my group was there. The others were from another group and they are not here. All of these men work directly for me. You can trust them as much as you trust me."

Robin looked steadily into Alex's eyes. "Since I trust you with my life, I feel much better."

Alex held Robin's gaze. "And I trust you with my life. We are soldiers in a dangerous and complicated world. It is good we are comrades."

The two men kissed each other on the cheeks, the traditional Russian expression of friendship. They did it as a display of unity to the other men as well.

Three hours later, Robin walked with Alex and Ernie across the flight line when he heard a commotion from where the Guardians and Spetsnaz were working on coordinating small team tactics. "What the hell's going on?"

The three men walked over to a widening circle of men. In the middle of the circle, Burke was squared off with the Spetsnaz First Sergeant. The Sergeant was a full inch taller than Burke and built like a brick wall.

Robin tapped Rocky on the shoulder. "What the hell is going on, Rock?"

Rocky turned to Robin. "The First Sergeant and Burke had a discussion about hand to hand combat. They decided to test each other's theory."

"Shit, they may kill each other!"

"They agreed there'd be no punches, just moves and holds." Rocky had a big grin on his face.

Alex started forward, but Robin grabbed his arm.

"Let 'em go, Alex. They know what they're doing."

"But Robin..." A look of realization came over Alex's face then he smiled and relaxed.

Burke and the sergeant started circling each other, looking for an opening. The sergeant grinned at Burke, taunting him in Russian. Burke answered, telling the sergeant to stop talking and start fighting. The sergeant feinted and then moved like lightning, burying his shoulder into Burke's solar plexus knocking him down. Burke rolled and sprang to his feet and in an instant he swept the sergeant's feet from underneath him while lifting him by the belt and slamming him to the ground. The sergeant sprang to his feet before Burke could move in. The give and take battle went on for fifteen minutes. Both men were nearing exhaustion, but at the last moment the First Sergeant tried to kick the inside of Burke's knee...a move that violated the informal rules. Robin could tell by the look in Burke's eyes that he took the move as a green light. Burke made a circular motion with this left arm, catching the sergeant's foot in the crook of the outside of his wrist and then completing the movement to spin the First Sergeant's body in midair and slamming him face first into the ground. The sergeant laid there for a long moment.

Burke moved to the sergeant's head and he looked up. Burke offered his hand. A stillness filled the air as no one breathed, waiting for the sergeant's reaction. A puff of breeze raised a small cloud of dust in front his face and spun away. He shook his head, slowly raising his hand and Burke took it, pulling the sergeant to this feet.

The two men looked at each other and then the sergeant gave Burke a bear hug and rubbed the top of his head. The group broke out in cheers and laughter and crowded around the two combatants.

"Looks like we're a team, Alex!"

Alex grinned at Robin and nodded with approval.

ROBIN GAVE the last comments of the briefing. "We'll infiltrate in three flights. One plane will land at Kohrat, one at Risālpor and one at Minhas. Getting off the planes and getting them back in the air in under three minutes is critical. That way we'll be off the airports before anyone can react, if they will at all. The Paks have C-130s, so if anyone sees one of our planes, hopefully they'll think it's just a C-130 on a training mission and let it go. Does anyone have any questions or concerns?" No one spoke up. "All right, assembly is at 2100 hours." The meeting ended and the men headed to complete final preparations for the mission.

Alex came up to Robin.

"It sounds like we are on the right track. At least we're doing something and this information cannot be ignored."

"That's our opinion, too. My team needs some sleep before we launch tonight. It will probably be awhile before we get to sleep again. I'll see you this evening."

ROBIN WOKE to Ernie shaking him. "Wake up, Rob. We've got a problem."

Robin instantly woke and sat on the edge of his cot. "What's up?"

"Grassley is calling and demanding to talk to you. He sounds pissed."

Robin looked at his watch and saw it was time to start getting ready for the mission. "That's not a problem."

"Are you going to talk to him?"

"In a while. Let's get ready for the mission."

JONATHAN ADJUSTED himself in the hard wooden chair. He

smiled at the sound of Colin's snoring as he slept on the floor. He picked up his radio.

"Jonathan to Doug, radio check."

"I'm awake." Doug answered.

"Roger."

Jonathan felt sorry for Doug. He sat in a car a few blocks away, ready to start following Bacla when he left for Peshawar. Doug had to move often to avoid detection.

Jonathan leaned back in his chair. The sun sank to the horizon, bringing an end to the day Ahmed's brother was supposed to leave. He was getting a little concerned about following their man in the dark with only two vehicles. He was also concerned that Ahmed's information may be false.

During the surveillance, the team had seen Ahmed, an older woman they surmised to be his mother and another young man who appeared to be Ahmed's brother. The brother only appeared twice in two days and didn't seem to be in a hurry to go anywhere. Jonathan let out an exasperated breath. Surveillance can be so boring.

CHAPTER FORTY-ONE

"Grassley here. Is that you, Rob?"

"It's me."

"You want to tell me what the hell you're doing?"

"Not necessarily."

"Goddammit, Rob, I can't cover your ass if you insist on playing games."

"I'm not playing games...I'm avoiding them."

"Okay, let me ask you this. Are you working on the missing items?"

"Yes, we are."

"Can you tell me where you are?"

Not yet." "

"Jesus, Rob, if you're where I think you are, there'll be hell to pay."

"Don't jump to conclusions, Bill. We're just following a lead."

Bill didn't respond right away. "I assume you're working with other clients."

"Bill, I'm doing the best I can here. We're dealing with an

extraordinarily dangerous situation and it benefits the entire world for us to be successful on this mission. Your cooperation gives us an extra margin for success."

Bill replied after a brief pause. "I'll get back to you."

Robin took off the headset and looked at Jamie. "What do you think, Jamie?"

"I think the whole thing is crazy, but I don't see any other alternative to what we're doing now."

"My sentiments, exactly. We'll keep in touch."

"I'll be here, boss…and please be careful."

"How 'bout I promise to be tactically sound."

Jamie laughed. "That'll do, Rob."

FORMER RUSSIAN GENERAL IVAN PICUSHKIN fidgeted with his watch. In a few hours, it will be time for the final transfer of two weapons to the terrorist organization known as Al Qaeda…a very dangerous time for him and his men. Picushkin knew these terrorists were ruthless and considered him an infidel, but he possessed things they wanted very badly. They were willing to buy all four weapons, but Picushkin knew if he gave them all up, he wouldn't likely survive another ten minutes, so he arranged to sell the other two weapons one month after the first two were used. Even that didn't make him feel certain they wouldn't kill him, so he had one more card to play they didn't know about.

Picushkin took a sip of his tea. His stomach constantly ached since he and his men made their move and he knew the Russian government was scouring the world for him. If they ever found him, it wouldn't be a pleasant experience, but he had a contingency for that problem too. Former Russian Major Igus "Poppy" Popovitch came into the room.

"The counter surveillance is in place, General."

"Very good, Poppy. We can't be too careful with these people."

"I agree, sir and we have four hours before we begin the exchange. That gives us plenty of time to decide whether things look safe."

"Monitor the situation carefully, Poppy. The slightest sign of trouble and we will quickly disappear."

"Yes, sir."

"JONATHAN TO DOUG, standby to move. A white Mercedes sedan has pulled up to the Ahmed's house. Vehicle is facing north."

"Roger, I'm ready."

"Wake up you English dog, we'll be moving."

Colin groaned as he got to his feet. "Buggers, it's been a long time since I've slept on something so hard!"

"If you were a Legionnaire, you could still do it without pain."

"That'll be the goddamn day."

"Better get down to the car. Here we go! Jonathan to Doug, the brother is getting into the car...Oh, shit, they're forcing Ahmed into the suspect car!"

"Doug has the eyeball."

"Colin to Doug, we'll be behind you in a few seconds."

"Good idea."

ROBIN WAS JARRED in his seat as the AN-12 landed on the strip at Risālpor. The pilot executed a short field landing and the plane shuddered as the engines screamed in reverse. The loadmaster and his crew started popping the turnbuckles on the restraining straps holding the Land Rovers as the rear door slowly opened. On the loadmaster's signal, Mike Collins started the engine and drove off the ramp into the night. Robin scanned the area to his right with his night vision goggles.

"I don't see anyone around."

"Looks like we're clear on the left," Marv offered from the back seat. A Spetsnaz soldier was the fourth man in their vehicle. Each vehicle had four men, with a mixture of Guardians and Spetsnaz.

"All vehicles clear the aircraft," Emmett advised.

The three Land Rovers turned left onto a dirt road that went onto a feeder road to the N45 highway. The AN-12 roared off the runway and banked north to Osh. Less than two minutes had elapsed. Robin admired the pilot's skill. He did both a successful short field landing and a short field takeoff on a one mile secondary runway, chosen because it was almost a mile from the nearest building.

Rob keyed his mic. "Road looks clear. Maintain blackout."

The vehicles turned onto the N45 and headed south. "Spread out. When you have half mile separation, turn your lights on."

Robin breathed a sigh of relief. At least his team's insertion went well. Burke's voice came over the radio. He and the First Sergeant Setchinko landed at Minhas Air Base.

"Burke to Robin."

"Go ahead, Burke."

"Insertion successful. Doug says the suspect vehicle is thirty minutes out. I've sent a team to Peshawar."

"Roger. We'll have one team standing by to join you on the surveillance. The rest of us will head to Peshawar."

"Roger."

Robin looked at Mike. "I hope Ernie and Alex made it in."

Robin's satellite phone beeped. "Speak of the devil...you guys okay, Ernie?"

"Yeah, we're good. Had a guy shine a light on us. We waved, he waved back and that was that. We should be in Peshawar in about an hour."

"Good. Contact me when you get there."

"Roger."

COLONEL RASHA BULECHEKURA reached for the phone that jarred him out of a deep sleep.

"What is it?!" He barked

"So very sorry to disturb you, sir. This is Lieutenant Salishura."

The colonel sighed deeply. "Yes, Lieutenant." He didn't want to dampen the enthusiasm of the good lieutenant, his most loyal and conscientious officer at Kohrat.

"Sir, we heard a multi-engine aircraft land on the field and then take right off again. The only thing we saw was the exhaust flame from his engines."

"Is that it?"

"No, sir. One of our sentries encountered three vehicles leaving the east side of the base."

"What happened?"

"Well...ah...they waved at each other."

"Thank you for the alert, Lieutenant. I'm sure it's just those arrogant special forces practicing their missions without telling anyone."

"Oh, well, I'm so sorry for disturbing you, sir."

"Don't worry, Lieutenant. You did the right thing. Just note the activity in the log."

"Yes, sir. Thank you, sir!"

The colonel laid back in his bed and soon fell back asleep.

ALI AL-SHALABAD KEPT an eye on the rear view mirror as he drove on the N5 highway towards Peshawar. He was relieved no blue lights were behind him. The operation was already running into problems.

When he and Soli went into the house, the old woman started yelling, telling them to get out of her home. Then she grabbed Bacla and wouldn't let go. Ali pulled out his silenced Czech 9mm pistol and shot the old woman in the head. The young brother jumped on him and it took himself and Soli to knock the boy off and tie him up. They were going to take the younger brother all along as insurance to make sure Bacla would complete the mission, but he didn't plan on killing the mother. He looked in the rear view mirror again and saw the younger brother's eyes staring at him with burning hatred. *He is going to be a problem.*

ROBIN ASSIGNED surveillance positions as the vehicle teams came into Peshawar. All teams were in position as Burke informed him the suspect vehicle was five miles from the city and still on the N5. His apprehension steadily increased. Conducting vehicle surveillance in the areas with narrow streets without being spotted was going to be tough. He planned to set up a perimeter around these kinds of neighborhoods and then deploy foot surveillance. This procedure would hopefully minimize the chance of detection.

The suspect vehicle entered the city and immediately turned into an older neighborhood, with very narrow streets. Robin began setting up surveillance posts in an inner ring and an outer ring. Before he could deploy foot surveillance, the vehicle came out of the neighborhood.

"Everyone watch it. He's checking for a tail."

At two in the morning, traffic was light, making it difficult for the team to change eyeball positions without being obvious. After going another mile on the main boulevard, the vehicle ducked into another neighborhood with narrow streets. Robin set up the posts and deployed foot surveillance. Several minutes passed without the suspect vehicle being spotted. Robin became very nervous. Then a Spetsnaz soldier came over the air in a whisper.

"Bear Six, the vehicle is parked with lights out in an alley. He appears to be waiting to see if any surveillance comes by."

"Roger, Bear Six," Robin answered. "Are you in a good position to maintain eyeball?"

"Yes, sir."

"Good. It's your call."

More time went by, then the Spetsnaz soldier transmitted again. "Bear Six, the suspect vehicle is getting ready to move. He is heading out of the neighborhood the same way he came in."

"Roger, we'll pick him up when he comes out."

The suspect vehicle came out of the neighborhood and headed west at a speed faster than he had driven since he came into town. He stayed on the boulevard until he came to an industrial center near the airport and then turned onto a back street. He drove two blocks and pulled up in front of a loading door to a warehouse. A few seconds later, the door opened and the vehicle drove into the warehouse.

"We've established our target location. I want the four closest teams to each drop off one person to set up a four point observation on the building. Watch out for counter surveillance," Robin ordered over the radio.

Four men jumped out of vehicles and moved quietly to the area surrounding the building, each taking up a position to watch a corner.

"Okay, everyone else meet me three blocks to the south of the target."

The teams met Robin and he, Alex and Ernie made final assignments. Robin and Alex would lead a ten man assault team into the building upon Picushkin being identified as present. Burke and First Sergeant Setchinko would standby with a six man backup assault team. Ernie would lead the surveillance team ready to cutoff any escapes, if necessary. All teams deployed to their standby positions.

A Spetsnaz man came on the radio. "There is a man sitting in a car near me. I believe he is counter surveillance."

"Has he seen you?" Robin asked.

"Negative."

"Terminate him just before we move in."

"Roger."

"I have one too," Willy advised. "I understand the order."

MIKE COLLINS' voice came over the radio, barely above a whisper. "Mike to Robin, another vehicle has pulled up to the loading door...standby...someone just came out of a side door and is shining a light into the vehicle...he's gone back into the warehouse, aaannnd the loading door is opening... looks like the dope is here!"

Robin laughed at Mike's reference to their former jobs as narcotics officers. "Roger, Mike, can you get a closer look-see?"

"Standby."

MIKE COLLINS TOOK a moment to listen to the environment around him and do a visual 360° check. Satisfied it was clear, he moved in the shadows to the edge of the street. He looked and listened again then moved quickly to the west side of the warehouse. Laying down, he low crawled along the foundation to defeat any possible video surveillance. Mike came around to the north side where the doors were and inched up to a side door which had a window. He slowly raised up and looked in.

Mike's pulse rose sharply. He saw what appeared to be two backpack nukes. An Anglo man showed Arab men the inside of one backpack. Another Anglo man stood with his arms folded and Mike recognized him as Picushkin from the pictures at the briefing. There were more armed Arab men in the area also. Mike tried the door knob and smiled as it moved. He backed away from the window and dropped down, pressing his transmit button. "Targets are on scene with two visible babies. Numerous armed suspects. Door is unlocked. Time to rock 'n' roll."

"Roger, Mike, we're inbound."

PICUSHKIN WATCHED as Poppy explained the mechanism sequence to the Arab teenager while another man translated. The boy's face was passive as he listened and Picushkin couldn't be sure the boy understood the explanation. Poppy finished and asked the boy if he understood. The boy nodded and then asked, "What is the code?"

Poppy handed him a piece of paper and the boy looked at it for a moment and then said, "I thought there were twelve characters in the code. This paper only has eight." Ali grabbed the paper.

Poppy looked at Picushkin who stepped to Bacla and handed him a card. "When you are ready to detonate the bomb and have entered the first eight characters, call this number. I will give you the final four characters." Picushkin suddenly pressed the radio earpiece deeper in his ear. "There's trouble outside!" He yelled.

Furious, Ali went for his pistol. His hand wrapped around the grip when he caught a movement in his peripheral vision. He turned and saw men coming quietly through the side door, one of whom pointed a submachine gun at him. The barrel flashed. It was the last thing Ali ever saw.

WHEN MIKE MADE THE CALL, Robin and the assault team moved quietly to the warehouse from their staging area just across the street. They stacked up at the door and Mike opened it. The team moved in and shooting immediately erupted with the muffled staccato of suppressed automatic weapons mixed with those loud reports from the terrorists' AKs. Robin was the fourth man and scanning through the gun smoke and din he saw an Arab man dragging a teenaged boy toward an inside door. Robin acquired the man's head in his sights and squeezed the trigger. The Arab's head flew apart and the young boy collapsed to the ground. Robin scanned right and then left. Then the lights went out.

Men yelled and several flashlights came on followed by more machine gun fire. In the glow of the flashlights, Robin caught a glimpse of a man coming at him from close quarters. He was so close Robin had to fend him off with the butt of his submachine gun. The man fell backwards and Robin fired a burst into the man's torso. The lights came back on.

The Al-Qaeda guards were no match for the professional operators and all but two lay dead. The gun battle lasted less than a minute.

Robin keyed his mic. "Warehouse is secure. Where's Picushkin?"

A few seconds elapsed and then Ernie came up on the radio. "We're on him. A Mercedes sedan picked him up."

"Everybody please clear the frequency!" Gary called.

"Go ahead, Gary."

"I'm following Picushkin. Ernie you're following what I think is an ISI agent and he's setting us up."

Robin's breath caught. "Shit, if he's right, we could be royally fucked!" Robin knew Gary well enough to know he wouldn't lay down bullshit at a time like this. He keyed his mic again. "All teams clear the area! Ernie, break off your surveillance! You've been compromised by ISI. Everyone get scarce!" Robin looked over and saw Jonathan with the older boy. "You know what to do with him."

"But Ahmed!" Jonathan protested.

"We'll get Ahmed!"

Jonathan saluted and headed for the door with Bacla.

Alex had the Russian called Poppy and he and a soldier dragged the wounded man to the door. The backup assault team brought the vehicles up and everyone piled in to the car closest to them. Robin got in with Burke, Rocky and a Spetsnaz soldier. Alex and a Spetsnaz soldier took Poppy into First Sergeant Setchinko's Land Rover.

"Where are you, Gary?"

"We're headed into the airport. I'll keep you posted."

Burke pulled onto Airport Road and headed north. They had gone a mile when two police cars went speeding by them with lights and sirens on. Robin looked back to see if they would turn around, but they didn't. He also looked back at the First Sergeant's vehicle. "I wonder what's happening in that car," he mused.

The Spetsnaz soldier shrugged and said, "Major Popovitch will talk."

Robin turned around. "I have no doubt about that." He keyed his mic. "Gary, where can we meet you?"

"Turn right on Rafiqui Road. It's across from the entrance to the air base."

"Roger. Alex, you copy?"

"Roger."

They met Gary on a darkened street just off Rafiqui Road. Alex walked up to Robin.

"Picushkin went to Karachi. That's where the other two bombs are."

"Yeah, they got into a private jet. I got a partial tail number," Gary said.

"Alex, did he tell you where the bombs are?"

"He said they were on a boat, but I don't know if he lied."

"How can you find out?"

"I can't. Popovitch is dead. He bled to death from his wound, but he did say something that has me worried."

"What's that?"

"He said, 'Worse than Tunguska.'"

"I don't know what that means."

"In the early nineteen hundreds, scientists believe a huge asteroid hit Siberia completely wiping out everything for over eight hundred square miles."

"Damn, we've got to get to Karachi and we better do it now, before the ISI gets a bulletin out on us. Alex, you and I need to catch a plane from here. Burke tell Ernie to get the team back to Osh and get the boy from Jonathan. Tell him to do what he thinks is best when you guys get to Fatboy." Robin looked at Alex. "Alex, I'm going to ask the CIA for help. Hopefully, they can pick up Picushkin at the airport and follow him. I think I can convince them not to talk to the ISI."

Alex shrugged. "We don't have much choice. Our closest assets are in India."

Robin got into the car and called Grassley.

"Bill Grassley."

"Bill, it's Robin."

"I've been sitting here hoping you'd call."

"Do you have reliable assets in Karachi?"

"We have a station there."

"Okay, Picushkin will be landing in Karachi in about two hours in a private jet...or more accurately, an ISI plane with a tail number ending with 712A. We need someone to pick up surveillance. We'll be there in two to four hours."

"Where are you?"

"Moving and dodging the ISI. Bill, you can't call the Paks."

"I have to, it's protocol and I have no doubt we will soon be receiving inquiries about your activity."

"Lie to them. Do you want these Paks to get backpack nukes?"

Grassley didn't answer.

"Look, Bill we'll recover the nukes and take care of Picushkin. We'll be out of Pakistan in twelve hours. Work with me on this."

"All right, Rob. Call me when you get to Karachi."

CHAPTER FORTY-TWO

R obin drove a rental car slowly through the Karachi Airport looking for Alex. He flew in on Pakistan International Airlines while Alex took a flight with Shaheen Air. He stopped in front of the terminal area for Shaheen. A few seconds later, Alex appeared and Robin honked his horn. Alex jumped in the car.

"Any problems getting here?"

"There was interest in me when I bought my ticket, but nothing came of it. Did you have any trouble?"

"Like you, I got asked some strange questions and a guy tried to get someone on the phone, but he never connected. So, they let me go. Just the same, we should check for a tail. I'm going to stop up here and you need to take over driving while I coordinate with the CIA."

Robin pulled over and the men changed positions. Robin called Grassley.

"I hope that's you, Rob."

"It is."

"We picked up Picushkin at the airport. He was with a man our guy says is a rogue ISI agent, whose job is to assist

Jihadist terrorist groups. The ISI doesn't admit he's theirs, but he is. There was also an Asian man and they had a young boy. Standby while we connect you to our agents."

Robin heard some clicks and static, then a voice.

"Hello?"

"Hello, I'm your contact. I'm Rob."

"Hi Rob, are you at the airport?"

"Yes, how do we connect with you?"

"Okay, the targets split up. Picushkin and the Asian guy went down to the Karachi harbor at The Defense Housing Authority Marina."

"Did they have the boy with them?"

"Yeah, he was with them."

"How do we get there?"

"I assume you have a map?"

"Yeah, I picked one up from the rental agency."

"Look southwest from the airport to the water and you'll be in the general area."

"Okay, I see it."

"You want to get on Shahrah-e-Faisal Highway and head west."

"I see that."

"Then come south on Creek Avenue."

"Yep, I got it."

"You'll come to Zulfigar Street 1. Go down that street until you get to the Carlton Hotel. I'll be in the hotel restaurant. You better get moving. Shahrah-e-Faisal can get really jammed up."

"We're on our way."

The trip was twenty miles, but took an hour. The Karachi drivers drove like they were in a road race with a mix of bumper cars. Robin was glad Alex drove because they went through several serious traffic jams that would have tested Robin's patience, but Alex seemed unfazed.

The two men pulled into the parking lot of the Carlton Hotel and made their way to the restaurant. A man in a tan suit with an open collar waved them over to his table.

"Good afternoon, gentlemen. I don't believe introductions are necessary."

"Good afternoon. What are we eating?" Robin asked.

"I recommend any seafood here. You don't want to try their meat. It can be an iffy proposition sometimes."

The waiter came over and Robin and Alex ordered grilled tuna steaks. When the waiter left, the CIA agent pointed his thumb over his shoulder towards the bay, which spread before them in panorama through large picture windows.

"The eighty foot yacht to the right is your boy's boat. He, the Asian and the young boy are on board and have been for several hours. I haven't seen any activity indicating they're getting ready to leave."

Robin studied the geography and the tactical situation. "We're going to have to do a seaborne assault. Can you provide us with scuba gear, weapons and a RIB?"

The CIA man gave Robin a hard look. "Not without permission from Langley and a RIB on this short notice will be tough."

Robin looked around. "I'll be right back." He went down the stairs and through the lobby to the front desk.

The clerk looked up. "How may I help you, sir?" He asked in Arabic.

Robin replied in the same language, "My friend and I are staying at the Hilton, but we like your hotel so much, we'd like to get rooms here. Do you have any available?"

The clerk gave a condescending smile. "The only room I have available is one of our Royal Suites, which is quite expensive."

"On the top floor?"

"Why yes, sir."

"Fine, we'll take it."

"How long will you be staying?"

"A week."

The clerk raised his eyebrows. "I will need the room rent in advance."

Robin handed the man a credit card.

The clerk looked at the name on the card. "Well, Mr. Al-Alani, you don't look like you're from the Middle East."

"My father is Saudi, but my mother is Irish. My father is of the royal family."

"Oh, I'm so sorry to have questioned you, sir!"

"Apology accepted."

The clerk looked relieved as he handed Robin two keys.

Robin made his way back to the restaurant and sat back down at the table.

"You can forget about the RIB. We'll launch the assault from here."

"How are you going to do that?" the CIA man asked.

"I just got the penthouse here for a week. All you need to do is get us scuba equipment, a couple of hundred feet of rope and suppressed weapons. If you need juice to get authorization, call Grassley."

"My boss doesn't like jumping the chain of command."

Robin sat back and drummed his fingers on the table. "What's your boss' phone number? I'll have Grassley call him."

"All right, all right, calm down. I'll get the gear. It's just doing this op without telling the Paks is downright dangerous."

"And if we told them, the ISI would warn Picushkin and get him out of here."

The CIA man took a deep breath. "What time do you want the gear?"

"After dark."

"I'll be here." The CIA man rose to leave and reached for his wallet.

Robin held up his hand. "Don't worry about it. I'll bill the room."

The CIA man nodded and left. Robin and Alex went up to the suite, which was spacious and had a balcony overlooking the bay. It gave a direct view of Picushkin's yacht.

"Well Alex, we have a great surveillance location."

Alex laughed. "You're truly an amazing person, Robin."

"What do you mean?"

"I would have never thought about renting a room here and you had the CIA man terrified of you when he left."

"I don't know about that. We need to be careful. He might just decide he needs to tell the Paks what we're up to."

"Do you think he will?"

"Not really because he probably believes we'll kill him if he does."

Alex broke out laughing. "Yes, he had that look in his eyes."

Robin reached into his bag and pulled out a pair of binoculars. "I'll take the first watch. You get some sleep."

Alex reached for the binoculars. "No, my friend, you have done most of the work today. You get some rest. I need that crazy mind of yours working in high gear tonight."

Robin shrugged. "All right, partner, I'll grab some shut eye."

Alex laughed again. "Sometimes you sound like the cowboys in American westerns."

"That's because I am a cowboy at heart."

ROBIN GLASSED the yacht as he saw a motorboat heading out to it, its wake jumbling the reflection of the lights on the other side of the harbor. He had relieved Alex four hours before. It was dark, but he could see the boat pulled up alongside the yacht. Robin could make out a man climbing on board. The lighting on the yacht revealed a well-dressed man whose head moved surveying the area. Definitely an operator and probably Pakistani ISI. Picushkin appeared and warmly greeted the ISI man. They went below.

Robin walked to the room where Alex rested. "Hey partner, wake up. We have activity."

Alex immediately jumped to his feet. "What is it?"

"It looks like Picushkin's ISI contact has showed up. It's time to go to work."

They moved swiftly, packing the gear delivered by the CIA man. They were already in the wetsuits. They put on their air tanks and masks. Robin stepped out to the balcony and looked four stories down. The area below was clear and quiet in the sticky warm air. The area was basically under construction. The hotel was new and the grounds around it didn't have much in the way of shrubbery for concealment, but there wasn't much in the way people traffic.

Robin secured a rope on the balcony railing and threw the other end over the side. Alex slid down the rope first and disappeared behind a small building. Robin went next and knelt down next to Alex. The water was one hundred yards away.

The men remained still, listening and surveying the area. Minutes later, Robin looked at Alex and gave a thumbs up. Alex returned the hand signal and they crept across the barren dirt using shadows for concealment. They reached the beach and slipped into the water.

Once in the water, Robin put his flippers on and started towards the yacht on a compass bearing he previously plotted. A long cord connected him to Alex. Robin barely surfaced twice to check their course. Twenty minutes later, they were at the swim platform of the yacht. They took off their tanks and removed their weapons from waterproof bags. Each man had a suppressed MP5 submachine gun, a suppressed Glock 9mm pistol and KaBar knives. They put their pistols in thigh holsters.

The only sound they heard was water lapping against the hull of the boat. Robin raised his head over the stern and covered the area with his submachine gun as Alex climbed over the gunwale and ghosted to the cabin door. He knelt ready to shoot and waved Robin over who went to the other side of the door and knelt. Alex rose to the bottom of a window. He quickly looked and then dropped back down. Turning to Robin, he put his fingers to his eyes and then held up one finger, indicating he saw one bad guy. He then made a throat slitting motion indicating he would use his knife to kill the enemy.

Robin held up his hand for Alex to wait and pointed up to the bridge of the yacht. He wanted to clear high ground before they assaulted the main part of the boat. Alex nodded.

Robin turned and climbed the ladder to the bridge. He approached it in a crouch and then rose slowly to look through the door window. He saw a large man bent over the chart table. He also saw Ahmed sitting on a chair, his feet and hands bound. Robin tried the door handle and it moved. He thumbed the selector switch on his submachine gun to semi-auto, raised it to eye level and silently entered the bridge. The man started to straighten up and turn as if he sensed something. Robin squeezed the trigger and shot the man with one bullet into the base of the brain. The man pitched forward, but Robin caught him before he crashed onto the chart table and quietly lowered the body to the deck.

He turned to Ahmed, whose eyes were wide and terrified. Robin put his finger to his lips and moved next to Ahmed and spoke in Arabic.

"I'm Rob and I'm a friend of Jonathan. I'm going to get you to safety after I take care of the others on the boat. Do you understand?"

Ahmed nodded his head.

Robin looked around and saw a hatch. He went over and opened it and saw a hold large enough for Ahmed to hide. He went back and untied Ahmed. "Ahmed, you're a brave boy. I want you to hide in that hold until I or another man named Alex comes for you. Will you do that for me?"

Ahmed nodded again and then asked, "Is my brother safe?"

"Yes, Ahmed, he is with Jonathan."

Ahmed got up and went to the hold and crawled in.

"Remember, Ahmed. Don't come out until I or a man named Alex comes for you. You're going to hear some bad things, but just stay here."

"I will."

Robin rubbed the boy's head. "Good boy."

He closed the hatch and looked around and saw where a flight of stairs went down to the main cabin. He crawled to the edge of the stairway and listened. He could hear voices in serious discussion. He backed off and called Alex on the radio.

"Alex, do you copy?" Robin whispered.

Alex's whisper came through Robin's earpiece. "Roger, good signal."

"Still got the drop on your guy?"

"Roger."

"I took one out here and found Ahmed. Take yours out and re-contact me. We'll recon and then do the assault."

"Roger, standby."

Robin stood back and gripped his weapon, ready to charge down the stairs if Alex ran into trouble. The seconds ticked by...

"Bad guy down," Alex finally whispered. "I see two people, an Asian and probably the ISI man talking to someone across the room I can't see. There's a guy with an AK shorty, probably a bodyguard, standing behind them."

Robin crawled back to the top of the stairs and looked. "There's another bodyguard with an AK shorty standing to the left of where you'll come in." Robin moved his head to the right. "The guy the others are talking to is Picushkin, who is sitting on a settee. I'll take out the bodyguard I see, you take out yours. Let's try to take everyone else alive."

"Roger, I'll move to Picushkin, you move to the others."

Robin pointed his submachine gun at the head of his bodyguard and switched the selector to full auto. "Roger. Are you ready?"

A few seconds went by. "Roger."

"On the three count...three...two...one." Robin squeezed the trigger and sent a two round burst into the side of the head of his first target. He leaped onto the stairs, wrapping his left leg around the railing and slid down on his left leg facing backwards so he could train his weapon on the Asian and the ISI man. He landed on the deck to the left and slightly behind Alex, who advanced on Picushkin. The ISI man reached into the left side of his suit coat. Robin advanced on his two targets and shouted, "Don't move!" The ISI man continued to go for his gun. Robin fired a three round burst and shredded the ISI man's right shoulder sending blood, bone fragments and muscle tissue flying. The man screamed and fell back against his chair while his gun clattered onto the deck. The Asian didn't move. Robin moved behind the two men. He now faced Picushkin and saw he held a satellite phone with a calm face and his index finger on the keys. Alex was next to him with his submachine gun pointed at Picushkin's head at point blank range.

Aside from the sounds of pain coming from the ISI man,

silence settled in the room. Robin kept his submachine gun pointed at Picushkin and searched the Asian for a gun. The man was clean, but Robin found a passport identifying him as Bao Ma Teo, a Chinese citizen. He also searched the ISI man. He had no more weapons, but Robin removed a cell phone from his coat pocket.

Picushkin looked at Alex and smiled. "Well, Alex, I must admit you moved much faster than I expected."

"I'm taking you back to Russia."

"Oh, I don't think so. All I have to do is push the pound key on this satellite phone and a signal will be sent to a backpack nuclear bomb in the main nuclear weapon storage facility at Saratov-63. Do you know what that would mean?"

"Worse than Tunguska."

"Very astute, my boy, very astute! And of course you can't kill me, because you need what I know. So we have a predicament."

Robin pretended to be occupied with putting plastic handcuffs on his prisoners. His mind raced, weighing the odds of a shot to knock the phone out of Picushkin's hand. He had to get far enough to the right to take the shot without hitting Picushkin in a vital area...and he had to be sure he could do it. If he missed, a whole bunch of Russian people would disappear. He made it to a position where the phone was clear of vital areas on Picushkin's body. Robin breathed deeply and slowly. Slow is smooth, smooth is fast.

Picushkin continued to taunt Alex. "Maybe you should call your dear Yosef and get some direction on what you should do, Alex. There is so much and so many lives at risk..."

Robin's hands and arms moved the MP5 smoothly to the shooting position as his trigger squeeze already started. By the time his sight picture settled where he wanted it, the trigger cleanly broke and two rounds smashed into the phone and Picushkin's hand. Robin came off the sights seeing Alex and Picushkin in what seemed like a slow motion ballet of Picushkin trying to catch the phone and Alex thrusting the butt of his MP5 into Picushkin's face. The former general went flying over the settee. Alex jumped over the furniture and quickly put plastic cuffs on Picushkin.

Robin moved to the center of the room so he could watch the other two men and give help to Alex if he needed it. He didn't. Alex rose up from behind the settee dragging Picushkin by the scruff of the neck. He threw the hapless general at the feet of the other two men.

Robin put his hand on his friend's shoulder. "You okay?"

"Yes, thanks to you. I made a stupid move by getting too close to him."

"It's the end result that counts, my friend. I'm going to get Ahmed. I trust you can get the general to tell where the other two bombs are."

"No problem."

"I didn't think so." Robin hurried up the stairs to the bridge. He reached down to open the hatch. "Ahmed, it's me, Rob. I'm opening the hatch."

"Okay, Rob."

Robin opened the hatch and Ahmed crawled out and immediately wrapped his arms around Robin. Robin could feel the boy shaking. "It's all right, Ahmed. We're getting out of here."

Robin went over to the captain's chair and surveyed the controls and the instruments. He turned the engine batteries on, activated the power and began the startup procedure for the diesel. He cranked the engine and the instruments came to life all in the green.

"Ahmed, I hereby designate you the First Mate. Do you know anything about boats?"

"No, sir."

"Well, just do as I say and you'll be fine. I want you to stay here and make sure the dials all stay in the green. If one doesn't and goes into the red, pick up the microphone and call my name. This is the boat's intercom and I should hear you."

"Okay, sir."

"Good boy. I'll be back in a couple of minutes." Robin went back down the stairs and saw Picushkin bent over sobbing.

Alex looked at Robin. "The other two bombs are in the master stateroom in a compartment under the bed."

"Roger." Robin worked his way to the master stateroom, clearing every area along the way and after a brief search, found the compartment and removed the backpack bombs. There were also two large briefcases. Robin opened them and saw they were full of US dollars. He looked deeper into the compartment and found another briefcase. He opened it and an involuntary, "Son of a bitch," fell from his lips. The briefcase contained the Soviet Union's order of battle for a nuclear war with NATO. Robin knew he had a real predicament. He shook his head. *How did I go from being a raggedy-assed street cop to being in possession of this pile of monstrosity?*

He stood up and looked at the heap of backpacks and briefcases, wrestling with the conflicting loyalties inside of him. He rubbed his temples and stood still for a few moments. Then he reached down and picked up the backpacks and carried them back to the main salon. As he entered the salon his eyes met Alex's.

"You found them!"

Robin put the bombs down. "There's more. I'll be right back." He went back and retrieved the two money cases.

"What is in those cases?"

"The general's loot. I've got one more to get." Robin

retrieved the case with the secret documents and brought them into the salon.

"More money?"

"No, we'll talk about this later." Robin pulled Alex closer and whispered, "Get a hold of Yosef and see if you have any ships in the area. We have to get out of here immediately. I'll watch these morons."

Alex gave Robin a puzzled look for a moment and then went into another room. He returned a few minutes later and leaned to Robin's ear. "There is a submarine two hundred and fifty miles away. It has been ordered to come to us."

"I'm going to get this boat underway. I'll be back in a bit." Robin went up the stairs.

"How we doing, First Mate?"

"Everything is green, sir."

"Good." Robin looked over the control panel again. He sat in the captain's chair and engaged the forward gear. The boat started slowly forward. "Okay, Ahmed, keep the bow of the boat headed toward the bay entrance. I have to go forward and stow the anchor. Watch me and when I hold my fist up like this, you ease this lever to the neutral position. Understand?"

"Yes, sir."

Robin hurried forward and looked over the bow, stepping on the switch for the anchor winch and the anchor started rolling in smoothly. He raised his fist and the forward motion of the boat slowed to a stop. The anchor soon came up and locked itself into place at the tip of the bow. Robin hustled back to the bridge and put the engine back in gear, pushing the throttle forward. "Okay, Ahmed, steer for the bay entrance again."

He went to the stern and loosened the motor boat the ISI man came in. When it floated a safe distance from the swim platform, he tied it off. The boat now trailed behind the yacht by a short distance. He surveyed the bay and saw no activity indicating anyone chased after them. He went back to the main salon and pulled Alex aside.

"We're probably going to have company in a while. We need to get the bombs and cases near the stern."

"Why?"

"This yacht isn't built for speed. We can't outrun anything. If we get chased before the sub gets to us we could be screwed."

"I wonder how long before the ISI misses their man?"

"I don't know, but I do know we have things the ISI, the CIA and your government want and not for the same reasons. We've got to get to that sub or things could get ugly."

Alex studied Robin's face. "You're a complicated man, my friend."

"Jesus, you're beginning to sound like my wife! Look, I'm going to move all this stuff to the transom. If we see anything suspicious, we'll put this thing on auto pilot, load up the motor boat and head out to sea and hopefully the sub. You with me?"

"Indeed I am."

CHAPTER FORTY-THREE

Burke Jamison listened carefully to the air as he stood on the tarmac of the Saidu Sharif airport near Mingora, Pakistan. He thought he could hear a faint rumble of a multi-engine aircraft. He turned to Ernie Jackson who stood next to him.

"Hear that?"

"Yeah, they're coming." Ernie turned to First Sergeant Setchinko. "Sergeant, get your men ready."

"Yes, sir."

The rumble grew louder and the team quickly prepared their vehicles to load onto the planes. Then the rumble ceased. Burke strained to listen and was jolted as an AN-12 appeared out of the darkness and screeched onto the runway. One half of the team started their vehicles and raced after the plane.

Burke caught a light out of the corner of his eye, turned and saw headlights coming toward the airport. Then blue lights lit up on top of the car. "Shit!" Burke jumped out of the Land Rover and started running toward the police car.

"I'm behind you, Burke!" Mike Collins yelled.

"Just knock 'em out! Don't kill them!"

"Roger!"

Burke began waving his arms and yelling in Arabic. The police car stopped and Burke went up to the driver's door and started saying he needed help. He saw Mike come out of the shadows behind the passenger. When Mike reached the door post, Burke grabbed the driver around the neck with his right arm and opened the door with his left, dragging the officer out of the car. He punched a power syringe into the officer's neck. The man struggled for a few seconds and then went limp.

"Mike, you okay?"

"Yeah, I'm good here."

Burke looked in the car and heard someone calling frantically on the radio. "We better get out of here. We're going to have company soon."

The two men ran back to the rest of the team. The first AN-12 took off. As it lifted and flew away, Burke could hear sirens in the distance. The second AN-12 came in for a landing.

"Come on, move it!" The team sped to the second plane. It spun around at the end of the runway as its cargo door lowered. Burke saw multiple flashing blue lights coming to the airport. He jumped out of the Land Rover. "Get in the airplane!" he yelled at Mike. Burke knelt down as a police car charged toward the plane. He fired a good burst from his Colt Commando at the engine of the car. The police car braked hard, did a sharp turn and sped away, steam coming from the engine compartment. The other police cars stopped moments later.

Burke heard the plane go to full power. He jumped up and ran for the ramp. A bullet went by his left ear. Mike and Emmett were at the end of the ramp which slowly rose up. Burke slung his carbine and sprinted as fast as he could go and grabbed Mike's waiting hand. He felt the strength of Emmett's huge arms grab and pull him onto the raising ramp. The angle of the ramp reached a point where all three men rolled down it onto the cargo deck in a heap. As the plane lifted off, they looked at each other and broke out in a fit of laughter.

ROBIN SAT at the helm of the Picushkin's yacht. They were ten nautical miles from the bay heading into the Arabian Sea on auto pilot. So far no one came after them that he could see. He used a small camera and began photographing the pages of the Russian order of battle. He got that done and placed the book back into the briefcase. Then he picked up his satellite phone and called Ernie.

"Rob, where are you?"

"Alex and I are fine and we have the goods. Listen to me. You need to stay in Osh or go to Zurich. It's your call. Whatever you do, don't go to a country allied with the US or NATO."

"Why?"

"My guess is you'll be arrested."

"Damn, Rob, what kind of mess did we get ourselves into?"

"We'll be all right. Just don't do anything other than what I just said until I contact you."

There was silence for a moment. "Roger. We should be in Osh soon."

"Good. Hang in there, brother."

"Same to you."

WHEN ROBIN TOLD him to get the team back to Osh earlier that night, Ernie felt sick. On one hand he knew Robin was right. On the other hand he worried about his best friend being alone in a hostile country with a Russian GRU agent as his only ally.

Reluctantly, he had First Sergeant Setchinko contact Osh and arrange the pick-up. Osh came back and told them to make for the airport near Mingora, north of Peshawar on the N95 highway. The pick-up would occur the next night, which meant the team had to lay low for a day. This wasn't a comforting thought for Ernie. The team was being hunted.

The Peshawar Police were all over the place...looking. Fortunately, it appeared they really didn't know what they were looking for. Ernie knew the ISI, on the other hand, did have an idea of what they were looking for and the two helicopters in the air indicated they were indeed looking. Ernie fervently hoped the ISI didn't tell the police much...which is usually the case between intelligence agencies and the police.

Ernie gave the order to exfiltrate to Mingora and the team performed like the true professionals they were. They spaced themselves on N95 and some stopped and acted like tourists every now again. This allowed the team to make sure they weren't being followed. Once in Mingora and the surrounding area, they mingled in the towns or stayed in the countryside until time to gather at the airport that night. Although, the second plane nearly got nabbed, Ernie felt good about how the operation went.

Robin said he had the goods and Ernie and the team captured two Al-Qaeda operatives, in addition to the several they killed in the warehouse. But Ernie worried about Robin. He had learned much from Robin, but he couldn't quite bring himself to be as eclectic about the world as Robin had come to be. Robin usually briefed Ernie on his conversations with

Grassley, but Ernie knew he didn't tell him everything because he was protecting him. Robin made sure if there had to be a sacrificial lamb, it would be him and no one else.

The more he thought about it, the more he decided he would hold a council with the rest of the team when they got to Osh. They just may not lay low. There were a lot of devious minds in the Guardians.

CHAPTER FORTY-FOUR

They had been underway for twelve hours and were one hundred and twenty nautical miles from Karachi, so Robin got more hopeful things were going to work out. They were in international waters, but a turn to port could put them in Indian waters in a couple of hours. He traded places with Alex every so often so Alex could take a break from watching the prisoners and interrogating Picushkin, as only Alex could do. It also gave Robin time to properly dress the ISI agent's wound.

Picushkin talked. He didn't like pain. When Alex asked him about the others involved in this plot, Robin sensed Picushkin held back from telling everything. Robin didn't really care. That was between him and his country.

It was during those breaks Robin was able to move the briefcase with the nuclear order of battle to the bridge and back without Alex noticing. In fact, the only one who knew was Ahmed, but he had seen his mother murdered and he now considered Robin his family... another worry for Robin as he knew he was far from a hero to the US Government at the moment and getting Ahmed into the country could be a problem. *Ease up brother...one step at a time.*

"Ahmed, I'm going down to give Alex a break."

"Yes, sir."

"Ahmed, you've been through a rough time and I know you're confused and hurt, but you need to just call me Rob."

"Yes, sir."

Robin laughed. "Oh, well you'll get the hang of it." He went down the stairs.

"You ready for a break?"

"Yes and we need to feed these guys again."

"Okay, take a break and then we'll get some food."

Suddenly an explosive roar blasted over the yacht. The two men looked at each other.

"Sounds like jet fighters!" Robin yelled as he ran for the rear door. He went out on the deck and caught a flash of sunlight off the canopies of two U.S. Navy FA-18 fighters in a climbing right turn.

"Damn, they found us," he muttered to himself. He knew they wouldn't fly that low and close to a yacht unless they considered it hostile. He ran back into the main salon.

"It's the U.S. Navy, Alex! Find out where that sub is!"

Robin ran up to the bridge and found a terrified Ahmed. "Don't worry Ahmed. They aren't going to attack us." *I hope.* Robin turned on the yacht's radar. He had kept it off to minimize them being seen, but now it didn't matter.

Damn, we got a crowd coming! The radar showed a contact behind them and closing fast. He also had several contacts off the one o'clock position.

"Alex, where the hell is the submarine!"

Alex, poked his head through the stair hatch. "They are close, Robin. What are we going to do?"

"We're going to try to create a Mexican stand-off."

"Look, sir! There's a submarine!" Ahmed exclaimed.

Robin heard a familiar noise and looked to the right. "Yeah, and here comes two Sea Stallion helicopters, probably loaded with Marines." He reduced the throttle as the submarine came closer.

"Alex, get Picushkin and all the cases on the sub! Just leave me one of the money cases."

Alex poked his head up again. "What about the other two prisoners?"

"Leave them for me. I need the bargaining chips."

Alex's head disappeared, but then popped up again. "Robin!" Robin turned and met Alex's eyes. "Пожизненные братья!"

"Brothers for life, Alex. Now get your ass outta here."

Another set of jet fighters roared over the yacht, but this time they were Indian Mig 29s.

Damn, we got a regular international convention!

The Navy jets blasted for higher altitude. The Indian Migs stayed at low altitude and circled the spectacle building around the yacht, submarine, Pakistani destroyer and the US Marine helicopters. The submarine crew tied the yacht to the sub. Robin put the boat in neutral, grabbed Ahmed and took him down to the rear deck.

"Stay here, Ahmed!"

Robin went into the main salon and moved the two prisoners to the rear deck. When he came back out, Robin saw the Russian submarine crew pointing weapons at the US Marine helicopters and the Marines pointing weapons at the Russians. *Jesus, this is insane!* He tried Grassley's number again and got the same message saying the number was no longer operational. Then he dialed Ernie.

"Rob! Are you okay?"

"I'm on the deck of Picushkin's yacht with four countries surrounding me. Have you heard from Grassley?"

"Rob, Jordan Yates and Bill were fired. They're no longer with the CIA."

The words stung Robin. He knew now the situation neared a deadly and catastrophic stage. "Ernie, if this doesn't work out, tell Karen and the kids I love them." Robin pushed the end button.

ADMIRAL JAMES ELLISON listened to the conversation between the president, the Chairman of the Joint Chiefs and the Director of the CIA on his secure satellite connection. He waited for orders. He relayed to the group a standoff was in progress around the yacht. From the conversation, he could tell they were really pissed off at this guy Marlette.

"Admiral Ellison, this is the president. You are ordered to terminate Robin Marlette with prejudice."

CHAPTER FORTY-FIVE

Marine Sgt. Enos Barclay couldn't believe what he heard over his headset.

"Wolfhound One, you have a green light on target one."

He looked over at his spotter, Sgt. Jeff Smiley. "Did I hear that right?"

"They're saying to take him out, Eno."

"Fuck me! Didn't they say that guy Marlette was an American citizen?"

"Eno, they're not asking for our opinion. It's an order. We gotta take him out!"

Sgt. Barclay felt a tight knot building in his stomach. *This isn't what I signed up to do as a Marine sniper. I'm supposed to be taking out the commies and terrorists!*

He shook his head to clear his mind and took several deep breaths. He made slight adjustments to his body position and settled his head behind the scope on his Barrett .50 caliber rifle. He began melding his mind to the rhythms of the yacht and the helicopter. He vaguely heard Sgt. Smiley tell the pilot to steady the chopper for a shot. Barclay acquired Robin in the crosshairs. Smiley gave him the final dope...range, wind, temperature. Barclay made two scope adjustments and took a deep breath and then slowly let it out while starting the squeeze on the trigger. He had the rhythm synced and the target's head in the crosshairs. Then the target turned and looked directly at him.

ALEX SAW the sniper in the helicopter focus on Robin and realized the he was preparing for a shot. He yelled at Robin and pointed to the helicopter and then screamed to the Captain of the submarine to open fire on the Americans. He saw Robin look towards the chopper.

JAMES CHAPPLE, the new Director of the CIA frantically waved at the president as he talked to someone on the phone.

"Stop the shot! Stop the shot!"

The president didn't understand what the director was trying to say. "What are you talking about?"

"Tell them not to kill Marlette!"

ERNIE WAS furious and screamed into the phone to the Director of the CIA.

"If you sons of bitches have killed Robin, we will bring you down! All I have to do is push a button and everything we know and have done will go to every major newspaper and media outlet in the world!"

"I'm trying to stop it, I'm trying!"

"Trying isn't good enough!"

ALEX GLARED AT THE CAPTAIN, Dimitry Anglov.

"Shoot down the helicopters!"

"I am not going to risk my men and this submarine over one American spy," the captain calmly replied.

"That man saved millions of Russian lives and helped me recover these nuclear weapons! Shoot down the helicopters!"

"I'm sorry. I'm not going to give such an order and you will not shoot either."

ADMIRAL ELLISON overheard the commotion in the White House situation room. He didn't need to be told what to do. He repeated his order.

"Do not shoot Marlette! Did you get my order?!"

Silence was his answer.

CONFUSION REIGNED on the Marine helicopter. The shot had gone off. The pilot screamed into the intercom. The Marine Captain yelled over the tactical net. Sgt. Barclay held his head over the edge of the helicopter floor and puked over the side. He felt a hand on his shoulder.

"You okay, Eno?" Sgt. Smiley asked.

"F-f-fuck no, I'm not okay! I just killed someone who shouldn't have been killed!" Tears were streaming down Barclay's face.

"Hate to break the news to you sport, but you missed Marlette."

"What?!"

"You missed Marlette and shot the Asian guy. That son of

a bitch jumped Marlette and knocked him down just at the right time and you hit him instead of Marlette...and you tore a big hunk out of the gunwale of the boat and hit the sub, too, but it doesn't look like it did any damage to the sub."

THE INSTANT ROBIN saw the sniper, he was slammed to the deck from the back. He thought he had been shot at first, but realizing he wasn't hit, he looked over and saw the Chinese agent's body lying on the deck with everything above the chest missing. Ahmed was on his knees screaming. Robin grabbed Ahmed and jumped through the door into the weather room and went prone next to the wall. He pulled Ahmed close to him and felt the boy trembling. He kept his MP5 trained on the ISI man. A large hole was in the gunwale near where he last stood and the remains of the Korean's head and shoulders were sprayed all over the deck. Anger surged through him. He considered crawling to the door and emptying a magazine at the chopper, when he heard the noise of the helicopters fading. His satellite phone beeped.

"Hello."

"Colonel Marlette?"

"This is Robin Marlette, but judging by the last few seconds, I don't think I'm a colonel anymore, but I am one hundred percent pissed off! Just who in the hell thinks I need to die! Have you idiots gone fucking nuts?!"

"This is Admiral Ellison. I command Task Force Sea Strike One and now I'm finally in full control of this operation. I apologize for the attempt to kill you. It's not something I would've recommended. Can we discuss this situation?"

"You picked a hell of time to tell me you want to talk, Admiral. Sixty seconds ago would have worked a lot better!"

"Bear with me here, Colonel. Things have not been going

the way I wanted it. You have my word on that, but as I said, I have full control now. I'd like to talk man to man about this."

Robin winced at these words. He'd heard them before. "What's your combat experience, Admiral?"

There was a pause. "Well, I fought in Vietnam in the Mobile Riverine Force on the Mekong Delta. I commanded a patrol boat as a junior officer and a lieutenant. From there I went into the SEALs and saw action in several places, including Panama and Grenada. Then I was assigned as the executive officer to a Marine Expeditionary Unit task force and now I command one."

"When you were in the Riverine Force, did you know Bud Hallen?"

"Damn sure did! He served on my second boat! How do you know Bud?"

"He's on the Arizona Highway Patrol. I used to work with him. He used to tell me about his boat commander. He spoke highly of you."

"Well I'll be damned. I'd like to see that man again."

"I'm sure he'd like to see you too, sir." Robin took several deep breaths. "Okay, I'll listen."

There were several minutes of silence. "Well, Colonel, let's start with you telling me what's going on."

Robin took another deep breath. "Admiral, we're going to get along a lot better if you just tell the FBI negotiator to go home. If we can't talk as fellow warriors, then this conversation is going nowhere."

Another period of silence went by. "Okay, Colonel, he's gone."

"Call me Robin, Admiral. Like I said, I don't think the colonel title is valid anymore."

"Okay, Robin, let's start over. As I understand it, you are in possession of items a lot of people want, including nuclear weapons. Unfortunately, no one has really explained to me what they are and who owns them."

"Myself and Colonel Alexander Prokenzi from the GRU, we're in possession of two Russian tactical nukes stolen from the Soviets by a renegade general named Picushkin. We stopped him from delivering them to the Al-Qaeda terrorist group. We also seized fifty million dollars in cash. Alex has taken the two nukes and twenty-five million dollars onto the sub along with General Picushkin. I have the other twenty five million."

"I was told there were other top secret documents on the yacht."

"We'll have to talk about that if and when we meet. I also have a wounded Pakistani ISI agent in custody with me. I did have a Chinese Intelligence agent in custody also, but you guys just killed him. Lastly, I have a young Pakistani boy who was made an orphan during this whole mess and who you guys have managed to scare shitless. That's the score so far."

"You stopped the delivery of nukes to Al-Qaeda?!"

"My team and Alex's Spetsnaz team did. Then Alex and I recovered two more on this yacht. Call the Russian sub and ask for Colonel Prokenzi. He'll verify what I just told you."

"Can you standby for a few?" Robin's phone was beeping an incoming call from Ernie.

"Well, I was planning to drop a line in the water and see what I could catch, but I'll wait."

The Admiral laughed. "Okay, Robin. I'll get right back with you."

"Yes, sir."

Robin switched calls.

"Hey, Ernie, are you guys all right?"

"Us?! Did they try to kill you?"

"Indeed they did."

"That does it. I'm going to the media."

"Hold on, ol' buddy. Things have calmed down. Just hang loose until I get back to you."

"Are you sure?"

"I'm sure."

"Okay, if you say so Rob, but personally I think we should blast everything to the media."

"Don't do anything yet."

Robin ended the call. He looked at Ahmed, who still trembled. "Ahmed, it's going to be all right. I'll take care of you. Do you have any family in Pakistan now?"

"I have an uncle, but he is mean. He beats my aunt and my cousins."

"What about grandparents?"

"They died."

"Okay, one way or the other I will make sure you and your brother are going to be safe."

Ahmed hugged Robin tight. "I want to go home with you!"

"I'd like that myself, Ahmed, I just don't know if I can swing it, but we'll give it the ol' college try."

The phone beeped.

"Hello."

"Robin, I just talked to Colonel Prokenzi and he verified everything you told me. I can't tell you how upset I am this situation got so far out of hand and I will tell the president he needs to fire whoever recommended you be targeted."

"Okay, Admiral. Where do we go from here."

"Can we give the ISI agent back to the Pakistanis?"

"Admiral, this asshole is the main contact with Al-Qaeda for the ISI. He is an intelligence bonanza, if we can hang on to him."

"As much as I would like to keep him, the Paks are raising hell and threatening to sever ties with us if we don't give him back."

"Of course they are. They don't want us to know what they've been up to."

"Robin, I have to give him back."

Robin took a deep breath and shook his head. "You're running the show, Admiral."

"Good. They're sending a boat over now. The choppers are coming back, but this time it's to protect you."

"I can take care of myself, thank you."

"Work with me, Robin."

Robin weighed his options...there weren't many. "All right, Admiral. I'm putting a lot of faith in you."

"I know, Robin. I know."

A few minutes later the helicopters came back as a tender from the Pakistani destroyer that came alongside the yacht. Four unarmed sailors came aboard, put the ISI agent on a stretcher and took him off the yacht. Ahmed started trembling more and held tightly to Robin.

"Robin are you there?"

"I'm here, Admiral."

"Are you ready to be picked up?"

"The boy and I are ready."

"The Russians say they'll take the boy. They have his brother at Osh."

Alex came over the gunwale from the sub. Robin stood up with Ahmed. Alex gave Robin his usual bear hug.

"I thought they were going to kill you. I demanded the submarine captain shoot down the helicopters, but he refused."

"Well, that just means he's a lot smarter than both of us. Why do you want Ahmed?"

Alex grinned. "My Sergeant Major must retire because of his age. He has no family. He wants to adopt both boys and teach them what he knows."

"Damn, that could be one hell of an education!"

Robin put his hands on Ahmed's shoulders and translated what Alex just said. Ahmed began to cry.

"I want to go with you!"

"Ahmed, I'll find a way to make sure we're not far apart. It's a promise. Right now, I need you to go with Alex."

Alex knelt down and faced Ahmed. "We will take good care of you and your brother, Ahmed. Come with me and we'll get a good dinner and some ice cream and in a few hours you will be with your brother."

Ahmed looked at both men. He turned to Robin and hugged him. Alex held out his hand and Ahmed took it. Robin watched as the giant of a man gently took Ahmed away. As they were walking to the conning tower of the sub, Alex turned and saluted Robin. He saluted back. He ducked into the salon and retrieved his gear and the other briefcase with the money and went back out on the deck. One of the helicopters lowered a penetrator seat and Robin climbed in. Moments later he was on his way to Admiral Ellison with an uneasy stomach.

CHAPTER FORTY-SIX

Robin lay on the bunk in the stateroom the Admiral assigned him. When he arrived on the carrier, Admiral Ellison met him on the flight deck and took him to his stateroom. There Robin gave him a complete debriefing on all the missions that began three months before. When he finished, Admiral Ellison was furious...at Washington. When he got around to asking Robin about the Russian battle plans for conflict with NATO, the discussion became a little tense.

"Yes, Admiral, the plans were on the boat."

"Where are they?"

"I'm a little curious, sir. How did you know the plans were on the yacht?"

The Admiral shifted uncomfortably in his seat and drew a deep breath. "NATO made a deal with Picushkin to buy the plans."

Robin was stunned, angry and confused all at once. "Wait a minute, then why did the CIA give us the equipment to take down Picushkin?"

"Compartmentalization. The CIA didn't know until after

you took off with the yacht…something they didn't expect you to do. They expected you to take Picushkin to the airport and be picked up by your plane. The NATO op was being run by MI6 and Germany's BND. When they learned you and your friend had stolen the yacht and Picushkin, they went ballistic and started looking for blood. Apparently the CIA Director agreed."

"What a mess."

"I agree, but I need to know what happened to the plans."

"Alex took them. After all, they belonged to the Soviet Union."

Ellison let out an exasperated breath. "NATO is really going to be pissed."

"Really?! What's that bunch of little ol' ladies going to do? They are so politically correct, they're worthless. It serves them right for playing bullshit games."

Ellison broke out laughing. "Well, you're probably right."

"Look Admiral, isn't it the accepted philosophy the cold war stays cold because of the balance of military power?"

"Yes, of course."

"Well, it seems to me if NATO had bought those plans from Picushkin, the balance of power would be drastically altered and that wouldn't be a good thing."

Ellison looked at Robin for a moment. "I'm beginning to think a lot of people underestimate you. I promise I will never make that mistake."

Robin smiled as he remembered the admiral's comment, but at this very moment he was starving. During the debriefing with the admiral, Robin only asked for coffee. He didn't dare leave his stateroom. He figured he was in enough shit. He heard a knock at his door. He got up and answered it. A young Marine sergeant stood at attention before him. The man looked nervous and ill.

"What's up, Sergeant?"

"Sir, Sergeant Enos Barclay requesting permission to speak with you, sir."

"Come on in, Sergeant."

Robin waved the Marine in and sat on his bunk. "Have a seat at the desk."

Barclay stood at attention. "Sir, I think it's best for me to remain formal."

"Sergeant, I've had one hell of a day and formality really isn't on my list of things I need. Will you please sit down?"

Barclay seemed to deflate and he almost collapsed into the chair.

"Are you all right, Barclay?"

"No, sir, I'm not. I came here to apologize, sir." Barclay took a deep breath. "I'm the sniper who tried to kill you today." Tears started streaming down the Marine's face and he blurted, "In my heart I knew it was a bad order, sir, but I went ahead and took the shot anyway. I'm so ashamed."

Robin was taken aback and didn't know what to say to Barclay.

The Marine took a deep breath. "I've told my lieutenant I'm quitting the Marines and I'm here to ask you to forgive me, sir."

Many thoughts went through Robin's head before he could formulate a reply. "What do your friends call you, Barclay."

"They call me Eno, sir."

"Well, Eno you can call me, Rob. Were you given a direct order?"

"Yes, sir and I did question the order, but I was told they didn't want my opinion."

Robin chuckled. "I'm sure that's the case. Well, here's the deal, Eno. Apparently, someone advised the president I was a proven traitor. I don't know exactly who just yet, but that's the scoop I've received so far. Would you have a problem shooting a traitor?"

"If they're an American citizen, I think they should be convicted in court before we decide they're a traitor."

"I like your thinking, but what if the traitor possessed nuclear weapons and intended to use them against innocent people?"

"If that were the case, I believe I would have to shoot."

"I do too. That's what the president was told. It's not true, but that's what the president thought he was acting on."

Barclay looked at Robin. "Still, I have a problem shooting American citizens. I signed on to shoot communists and terrorists."

"Think about this. Police officers kill American citizens all the time, in justified shootings. Why should you be any different? It's been my experience, that if you're going to be a shooter on behalf of the government, you can't think in black and white. The world is too complicated and you have good sensibilities. I wouldn't quit the Marines, if I were you."

Barclay looked at the floor in thought.

"And one more thing, Eno. Always look at the end result. You said you signed on to kill communists and terrorists, right?"

Barclay nodded his head.

"Well, the guy you whacked was a Chinese intelligence agent working with Al-Qaeda terrorists and let's not forget he tried to kill little ol' me, by the way. So, you actually saved my life and killed a guy who was a communist and a terrorist. The way you got there may not be pretty, but it sounds like a good day's work to me."

Barclay looked up and shook his head smiling. "I came here thinking you would hate me and instead you're making me feel a whole lot better."

"Well, I do hate you, Eno, but I'll stop hating you if you

can get me some place where I can get something to eat. I'm starving!"

Both men laughed. "Can I do that? Will we get into trouble?"

Robin shrugged his shoulders. "I'm not under arrest and no one told me I couldn't leave my stateroom, I just didn't think I should be roaming around without an escort."

Barclay stood up. "Well, then let's go!"

"Good, but let's stop in to see your lieutenant first and tell him you've changed your mind."

"Okay, Rob. Thank you."

ADMIRAL ELLISON WROTE a full report of his interview with Robin and sent it directly to the White House. An hour later he received a coded message from the president relating several high ranking individuals in the CIA and the White House staff were fired, including James Chapple. The admiral learned Jordan Yates had been appointed the new Director of the CIA and a William Grassley was named the new Director for Operations. The president asked the admiral to give a message to Robin. A message the admiral was happy to give.

He went down to Robin's stateroom and when he couldn't find him the admiral found out Robin was in the galley with a group of Marines. As he neared the galley, the admiral heard loud laughter, which abruptly stopped as he entered the door. All the Marines stood at attention as did Robin.

"Why is it every time I show up the fun stops? Please be at ease gentlemen."

"Care to join us for a cup of coffee, Admiral?" Robin asked.

"Actually, I think I'll see if I can get a hamburger."

Sgt. Smiley turned to a very young private. "Cameron, get

the admiral a hamburger. Want some fries with that Admiral?"

"I can get my own food, Sergeant, but thank you."

Smiley indicated to Cameron to still get the hamburger. "Ah, sir, we don't get to talk to you that often and well, sir...we've had worse admirals. Just consider it a token of our appreciation."

Admiral Ellison smiled. "Okay, that would be great, Sergeant." He sat next to Robin. "So Robin, have the Marines been telling tales of their combat prowess?"

"Actually, sir," Barclay said, "Robin has been telling us cop stories."

The Admiral gave Robin a surprised look.

"My prior life, sir."

"Oh yeah, you did mention you worked with Bud Hallen on the highway patrol."

Robin shrugged. "Seems like a long time ago."

The master chief of the galley delivered the Admiral's hamburger and stood by, a little nervous, to see the Admiral's reaction. The chief left with a smile on his face when the Admiral said, "Damn good burger, Chief."

As the admiral ate his burger, Robin resumed answering questions about police work. Several of the Marines said they intended to apply for a law enforcement job when they left the military and Robin gave them some advice. Then a Marine asked Robin about what he did now. The admiral interrupted.

"Gentlemen, as you can imagine, the colonel, cannot discuss his current assignment. What he does now for a living is even beyond my security clearance."

Silence descended upon the group. Then Robin spoke up. "Hell, guys, are you going to let rank destroy a blooming friendship?" The group broke out in laughter.

The admiral stood up. "Gentlemen, I have sincerely

enjoyed your company, a welcome break for me. Unfortunately, I must steal the colonel from you. We have some important matters to discuss."

Robin stood up and shook hands with the Marines. The one who asked about his current assignment took his hand and looked him in the eye. "If you need a good man, sir, I'd like a shot at your unit."

"What's your specialty, Marine?"

"Sneak and peek," a voice said from the group. The others laughed.

"That's a good specialty in my kind of work, Marine." Robin looked at his name tag. "I'll keep you in mind."

"Thank you, sir."

WHEN THEY WERE in the admiral's stateroom, he reached into a cabinet and produced a bottle of Jack Daniels Tennessee Whiskey. "I don't know about you, but I could use a drink after today."

"Amen, Admiral. I came real close to dying today."

The admiral poured two fingers of whiskey in the glasses. He held up his glass to toast. "I salute an American hero."

Robin was momentarily confused. "Are you referring to me, Admiral?"

"Yes, I am, Robin. What you did these last couple of days was nothing short of heroic."

Robin took a sip of his whiskey. "I'm no hero, Admiral. Certainly, not an American hero. We were once cops who tried not to hurt anyone, including suspects. Now we kill just to survive and it has reached the point where killing has become a mere afterthought. I've killed sleeping men, men who didn't know I was near them and men who were simply doing an assigned task at a particular moment. They were all involved in acts threatening innocent people, but I gave them no warning...no chance to surrender. I just killed them." Robin's eyes met the admiral's. "My men and I have become dark and dangerous shadows moving through the night grappling with a squirming underworld. I've become unsure of just what and who the enemy really is...I just react to threats to the innocent people on this earth."

The admiral looked at his glass. "We did the same in SEALs. I've killed in the same way and you're right, we can't consider ourselves heroes for those kinds of acts. But in a very short period of time, your team has prevented large scale violent acts and probably prevented a nuclear war. At the very least, stopping Picushkin saved hundreds of thousands, if not millions of lives. That makes you a hero in anybody's book...it's just no one will know, except a few. I'm lucky enough to be one of those few. I salute you." The admiral raised his glass again.

Robin smiled and touched the admiral's glass with his. "Thank you, Admiral."

"Now, the president has asked me to convey to you his deepest apologies and he wants you to know he was told lies."

"But why? Who would do that?"

"Apparently, there was a rift in the CIA that reached to the White House staff. The new CIA Director felt threatened by Jordan Yates and William Grassley and I guess, especially about the existence of your team. The director had close supporters on the White House staff. They concocted the story that your team are rogue traitors and that Yates and Grassley couldn't control you."

Robin chuckled. "Well, to be honest Admiral, there's a grain of truth in the idea they couldn't control us. The rest is bullshit."

It was the admiral's turn to laugh. "Yes, you were described to me as an, 'independent son of a bitch'."

"Well, I'm probably guilty as charged."

"I have no doubt. The president also wanted me to tell you your status has not changed in any way. Suffice it to say your team is still activated...and according to the president, desperately needed."

"I hope you won't be offended if I take all this with a grain of salt."

"Not in the least. I would too, if I were you."

The two men touched their glasses again and finished their whiskey. "If you don't mind, sir, all this is catching up with me and I'm ready to drop."

"I understand."

CHAPTER FORTY-SEVEN

Robin sat next to Rick as Fatboy winged its way back to the United States and home. He was played out. Admiral Ellison authorized a flight for Robin to fly to Mumbai International Airport in India where Fatboy picked him up. Then they immediately flew to Taipei to pick up Rick, Lucy and Maria. Maria sedated Rick for the move and now Robin sat patiently waiting for Rick to regain consciousness, his mind replaying the last month in a constant stream of chaotic images and recalled conversations. All of this was overlaid by a desperate longing for Karen, his children and the peace of their home.

Ernie came into the cabin and sat down.

"How you feeling, Rob? You've been pretty quiet since we picked you up."

Robin drew a tried breath. "I'm still trying to process everything that's happened in the last month. It all seems like a crazy, confused dream."

"Well it wasn't a dream, but it sure as hell was crazy and confused!"

A groggy voice interrupted them. "Don't you assholes have better things to do than keep me awake?"

Robin stood up and stepped next to Rick. "How are things, Rick?"

"Not worth a damn, Rob. I heard you guys talking. I guess I missed a lot."

"We just decided to get into a bunch of shit to see if we could do it without you."

"Oh, well I guess you did then."

"No, we learned we need you and Mark on every op. Otherwise things get just a little bit too hairy!"

"Why did you say Mark? Is he all right?"

"He got hurt pretty bad, but he's recovering. He's like you. He'll be okay, but it's going to take a while. Everyone else is okay."

"Except for you, Rob," Ernie interjected.

"Oh, I'm doing fine, Ernie. Cut the shit."

"Maria says you need rest and you need to have your injuries tended to. The injury to your back is getting infected."

"Jesus, Mary and Joseph, you guys must have had a rough time!"

"You got it the worst, Rick. Other than Mark, the rest of us are just fine."

Ernie rolled his eyes and gave Rick a knowing look.

"How did you get shot up so badly?" Robin asked Rick.

Rick started to laugh, but it turned into a cough. "I got to the door of the engine room and came face to face with a bad guy with an AK-47. I knew Emmett and Doug were concentrating on setting their charges and weren't paying attention to the engine room. So, I couldn't let the bad guy get through the door. He had to reach for his gun and I figured I could draw and nail him before he could get his gun up...and I did! I just didn't count on his reflexes pulling the trigger. As he fell back, the damn gun cranked full auto and came right at me. That's all I remember until the hospital in Taipei." Rick took a deep breath. "I'm feeling pretty sleepy, Rob."

"Go back to sleep, Rick. I just wanted to say hi to you."

"Thanks, Rob. Make sure Lucy's okay will you?"

"She's doing fine. Maria gave her something to help her sleep and she's doing just that. You do the same."

Rick nodded and closed his eyes. Robin and Ernie walked out of the cabin. "By the way, Ernie, thanks for throwing shit into the CIA's game with the threat to go public. You probably saved my life."

Ernie put his arm around Robin's shoulders. "If I let anything happen to you, a whole lot of Marlettes and Jacksons would kick my ass!"

"It's pretty interesting that we started out as friends and now we're family."

"Yes it is, Rob and a growing family at that. I'm pretty damn proud of that fact."

"Me too, Ernie. Me too."

KAREN, Laurie and Eddie all held tightly to Robin at the front door of their home. It was a tearful reunion. Robin hurt inside for all the worry and fear he'd caused his family. Karen recovered quickly, however, and didn't let the family dwell on their worries and fears. She immediately put Robin to work on the barbeque and made sure he had a glass of wine in his hand.

As Robin looked out over the Strait of Juan de Fuca, he felt a calming effect seeing the setting sun casting an orange and golden glow over a peaceful sea. The weather was cooling and Robin thought how he hoped the world was cooling also. He wanted to be home.

Eddie came out on the deck and Robin started to pay attention to the salmon on the grill.

"Hey, Dad, I need to tell you something."

"Sure, son, what's up?"

"I got suspended from school two days ago."

Robin couldn't believe what he just heard. "You... suspended from school! Eddie, how did that happen?"

"I got into a fight."

"Over what?"

"There's a girl at school whose...well, she's kinda slow and she's in special ed classes. I saw some guys making fun of her, so I went over there and told the jerks to cut it out. They just started mouthing off and I was moving the girl away from them, when the main guy shoved me from behind." Eddie took a breath at this point.

"And...?"

"Well, I was already mad, so I turned around and sort of hit him."

"Explain 'sort of hit him'."

"I knocked him on his butt."

"That's it? That's what you got suspended for?"

"Well, not exactly. After I hit that guy, his buddies jumped us..."

"Whoa, who's 'us'?"

"Ilya and me."

Robin looked at his son. "Did Ilya get suspended too?"

"Yeah."

"Wonderful. Go ahead."

"Well, Ilya and I took them all on."

"How many?"

"Six, including the first guy I hit."

"Did you win?"

"Yeah, none of them really knew how to fight and they gave up pretty fast."

"What have I told you about getting into fights?"

"Never to start one, but always finish the ones I do get into."

"Was the shove hard enough to warrant the punch?"

Eddie looked down. "No, not really. I was just mad."

Robin put his arm around Eddie's shoulders. "I'm proud of you for sticking up for the girl. Next time wait until the other guy tries to hit you or hurt you before you kick his ass."

Eddie smiled. "Yes, sir."

"And don't tell your mother this, I'm also proud you won the fight. I doubt if they will be bothering you again."

Eddie laughed.

"What's so funny?"

"Mom said the same thing, only she said not to tell you!"

LATER IN THE EVENING, Robin and Karen were sitting in the reading alcove in their bedroom. Karen looked up from her book.

"I met with the principal about Eddie."

"How'd that go?"

"I agree with part of what he said about not tolerating brawls on campus, but he seemed more concerned about that than the harassment of the poor girl."

"That's not right."

"No it isn't. He went on a rant about violence and when I asked about the girl, he said they try to prevent harassment, but they can't be everywhere."

"Are you serious?"

"Of course, I'm serious. The whole conversation is still bothering me. They suspended the other boys for fighting too, but no one was disciplined for the harassment."

"We need to talk to the superintendent."

"I'm doing something better. I'm going to run for the school board."

Robin looked at Karen. "My wife is becoming a politician?!"

"Yes, I am. The school board makes policy and there needs to be some policy changes in this district."

"Well, I guess we better get our election machine up and running! Who is going to be your campaign manager?"

"Laurie, of course. Do you know anyone more organized than our daughter?"

"No I don't. Good choice."

Karen got up and sat on Robin's lap. "Are you going to stop loving me if I become a politician?"

Robin put his arm under her legs and stood up cradling her in his arms, carried Karen to their bed and laid her down. "I will never stop loving you. I love you more today than I did yesterday and I didn't think I could love anyone as much as I loved you then...and I will never stop wanting you." Robin turned out the lights and laid down next to Karen.

"Rob, I'm scared to death."

Robin didn't reply. He just put his arms around his wife.

"Are we going to get through this? Are you going to make it out the other side alive?"

"What do you want me to say? What we do is dangerous... necessary, but dangerous. All we can do is the best we can."

"That's not a damn bit reassuring, Robin Marlette."

"All we can do is follow one of the truest mottos of all time."

"What's that?"

"One day at a time."

Silence followed and they fell asleep in their clothes.

CHAPTER FORTY-EIGHT

Karen curled up against Robin as they lay in front of their fireplace. Rain beat against the windows and the wind surged across the Strait of Juan de Fuca with a dull roar in the darkness. The grandfather clock chimed midnight. She pulled herself closer to him as if she wanted to meld her body with his.

"It's so good to have you home. I can't believe it's been three months without you going anywhere."

"It's very nice, honey, especially being with you. I'm beginning to feel myself unwind."

"I'm enjoying not worrying about you."

"I know you worry, but you shouldn't."

Karen sat up. "I shouldn't?! You were nearly killed several times in these last operations. Our own country tried to kill you! Mark and Rick were seriously wounded. How can I not worry?!"

"It's just that worrying doesn't do any good. There's no getting out of this anytime soon. We know what we're doing and we do it well. That's about as good as it gets."

Karen laid her head back on Robin's chest. "It's as good as

it gets as long as politicians don't interfere and you know they will."

"Probably, but at least this president learned a good lesson."

"I'm not sure any politician learns lessons unless the lessons get them reelected."

"Why don't we talk about us and how wonderful it is to be married to the person you truly love."

"Is that a signal you want me to be quiet?"

"No, it's a signal we have a nice fire in a nice home on a stormy night and I'm with the most beautiful woman in the world. I want to enjoy it."

Karen laid her head back down. "I saw Rick and Mark walking yesterday. They seem to have developed a close bond."

"Yeah, they've really been good for each other. So far Maria says they'll fully recover, which is a miracle, if you think about it."

"Speaking of miracles, how is Tim doing?"

"It didn't take long for him to get things under control. Pat was right. The man probably is a genius. The only problem we have left is hiring dock workers."

"Can't you hire disabled cops and soldiers?"

"Not for that kind of work. There's a lot of heavy lifting and other physical work."

"Oh, yeah, I see what you mean."

"Well, I set Burke and Rocky to work on the problem. They'll get it solved."

Karen snuggled closer. "I love you, Robin."

"I love you, honey."

They became quiet listening to the fire crackle against the stormy night and enjoying the closeness of each other.

ROBIN AND BILL GRASSLEY sat on the deck of Robin's boat at the Cap Sante Marina in Anacortes. The conversation was a rambling one with Robin wondering why Bill had come to visit.

"Bill, do you want to tell me why you're really here?"

"Two things. First I've waited patiently for you to come clean about the Russian battle plans."

"What about them?"

"I know what you told Admiral Ellison, but I also know you. I don't believe for a minute you didn't look at those plans."

"I never said I didn't."

"True, but you never said you did."

"I don't think it matters anyway."

"Why? Those plans could mean the difference between victory or defeat if war broke out."

"I doubt it. I think the Russians would've changed the plans just to be safe."

"You don't know that for sure."

Robin looked at Bill. "What would you do?"

"Change the plans, of course."

"Thanks for making my point."

Minutes of silence passed between the two men. "Okay, Bill, let's say hypothetically, I had the plans memorized or I even took notes. I still believe in the balance of power, but if it looked like the Russians were going to launch a war, I'd give them to you...hypothetically speaking."

"Of course...hypothetically." Bill smiled at Robin.

"What's the second reason?"

Bill looked at his watch and then at the marina entrance. "Ah, I think the second reason is just now coming into the marina."

Robin looked over and saw a Nordhaven trawler coasting in. He watched, a little confused, until it hit him...Picushkin's yacht! A large man came out of the bridge and saluted. Robin recognized Alex and jumped up.

"Well, I'll be damned."

The yacht headed for one of the empty berths where a fishing boat used to moor. Robin hurried over to the slip in time to catch a line from Alex.

Alex's deep voice boomed. "Good afternoon, my brother!"

"It's very good to see you, brother!"

Ahmed came running to the bow. "Robin!"

"Hello, Ahmed." Ahmed's brother came out behind Ahmed and waved. Robin waved back. When the boat docked and the engines turned off, First Sergeant Setchinko came out of the bridge. Robin and Bill boarded the yacht at midship.

Robin and Alex hugged each other and then Ahmed embraced Robin tightly. He rubbed Ahmed's head.

"How are you doing, my young friend?"

Ahmed's face beamed. "I'm doing very well and even better now we are here with you."

"That's good to hear." Robin reached over and shook the brother's hand. Setchinko walked up and warmly greeted him.

Bill Grassley spoke up. "Let's go into the salon and talk."

When everyone was seated, Bill spoke. "Rob, as you know the Soviet Union is collapsing. The country is broke. Many government employees aren't getting paid...no retired government employees are getting paid."

Robin looked at the First Sergeant. "Does that include you?"

"Da."

Bill continued. "Yosef contacted me and asked me if I could get First Sergeant Setchinko and the boys into America. The boys have gone through hell and now First Sergeant

Setchinko has no way to support them. I thought you might have a position for the First Sergeant."

"Are the immigration issues resolved?"

"Yes, like we've done before."

Robin stood up. "First Sergeant, will you please come with me?"

Bill gave Robin a questioning look.

"Job interview."

Bill shrugged his shoulders.

Robin and Setchinko walked out onto the deck and leaned over the rail. "Sergeant, I never learned your name."

"My name is Nikolaj Setchinko, but I am called Nikky."

"Pleased to meet you, Nikky. How do you feel about this?"

"I really have just been going along with the tide. I have no money and there is no work in Russia, especially for a used up soldier. I have to take care of my boys."

"You're well aware of what our company does. How does that sit with you?"

Nikky shrugged. "You impressed me when you helped Russia stop Picushkin. You did not worry about ideology, you just wanted to stop a greedy madman." Nikky turned to Robin. "We are not much different, you and I. Yes, I was a soldier for my homeland for many years and I was a good soldier. But I never hurt innocent people, no matter where they lived or what country they came from. As Spetsnaz I was ruthless with our enemies...but only enemies, not innocents."

"Do you trust me?"

"Alex says you are brothers and he would give his life for you. There is no higher recommendation of your character. Yes, I trust you."

"Okay, you're hired."

"What will you have me do?"

"Well, besides covert ops, what do you want to do?"

"You mean I can still do soldier work?"

"Nikky, in our organization, there is no such thing as a used up soldier."

Setchinko broke out in a grin.

"But we don't do ops all of the time, what do you want to do during our down times?"

"Well, I like your new boat. The boys and I can take care of it."

"What boat? You mean this one?"

"Yes, it is a gift from the Russian government to you."

"We'd better talk to Bill and Alex."

The men went back into the salon. "Okay, what's up with the boat?" Robin asked.

Alex stood up and put his hands on Robin's shoulders. "It's yours, if you want it, Robin. A gift to you from our country for saving so many Russian lives."

"I don't need any gift, Alex. I wouldn't have been able to live with myself if we hadn't stopped the idiot from detonating that bomb." Robin looked over at Nikky who had an expectant look on this face. "I will accept it as a symbol of what our two countries can do when we work together."

Alex grinned broadly. "That is a fitting sentiment, my brother."

Robin turned to Nikky. "Captain, you may take control of your ship and assign your crew as you see fit."

Nikky took Robin in a bear hug. "Thank you, Robin."

"My pleasure. Now, I smell meat and potato pie."

Alex laughed. "Our cook has prepared your favorite Russian food. I thought it would remind us of our first dinner."

"Ah, yes. That was an interesting dinner."

Alex laughed again. "A favorite memory of mine!"

"What are we drinking?"

Alex walked to the bar and produced a bottle of Jack Daniels whiskey. "I thought we would drink American this time."

"Sounds good to me."

Dinner was served and enjoyed by all except Robin detected some reservation on the part of Bacla. He wondered if the young man still believed in jihad. After the dinner, Robin walked out onto the rear deck. Bacla followed him out.

"May I speak to you, sir?" Bacla asked in broken English.

Robin replied in Arabic. "Call me Robin or Rob, Bacla. You don't need to be so formal. What's on your mind?"

"Thank you for rescuing my brother."

"You don't have to thank me. Ahmed is a good boy, I'm glad we got him away from all the violence. What about you? Do you still believe in jihad?"

Bacla seemed taken aback by Robin's blunt question. He looked down. "I am ashamed I considered those men my friends and mentors. They had no reason to murder my mother; she only tried to protect us, like any mother."

"It seemed to me you wanted to know the code to arm the bomb in the warehouse."

"I did. I wanted to arm the bomb there and kill everyone for what they did to my family. I was so angry, it was the only thing I could think of doing."

Robin considered the boy for a moment. "Bacla, you're going to be living in the United States now. You'll find out that there's more opportunity to do whatever you want than in any other country. It's not a perfect place by any means, but you can make your life whatever you want it to be. You're also lucky to have Nikolaj as a father now. He has much he can teach you about the world."

"He is already our Poppa. We love him."

"And I'm sure he loves you. I can also introduce you to

young people like my son and daughter. They can help you get acclimated to American ways."

"Ahmed and I need to learn to speak better English."

"We'll get you into classes right away, although I can tell your Poppa has already started teaching you."

"Yes, I can read it well, but I can't speak it very well."

"It'll come to you, don't worry."

"Well, thank you for everything...Robin."

"You're welcome, Bacla."

Bacla left and Alex came out. Robin noticed Bill talking to Nikky and some of the boat crew Alex brought with him.

"Thank you for the wonderful dinner, brother. I also need to pay you back for the dinner in Vladivostok."

Alex grinned. "I believe Picushkin's twenty-five million dollars is more than adequate repayment."

"Before you leave, I want to give you money for the doctor who treated Mark. Can you get it to him?"

"I'll take care of it."

"What did you do with Picushkin?"

"After interrogation, he was to be executed by a firing squad for treason, but the Chairman intervened and Picushkin is in a Siberian prison."

"Did you get any good intelligence from him?"

"Yes, for us and for your country."

"Why did the Chairman intervene?"

Alex shrugged.

"You need to watch him, Alex."

"That problem is very much above my level."

"Nevermind. I have a question for you. Why did Yosef call Bill and not me?"

Alex gave Robin a whimsical look. "Why Robin, we did not know you were American."

"Ahh, touché, Alex."

"Now, I have a question for you."

"Yes, I took pictures of the battle plans."

"Ah, you knew Ahmed would tell us."

"Of course he would, he's a good boy." Robin's eyes met Alex's. "I didn't give anyone the photos. I still have them and they are safe and I won't give them to anyone, unless Russia initiates a nuclear conflict."

"We would never initiate a nuclear war."

"It doesn't matter, Alex, you know and I know you've already changed the plans."

"I can't say."

"I didn't expect you to and quite frankly, I don't want to know."

"So, as you say, the balance of power is intact."

"As far as that goes. Your greatest national security threat is your economy."

"Do you think the U.S. will do something?"

"Of course, the U.S. will offer help."

"They will not attack?"

"I can't see that happening. Most people in the government didn't see the collapse of your economy coming and I can't see our military contemplating a ground war in Russia. Hopefully, they learned from Germany's folly in the Second World War. No, America will offer help, not war."

"Russia will never take help."

"Why not? You took it during the Great Patriotic War."

"It's different now. Our countries have been enemies in the Cold War for too long."

"How about you? Do you want to go back? I'm sure Bill can arrange for you to stay."

"It's different for me. My country needs me and I'm still getting paid a little. My men count on me to take care of them. I use Picushkin's money."

Robin smiled. "That's what I thought you'd say...especially the last part."

Bill came out to the deck. "Rob, we need to go. We have some things to take care of before I head back to Washington."

When Robin and Bill were back at Robin's boat, Bill laid out some plans.

"I arranged for the Bremerton Navy Yard to make alterations to your new boat. I think your team can use a seagoing platform."

Robin thought about this for a moment. "I don't know. I don't feel comfortable getting into a tactical situation on a boat with a top speed of twelve knots."

"The yard says they'll increase the speed of the boat considerably. They will also build in weapons and military grade sensors."

"Have them also sweep the entire boat for hidden transmitters."

"I thought you trusted Alex."

"Oh, I do, but he wasn't on the boat all the time the Russians had it."

"Good point."

"Am I going to have input in the refit?"

"Yeah, I'll put you in contact with the commanding officer at the yard."

"Thanks."

"I need a ride to the airport. A chopper will be coming for me soon."

"Okee dokee."

EPILOGUE

James Chapple guided his small fishing boat to his favorite spot on Lake Eaton as the sun was just starting to glow behind the eastern forest. The water looked like glass and the mild chill in the air was invigorating, rather than uncomfortable. Chapple spotted the cove where he always caught good sized bass. As he nosed in to the isolated eddy, he was slightly concerned his boat seemed to drag a little bit. He made a mental note to check the bottom when he got back.

He baited his line and flicked it into the water. He took a deep breath and let tension flow out of his body. It had been a tough nine months. Getting fired as Director of the CIA embarrassed him, but the subsequent criminal investigation terrified him because Chapple had much to hide. He pulled as many political strings as possible and the criminal investigation went nowhere. Then his political contacts went to work and got him a nice, cushy consultant job with a defense contractor. He smiled. More secrets I can sell to my Chinese friends.

All in all, Chapple felt good about his future and now

considered the trouble he went though as a minor setback in his life...well, almost. His wife left him when a nosy newspaper reporter uncovered several of his extramarital affairs. In the end, he just considered the whole mess as his freedom. Now, he could have his affairs without worrying about his marriage.

Chapple felt a tug on his line and leaned forward in anticipation. Then a stronger tug hit his line and he leaned more forward. Suddenly, two black clad hands exploded out of the water and grabbed him by his jacket, pulling his body violently into the lake. He kicked and swung his arms at the assailant, but the hands were strong and they took him further under the water. The man pushed him through an icy cold layer that made him take an involuntary breath...of water. In panic he flailed his arms and legs, his lungs screaming for oxygen. Then he was gone.

THE MAN WAS clad in a wetsuit and used a rebreather, leaving no bubbles to rise to the surface. He pulled Chapple's body to the bottom and looped a cable around a large dead tree and wrapped the other end around the body. He put a waterproof time lock through the end loops and fastened it. Pushing a button on the lock, he started a thirty-six hour countdown.

The diver swam back up to Chapple's boat and took the rope he had used to hitch a ride during Chapple's run to the cove. He used it to pull the boat to another area of the lake, where he pushed it into tanglewood close to the shore so it couldn't go anywhere. The diver then swam to the small backwater where he had entered the lake.

He carefully surveyed the area before emerging and going ashore. He immediately disappeared into the woods. A short time later, he reappeared dressed in hiking clothes and carrying a large pack. Ten miles and two hours later, he stepped out onto a forest road as a Range Rover approached. The car pulled over and stopped. The man opened the back door and put in the pack and then climbed into the front seat.

"You okay, Rob?" Burke asked.

"Yeah, I'm good." Robin punched Bill Grassley's number on his satellite phone.

"Hello."

"Can't make it today."

"Thanks for letting me know."

Robin looked into the side mirror and saw his face bore the look of grim satisfaction.

BILL PUT DOWN HIS PHONE. "It's done, sir. The body will surface in thirty-six hours."

The president turned and looked out the window. "I don't relish what we've done, but there just wasn't any other way."

"No there wasn't, sir. What Picushkin told the Russians was unnerving. Chapple's work for the Chinese was very damaging. A trial would have put several of our operatives in extreme danger and exposed top secret programs."

"We're damn lucky the GRU thinks enough of Marlette to tell us about Chapple. We should've known something was wrong from his conduct during the standoff."

"That's a lesson we need to take to heart."

The president turned back to Bill. "How do we really thank men like Robin Marlette and his team?"

"With Robin, I don't think he wants or expects thanks. I think the best way to thank them is make sure when we ask them to go into harm's way, it's for a good reason."

"I hope we always know what a good reason is in this complicated world."

Bill looked past the president through the window and into the world. He let the silence resting on the Oval Office be his answer.

THE END

A PREVIEW OF BLOOD WEALTH BY MICHAEL E. MCNEFF

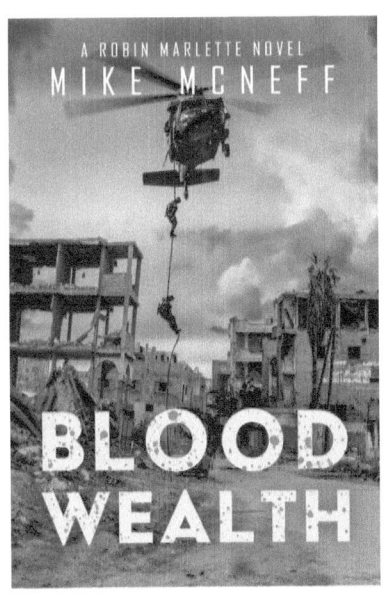

BLOOD WEALTH

Chapter One

June 7, 1977

Jonas Carrington held the group of agents in a friendly spell as he spun another tale about the bureau "in the good old days" as only Jonas could. Jonas was a legend because he had done it all. Every assignment an FBI agent could catch, from the plum assignments to the garbage ones, because Jonas *could do* them all.

They were in an historic saloon-turned-restaurant in the Valley of the Sun foothills near Scottsdale, Arizona, with its roughhewn walls adorned with six-guns and pictures of Wyatt Earp, Bass Reeves, Bat Masterson—and John Wayne. Harry Meridan thought it a fitting setting for the retirement of what was a true legend of the FBI, akin to the last western gunfighters.

A wave of sadness flooded over Harry as he watched his partner weave his magic over the younger agents crowded around him, all leaning in so they wouldn't miss a word.

There was also a mild sense of insecurity as Jonas's unofficial retirement party wound down. Harry and other fellow agents from the Phoenix FBI office had kidnapped Jonas and had taken him out on the town. They had treated him to a fine dinner and good drink while they royally roasted him. After ten years as partners, Harry was troubled about facing the job without Jonas.

An older agent, Randy Coloso, plopped down beside Harry. "So, how you gonna do your job without Carrington holding your hand?"

"Not as well."

"Oh c'mon, don't give that old fart so much credit. I bet he bored you half to death with recounts of his career while you guys were on surveillance."

"Only what I needed to know to do a better job."

"You seriously expect me to believe he didn't give you every detail about his days investigating the Nazis at Nuremberg after the war?"

"He has never spoken of Nuremberg to me, but then, Coloso, Jonas doesn't need to brag because he actually did investigations."

A deep shade of purple crawled up Coloso's face. "Fuck you, Harry." He abruptly stood and walked away.

The conversation did nothing to quell the uneasiness in Harry.

The laughter was dying down after the last tale when Jonas leaned over to Harry. "I think it's time you drove me home."

Harry put his arm around Jonas's shoulders. "Runnin' out of steam, old man?"

"I have a belly full of good food and good booze. It's been a great time, partner, but we have some unfinished work to do."

"What work? You're officially retired now."

"Some business never ends. C'mon, we gotta go while I can stay awake."

The two men walked into Jonas's house, where he lived alone. Harry always felt comfortable in the orderly and simple home. His favorite place was Jonas's office, the one place the older agent splurged. It was furnished with an oak roll topped desk and oak chairs, lined with rosewood paneling and a hardwood floor decorated with a beautiful Navajo rug. A fireplace added to the comfortable feel, although in Phoenix it didn't get much use.

"Pour us a drink while I get some stuff out of the safe."

Harry walked over to the bar cart and poured two whiskeys.

Jonas emerged from the closet, where he kept a walk-in gun safe, carrying a large file box. He did this three more times until the boxes were stacked on his desk.

"I've always wondered about those boxes. What's in them?" Harry asked.

"A curse I'm about to bestow upon you."

Harry was about to make a wisecrack until the look in Jonas's eyes shot a shiver of disquiet through him. They sat down at an oval table in front of Jonas's desk.

Jonas took a deep breath. "We've been partners for ten years now. Even though you were a pain in the ass, fucking new guy when we started, I've come to love and trust you like a brother. I've also come to respect you as an agent. You do damn good work."

"Thanks, Jonas...."

Jonas held up his hand. "I'm telling you this because I want you to know why I'm passing this curse on to you. The information contained in these boxes will shake you to your very core. The mere possession of this stuff could be a death sentence."

Jonas opened one of the boxes and handed Harry an envelope. "Here's a letter that explains how I came to possess the original documents. The rest of the information is work I've done as follow up. No one knows I've done this until now. The letter is just as relevant today as when I received it. Let it be your guide."

Harry looked at the envelope.

"Go ahead and read it," Jonas said.

Harry opened the envelope and unfolded the letter.

July 12, 1946

Nuremberg, Germany

Dear Jonas,

We are a group of people involved in the investigation of the crimes of the Third Reich. You know many of us, but there are many you haven't met. In a way, you have been a member of our group, but we kept you out of our secret operations because we knew the time would come to lay a heavy responsibility on you.

You have been chosen to be the bearer of the truth. The documents now in your possession are excerpts from many investigations. Each excerpt can stand on its own, but each excerpt also tells you the location of related reports and how they can be recovered. We have all gone through what you have endured here at Nuremberg, some worse than others. Evil people have been released. Investigations have been stopped or diverted with the evidence and records confiscated. There are forces at work here that make the military power of the allied nations look like a wooden sword against an armored division.

There is nothing any of us or you can do about this at the present time, or in the foreseeable future. The distant future is a different matter. You were chosen to carry the torch because you are a fair, honest and honorable man—and fearless. You were also chosen because the FBI seems to be the least corruptible of all the agencies at work here. Take this package and expand it when you can. When you've reached the end of your career, pass it on to a man like you with the instructions to do the same. It is our hope that someday the person holding these documents will realize the time to act has come and use the information to take the power from the few and give it back to the people.

If you begin to believe this mission is impossible, do not despair. You are the tip of the spear.

Harry put the letter down, sipped his whiskey and searched his partner's face. Jonas's brown eyes were sad and tired. His wispy, white hair was thinning. There were no laugh lines around his mouth, just lines of worry carved into this face. He seemed to have aged ten years in ten seconds.

"Harry, these boxes contain information about crimes committed by the most powerful people in the world. They are so powerful that even when some of their most horrendous crimes became publicly known, nothing could be done about it. When the time is right, they and their organizations need to be destroyed. I've done a lot of work on them. Now it's your turn."

"We can do this together, even if you're retired."

"I can't, partner. I'm not going to be around much longer."

"What? What are you talking about?"

"The big 'C' has got me. I'm dying of cancer."

Harry jumped to his feet. "Jesus, Jonas, I'm your partner, your best friend, and you couldn't tell me this?"

"Calm down, I just found out myself."

Harry fell back in his chair, trying to hold back the tears. "Hell, I'm not even sure I want to continue on in the bureau without you. Why would I want to take this on?"

"Okay, number one, you *are* going to stay with the bureau. You're an outstanding agent. You'll do fine without me.

Number two, you need to continue my work. It's more important than you can imagine."

"Aren't you going to give me a choice?"

Jonas looked off into the past. "I wasn't given a choice. I'm passing this on to you for the same reason others passed it to me. You're the only one I know I can trust to do what's necessary."

"What *is* necessary?" Harry stood and walked over to the boxes. "Can you give me an idea of what's in here?"

"The original information detailed the crimes of the military and industrial leaders of Nazi Germany and how the United States, Britain, Russia, and the Catholic Church worked to get many of the suspects free."

Harry met Jonas's eyes. "If you weren't the one telling me this, I'd smack you in the face."

Jonas smiled. "Thank you for that."

"What did you find out?"

"For starters, how about the fact that the Nazi party is alive and well- financed thanks to Hjalmar Schacht and Martin Boorman? Schacht was the Nazis' banker and economist. Boorman was Hitler's right-hand man."

"But the official position of the United States is the remaining Nazis are just a cult...oh fuck, Jonas. Is it that bad?"

"No, it's much worse. We now know that about a year before the war ended, Schacht and Boorman worked with bankers and industrialists around the world to form as many as seven hundred and fifty corporations all over the world. They moved Nazi assets worth hundreds of millions of dollars—billions in today's dollars—into these corporations and hid the ownership through a maze of bearer bonds and stock transfers. American intelligence knew all this."

"And they did nothing?"

"That's right. They didn't because we imported thousands

of Nazis into the country to work on our space program, aeronautics, pharmaceuticals…and my personal favorite, our intelligence services."

"Why the hell did we put them in our intelligence services?"

Jonas gave Harry a cynical smile. "To fight communism, of course."

"Jesus, you're right. I need to read this stuff." Harry pulled out a folder from the first box and opened it. A photograph of a SS officer was on the top. "Who is this?"

"Hermann Schinner. He's one sick, vicious piece of work. A member of Hitler's inner circle. He's still alive, living near Vienna. I would be forever grateful to you if you could find a way to make him die a slow and agonizing death."

"Jonas!"

"Don't worry. It's just wishful thinking." Jonas winced as he forced his trashed knees to get him to a standing position with a long groan. "There's another reason why I need you to do this."

"What's that?"

"I'm not dying from natural causes. I've been murdered."

Harry jumped to his feet. "Who? How?"

"Someone got me to ingest a radioactive isotope that started the cancer, according to my doctor. He says the concentration indicates food or drink. So, in addition to working on Nazis and terrorists, I'd like you to try and find out who did this."

"We need to report this, so a bureau investigation can be started."

Jonas shook his head. "No, my doctor wanted to do that, but that would lead investigators to these boxes and that wouldn't be good. All my work would disappear. Plus, whoever did this is in the FBI."

"Goddamn, you're piling a load on me."

"I know, but you're the only one I can trust."

Harry looked at his partner and the anger that was growing inside of him subsided. They had been through too much together. He reached out and put his hand on Jonas's shoulder. "I'll do my best to live up to your trust, Jonas."

The older man pulled his friend to him in a bear hug. "I know you will. Just one more thing."

"What's that?"

"This curse is why I don't have a family. I can't tell you what to do, but anyone close to you will be in danger. Once you read all of this, you'll understand."

"Is this also the reason why you always took vacations alone?"

A sly smile crossed Jonas's lips.

"I'll keep all of that in mind."

"Okay, enough of this serious shit," Jonas grinned. "We have to go on one last weekend deep-sea fishing trip."

"Are you crazy? You could get sick and die out there before you tell me everything you need to."

Jonas broke into a larger grin. "Well if that happens, you can throw me overboard for chum."

Get Blood Wealth on Amazon today!

BOOKS BY MIKE MCNEFF

GOT-U

Necessary Retribution

Blood Wealth

Other Titles

Hard Justice: The Legend of Jasper Lee

ABOUT THE AUTHOR

Mike McNeff a retired police officer and lawyer who always wanted to write novels. So when he retired that's just what he started doing. His novels draw from his law enforcement experiences which included working on SWAT and training with special forces. They also reflect his obsession with history and current events.

Mike has worked as a state trooper, a deputy sheriff and a city police officer. He's been a prosecutor, police legal advisor, defense lawyer and a civil trial lawyer, using each experience to learn great lessons about life.

Mike is married with four children and seven grandchildren. In addition to writing, he does volunteer work and spends time teaching folks about firearms and shooting. He enjoys hiking, biking, fishing and playing guitar. Mike lives on an island off the coast of Washington State.

His books can be found on Amazon at http://bit.ly/1kUw97G and Barnes and Noble at http://bit.ly/1kUvSld

ACKNOWLEDGMENTS

This is my second book. I had a lot of fun writing the story. But I've learned a lot since writing GOT-U and that knowledge made the hard work of getting the book finished as a novel people would read much harder. There were many rewrites and story changes based on suggestions from Hannah Barnes, Cathy Shaw, Mare Chapman and Michaelene McElroy. I also received great suggestions from my friends in Whidbey Writers Group who reviewed many chapters and provided honest assessments. Writing is an enjoyable endeavor with friends like these.

Of course, my wife Linda, is the best help of all. Her unwavering support for my writing and the honesty of her critiques of my stories, and my life, are priceless commodities. I love you.